Damien Larkin

DANCING LEMUR PRESS, L.L.C.
Pikeville, North Carolina
www.dancinglemurpress.com

Published by Dancing Lemur Press, L.L.C.
P.O. Box 383, Pikeville, North Carolina, 27863-0383
www.dancinglemurpressllc.com

ISBN 9781939844958

Cover design by C.R.W.

Library of Congress Cataloging-in-Publication Data:
Names: Larkin, Damien, author.
Title: Blood red steel / Damien Larkin.
Description: Pikeville, North Carolina : Dancing Lemur Press, [2023] |
    Summary: "Blood alone decides the fate of Mars For two years, the Mars
    Expeditionary Force has held the line against the last remnants of the
    Third Reich. McCabe, Jenkins, and the Second Battalion long for home.
    Reinforcements have arrived, but the veterans of the MEF have one final
    mission. Defend Forward Base Zulu at all costs. While
    Generalfeldmarschall Brandt plans a decisive showdown at Forward Base
    Zulu, Reichsführer Wagner celebrates the activation of the first
    generation of the Hollow Programme. Surrounded and cut off, McCabe and
    Jenkins once again find themselves in league with the MAJESTIC-12
    operatives known as the Black Visors. Now the future hinges on the
    sacrifices of a few determined soldiers"-- Provided by publisher.
Identifiers: LCCN 2023013181 (print) | LCCN 2023013182 (ebook) | ISBN
    9781939844958 (trade paperback) | ISBN 9781939844965 (ebook)
Subjects: LCSH: Nazis--Fiction. | Mars (Planet)--Fiction. | LCGFT:
    Alternative histories (Fiction) | Science fiction. | War fiction. |
    Novels.
Classification: LCC PR6112.A746 B59 2023 (print) | LCC PR6112.A746
    (ebook) | DDC 823/.92--dc23/eng/20230331
LC record available at https://lccn.loc.gov/2023013181
LC ebook record available at https://lccn.loc.gov/2023013182

"Dedicated to the men and women of the 20th Infantry Battalion (Fórsa Cosanta Áitiúil) and the 62nd Infantry Battalion (Reserve Defence Forces of Ireland). It was an honour and a privilege to serve alongside you."

Other titles by Damien Larkin

Big Red
We have always been here...
Print ISBN 9781939844606
eBook ISBN 9781939844613

"There is drama and heartache here, insights in the light and darkness of humanity's soul. This book makes you think." – Phil Parker, author

"This is a military sci-fi that reminded me a lot of Heinlein's Starship Troopers." – Lynda R. Young, author

Blood Red Sand
Mars will run red with Nazi blood...
Print ISBN 9781939844781
eBook ISBN 9781939844798

"The many combat scenes keep the pages turning..." - Publisher's Weekly

"Brilliant follow up to Big Red." – Tripp Ainsworth, author

STROLLING PAST THE CUTLINE

OUTSIDE NEW BERLIN COLONY, MARS
18th MARCH 1956
08:58 MST (MARS STANDARD TIME)
DAY 727 OF THE OCCUPATION
23 DAYS UNTIL THE FIRST TERRAN – MARTIAN WAR

Four hundred eighty-eight men of the Second Battalion waited beyond the gates of New Berlin, on soil where their brethren had died two years earlier. They each stood at attention, staring at the vast, dented main entrance to the colony. Lieutenant William McCabe lingered in a line at the front, the surviving lieutenants and acting captains to either side. Their commanding officer, Lieutenant Colonel "Mad Jack" Wellesley, faced the unopened doors. He slid his sword free and held the blade aloft.

"Strike banners!"

McCabe, officers, and NCOs repeated the order. A line of men behind Mad Jack reacted. In well-practised motions, they hoisted the colours of their nations high, but without any wind, the flags flopped. After eight months of hunting werewolf units and ambushing Wehrmacht forces across the barren Martian terrain, McCabe had hoped for even a light breeze to see the British flag flutter in all its glory. He gazed across the French, Polish, Soviet, West German, and Irish flags representing the make-up of the battalion and imagined the scene of the banners fluttering at full strength.

"Raise the standard!" Mad Jack said, and again, his order echoed.

One soldier stepped forward from the line and hoisted a pole with a wolfskin dangling from it. Macabre as the spectacle appeared, their wolfskin standard had become a rallying point for the beleaguered battalion after months of death and destruction. They'd liberated it from an SS bunker out in the Badlands at the start of their mission, and it seemed fitting for their operation. Since tasked with hunting and exterminating the werewolf terrorists fuelling the insurrections across the colonies, they branded themselves wolf hunters.

"Battalion, prepare to march. March!"

As one, four hundred eighty-eight feet thudded on the blood-red sand. The reinforced doors to New Berlin lumbered open. McCabe took a deep breath, fighting the growing tightness in his chest. The strange, light-headed dizziness that seized him from time to time seeped into his skull. Focusing on his breathing, he maintained his gaze on the opening doors ahead. Jenkins cleared his throat across the open common channel and prepared to sing the battalion anthem.

"Oh, King Ares wades in blood to his knees, a warrior is he."

A momentary pause before the battalion repeated his words in a thundering, unified voice.

"Oh, King Ares wades in blood to his knees, a warrior is he."

"He calls for his knife, he calls for his rifle, he calls for the Second Batt infantry."

"He calls for his knife, he calls for his rifle, he calls for the Second Batt infantry."

"New Berlin is ours, says the colonel!"

"New Berlin is ours, says the colonel!"

"It's raining lead, say the captains."

"It's raining lead..."

The tightness in McCabe's chest intensified when they entered the tunnel leading to the airlocks into the colony.

6

His hands shook in the strange involuntary way they did at random intervals. He could hear his heart pounding but knew if he checked his pulse, everything would be fine. Sounds of gunfire, explosions, and screaming rattled through his skull.

"First o'er the top, say the louies."

"First o'er..."

The main entrance slammed shut behind the battalion, and the first armoured airlock door rose. Two years ago, McCabe had led an assault on the command station above, seizing control of it with the mysterious Black Visors. Three days of brutal fighting in the Battle of New Berlin preceded an unimaginable cycle of violence, costing him the lives of countless good men. Images of butchered Nazis and his own slaughtered soldiers danced across his vision. He tightened his grip on the butt of his Lee-Enfield to ease the trembling in his fingers.

"Don't get paid to slack, says sar'nt major."

"Don't get..."

Shame filled McCabe when the dizziness blurred his eyesight. His lads relied on him to be their strength, yet his own body betrayed him. He experienced fear in battle like many men, but it never engulfed him. Why now? Why when no shots erupted, with none of his soldiers dying, could he hear those awful screams?

"Fix bayonets, says the colour."

"Fix bayonets..."

The airlock door thumped down behind the marching battalion, leaving one more between them and the colony. McCabe fought to reassert control before they entered. Thoughts of losing command of himself, of collapsing in front of his men without any physical wound, mortified him. They'd never look at him the same way again. As one of Her Majesty's soldiers, he needed to pull himself together and act like it.

"Boots, one size fits all, says the BQ."

"Boots, one size..."

Sharp pain ate into his torso, and everyone carried on marching. McCabe concentrated on the airlock door, knowing the phantom shrapnel pieces paining him weren't real and fought the sensations telling him otherwise. If he sustained such an injury again, he knew he wouldn't be capable of walking, so he kept his gaze fixed and refused to look down at his undamaged EVA suit. Faces of snarling Nazis trying to stab him crossed his thoughts, each one long dead. Sweat dripped across his brow. The dying called his name.

"Kill them all, say the sergeants."

"Kill them all..."

Bodies slumped across the Martian landscape, friend and foe alike. McCabe battered a Nazi soldier's helmet in with a rock and let the bastard suffocate. Enemy artillery pounded the soil, sending columns of copper dirt high into the sky. Pieces of metal burst through EVA suits. Wails rang out as McCabe crawled, no ammo left, with only a knife. A figure emerged from the shadows, gun raised, and he stabbed.

"Should have been a vet, say the corporals."

"Should have..."

The final airlock rose. Scenes of the devastated colony beckoned. When the SS surrendered, many thought the worst was over, just a matter of hanging on until reinforcements arrived. The insurgency took its toll. Civilians on both sides armed themselves, spreading strife and disruption across the colonies, and the werewolves launched suicidal attacks on the Mars Expeditionary Force. The Wehrmacht cut supply and communication lines, the perpetual thorn in the side of the victorious Allies.

"Booze, booze, booze, say the privates."

"Booze, booze, booze..."

At knee height, light flooded in from under the airlock, golden and blinding. McCabe blinked from the sudden brightness, fighting the urge to rip his helmet off in the hope the fresh air could steady his nerves.

"For warriors are we."

"For warriors are we."

"They stop and stare. Fall dead right there. Facing Second Batt infantry, aha."

"They stop and stare. Fall dead right there. Facing

8

Second Batt infantry, aha."

Two columns of soldiers lined the street ahead, dressed in red and black khaki uniforms, rifles with bayonets attached raised in salute, all standing at attention. When Mad Jack placed his foot on the concrete ground of New Berlin, flags rose high, fluttering in the artificial wind. Music rang out from somewhere. Newly arrived civilian scientists, engineers, and bureaucrats waved banners from apartments and houses. Fresh paint covered once battle-scarred buildings. No piles of rubble anywhere.

On Mad Jack's order, the battalion came to a halt in front of a stage. Flanked by senior officers and representatives of the Jewish communities, Major General Hamilton stood behind a podium and accepted Mad Jack's salute. After impromptu cheers from the gathering civilians, the leader of all Allied Forces in New Berlin broke into a long-winded speech, emphasising the virtues of their work and the long struggle ahead.

The words meant nothing to McCabe. His body finally obeying him, he focused his thoughts on the one thing that had kept him going for so long. Home. After two bloody years of non-stop fighting, they were going home. The reinforcements who had arrived five months earlier were several times the number of the original invasion force. It was the Mars Occupation Force's time.

In a couple of days, Lieutenant William McCabe and the Mars Expeditionary Force would be going home, and that's all that mattered.

BARRACKS SECTION, COMMAND AND CONTROL BUILDING, NEW BERLIN
21:59 MST
DAY 731
(-19 DAYS)

Corporal Peter Jenkins sat on his bunk polishing his boots. Every so often, he glanced at the Lee-Enfield perched against the locker, well within hand's reach. Even though they resided in the barracks, surrounded by reinforced walls of concrete and steel and protected by layers of armed soldiers, the sight of his trusty rifle relieved him. Having narrowly survived the Battle of New Berlin as a private, he had learned to keep his gun close.

Out in the field, his weapon and his wits kept him alive. In many ways, it had become an extension of his person. To not have the strap dangling around his neck almost felt like he was missing a hand. But he rested in the barracks, safe. After eight months of stalking the Martian wastes, he needed to adapt to setting his weapon down from time to time. Still, it reassured him to check it hadn't grown a pair of legs and walked off.

Fidgeting on his mattress to get comfortable, he felt cold steel pressed against the small of his back while he wiped the polish. The handle of the blade he had taken from the Nazi soldier he killed during the Battle of New Berlin prodded him every time he shifted his weight. He didn't mind, though.

Most soldiers preferred to wear their captured German knives and guns on their belts for all to see. Jenkins favoured keeping his concealed. Not out of shame or regret, but as a constant reminder of the things he did. The actions he committed were his and his alone. When he returned home, back to Bristol, he planned to take every memory from the accursed war, place it in a box in his mind, and throw away the key.

"Drink."

The sudden utterance from the darkened bed beside his caused Jenkins to drop his brush and boot. Shaking himself back to reality, he reached out, took the shot glass filled with vodka, and threw the contents down his throat. It burned as it worked its way down his gullet, but the taste was starting to grow on him. Not that he'd been much of a drinker prior to arriving on Mars. He replaced the glass on the table and glanced at Sergeant Boris Alexeev sitting bolt upright on his bunk, empty glass in hand, staring unblinkingly at the far wall.

Alexeev picked up his bottle of vodka, filled Jenkins's glass before his own, and returned to staring at the wall. Whenever Jenkins glanced at his expressionless face, he could almost hear the rattle of machine gun fire emanating from Alexeev's skull. Those eyes saw past the concrete, across time and space, replaying battles that would most likely never be written in history books.

Inspiration took him, and Jenkins quickly snatched his notebook and pencil from his trousers pocket. Although they had little free time out in the field, he had made it a point of jotting down everything he could about his experiences on Mars. Admittedly, he'd never possessed much of a head for schooling, but with each passing day, he grew more tempted to turn those notes into a memoir. He jotted down the titles floating in his mind: *How to Hunt Werewolves on the Red Planet* and *Red Werewolf Hunters*. Both sounded catchy, but while he mulled it over, he returned his notebook to his pocket.

"Drink."

Jenkins threw back the shot, then turned his glass upside down when he replaced it on the table. That, he had learned, was the only way to stop Alexeev from pouring him any more. Standing smaller in height and far thinner, he couldn't hope to match his burly colleague's ability to consume alcohol. Alexeev could drain two bottles of vodka and still be fresh as a daisy with four hours sleep, primed to prowl the halls for any unsuspecting soldiers sneaking in after curfew.

Rapping on the door caused Jenkins to jump to his feet, hand already on his rifle. Talking himself down, he loosened his grip and told himself he was safe. The insurgency inside the colony had long since ended. The Wehrmacht soldiers captured during the Battle of New Berlin were still in their de-Nazification camps.

"Expecting company, Boris?" Jenkins said as he approached the door.

"*Nyet.*"

It could have been someone from the platoon checking in, but Jenkins's instinct flared to life all the same. He slipped his boot behind the door and opened it a few centimetres. In the corridor, he recognised an officer and two armed soldiers in Soviet uniforms.

"Sergeant Boris Alexeev," the officer said.

Jenkins began to speak when one of the soldiers pulled

back his foot and crashed it at the door. It caught against Jenkins's boot, stopping it from swinging wide open. The two soldiers barged in all the same, one rifle barrel aimed at his face, forcing him back. The officer marched inside, stood at the end of Alexeev's bed and exploded into a tirade in Russian. The second soldier swung around the room, but, seeing no one else, fell in beside the officer, gun aimed at Alexeev. Anger rushed through Jenkins as he stared down the barrel, the Russian soldier smirking.

"Boris, what's going on?" Jenkins asked, his gaze locked on the weapon pointed at his face.

The officer maintained his steady stream of words, Alexeev answering in one or two syllables and remaining seated on his bed. Fury at the disrespect shown to them both tightened in Jenkins's chest. The smile curling on the soldier's face became a flaming match to the oilwell of hatred within him.

Jenkins waited until the soldier shifted his gaze to glance at the officer. He lunged, grabbed the rifle, and jabbed the butt of the weapon into the Soviet soldier's face. Blood spurted from his nose, and he fell to the ground. Stepping across him, Jenkins hammered the butt again into the skull of the second soldier.

He, too, collapsed, but the startled officer reacted and tried to grab at the weapon. Jenkins let it slip from his fingers, pulled the knife from the back of his belt, and rammed it against the officer's throat, his left hand grasping his forehead to expose his neck even more. Without hesitation, he swung about to gain a better view of the downed soldiers and pressed the edge of the blade against the officer's skin until a trickle of blood slipped free.

"I'm going to say this once," he said into the officer's ear. "You speak the Queen's English, or I'll cut your throat right here and now. You're not the first Russian I've gutted, you red commie piece of shit."

The bile in Jenkins's words startled him, especially in the presence of his friend Alexeev, but the intent was true. Many pro-Nazi Russians had died in the Second Battalion's first firefight after crashlanding. Plenty of them by Jenkins's own hand. He pressed the blade harder, the hatred threatening to spill over.

"Peter Jenkins, stand down," Alexeev said, rising from his bed. "This lieutenant and these men are Cheka. They are here to take me back to Soviet Zone for questioning."

"Questioning? Over what? We're back a couple of days, and you've spent every minute in the barracks."

Alexeev approached and, reaching out a meaty hand, loosened the blade from the officer's skin. "I have spent too much time with imperialist dogs like you, Peter Jenkins. Now that the Cheka have arrived with the reinforcements, I am to be relocated to the Soviet Zone where I will be interrogated and found guilty of crimes against the Soviet Union."

Jenkins blinked at Alexeev's response. Everything about his answer seemed wrong, yet the Russian appeared unfazed, even going so far as to help the soldiers back to their feet. Unsure of what to do, he loosened the blade further but kept it close enough to kill the officer if he needed to.

"Mate," he said. "That makes no sense. How can you be guilty before you've even had a court martial? There're so many things wrong about what you just said."

"The State is never wrong, Peter Jenkins. Now, I am still your sergeant. You will drop knife and step aside."

Gobsmacked, Jenkins stared at his colleague, but Alexeev focused his glare on him. With great reluctance, he released the Cheka officer, slipped his blade back into its sheath, and took a few steps towards his bunk with the rifle leaning against it. Shaking his head, Alexeev warned him off. The two bloodied soldiers prodded their weapons and shepherded him out the door, the officer following close behind.

Shocked by Alexeev's words, Jenkins downed his shot of vodka and raced into the corridor to find Lieutenant McCabe.

MEDICAL BAY, COMMAND AND CONTROL BUILDING, NEW BERLIN
07:38 MST

DAY 732
(-18 DAYS)

Sitting on the hospital bed, McCabe pulled out a cigarette and glanced again at the curtains surrounding him. He lit up and took several rapid drags while Dr Fawcett paced around, studying his charts. He had snuck into the medical bay early, hoping to avoid seeing anyone who might know him. The elderly doctor tested his blood and ran him through a variety of checks. Even in full British battledress, McCabe felt more exposed than when he stripped himself down.

"And you say you feel the sensations of not being able to breathe, even though you can?" Fawcett said, squinting over his spectacles.

"Yes, sir. It's like I know I'm breathing normal, but this feeling comes from the inside and makes me think I'm not. It's the same with my heart. It's like it's hammering, but if I check my pulse, everything is grand."

"Interesting. And do these sensations occur when you're under fire?"

"No, sir. Never. It happens at random intervals, normally when things are going fine and dandy. That's what makes it so strange."

"Well, it's nothing physical," Fawcett said, resting the chart on a nearby table. "I doubt it's battle shock, considering it's not affecting you when under attack. May I ask how many cigarettes you smoke and how much alcohol you consume?"

"Yes, sir. About a pack a day and five or six pints a week. When not in the field, of course. They haven't built an EVA to facilitate the smokers in the battalion yet."

"Well, there's something we can start with straight away then, Lieutenant. I want you to begin smoking two packs a day and move on to hard liquor. Whisky, perhaps, or brandy. Cigarettes are an excellent way of relaxing the mind, while a nice scotch can ease it of any undue worries and concerns."

McCabe nodded, not entirely convinced of the doctor's reasoning. The sensations and uncontrollable

14

hand shaking had happened twice since settling into the barracks and neither a cigarette nor a stiff drink made him feel any better. Still, with no other remedy suggested, it limited his options. As medicines went, at least he'd enjoy this prescription.

"Thank you, sir," he said and rose to exit.

Flapping his hands, Fawcett mumbled a reply while McCabe slipped out from behind the curtains. Puffing on his cigarette, he glanced about and relief washed through him at not seeing anyone he knew in the empty medical bay. Somewhat placated, he turned his thoughts to Sergeant Alexeev's predicament and that of the other Soviet-aligned soldiers recalled after returning from the field. He'd attempted to inform Mad Jack the moment Jenkins told him but, so far, had been unable to reach their commanding officer. He stepped out into the corridor, flicked his cigarette away, and stopped in his tracks at recognising a face he hadn't seen in a while.

"Colonel Henke," he said, saluting the West German officer.

"Lieutenant McCabe," Henke said, returning the gesture. "I heard about your battlefield promotion. My congratulations."

"Thank you, Colonel."

Henke extended a gloved hand to the auburn-haired woman standing next to him. Piercing, cool granite eyes stared back at McCabe. It took a moment to place her face, but he recognised her from the battle outside the government district.

"I trust you remember the Army of David leader Miss Zofia Nowak?"

"Captain Nowak," she said, eyeing McCabe.

Blinking at her words, McCabe enacted a confused salute and brought his hand back down.

"Of course," Henke said. "Please, forgive me. Captain Nowak. As you can see, Lieutenant, old habits die hard."

"Congratulations," McCabe said. "I wasn't aware the Army of David had been incorporated into the Mars Occupation Force."

"The MOF leadership would never make such a wise

decision," Nowak said, her lips curling into a snarl. "With Colonel Henke's assistance, my fighters have formed a Freikorps battalion alongside the West Germans. We operate outside the normal chain of command and provide security within the colony."

Not for the first time since arriving on Mars, McCabe found himself caught off guard with their unique alliance. Colonel Henke had been an officer in the Wehrmacht during the war back on Earth. Although he served with distinction throughout the Battle of New Berlin and had since sworn allegiance to West Germany, McCabe had never been able to shake off his mistrust of the man's previous commitment to the Third Reich.

Nowak, on the other hand, had been a slave for at least ten years and, under Nazi boots, had built the Army of David. Those fighters had engaged in some of the bloodiest encounters to seize the colony. Given both groups' history, it would have been natural for them to be enemies. Yet the two opposites stood side by side in front of him.

"I take it from your expression you haven't heard of our work?" Henke said.

"No, sir. Then again, I've spent eight months hunting down werewolves out in the Badlands. I did notice there're considerably less explosions than the last time I was here."

"I must give full credit to Captain Nowak for that," Henke said, drawing out his cigarette case and offering one to McCabe and Nowak.

Both accepted, and after lighting them, Henke continued. "After the insurgency started dying down, we still had daily clashes between the Jewish and German populations, sometimes even against the MEF peacekeepers. Nowak suggested we form an all-German-speaking battalion to try and forge a bridge between these disparate communities. We took her fighters, a handful of recruits from the anti-Nazi minority here in the colony, and former Wehrmacht and Volkssturm soldiers deemed sufficiently de-Nazified. Staffed and led by my West German NCOs and officers, we kept a lid on the violence and perhaps even prevented some atrocities."

"My compliments to you," McCabe said and dragged

on his cigarette. "Whatever results in fewer bullets flying around is a win in my books."

"Speaking of which," Henke said, leaning in close. "I hoped to speak with Lieutenant Colonel Wellesley about our up-and-coming assignment, but I haven't been able to get a hold of him. Perchance you could ask him on my behalf? There is much that needs to be discussed."

"I'd be happy to, sir," McCabe said, tapping the ash off his cigarette. "The Colonel has been busy..."

He trailed off, mind focusing on Henke's words. As he replayed the sentence over in his head, a lump of ice formed in his stomach.

"If I may, sir. What assignment?"

"The Second Battalion being deployed to Forward Base Zulu for operational experience and training up the new MOF arrivals. The First New Berliner Freikorps Battalion will be sent, too. I'm sure you're sick of the field after your last stretch, but for me, it will be good to get out of the colony for a little while."

The world collapsed around McCabe. Head spinning, he battled to maintain his composure. Two years. For two years, he had fought and bled on Mars. Reinforcements had finally arrived, ships orbited the planet, and each one had ferried thousands of soldiers to Mars, which meant they had vacancies to ship the veterans of the Mars Expeditionary Force back. Especially considering only a fraction of their original number still lived. They couldn't keep him there any longer. Could they?

"Excuse me, sir," McCabe said, flicking his cigarette away. "I must speak with Colonel Wellesley immediately. I'll be sure to pass on your message."

Without pausing to salute, McCabe took off down the corridor at the fastest pace he could muster short of sprinting. His mind raced. The tightness in his chest squeezed its iron grip around his lungs, and dizziness cascaded through his vision, but he pushed on. The MOF had to send them home. They had fulfilled their obligations. Served Queen and country.

They had to let them go. They had to.

FORWARD BASE ZULU, THE CUTLINE BORDER
03:17 MST
DAY 737
(-13 DAYS)

Against the bleak Martian landscape, one structure towered over all. Adjusting the binoculars, Generalfeldmarschall Wilhelm Brandt soaked up the sight of the building situated on plain, open land with a spine of hills and peaks on its east where he hid. He had studied the plans smuggled out of New Berlin but seeing it with his own eyes brought the Allied construction to life.

"Forward Base Zulu," General Fischer said from his side. "I do not like to give the Allies credit, but to construct such a thing in five months is impressive."

"Never underestimate the enemy," Brandt said, lowering his binoculars. "My predecessor made that mistake once, and it cost us everything."

The thoughts of that old fool Generalfeldmarschall Seidel caused Brandt's blood to boil and the shrapnel scar covering half his face to ache. He glared at the shadowy outline of Forward Base Zulu, wishing his unadulterated hatred alone could obliterate such an eyesore from the face of Mars.

Two years had passed since Seidel's defeat at the hands of the Mars Expeditionary Force. The traitor General Schulz's surrender was the final nail in the coffin of the Third Reich's grip on the planet. In that time, werewolf agents fought bravely to disrupt the enemy's occupation. Hit squads targeted the MEF's leadership and the prominent Jewish activists. Bomb attacks spread even more disruption, but it wasn't enough.

Singlehandedly, Brandt took the disorganised remnants of the Wehrmacht and built them into something new. Even some SS units, still loyal to the Führer, came over to his side. During that time, he invested every waking minute in gathering these disparate elements and forging them into one unstoppable force. It meant laying low, staging minor operations to keep the enemy engaged and even causing grumblings from his officers, but it was

18

worth it. Soon, they would lead an all-out offensive against the invaders, aided by millions of the natives about to cast their lot with the German Volk.

Keeping low, Brandt slid down the hill out of view of the base and circled back around a rocky outcrop. He paused long enough for Fischer to catch up and then carried on down the path. In the dark, it took them longer to navigate, but within five minutes, they reached the hatch leading into the underground installation established by their native allies. He marvelled at their ingenuity in building an extensive network beneath the surface to counter the MOF's air superiority. Such tenacity reflected their status as honorary Aryans.

Fischer unlocked the outer airlock, allowing Brandt to climb down first. They worked their way through the narrow shaft and waited for the airlock below to pump atmosphere in before they removed their EVA suits. Brandt took a moment to adjust his uniform, fix his cap, and wipe dust from the medals dangling from his chest. As the highest-ranking member of the Wehrmacht, it was on him to set a good example and become the beacon for their dreams of revenge.

Walking into the corridor, he snapped up his hand in anticipation of the salute from his personal guard. They trudged on down the hallway, soldiers and native militia stepping aside and coming to attention in his presence. When he entered the command centre, all rose and lifted their arms.

"Heil Hitler," every voice echoed.

"Heil," he said and waved for everyone to stand easy.

Along the flanks of the room, radio operators relayed orders and jotted down updates. Junior officers used counters to move the positions of enemy and allied forces across a huge map that took up the centre of the room. All stepped aside at his approach, and he glanced down at the latest reports. He studied the entire area of MOF control and the disputed zones along their so-called Cutline border. Smiling, he wondered if they even knew how many native units had infiltrated their territory in preparation for the offensive.

"Herr Feldmarschall."

Brandt turned and accepted the salute from Oberst Walu. Despite his stature, the Native Martian officer looked prim and proper in his officer's uniform, chin tilting up with pride. Initially, Brandt had been hesitant to allow natives into the Wehrmacht, but the need for manpower overruled any reluctance. Their conduct, zeal, and adherence to National Socialist ideology dispelled any notions of incompetence, and he remained grateful for their commitment to defending the Reich. In many ways, he had taken Walu under his wing, training him to be the ideal leader of the native militia who would spearhead the up-and-coming offensive.

"Stand easy, Oberst."

"Thank you, Herr Feldmarschall," Walu said in the accented German twang the natives spoke. "The reports you asked for."

After accepting the files, Brandt flipped them open and skimmed through the requested information. Every day, the native militia, known amongst their own people as the Red Blades, grew in strength. Volunteers flocked from across the twenty-three clans, eager to join the struggle against the Jewish-Bolshevik invaders and their Mars Occupation Force puppets.

"Have you any reports on your leaderships council meeting, Oberst?"

Walu's demeanour changed ever so slightly, chin lowering, shifting his weight from side to side. "No, Herr Feldmarschall. Eleven clans stand with us, ten against, with two undecided. Unless we can convince the remaining two to vote for the Red Blades' plan to commence the war of liberation, the legitimacy of our actions remains in question. Volunteers will join us, but without a council majority devoid of abstentions, we will not have official support."

Returning his attention to the map, Brandt focused on New Berlin. Without the mass mobilisation of millions of Native Martians to aid the cause, the outcome of the war lay in jeopardy. He would not allow another defeat to taint his honour. The time to cast the dice and strike had arrived. Any further delay threatened their morale and could permit the initiative to slip to the MOF.

"Do what you must," he said, facing Walu again. "Take any and all actions necessary to persuade the council to support our efforts. Do I make myself clear, Oberst?"

"Yes, Herr Feldmarschall."

Dismissing him with a hand flap, Brandt's gaze shifted to Forward Base Zulu on the map. Soon, he would have his chance to test his new fighting formations in the field. Many good men and natives would die in the approaching conflict, but their blood would cleanse the Martian soil of its occupation by the decadent Western Democracies and their Red Horde allies.

Revenge drew near. Sooner than they expected.

423KM EAST OF NEW BERLIN, FORWARD BASE ZULU
08:55 MST
DAY 739
(-11 DAYS)

Hopping out the transport door, Private Shirley Watford soaked up the hustle and bustle of the hangar bay and tried to stop grinning. Adjusting the bag straps on her shoulders, she fell into line and followed her comrades as they trekked across the bay to the waiting officers.

Rows of vessels lined the floor. Teams worked in precise movements, unloading crates of ammunition, food, and equipment. She glanced up at the ceiling at least three stories above her. Marvelling at the sheer size of the hanger bay, she pondered how vast the levels above her must sprawl.. To think its construction took five months astounded her. It spoke volumes on the British ability to roll up its sleeves and get the job done.

The line halted at three desks manned by officers. For the dozenth time in the last hour, she patted down her red and black Mars Occupation Force uniform. As she gazed at the women in front of and behind her, a smile crossed her face again. She knew she had to wipe it away before facing the officer, but she allowed herself a moment of triumph. Shirley Watford from Manchester — an actual, real-life soldier.

The sense of glee faded when she thought of the day she came across the advertisement. Tears still in her eyes from burying her father, she noticed the flyer hanging from the lamppost calling on volunteers to do their part and offering a challenging adventure. With her two brothers killed in the war and her mother long since dead, Watford took the leap. She was surprised to learn the job was affiliated with the army and even more so when they accepted her after all those interviews and tests. No women were allowed to serve in the British Army outside of wartime, so at best, she expected to be relegated to a support role. For once in her life, a man held the door open rather than slamming it in her face.

"Male or female, it makes no odds to me," her instructor, Lieutenant O'Reilly, barked at her recruit platoon. "You're all equal piles of dog shit in my eyes."

The training nearly broke her, but she clung on. Nowhere else to go and no prospects, she dug in with an animalistic ferocity, even when men and women she considered stronger than her gave up. She endured the catcalls and wolf whistles. The eyeballs soaking up her figure, staring at her curves, and the snickers behind her back. Being called "princess," "sweetheart," and "darling." She took it all on the chin, gaze set on the prize. Shirley Watford — an actual soldier.

The line inched forward at a snail's pace, but Watford used the time to attempt to suppress the growing giddiness building within her chest. She'd survived the gruelling training at the Atacama Desert base in Chile. Not only endured but flourished. No matter what her instructors threw, she took it with a calm head and achieved any objective they set. Even with her claiming the highest scores on the firing range, the old guard sought to demoralise her. Flabby, balding desk jockeys tried to tell her and the other gals it was all an experiment gone wrong. Women couldn't serve in frontline roles.

"It would be bad for unit cohesion," they said, singing from the same hymn sheet.

As she stood at the abyss of uncertainty, her dream

fading before her very eyes, someone behind the scenes threw them a lifeline. Combat medic. They'd allow females to participate if they trained as combat medics.

Some quit soon after, and Watford couldn't blame them. Bitterness lingered at realising they wouldn't be regarded the same as their male counterparts. Watford persevered. She took the sneering disdain and used it for fuel. Understanding she had to prove herself, to work harder to receive equal treatment, she threw herself into the medical course, and it paid off. Five months of scrubbing bedpans in New Berlin's military hospital, and there she was. Finally on the frontlines, attached to an actual combat unit. Shirley Watford — a soldier.

"Next."

Exhaling, Watford ordered her thoughts, approached the desk, and stood to attention.

"Papers."

She saluted the seated lieutenant, noted his name tag read Barrymore, and passed him her orders and identity documents. While he perused everything and studied a list, she picked an imaginary spot on the wall and stared. A corporal behind Lieutenant Barrymore smirked and blew her a kiss.

"Right, Watford, I have you here," Barrymore said. "Same as the rest. You'll be reporting to Lieutenant Tracy in the medical bay for nursing duties. Next."

"If I may, sir," she said, accepting her documents back. "How long until we get to go into the field?"

"Nurses don't get to go on ops," Barrymore said without looking up. "No matter what good old Fighting Bill Tracy says about it. You're assigned to the medical bay, and that's where you'll stay, twelve hours a day, five days a week. Next."

The woman behind Watford tried to step past, but she stood her ground. Unadulterated fury pumped through her veins. She had done everything they asked and more. Every task completed to the maximum standard, no stone left unturned. Absolutely every objective exceeded without a flaw. For this?

"Excuse me, sir," she said, fighting the urge to scream

until her lungs burst. "I'm a combat medic, not a nurse. I've been trained to perform battlefield surgeries to stop men from dying before they can be evacuated. I was assured this assignment would involve me being attached to a combat unit."

Barrymore dropped the pen from his hand and met her gaze. His jaw tightened when he stared into her eyes, but she refused to flinch. They'd promised her. They made her jump through hoops. She earned the right to be treated with the smallest amount of respect.

"Listen here, missy. This is the Mars Occupation Force, not a little princess party for your dollies. You have been assigned as a nurse at the medical bay, and that's exactly what you'll bloody well do. Now, be a good girl, unscrunch your panties, slip into something a little less comfortable, and run along."

It took every ounce of Watford's reserves not to punch him there and then. Her entire body trembled from the sheer flood of anger rushing through her limbs. Balling her hands into fists, she imaged pounding Barrymore's face into the dust and tearing his innards out with her fingers.

"Walk it off," a voice whispered from behind.

She turned about and glared at the woman standing there. Half-expecting a smug smile, she readied herself to throw a punch. Instead, she looked over the faces of a dozen angered women, jaws set, shaking their heads, and staring in contempt at the officer.

"Walk it off," the soldier closest to her said again. "Don't let them get under your skin. Take a deep breath, exhale, and we'll figure it out later."

Somehow, those words cut through the tsunami of frustration smashing through her body. She turned about and, biting her cheek to stop from screaming, walked out of the line to find the medical bay.

"Smile more, darling," Barrymore called after her, half-chuckling. "You'll look prettier."

Nipping the inside of her mouth harder until she tasted blood, Watford ignored his words.

"I'm a soldier," she whispered to herself. "I am a

soldier."

EISENHOWER COLONY, US ZONE OF OCCUPATION
12:03 MST
DAY 743
(-7 DAYS)

Devoid of his SS uniform, Reichsführer Ernst Wagner felt almost naked. For years, he'd commanded the SS across the colonies, but those days were long over now. He ran a gloveless hand down his shirt and tie and fixed the creases on his jacket. The fabric itched against his skin, but he pushed such irritations aside. That day marked the pinnacle of his achievements, and it wasn't like he'd be in that body for long. The longer he stayed in any given time period, the higher the chances Anna Bailey or the Core Cadre would attempt to kill him. His death wouldn't have a serious impact on the primary timeline, but he enjoyed being alive and admiring his work. After years of experiments and failures, his dreams were finally coming through.

"When you're ready, Herr Reichsführer," Dr Elizabeth Rimes said in her bastard American accent.

Forcing a smile, he gave the slightest of nods. "Thank you, Doctor."

They walked through a narrow corridor in the underground facility and stepped into the training hall. Wagner paused mid-step, gasped, and gazed across the rows of uniformed teenagers all standing at attention, eyes straight forward, unmoving. Tears welled up in his eyes when he took in those youthful faces, each one representing the next generation of soldiers. Engrained warriors, all.

"Is it everything you imagined, Herr Reichsführer?" Rimes asked.

He held up a finger to silence any other questions and took a cautious pace forward. Not since activating Anna Bailey had he experienced such joy. His run-in with the group of Core Cadre soldiers in the last moments of the Battle of New Berlin confirmed his righteousness. The

Hollow Programme would be a resounding success. All the trials, all the errors. All worth it.

"One hundred in total," Rimes said. "No losses. Every one of them from the genetic profiles you provided, all aged between ten and fourteen years and in perfect health. Interestingly enough, a significant portion were strays and orphans. The rest, well, as far as their families are concerned, they simply vanished. Each specimen has had their memories wiped to remove any attachment to their previous lives."

Wagner approached a boy of not more than twelve years and studied him. Aside from his chest rising and falling and the odd eye-blink, he didn't move, even with his proximity. He pushed on, strolling down the front line, taking in each face as he passed, heart threatening to burst with joy.

"Are they combat-ready, Doctor?"

"Yes, Herr Reichsführer. Since their activation five months ago, they've endured rigorous preparation in the Rigs and the real world. All of them are trained up to the level of special forces operatives. They are beyond proficient in every weapon at our disposal and hand-to-hand combat. Don't let their young faces fool you, Herr Reichsführer. These are flesh and blood killing machines. Would you care for a demonstration?"

"Nothing would please me more," Wagner said and stepped back.

"Holly, Ashe, step forward."

Two girls from the first line stomped their feet, marched, and came to a stop in front of them. Raising an eyebrow, Warner looked them over and turned to Rimes.

"You gave them names?"

"Designations, Herr Reichsführer. Although we've removed their memories and conditioned them to obey, our early psychological studies indicated a certain... subconscious rejection of being labelled as numbers. We may treat them like machines, but they are still human. We found they gel together more efficiently if they can relate to each other on a more natural level. Hence, designations."

"Very well. Proceed."

Extending a hand, Rimes pointed out the girl on the right. "This is Holly. One of our first activations. We located her outside a Choctaw reservation. She's one of our finest trainees. To her left, we have Ashe, originally from Mexico City and a top contender to become senior private within the company. Both girls are quite close to each other and spend a lot of time training together. I'm hoping this will make it a bit more interesting. On your command, Herr Reichsführer."

"Very well. On my order, you will fight. The victor is the one still breathing at the end. Begin."

Holly lunged first, her fist a missile aimed at Ashe's head. Ashe pulled back and swung a hook, catching Holly on the jaw and forcing her back. She threw another punch, but Holly blocked and countered with a spinning kick to her head. Again, Ashe dodged and, with spectacular speed, closed the distance and levelled a vicious whack to the gut. Holly managed to grab her wrist, turn her arm, and force Ashe face-first to the floor, but she wrenched her limb free, rolled over and threw a kick.

Holly evaded the blow, and both young women scrambled to their feet again. She closed the distance, jabbing while Ashe deflected every strike. She fell, swung her leg, and swept the legs from under Ashe, who thudded down but lashed out a foot, catching Holly in the stomach. Undeterred, Holly surged forward again, slapping away Ashe's legs, and dropped her weight onto her, smashing her knee into her groin.

Ashe grabbed her shoulders, hooked her legs around Holly, and attempted to hurl her to the ground, but Holly held her position. She slammed her knuckles, the shot absorbed by Ashe's forearm. She slipped a hand under her guard and inched up closer while she drove her forehead downwards, smashing her on the nose and splattering blood across her face.

With Ashe dazed from the blow, Holly raised her hand and punched, catching her again on the face. Fists pounded against flesh, a slapping noise echoing throughout the room. Following every attack, Ashe's body turned limper, her face deteriorating every second. When her arms collapsed unmoving to her sides, Holly paused, primed to strike, but frozen as she stared down at her colleague.

"Finish it," Wagner said.

Devoid of the slightest hesitation, Holly rained her knuckles down, splitting Ashe's face. She punched until she hammered through bone and brain and then stood bolt upright. Splatters of blood dripping from her hands, she came to attention.

"Excellent," Wagner said, clapping his hands. "How absolutely spectacular. You have outdone yourself, Rimes. MAJESTIC-12 will be most pleased with your progress."

Double doors on the side wall of the training room opened, capturing Wagner's interest. Rimes turned about and nodded as an MOF officer strolled in, pausing for a second to stare at the body before approaching them.

"Herr Reichsführer," Rimes said. "May I present General Hatfield, the US MOF liaison for the Hollow Programme."

Wagner extended his hand, but Hatfield glared back, his eyes narrow pinpoints of hatred. Taking the hint, Wagner lowered his hand and flashed a smile instead.

Hatfield turned to face Rimes. "Tell this baby murderer the signal he's waiting on came through. I want him off my installation ASAP. There's a lot of people here, myself included, who'd love to cut this SS sonofabitch into tiny pieces, nice and slow."

Hatfield spat on the ground and turned to exit the room.

"Herr General," Wagner called after him. "Be sure to send my regards to your superiors. Their assistance has been most exceptional."

Grinning to himself, Wagner turned his attention to Rimes. "It appears I must leave now, Doctor. Keep up the excellent work. I look forward to reading your reports. Please also ensure my Hollow body is maintained in this timeline. Should the Core Cadre attempt to disrupt my plans here, I may need to enact countermeasures."

Without waiting for a reply, Wagner sauntered back the way he had come. Everything he envisioned stretched out ahead of him, from that very moment to an empire inconceivable for anyone else of his generation. The threads tying them all together lay for him alone to see.

Every strand rested in his hands, the eternal puppet master.

APPROACHING FORWARD BASE ZULU
17:05 MST
DAY 745
(-5 DAYS)

A dark cloud hung over the members of Third Platoon, A-Company, Second Battalion. Jenkins suspected it emanated from Lieutenant McCabe and, from there, infected everyone else. Sitting in the transport, he glanced over the various morose faces. No laughter or banter broke out, and all avoided eye contact with one another. The men of the former Mars Expeditionary Force stared at nothing, lips clamped tight, sometimes shaking their heads slightly.

They weren't going home. Not yet. Despite the massive influx of reinforcements to bolster the colony defences, the powers-that-be insisted the reorganised Mars Occupation Force still wasn't combat-ready. Fewer than ten percent of the new arrivals had been assigned as replacements to the battle-hardened MEF formations leading the fight against the werewolves and their Wehrmacht allies.

More training was needed. Additional integration into field units to sponge up veterans' experience. Jenkins wanted to point out the MEF hadn't exactly gotten time to acclimate, with bullets blasting at them from the minute their boots touched Martian soil, but no one cared what a young corporal thought.

To his credit, McCabe fought for them. He rallied Mad Jack into broaching it with the leadership, to no avail. Even though the Second Battalion had lost half their number and battled constantly for two years, the decision was made, and orders handed down. The Second Battalion and the First New Berliner Freikorps Battalion were to be posted at some shithole backwater called Forward Base Zulu right on the Cutline.

The closest thing even approaching good news was that at least their numbers were finally being replenished with replacements. For the first time since arriving in orbit on the USAF North Carolina, the Second Battalion had a thousand soldiers swelling their ranks.

Across from him, McCabe fumbled for a match, cigarette dangling from his lips. Something had changed in his demeanour since finding out the news. The fire in his eyes petered out. He acted more withdrawn and less willing to help or answer any questions. Jenkins couldn't blame him. Everyone handled it in different ways. He experienced shock at learning their leave was being cut short and their return journey postponed, but he focused on his job. With Alexeev and the other Russians relocated back to the Soviet Zone, Jenkins found himself as acting platoon sergeant, which represented a significant increase in his workload.

"There it is," Private Wallace said, angling to stare out of the nearest window port.

Jenkins turned in his seat and glanced out the port behind him. When the transport circled to reach the external landing pad, he shifted his position until their new home for the next few weeks came into view. As bases went, it was one of the strangest he had ever been posted to.

Forward Base Zulu reminded him of a pyramid with the apex smoothed off. Reddish-brown coloured stone covered the smooth diagonal exterior, blemished by window ports and retractable gun emplacements. The flattened tip of the installation, which housed the Command and Control Centre, could be used as an emergency landing pad. The main one rested to the west, past where the structure met the ground.

Barbed wire fences and trenches ran around the perimeter, protected by a variety of heavy machine guns, mortars, artillery, and anti-aircraft pieces. Formations of EVA-clad soldiers marched along the open spaces between the emplacements. Smaller teams patrolled the sand outside.

Hills to the east looked like the only noticeable features

on otherwise flat land. In his mind, it didn't exactly look like a strategic piece of terrain. From the mission briefings, housing a base there allowed the MOF to project their power hundreds of klicks in every direction and reinforce the Cutline should the enemy ever attempt to attack en masse. With their use of transports, platoons and even companies could be deployed to a hotspot in minutes.

As the transport slowed for its descent, Jenkins again looked over the faces of his platoon, reminded for the millionth time of the soldiers no longer with them. Over half were replacements, the majority newbies, and in many ways, it was like looking at two distinct groups.

In a form of silent protest, the men of the Mars Expeditionary Force continued to don their home countries' uniforms beneath their EVAs and even on duty. British, French, West German, and Polish soldiers, all united by the common horror they had endured alone for two years. The replacements, on the other hand, all wore the so-called MOF Red'n'Blacks. Senior officers publicly and privately harangued the MEF veterans about it, but no official order came down to wear the MOF's uniform, most likely not to demoralise an already exhausted fighting force.

The transport thudded onto the landing pad, prompting Jenkins and the rest of the platoon to pull on their helmets. Grinding noises resonated through the hull when the pad lowered into the underground hangar bay. He stood and moved to the airlock door. McCabe alone kept his helmet off in clear breach of protocol, the only movement coming from his hand when he brought his cigarette to his lips. Jenkins said nothing and, gripping the handle, waited for the signal. The transport came to a standstill with a final bang. Three minutes passed until the light over the door flashed green. He yanked on the release, shoved open the airlock, and bellowed.

"Out! Out! Now! Get those arses off my transport."

With their equipment, bags, and weapons, the platoon raced out and formed up beside the craft. Egged on by the corporals, they removed their EVA suits and straightened their uniforms. McCabe stubbed his cigarette out and, without making eye contact, shuffled his way after them,

Jenkins following on his heels. Outside, the rest of the battalion, plus their Freikorps allies, arranged themselves into parade formation. Cajoling his soldiers to be on their best behaviour, he marched them on, taking their designated place within the Second Battalion lines.

Jenkins soaked up the size of the underground hangar and the sheer volume of equipment being unloaded. Weapons and ammunition of every kind poured from transports and shipped into the base in an unending stream of movement. It took five minutes for the battalions to form up, and when Mad Jack gave the order, they all came to attention. On a small podium set up in front of the assembled soldiers, an officer wearing the MOF Red'n'Blacks strode out and ordered them to stand easy.

"My name is Colonel Walter Penford, commanding officer of this installation and formerly of Her Majesty's Irish Guard. It is my distinct honour to welcome you to Forward Base Zulu, your new home for the next several months. During this time, I expect…"

Zoning out, Jenkins glanced over the mass of soldiers around him. Officers tended to drone on about things the enlisted took as obvious. Since no one had ordered him to hang on Colonel Penford's every word, he kept an ear out for anything of interest and utilised the time to get a closer look at the rest of the battalion and their new Freikorps allies.

"…decency, honour, and respect. I expect all my soldiers to adhere to these guidelines without…"

A quick estimate showed around half the Second Battalion wearing the MOF uniform, intermixed across all platoons and companies. Meanwhile, the Freikorps battalion all sported light grey khaki uniforms, almost British in design. He suspected the pattern helped them blend in better with the variety of buildings back in New Berlin. Recognising a few of the West German NCOs from past operations during the insurgency, he made a note to say hello after.

"…to not let our guard down. This may be a relatively tranquil area on the Cutline, but we must not surrender to complacency. Everyone should remain vigilant…"

Returning his focus to his own platoon, Jenkins once again thought of Alexeev. It didn't seem right to be on a mission without the burly Russian. Quiet as he acted on a day-to-day basis, he came to life under fire and had saved many of them countless times over. He glanced over at McCabe, who met his gaze. Eyebrows furrowing, he nodded back at Penford. Taking the hint, Jenkins looked up at the yammering officer and sighed.

"And remember," Penford said. "That we fulfil our obligations, not as British, French, Polish, or West German soldiers. We are one army. We are one people. We are Terrans!"

Unfamiliar with the last term, Jenkins turned to flash a glance at McCabe when half the battalion raised their rifles and shouted.

"Protect Terra!"

The unexpected thundering boom of so many voices caught Jenkins off guard. Veterans of the MEF exchanged glances, but those in MOF uniforms smiled from ear to ear, faces lighting up. Penford lifted his hands until silence crossed the floor.

"My sincere apologies to the majority of you who have been here far longer than us new arrivals," he said. "You must be unfamiliar with our slogans and protocols. Let us try again."

He unholstered his pistol, raised it into the air and shouted. "Protect Terra."

More people added themselves to the din this time, veteran MEF and Freikorps. Creases still crossed foreheads, and soldiers turned to mouth queries to each other, but they held their weapons aloft.

"Protect Terra!"

Goosebumps rushed across Jenkins's forearms. Waves of fervour surged through the battalions as two thousand voices merged into one.

"Protect Terra!"

Lifting his own rifle, he joined in the fray, still unsure of what he was cheering about. After three more rounds, Penford dismissed the men and returned them to their officers' control to seek out their accommodations and postings. On Mad Jack's orders, they broke down into their companies and marched into the main base.

Wondering who Terra was and why they needed protecting, Jenkins spurred his platoon on.

DE-NAZIFICATION CENTRE LIMA ONE, NEW BERLIN
20:13 MST
DAY 747
(-3 DAYS)

Former Wehrmacht commanding officer General Schulz lay on his prison cot, glaring up at the ceiling. When boredom really took hold, he counted the various scratches etched there, although the number never changed. Two hundred fifty-seven unique dents and splotches of mould all stared back.

Sensing a chill in the air, he tugged at his prison uniform and, not for the first time, noted how loosely it sagged. Though the Mars Occupation Force didn't have any plans to starve him to death, the slop they fed him offered far less nutritional value than he had become used to as an officer in the Führer's armed forces. He rolled over in his bed, the springs squeaking beneath, and glowered at the wall. One hundred thirty-eight marks on that one.

Boredom turning to irritation, he glanced at the two books sitting on his table and released a frustrated sigh. Both were given by his captors as part of their de-Nazification programme. Having to endure six hours a day of lectures, talks, and group sessions on the evils of National Socialism, he would have preferred to bash his own skull in with the tomes than read any more on the subject. The Allies had won their war. Their boot rested on his neck and on the throats of every German civilian residing on Mars. Must they own his thoughts too?

Fidgeting again, Schulz almost missed the sound of the bolt's release on the far side of the door. Curious at the break in his normal routine, he sat up, eyes locked on the metal frame. Another series of clanks brought him to his feet. He dusted himself off, again missing the feel of his uniform, and awaited the guards. A random evening interrogation, he guessed. Perhaps questions on yet another code the rebellious elements of his former army used to communicate under the noses of the MOF. Regardless, he doubted if he'd enjoy it. Good news seldom walked through his door.

He froze when a smiling face appeared as the door swung open. The devil in human form. The already chilly air in the cell dropped a few more degrees. Repressing a shudder, he tilted his chin up and tried to maintain what little dignity he had left.

"General Schulz," Mr. Myers said, flashing those impeccable, pearl-white teeth. "It's been a minute. I thought I'd stop by and say hello."

Dizzying torrents of hatred rushed through Schulz when the MAJESTIC-12 operative sauntered into his room, whistling to himself while he made a show of looking around. Two goons dressed in the same black suits with white shirts stood in the doorway, pistols strapped to their belts.

"Mr. Myers," Schulz said. "If I never saw you again, it wouldn't be long enough."

"Come now," Myers said, coming to a stop. "We're practically old friends, you and I. Together, we laid the foundations for something monumental. Centuries from now, scholars will marvel at what we started."

"You've built nothing," Schulz said, fighting the urge to spit in his face. "You only destroy. Neither of us will be remembered in the future, Mr. Myers. Of that, I am certain and grateful."

Chuckling to himself, Myers pushed a renegade strand of hair from his fringe. "Now there's one for the books. Getting lectured on morality by a card-carrying Nazi. Please, General, I didn't come here to spar. I came to deliver on my promise."

"I want nothing from you. Leave."

Myers took a step to the side and gestured at the open door. The goons stared at Schulz, leaving him no option but to obey or risk a beating. Hoping Myers's promise ended with a bullet to the back of his skull and the end of his miserable existence, Schulz complied. He trudged out the door, praying for a quick death.

Silence strangled the corridor outside and the surrounding empty cells. Schulz waited until Myers exited and then followed a step behind, head bowed. They walked through a security gate and took a right turn leading out into the main block housing his officers and senior NCOs. Bracing himself, Schulz took another deep breath. Flanked by Myers's goons, he stepped out onto the central floor.

Heads rose from pillows, card players swivelled about in their seats, and soldiers lounging against the walls stood and gaped. Everyone remained silent, the only sound coming from boots thudding across the concrete ground. Schulz forced his chin up, determined to at least appear defiant, but shame flooded him from those hundreds of sets of eyes. He could taste their anger. Each one of them willing to shove a knife in his back and kill the man who surrendered New Berlin to the Allies.

To Schulz's relief, they crossed the floor faster than expected, and Myers led them into another part of the complex housing the interrogation rooms. Schulz entered the first opened door. Like he had done many times before, he took the closest seat at the table and plonked himself down. Myers waved off his goons, selected a bag, and dumped it on the centre of the table before taking his own chair.

"Open it," he said.

"Tell me what you want, Mr. Myers. I have no time for games."

"Please, Herr General. Look inside."

Sighing, Schulz reached out, gripped the zip, and tugged it open. He drew it closer, gazed within, and paused at the sight. In disbelief, he prodded at the fabric and pulled the red and black khaki shirt free. Completely stunned, he stared at his medals pinned to its breast and the general's rank markings fixed to the collars.

"What is this?"

"It's your ticket out of here," Myers said, leaning in. "I told you I'd have need for you and your men in the future. The time has arrived. Feel free to try it on, although I'm certain it will fit."

Schulz dropped the MOF shirt back into the bag and shoved it away. "I'm afraid your American sense of humour eludes me yet again, Mr. Myers. I highly doubt your Mars Occupation Force will be welcoming to Nazis."

"You'd be surprised," Myers said with a shrug. "I mean, let's be clear. The Army of David has sentenced you to death. They've been calling for the executions of the Wehrmacht and SS leadership for two years now. Your deaths have been deferred on the grounds that MAJESTIC-12 needed your intelligence and insights to fend off the werewolves and the so-called 'True' Wehrmacht until reinforcements arrived. Now that they have, the real game begins. I need you and your forces at my disposal, fighting under the MOF banner."

"You're insane," Schulz said, shaking his head and wishing more than anything for a cigarette. "The Army of David will scream bloody murder over this. Even if your MOF soldiers were to accept us, which I sincerely doubt, what's to stop my men defecting to Brandt's Wehrmacht?"

Myers slipped a hand into his pocket, produced a cigarette, and offered it to Schulz. Grateful, he snapped it off him, placed it between his lips, and leaned in to take the match flame. Taking a few rapid puffs, he sank back in his seat and relished the light-headed buzz floating through his skull after so long.

"You let me worry about the Jews," Myers said, the corner of his mouth slipping up into a predatory snarl. "Same with the MOF. As for defections, I'll ensure appropriate countermeasures are in place for any operations to discount such a thing. You worry too much, Herr General, when you should leave all that to me. Now, do you accept my offer, or would you like to live out the rest of your days in your puny cell? I have an entire list of officers who I am sure would leap at the proposal I've given you."

Schulz took another long drag on his cigarette and exhaled. He stared at the bag, his thoughts resting on the hatred of his prison cell and the terror at living out his remaining days in such a place. Until the end of time, he would be known as the man who surrendered New Berlin.

A chance to redeem himself in honourable combat tugged at the last shreds of his pride. If he could at least die on a battlefield, then his tattered soul would know some form of peace.

"What of the Führer?" Schulz said in a quiet tone.

"As you know, we've been working with certain elements within the SS since the surrender, Herr General. If you're asking if your Führer approves of us utilising the Wehrmacht for operations, that is irrelevant. You are all property of the MOF. We can do with you as we see fit. I'm giving you the chance to be a soldier one last time. That's all there is to it. Do you accept?"

Mistrust of Myers swirled paramount at the forefront of Schulz's thoughts, but to escape his cell and receive an honourable death, he'd sign a pact with the devil himself. Still puffing on his cigarette, he reached out a hand and took the bag.

"Very well, Mr. Myers. I agree to your terms. Again. What would you have me do?"

"Excellent," Myers said and sprang to his feet. "At the moment, nothing. I'll have you escorted to accommodations more befitting a general. We'll talk more on what I need from you and your men tomorrow. In the meantime, eat a hearty meal and sleep on a soft bed. You'll need your energy for the days to come."

Schulz watched him stroll around the table and make for the door. As he walked, Schulz wondered if Myers really was a demon in human form. The man's very presence triggered a primal wariness within him, and those eyes held a darkened quality he had never seen before in his life.

"Oh, I can assure you I'm fully human," Myers said, pausing at the door and peering back. "Let's just say I've a bit more going on upstairs than the rest of you."

Stunned at Myers's words, he allowed the cigarette to slip from his lips. His guts twisted. How had he known what he was thinking? An educated guess? Cold chills ran up and down Schulz's spine when Myers left, laughing to himself.

He gripped the bag tighter when the goons fell upon

him.

FORWARD BASE ZULU
16:37 MST
DAY 749
(-1 DAY)

Lieutenant "Captain" Eddie Lockhart of the USAF North Carolina swayed and stumbled his way down the corridor. Gripping a wine bottle tight, he forced his drooping eyelids open. Strange music pounded through his skull from the mysterious box that was his most prized possession. At seventeen years old, he was the youngest pilot within the reorganised Mars Occupation Force. Due to his natural skill and vast experience, he was one of the best. But demons clawed at his cranium. Terrible faces of twisted and gnarled creatures from hell tortured him. The music, quite unlike anything he had ever heard in his life, helped. The booze did even more.

Leaning up against a wall, he collected himself as one song ended and another began. He smiled when he recognised the beat. Next to the songs the magic box labelled "heavy metal," he enjoyed "hip hop." Humming along to the tune of *California Love,* he pushed himself off and glanced around for any officers. If they caught him drinking again, he'd spend another night in the stockade. They'd threatened to take his ship, of course, but they never followed through. Drunk, hungover, or even sober, he was the best damn pilot the MOF had ever seen. They knew it. He knew it, too.

Three soldiers in British battledress came into view, so Lockhart averted his gaze. He often used the secondary corridors in the base to avoid detection but, from time to time, ran into others with the same idea. Hoping they weren't the type to report him, he kept his head down, but a sharp pain bit into his arm. He glanced down at the hand gripping him and found himself slammed against the wall, earbuds tumbling out.

"Well, well, well, lads," the British soldier pinning him said. "What have we got here?"

"He's little more than a bairn, he is," another one said, laughing. "Look at his face."

"Get off me," Lockhart said, his senses fighting to assert control over his alcohol-addled brain. "I'm an officer. Let go, now!"

The two other soldiers closed in, chuckling at his words. Their proximity triggered memories of what the Nazis did to him in New Berlin. Anger surging, he struggled to break the soldier's grip, but iron hands resisted and held him tight.

"Holy shit. He's a little *sceptic tank*," the soldier holding him roared. "The bloody Yankee-doodles have kids fighting for 'em. You believe it, boys?"

"Little 'ard man's drinking too," the second soldier said, snatching at his wine.

Lockhart struggled to grab the bottle when the first soldier punched him in the gut. Pain sliced up through his chest as the air left his body. Groaning, he wanted to keel over, but they held him in place.

"That is funny, innit? I thought Yanks only liked tea parties. How about we throw a tea party of our own, lads? Chuck this one out the nearest window?"

Laughter erupted but died quickly when a high-pitched whistle cut out. Teary-eyed and vision blurred, Lockhart managed to turn his head to see two figures in green battledress approach. Hands holding him slipped free. The three British soldiers turned to face the men.

"Let the yank go," an Irish-accented voice said.

"Mind your own business, paddy. We're just messin' around."

"Call me a paddy again. See what happens."

"All right. Get your spud-eatin', bog-lovin', paddy as—"

Commotion broke out around Lockhart. Winded and eyes watering, he couldn't make out the action, but heard grunts and groans and the slaps of knuckles pounding flesh. Disorientated and feeling the effects of the wine, he hardly noticed when two sets of gentle hands lifted him to his feet and guided him away. It was like he blinked, and suddenly, he was sitting at a table in the mess, a plate of food before him and a steaming mug of coffee beside it. He glanced up and studied the shaved-headed soldier across from him devouring his meal, while a much stockier one shook his head, face crinkled in disgust.

"Dub, mate. Show some decorum. There's people around."

"Relax, Mo. This isn't the Ritz Carlton. Anyway, I haven't eaten in two years."

"Here we go again. You ate yesterday, bruv."

"Yeah, in 1954. Two years ago."

Shaking his head, Mo shifted his attention to Lockhart and smiled. A vague familiarity came with that grin. Sensing no threat, Lockhart reached for his cup and sipped.

"Feeling better, Captain?"

At hearing his preferred nickname, Lockhart perked up. He couldn't place where he knew either soldier from but guessed he must have transported them on a mission at some point in the past. He took another sip of coffee and nodded.

"Yes, yes, I am. And my thanks to you. To both of you. Mo, is it?"

"Big Mo. Mo is fine, though," he said, pointing to himself and then gesturing at the Irishman. "This is Dub."

"No worries, Captain," Dub said, shoving his empty plate forward. "We owe you. You saved our lives. More times than you'll ever know. No thanks needed."

Nodding at his words, Lockhart brought the cup to his lips again. Eyes stinging, he could already feel the alcohol dissipating through his body, and even with the coffee, his brain calling out for sleep. Taking a sip all the same, he studied the bruises on the knuckles of both men.

"You been here long?" Big Mo asked.

"Couple weeks," Lockhart said. "They're trying to get the North Carolina fully operational again, so I was shifting between the Makin Island and the Bonhomme Richard for a while before they sent me down here. What about you fellas?"

"We have always been here," Dub said.

Big Mo slapped his hand over his face. "What my colleague means is, we've been here so long it feels like forever."

"This base in particular sucks," Dub said, looking around. "Proper shithole if ever I've seen one. Hard to believe what's about to kick off here."

"What's about to happen?" Lockhart said, leaning in.

"Nothing," Big Mo gasped, grabbing Dub by the arm and shaking him. "I mean, we have suspicions the Martians are going to attack at some point. It is a very isolated outpost when you take away air travel. Call it a soldier's hunch."

"Yeah, like instinct or some shit," Dub said. "Which reminds me. You have a flight scheduled in forty-five minutes back to New Berlin, right? You mentioned it when we were bringing you here."

The realisation of his oncoming departure sobered Lockhart up even more. He didn't recall mentioning it but considering the journey to the mess was a blur, it made sense. Downing another mouthful of coffee, he nodded.

"Yeah, you're right. Slipped my mind there for a minute. Why? You need a lift?"

"Nah, we're good," Dub said. "We're here for a while, but we're heading in the direction of the hangar bay. Good if we tag along, and swap stories on the way?"

"I'd like that," Lockhart said and stood. "You boys are all right. How about when I get back, I buy us all a round?"

"I don't drink," Big Mo said, smiling. "This one's a walking bottle of whiskey in human form, though. I doubt he'll object to a beer or seven."

The two rose and fell in beside Lockhart. In a weird way, he felt strangely safe in their presence. Even amongst his fellow American pilots, he struggled to make friends, except for his co-pilot Cheech. Giving a grateful nod, he exited the mess with them.

When he hummed along to the tune of *California Love*, they joined in.

WEHRMACHT OBSERVATION POST ALPHA ONE-ONE, NEAR FORWARD BASE ZULU
18:55 MST
DAY 749
(-1 DAY)

"No, no, no!" Brandt said and slammed his fist off the map. "Tell General Klein I need the Fifth Panzer four kilometres north of their current position. If he doesn't get them there within the next three hours, he is to be relieved of his command. I will not risk the northern pincer on his false concerns about the terrain."

Fuming at having to manage such a man-child, Brandt pushed himself up from the map while the lieutenant scampered away. Adjusting his uniform, he glanced over the various counters. Crimson represented the native militias fighting beneath the umbrella of the Red Blades, grey the Wehrmacht, SS, and Volkssturm under his command, black the werewolf units, and green the MOF.

Although the Mars Occupation Force outnumbered Brandt's forces, the natives dwarfed them when all combined. Easily twenty to one and growing. A mere fraction of them were trained to a standard he'd consider acceptable by modern equivalents, but the Native Martians possessed a surprise weapon he suspected would turn the tide of any battle. Even if they faltered, they possessed the resources to launch human wave attacks, if necessary, to wear down the enemy.

Turning his focus to Forward Base Zulu, he studied the mass of Red Blade militia already encircling it, concealed in their underground tunnels. The MOF soldiers were surrounded. They just didn't realise it. Based on the plans he had signed off on, he expected the installation to fall within a matter of hours.

Once that happened, the gates to New Berlin stood open. His panzers would strike hard and deep into enemy territory, flanking the MOF units on patrol before boxing them into a salient and destroying them piecemeal. The second surprise weapon the natives prepared lay ready to disrupt the Allied air superiority, rendering their orbiting ships' ferocious firepower moot.

"Herr Feldmarschall," Oberst Walu said and stormed towards him.

"At ease," Brandt said with a flick of his hand, pre-empting any salute.

43

"Herr Feldmarschall," Walu said, thrusting a datapad into his hands. "You must see this."

Taking the time to light a cigarette, Brandt eyed Walu. Letting the cigarette dangle from his lips, he inhaled, took the device, and tapped at the screen. Grainy black and white footage showed the interior of what looked like the natives' council room. Squinting, he even recognised several of the Native Martian leaders allied to his cause. The various councillors gestured with hands, rose, and sat, jaws continually moving. Even without any sound, he could see from their contorted faces and gestures their discussions were growing more heated. Perplexed at what he was watching, he nearly handed it back, but Walu spoke first.

"Wait for it, Herr Feldmarschall."

Brandt tapped ash from his cigarette, took another drag and focused again on the screen. The animated motions continued for several moments, and then everyone froze. After a brief pause, eyes glanced at each other. One of the council guards stepped closer to the door. It exploded in a flash of white light, knocking most of the councillors from their seats and hurling others across the table.

When the video footage stabilised from the blast, a small-statured soldier clad in an armoured suit walked through the smouldering doorway, strange-looking machine gun in hand. Brandt studied the unusual armour and weapon, perplexed at who could be behind the attack. Some of the councillors dragged themselves up and raised their hands in surrender, but the soldier levelled his gun and squeezed the trigger.

The muzzle flashes and bullets ripped through the bodies of the counsellors. Blood sprayed across the walls. Bullet-riddled corpses collapsed. A lone councillor to the soldier's right charged, but an armoured hand snapped out and grabbed him by the throat. Lifting him into the air, metal fingers twitched and squeezed before tossing the native away like a rag doll. After surveying the carnage, the soldier pulled out a grenade, tugged the pin, tossed it, and exited. The final flash caused the footage to end, replaced by static.

"What was that?" Brandt said, focusing on Walu. "I've never seen such an EVA suit. The council...are they all dead?"

"Yes, Herr Feldmarschall. All twenty-three councillors were killed in the attack. Intelligence reports indicate the operation was carried out by a covert unit based in the American Zone. Moles within Eisenhower Colony suggest these may be the result of something referred to as the Hollow Programme. Does this mean anything to you, sir?"

After stubbing out his cigarette under his boot, Brandt lit another and puffed while his thoughts raced. He did recognise the name. Back in New Berlin, officers often chatted about the secret experiments the SS ran on the Jewish population. Although much of it remained rumour and subjective, certain themes recurred in every retelling. Soldiers whose consciousness could be transferred to replicated versions of their own bodies, effectively staving off death.

Even more intriguing, one of these stories indicated the only ones capable of surviving such a process were people who inherited certain genetic traits. A throwback to a warrior class from a civilisation long since lost to the mists of time. He believed little of those tales, but the MOF's unprovoked attack on the Native Martian leadership played right into his hands. It certainly presented him with a handful of unique opportunities.

"My condolences on the loss of your leaders," Brandt said. "On behalf of the Führer and the German people, I vow we will take our revenge on the cold-blooded murderers who plague you and kill with impunity."

"Thank you, Herr Feldmarschall. I will transmit your words to the newly elected representatives who have tasked me with passing a message to you on the back of this most grievous attack. With the establishment of a new council, a vote has been tabled. By unanimous decision, the twenty-three clans have pledged allegiance to the Red Blades and endorsed your plan. We are with you, Herr Feldmarschall. My entire people stand with you and the Reich. The time to strike at the invaders draws near."

Masking his elation, Brandt gave a slight nod and

glanced at his watch. Hours away from the start of the operation, he had millions of people at his disposal. He marched over to the nearest radio, everyone in the room falling silent at his actions. After activating the scrambler, he opened a channel to all the waiting forces under his command, monitoring for his signal. Slipping his cigarette from his lips, he raised the microphone to his mouth and pressed down on the button with his thumb.

"Downfall. I repeat, Downfall."

Dropping the mic, he turned to see every officer, NCO, and soldier standing at attention, their arms outstretched in salute. Someone in the background started singing the Reich anthem, and within a heartbeat, a thunderous chorus of voices joined in. Smiling to himself, Brandt listened to their words and looked across their determined faces.

Remembering the vow he made to himself two years earlier, he added his voice to their song.

FORWARD BASE ZULU
21:23 MST
DAY 749
(-1 DAY)

Watford trudged across the storage room beside the medical bay and dumped another pile of ironed bedsheets onto the growing stack. She paused and looked over the other neat rows covering three of the four walls. It had taken two hours to organise it, not factoring in the five hours of ironing bed sheets before that. Task completed, she ran a hand over her face and adjusted her beret.

Over the past few days, ninety percent of her work involved some form of manual labour. Along with the rest of the combat medics relegated to nurse status, she mopped floors, washed clothes, made beds, changed bed pans, and organised the endless flow of paperwork crammed high on the admin desk. It wouldn't have been so bad if she could at least hone her skills with actual medical work, but the medical bay was surprisingly empty. Four soldiers were there with sprained or broken ankles, and a Scottish sergeant awaited transport back to New Berlin for surgery on his back. Two French lieutenants complained of chest pains earlier but left after Doctor Fawcett prescribed them a drop of brandy.

Frustrating as her duties could be, Watford was grateful for the company and new friendships. Thirty women had been assigned to the medical bay, all under the command of Lieutenant Tracy and Corporal Mick Owens.

"Fighting Bill" Tracy hardly behaved like an officer suited to a medical unit. Red-faced, fleshy, and constantly reeking of booze, if anything, he looked five steps away from a heart attack. Despite his appearance, he treated them with a surprising amount of respect while lamenting their status. Alongside Corporal Owens, he cared about the way they were being sidelined and the impact it could have on soldiers in the field should hostilities break out.

"Penny for your thoughts?" a voice said from the doorway.

Watford looked up and recognised the smiling face of the woman who had stood behind her in the hangar bay line. Private Anderson had fast come to be one of the more popular women in the platoon for her carefree demeanour and friendly attitude to everyone. More popularly known by her nickname "Smack," she had unofficially become the mother hen to them all and a good friend.

"Put a bullet in my head right now," Private Sheffield said, strolling up beside her. "I'm not built for giving a shit about this shit."

Sheffield, who went by the moniker of "Noid," was another story altogether. She and Smack were fast friends from a previous assignment, but Noid couldn't have been any more different. Although she pulled her weight and got her hands dirty, she was hot-headed and didn't take lip from anyone, fellow medic or officer. Qualities that made her a favourite with Fighting Bill.

"I'm just tired," Watford said and exited the storage room. "It's been a long day and an even longer week."

Smack and Noid fell in beside her, and they walked on to the medical bay. Pausing, she glanced over the sea of empty beds resting there, her section of medics alternating between menial tasks and checking on their five patients. Fawcett was nowhere to be seen while Fighting Bill snoozed loudly on his desk.

"Long left on your shift?" Smack asked.

"About an hour. Suppose I'll help Owens with admin stuff and then wander back to acquaint myself with the mattress and pillow."

"Where are you billeted?" Noid said, checking her nails.

"A dingy little closet down in section 18G. Level Two. I'd welcome you gals back for a cuppa tea, but I wouldn't inflict that place on my worst enemy."

The women glanced at one another and then back at her.

"There's a sewage leak in section 18. E, F and G compartments. Billets are fine, but the place stinks."

"What?" Watford said. "When did that happen?"

"About an hour ago," Noid said. "I know someone who lives in 18F. Told me the place smells like a sewer. Should be ok in a couple of hours, but I wouldn't recommend going back there anytime soon."

"Agreed," Smack said. "How about instead, I help you with that admin work and when your shift ends, we all go back to mine for a little while? You know...until the stink clears."

Eyeing the women, Watford shrugged. The last thing she wanted to do was go back to her shoebox and deal with any form of putrid smell. One of the secondary generators for Level 2 was right beside her room, so if they were trying to fix the sewage system, that would be kicking into overdrive anyway. Grateful for the offer, she nodded at Smack.

"Ok. Let's get stuck into those files, then. I mean, who needs sleep, right?"

With a smile, Smack rested her hand on her shoulder, and they walked over to join Corporal Owens. Noid glanced at her watch, took a seat in the corner, and glared at the door as if expecting someone.

Thinking nothing of it, Watford threw herself into her work.

WEHRMACHT OBSERVATION POST ALPHA ONE-ONE, NEAR FORWARD BASE ZULU
03:00 MST
DAY 1

"Downfall has begun, Herr Feldmarschall," Oberst Walu said. "All units have commenced operations."

Leaning in close to the reinforced window overlooking Forward Base Zulu, Brandt raised the night vision goggles to his eyes. He scanned the landscape outside the outpost and spotted the Red Blade teams infiltrating the perimeter fence while thousands of their comrades used the underground tunnels to attack from beneath. Across Mars, the Red Blades, supported by the Wehrmacht, mobilised to launch lightning strikes against bases, installations, and army groups. Behind the lines, the werewolves would initiate their sabotage operations and bombing campaigns to sow further anarchy.

"Excellent," he said, searching for any signs of discovery across the exterior of the base. "And the jamming signal?"

"Coming online now, Herr Feldmarschall. In a few minutes, all communications with the orbiting fleet will be jammed."

"May the Führer grant us success," General Fischer said.

"Providence walks with us," Brandt said and lowered his goggles. "Once again, the strength and purity of Aryan blood will guide us to victory. Heil Hitler!"

"Heil Hitler!"

A-COMPANY BILLETS, LEVEL 5, FORWARD BASE ZULU
03:03 MST
DAY 1

Sheets of thunder rumbling in the distance stirred McCabe from his light and dreamless sleep. His first thoughts were of being out in the harsh Martian landscape, huddling in caves with his battalion to seek shelter from the horrific storms the planet unleashed. Grown men cried at the sheer force of those ungodly winds, and in

49

the darkness, they sat together day after day. Blackness surrounded them at all hours. The light leaking in from under the door of his private room calmed him. Forcing himself up, he rubbed his face, wondering if the noise had even been real to start with.

Thoughts of being out in the field caused his chest to tighten and his skin to turn clammy. He eyed the half-empty bottle of whiskey perched on his nightstand and pondered indulging in a nightcap to soothe his disintegrating nerves and hopefully induce at least another hour or two of restless sleep. The rumbling started up again, leaking through the thick copper-coloured walls. Curiosity setting in, he quickly hauled on his battledress and boots and slipped his Webley revolver into its holster. He made for the door when the panel on the wall chirped to life. Lighting a cigarette first, he pressed the comm button.

"Lieutenant McCabe, this is Lieutenant Chang, USAF Makin Island. Do you read me?"

Curious why one of the orbiting ships would call him and not C&C or the duty officer, he exhaled. "Makin Island, send verification code."

Seconds later, the small section of the panel beneath the comm piece spewed out a string of green-coloured numbers. Head groggy from his two hours of uneasy sleep, it took him a moment to confirm the sequence as genuine, and he pressed down on the button.

"Confirmed, Makin Island. This is McCabe. Go ahead."

"Lieutenant, there's a large body of hostiles approaching Forward Base Zulu. We've been unable to reach your C&C. Has the base been attacked? Do you require aerial bomb—"

McCabe's blood froze and shook free any lingering cobwebs of exhaustion. He waited for Chang to continue his sentence, but the signal dropped. Numbness setting in, he pressed the button to re-establish the connection, but every attempt failed. He tried to contact C&C, the duty officer, or anyone else capable of receiving a communication. The line stayed quiet.

Revolver in hand, he dashed out into the corridor, half-expecting to see a werewolf hit squad waiting to gun him down. Aside from the soldiers posted outside the platoon billets, no one else stirred. He raced to their freshly assigned captain's room and pounded on Captain Chastain's door. When no answer came back, he waited three seconds and tore the door open, revealing an unoccupied bed. Heart pounding, he made his way to Mad Jack's room, repeated the exercise, and again found the officer missing.

"Everything all right, sir?" Private Doherty said from outside Sixth Platoon's billets.

"No," he said. "Reveille now. The entire battalion. Something's going on."

The soldiers on duty passed the order to one another and barged into their respective platoons shouting and roaring at everyone to wake. McCabe made his way to the nearest window port and glared into the darkness shrouding them. Somewhere in the distance, a flash of green lightning illuminated the terrain in an eerie glow. It took him a moment to realise the ships in orbit were firing at something outside the Cutline.

"What's going on, sir?" Colour Sergeant Brown said, pulling up beside him while soldiers, NCOs, and platoon commanders stumbled from their billets.

"Something's not right, Jim. I got a call from the Makin Island saying hostiles were approaching. Internal comms are down, so I can't reach C&C. Mad Jack and Captain Chastain are missing. Where's Sergeant Major Howells?"

"Not in his billets. You reckon we're under attack?"

"Could be. Find the BQ. I want the company stores opened and ready to go, just in case. Send a runner to the other companies too. Double time."

"On it, Bill."

McCabe strode towards the assembling platoon leaders and looked them all over. He gave them the information he had and then turned his gaze to Lieutenant MacDonald. As the next most senior officer, the company was his until they located Captain Chastain.

"You made the right call, Bill," MacDonald said. "Right now, we need to find out what the hell is going on. Lieutenant Barrymore, take a section and lead them to C&C. With internal comms down, we need to find out where we're needed. Lieutenant Hill, I want you to take the remainder of Barrymore's platoon and your own to post guards and begin recces of the level. Try to find out what's happening. McCabe, you, and Third Platoon will..."

McCabe zoned out of the conversation, his instincts flaring to life. He spotted two soldiers in MOF colours working their way through the assembling company. Everything about their gait appeared wrong. They slipped through the crowd, backpacks strapped tight, and entered the stores. The surrounding officers sensed it, and all followed his gaze. MacDonald broke into a sprint and, revolver in hand, roared at the soldiers nearest the storeroom.

"Get dow—"

Fireballs ripped through the stores and burst out into the corridor. Searing flames washed over stunned men, hurling fiery bodies through the air. The blast knocked McCabe from his feet and threw him full force against the wall. He crumpled to the ground, ears ringing and vision blurry. High-pitched screams cut over the whistling sounds carving through his skull, and he forced himself to blink his eyes clear. Muscles, back, and head aching, he pushed himself to his knees and glared at the devastation.

Smouldering, broken bodies lay scattered. Roaring soldiers dragged their wounded comrades away from the blast, while others attacked the blazing room with anything they could use to bat out the flames and smoke threatening their air supply. Charred limbs and smears stained the floor. McCabe rose and wobbled but managed to steady himself as warm blood dripped down his face. He stumbled forward and paused at MacDonald's eviscerated corpse and lifeless eyes.

"Sir, sir," Jenkins said, pulling up to his side. "Are you okay, sir?"

He nodded and, still stunned, looked over the carpet of bodies. At least twenty covered the scene. Another two dozen wounded to some degree or another. He replayed the images of those two soldiers entering the stores and clamped his eyelids shut. Werewolves. Nazi werewolves had infiltrated the base. Shedding any last shreds of doubt about their situation, he opened his eyes.

"Lieutenant Barrymore," he called out.

Barrymore helped up one of his wounded men, eased him into the arms of a waiting comrade, and turned to face him. Gashes lined his forehead and cheeks while soot stained the rest of his skin.

"The company's yours," McCabe said. "Orders?"

"Salvage what we can from the stores," Barrymore said with a cough. "Take your platoon to C&C, Bill. Do it quickly. I'll reach out to the other companies and the Freikorps. We need to establish a defence now."

"On it," McCabe said and turned to rally his platoon.

Jenkins corralled the surviving soldiers and privates while McCabe looked on. Through the window ports, he spotted more flashes of green. The concrete floor and walls rumbled, not from orbiting fire but from explosions all around. Intuition told him the situation was far worse than he expected.

Forward Base Zulu was about to be overwhelmed.

WHEN PLANETS COLLIDE

MEDICAL BAY, LEVEL 2, FORWARD BASE ZULU
03:10 MST
DAY 1

Snapping her head up from the desk, Watford wiped the drool from her chin and glanced around. She didn't recall falling asleep and shoved the mess of papers back into something of a semi-organised pile. To her right, curled up in a ball, Corporal Owens slept between piles of files while Fighting Bill continued to snore loudly from his desk. The medics on duty carried on their endless circling of the main area, wandering in between the empty rows of beds to glance over their five patients and keep themselves busy with whatever they could find. She couldn't spot Smack or Noid but assumed they'd gone back to their billets.

Yawning, she pushed herself up from the desk and contemplated the trek back to her own bed. She fixed her beret and was sauntering out when the flooring beneath her wobbled. Blinking, she wondered if she was half asleep when a series of booming noises echoed through the reinforced walls. Adrenaline coursed through her veins, and she raced back into the office and slammed the comm button. The panel refused to light up. She jabbed it again, but the silence lingered. Mind fully awakened, she shook Owens when a longer screeching sound rocked the base again. His eyes bolted open, and together they roused Fighting Bill.

"It's not artillery," Fighting Bill said, listening to the noise leaking through the walls. "Small arms, grenades. Maybe even medium-sized explosives. Werewolves, most likely. Ballsy bastards must've sent hit squads in to stir up trouble. Our boys will take care of 'em."

"I have no doubt, sir," Watford said amongst her gathered medics. "But if there's fighting within the base, then we're going to have injuries. With the comms down, we need to find out what's going on and where we're needed."

"Agreed," Fighting Bill said, scratching his chin. "Corporal Owens. Get up to C&C and find out what's happening. Private Watford, Private Roche, I want the two of you to head down to the hangar bay. If something's going on, it'll be coming from ground level. Treat any injured you come across, but I want you two back here if it sounds like trouble's heading your way. You're no good to me dead. Everyone else, prepare to receive casualties."

Heart pounding, Watford grabbed her medical kit and pulled on her helmet. Giving Roche a nod, she led the way and crept into the corridor. Lights flickered every time a rumble rang out, but she was grateful they held. They pushed on down the passageway and halted at the first stairwell. Watford took a few careful steps out and, gripping the railing, glanced up and down, seeking out any signs of friend or foe. Echoes of gunfire rattled from both directions. Had the enemy somehow gotten into the upper levels?

Confirming the coast as clear, Watford took point again and kept close to the walls, skulking down. Pausing at the ground level, she gave another nod to Roche and gripped the door handle. With a tug, she pulled it open and stepped into the hallway. Bullet holes riddled the walls. Smoke hung heavy in the air, clogging her nose, and scratching the back of her throat. Spying a body lying prone, she ducked down, crawled over to it, and rolled it over. Unmoving eyes stared up at the ceiling, blood leaking from a gash to the head. She stumbled when her gaze fell to the singed hole in the middle of the soldier's chest.

"What type of round could do that?" Roche said, leaning in. "A .5 cal?"

"No," Watford said and prodded at the charred flesh around the edges of the injury. "It seared the wound closed. Look, no blood at all. Bullets don't do that."

A pulsing surge of green light ripped through the smoke and struck Roche. Watford whipped about and dived towards her colleague. The gaping hole beneath her neck showed her as dead. She hit the floor when another flash cut through the space where she had knelt and zipped down the corridor. Unsure of what was happening, she rolled away from her murdered comrade and slammed back into the fallen soldier. She spotted the Lee-Enfield resting at his side, grabbed, cocked, and aimed it down the smoky hallway. Another flare lashed out, showing two tall silhouettes plodding towards her.

She shot once, knocking one of the shadows down with a guttural roar. Flaming energy zoomed over her head in response. Hammering on the trigger, Watford fired until the last enemy fell. She tapped at the dead soldier's belt, pulled out an ammo clip and slipped it into the rifle. Taking a deep breath, she eased herself into a kneeling position and waited, half-expecting another shot to ring out. Time dragged on until she forced herself up.

Keeping low, she rushed forward, Lee-Enfield at the ready, and came to a halt over the fallen enemy. She stumbled back at the sight of their unusually tall and thin dispositions, gaunt faces, and wiry limbs. It took her a moment to recognise them as the Native Martians she had learned about during orientation after arriving on the planet. Gazing over their copper-coloured uniforms, she kicked them for a reaction, but they lay lifeless. Realising she had killed them, she willed herself to push on just as a low moan echoed out from the end of the corridor.

Rifle aimed at the sound, Watford remained tight against the wall and crept on. She paused when the outline of a figure slumped on the floor came into view. As she approached, she made out the colours of the British battledress and lowered her weapon. A wounded private lay there, teeth clamped, hand pressed against the charred left side of his leg, a chunk of his outer thigh muscle missing.

"It's okay," Watford said, dropping to a knee. "You'll be fine."

"They're everywhere," he said, eyes bulging. "Bastards came out of the shadows and started gunning us down. We need to get out of here now."

"I'll get you out, but first, I need to find someone in command. If there're any more injured, we need to evacuate them too."

"You don't understand," the private said, grabbing her by the collar. "They've captured the hangar bay and most of Level 1. Captain Jones rallied a defence on the stairwells, but the Martians are still slipping through somehow. There's no wounded down there. Everyone's either dead or standing by to be killed."

Absorbing his words, Watford slung the rifle strap over her shoulder and slipped her hands under the soldier. She dragged him up while he whined at the attempt. Throwing an arm over her own shoulder for support, she grabbed him and hobbled him on a step. Moaning, he plodded another pace before his good leg buckled, and he tumbled over. She caught him, tightened her grip, and redoubled her effort.

"I'm too heavy," he said. "You'll need a bloody stretcher."

"You're not the first man I've carried," Watford said, "and you sure as hell won't be the last. Suck it up, princess. We need to move."

Grimacing, the private nodded, and they limped back down the murky corridor.

LEVEL 3, FORWARD BASE ZULU
03:37 MST
DAY 1

Ray guns. The bastarding Martians had ray guns. Jenkins threw himself up against the wall. Green flashes shot past him and pounded into concrete, blowing large, scorched chunks into the stone.

"FSG!" he shouted. "Suppressive fire on my order.

Everyone else, fix bayonets. Prepare to charge."

Attaching his bayonet to the end of his rifle, Jenkins looked over the remnants of his platoon. Murderous energy beams shot down an entire section while they recced Level 4. Two of the enemy killed nine men outright before they were put down. No one knew how many of the Native Martians had infiltrated, but they seemed to be everywhere. The Second Battalion and the Freikorps had cleared and secured Level 5 for the moment but reports of fighting above and below still filtered through. The only good news they had so far was that their shortwave radios worked, even if the base comms were down.

"Fire!"

The Bren light machine gun roared to life, three-second bursts ploughing lead back down the corridor and ceasing the enemy shots. Leading the way, Jenkins pushed out into the passageway. He stayed close to the wall, and bullets streamed passed him to his right, centimetres away, but he kept his gaze focused on the end of the hallway, scanning for any of the Martians risking a peek. Stopping a few metres away, he pulled out a grenade, ripped the pin and tossed it around the corner. The blast hurled two bloodied Martians to the ground and screams followed. The Bren fell silent, and Jenkins threw himself into action.

Swinging around the turn, he spied a wounded enemy fumbling to raise his weapon. Jenkins fired first. His soldiers swarmed into the position, blasting their rifles, gunning down the Martians without a single return shot. They scoured the fallen, plunging bayonets into flesh to confirm their deaths, and secured both ends of the junction.

Stooping over the larger of the downed Martians, he snatched up one of the weapons. Similar in style to a pistol, it had a cylindrical barrel and handle, and a single stud functioned as what he guessed to be the trigger. He slipped it into the back of his belt for examination and waved up the rest of the platoon. Waiting for them to gather, he pointed to his left.

"One Section, guard this corridor. No one gets past. Two Section, with me. We move to the end of the hallway on the right and secure the stairwell. FSG, at the front and ready to blast any of those Nazi pricks if they come at us. Make it happen, people."

The platoon split and swept into their respective sections. Bren at his side, Jenkins led them up the passageway, aware of how vulnerable they were in such a confined space. A handful of well-timed grenades from a patient team at the stairwell could wipe them all out, so he increased his jog to a sprint, gun levelled at the doorway. They reached the door without incident, and Privates Heaney and Patel took up positions on either side. On Patel's count, Heaney dashed through, Lee-Enfield turning about with Patel close on his heels. After four seconds of silence, Heaney flashed the thumbs up, and the section surged in.

Gunfire resonated above and below. From the external wall to their left, Jenkins sensed the vibrations of explosions leaking through the stone. Fierce battles were raging all around, and they still had no clue about the enemy's strength or disposition.

Flashing hand signals at the soldiers behind, Jenkins ordered the FSG to fall in on him and the rest of the section to guard their current position. Private Burke, lugging the Bren, aimed it down the stairs below while Private Pugg, carrying the ammo, took his place at the rear. A wall of rifles guarding their top and bottom, Jenkins crept down the metal staircase, expecting werewolf gunmen to open up from an unseen vantage point at every step. He reached the Level 2 door and paused, the sounds of battle leaking through.

Mouthing words of caution to Heaney and Patel, Jenkins yanked at the door, rifle seeking out any threat. Rows of wounded MOF soldiers lined the corridor, blood slicking the ground. He stepped through first, ears tracking the gunfire to his left. Urging his FSG team on, he followed them to the end of the hallway. An injured lieutenant propped up beside the opened door while clutching a silent radio brought Jenkins to a stop.

"Sir," he said, dropping to a knee. "I'm on orders from Second Batt HQ to find out what the hell is going on down here. How bad are we being hit?"

The officer groaned and shifted his weight. He dropped the unresponsive comm onto his lap. Blood soaked through the bandages on his shoulder and chest, and his pale skin dripped with sweat.

"I don't know the full scope," he said, gritting his teeth. "Somehow, they struck from the hangar bay and must've worked their way up. Level 1 has fallen, and this quarter of Level 2 is about all we have left. I have two platoons spread across the corridors around us trying to hold the Nazis back, but they're overwhelming us with those laser guns of theirs. They chew through skin and brick like it's nothing.

"There's also an allied force of unknown strength who have sealed themselves into the main storage bay beneath the central core. I have no idea how, but they're holding their ground. We need to stop them here, Corporal. If they take this hallway, we lose our last entry point to Level 2 and the medical bay's right behind us. I got wounded in there, and we know the Nazis don't take prisoners. At least not ones who'll live for long."

"Understood, sir," Jenkins said and pulled his notebook and pencil from his pocket.

He jotted down the main points, tore the paper loose and handed it to Patel. "Private, tell the platoon to hold their positions until further notice. The stairwell and corridors are not to fall. Take this message to Lieutenant Barrymore and request reinforcements. Double time, Patel."

"Yes, Corporal," Patel said, taking the note and slipping it into his uniform.

Without delay, he dashed back down the hallway and into the stairwell. After nodding at Burke, Jenkins shifted his attention back to the officer.

"Where do you need us, sir?"

"Take a right here," the lieutenant said, jabbing his thumb. "Follow the passageway for about a hundred metres. That'll bring you to the storage bay entrance. Whoever's left alive out there will show you exactly where you're required. Don't let the storage bay fall, Corporal. If the Nazis take it, they'll have a direct route up through the centre of the base. They'll catch us in the crossfire and cut us to pieces."

"On it, sir."

After signalling Burke, Jenkins stepped into the hallway and followed the gunshots. They reached a makeshift barricade set five metres outside the door to the storage area and dropped down behind sandbags peppered with bullet holes. Burke propped his Bren up and aimed down the corridor. Jenkins aided the one remaining soldier manning the post, trying to apply bandages to his bleeding chest. He fixed the bandage tight and, keeping low, took his place beside Burke, setting the ammo between them. Flashes of green light filtered through the window ports like some macabre lightning storm. Peering out, he noted the blazing explosions on the horizon as the orbiting ships bombarded the surface and the much smaller flickers raging from the land around the base.

"Anything?" he said to Burke.

"Nothing, Corporal. No movement at all."

"They're coming up through the floor," the wounded corporal rasped. "About forty metres out. Tricky bastards drilled their way up from under us."

While Burke altered his aim, Jenkins crawled back over to the corporal. Advising Burke to hold his position, he slid onto his back. Gripping the corporal by his webbing, he dragged him across the bullet-littered ground, back towards the relative safety of the other hallway. He'd just hauled him through the airlock when a flutter of darkness pulled his attention to the nearest window port.

For a split second, he thought it nothing more than another explosion from the aerial attacks, but a shadow lingered against the reinforced glass. He blinked and spotted a silhouette up against the frame and made out the outline of an EVA suit-wearing soldier attaching something. In the dim light, he recognised the style of the Wehrmacht's design, and his jaw dropped when he made out what looked like a bomb fixed to the exterior glass. Realising he didn't have time to reach the other hallway and make it back to Burke, he hauled the corporal back towards the storage bay.

"Bomb!" he roared and slammed the airlock shut.

The explosion rocked the entire corridor. Debris pinged and rattled as atmosphere leaked out of the ruptured exterior wall. Burke's Bren belched to life. Green energy bolts lashed out and blasted the sandbags to pieces. Jenkins pulled out a grenade, tore the pin and tossed it overhead. Lifting his Lee-Enfield, he waited for the boom. Shards of metal and flesh slapped against the walls. Wounded voices cried out.

Through the smoke, Jenkins aimed at staggering shadows and fired.

OUTSIDE COMMAND AND CONTROL CENTRE, LEVEL 10, FORWARD BASE ZULU
05:27 MST
DAY 1

"Sir, we're coming up now," McCabe said into the radio handset and then flung it at the operator.

Waving on the platoons, he rushed up to the soldiers at the intersection pouring fire down the corridor. Periodic green streeks of energy shimmered back, blasting lumps out of the wall between the two groups. Particle beams, McCabe remembered Dub telling him. He could still recall the devastating effect those weapons had on New Berlin's city centre when manned by four people. If the Wehrmacht had gotten their hands on such technology, it explained the sheer devastation of their lightning attack on Forward Base Zulu. Hours later, and the MOF were still trying to grapple with the assault and set up at least some basic defensive lines.

On his order, two soldiers with rocket-propelled grenades took up position at either corner, protected by blasts of Bren fire to keep the enemy at bay. Everyone else slunk back when the RPGs opened up and waited for the overwhelming booms. Howls of pain ensued, but the Brens suppressed them with another volley of short bursts. McCabe sprinted from his cover and, Webley drawn, he charged headfirst into the smoking corridor.

A stumbling shadow tumbled ahead, so he shot once,

dropping it. Energy bolts lashed out in response and went astray, but from the cries of shock, struck someone to his rear. Adrenaline pumping through his body, McCabe pressed on and fired into the smoke again before an enemy soldier lunged from the side. Dodging the strike, he tried to fire at the Nazi point blank. Bayonet steel bit into his hand, causing the pistol to slip. Lone bullets cracked back in defiance, but in such a closed area, no one risked hitting their commanding officer. Growling, McCabe grabbed the Nazi's K98k rifle and shoved him back against the wall. His soldiers raced past him and dived into the shadows, jabbing, and slashing at hidden opponents.

The Nazi tried to headbutt him, but McCabe avoided the strike and rammed his knee into the man's groin. When the German buckled over, he ripped the gun from his hands, pointed down, and shot him in the face. Another particle blast lashed out and decapitated Corporal Higgins, knocking his headless corpse into two of his privates. Grenade blasts from the end of the corridor sent smouldering figures crashing into the walls. Still hanging onto his new K98k, McCabe collected his revolver and pushed on.

Most of the bodies at his feet were charred and torn apart from the first barrage of RPGs, but some of his men rested with them, burnt holes in their torsos. He lowered his rifle at the sight of MOF uniforms surrounding two surrendering Wehrmacht soldiers, their hands in the air.

"What are you doing?" Colour Sergeant Brown said, strolling up to the captives. "Werewolf rules."

Private Doherty glanced at his colleagues and then back at Brown. "Sorry, Colour Sergeant, but what in the hell is that?"

McCabe took aim at one of the prisoners and pulled the trigger. The round punched through his face and sprayed his brain across the wall. Lowering his weapon, he stepped closer to the remaining prisoner.

"Leave only one alive to show we mean business. Extract every ounce of information from the survivor. Private Duplantier, are you still with us?"

"Yes, sir," the French soldier said, striding up.

"Good. Take him into the corner. Acquaint him with your knife, MEF style. I want to know everything about the enemy plans, strength, and movements."

"My pleasure, sir."

As Duplantier grabbed the crying prisoner and lifted him up, the blast barricades to their left rose. Guns clacked up in response. Holding his hand up to steady everyone, McCabe waited for the reinforced doors of C&C to fully open. Mad Jack stood on the other side, his head and left arm wrapped in bandages.

"Colour Sergeant," McCabe said. "Secure the outer area and await further orders."

"You got it, sir."

McCabe stepped into C&C and took Mad Jack's side. He glanced about at the rows of monitors and workstations lining the walls and the table in the middle of the room covered in maps. Wounded soldiers crammed the corners. He spotted Colonel Penford and Sergeant Major Howells amongst them, both men unconscious but breathing. Captain Chastain's unblinking eyes stared at the ceiling nearby.

Mad Jack led him to the table and pointed at a pyramid shape in the centre. McCabe smiled when he recognised a rough outline of Forward Base Zulu made with decks of playing cards. The outer ones had their insides cut out, giving an insight into the interior. Coloured buttons across the various levels showed an overview of the enemy's position as well as their own. After lifting a pencil, Mad Jack prodded at the structure.

"The hangar bay, Level 1, and Level 2 have mostly been seized by the enemy. They also have established footholds in every other level with the exception of 5, thanks to you, Lieutenant. Regular Wehrmacht forces for the most part, but they're backed by irregular werewolf packs and the Martian militia. Their strength outside the base is unknown, but we are still under limited artillery and mortar fire. We've also lost all contact with the units manning our artillery and anti-aircraft emplacements."

"Do we know how they got in, sir?" McCabe said, leaning into the stack of cards and studying the layout.

"We believe possibly through the hangar bay somehow, but they have affected multiple breaches through the exterior walls. This is a devastating tactic in itself. They detonate explosives, venting atmosphere, and then storm in from outside to seize control. If we are to retain command of Forward Base Zulu, we need to locate these external forces and eliminate them."

"Understood," McCabe said. "We could fight our way down and take one of the Level 1 airlocks, sir? We'd require a hell of a lot of men to do it, though, unless..."

"My thoughts exactly," Mad Jack said and jabbed a finger at their three-dimensional map. "We utilise one of the breaches, climb down, and sweep the surrounding area from there."

"We'd need a lot of cover," McCabe said and stuck a cigarette between his lips. "Otherwise, we'd be sitting ducks."

Mad Jack struck a match and waited for the cigarette to take light. "This installation already has defensive guns built into the walls for such a purpose. Unfortunately, the battalion assigned to base security was decimated, and the survivors are fighting on Level 2. However, we'll utilise who we can of ours and the Freikorps to man those weapons. Take A-Company and get down to ground level, Lieutenant. Clear the area and report back."

"Yes, sir," McCabe said and, after saluting, turned to leave.

"One more thing," Mad Jack said, halting him. "Before we lost all external communications, we received a transmission from Mr. Myers of MAJESTIC-12. He advised his...operatives may be on site. I believe you've had run-ins with this particular group in the past."

Exhaling smoke, McCabe took the cigarette from his mouth and met Mad Jack's gaze. The look in his eyes alone dispelled any doubt. After a two-year hiatus, they were back.

"The Black Visors."

"The Black Visors, Lieutenant. We are officially ordered to support them in any way they require, but I want to make it very plain to you. I don't trust them or

MAJESTIC-12. There's more going on in this place than you and I are privy to. We'll continue to do our duties as Her Majesty's soldiers but keep your eyes and ears open and watch your back. That'll be all, Lieutenant."

For two years, McCabe had expected the news. He often wondered why the Black Visors hadn't returned during the werewolf campaigns and the insurrection. Their return to this place, an outpost under siege, signalled something momentous on the horizon. If the Battle of New Berlin marked the ascension of the MEF to power, then what did Forward Base Zulu represent?

Doubting he'd ever truly know the answer, McCabe made for the exit. He didn't relish dealing with that git of an Irishman, Dub, but he hoped he could see Noid again. They'd kissed only once, a fleeting moment, but in the darkest hours of hunting werewolves across the barren Martian terrain, he often thought of her.

Pushing the memories of Noid aside, he returned to the task at hand.

SS RESEARCH FACILITY ALPHA ONE-THREE-ONE, AMERICAN ZONE OF OCCUPATION
06:45 MST
DAY 1

Reichsführer Wagner studied the grainy footage again and clapped his gloved hands in glee. He found himself mesmerised by the recording of the native council being wiped out by his Hollow creations. Thanks to his connections, he had access to all the video available and observed every movement and action within the operation in detail. A four-person team of teenage Hollows infiltrated a highly secure Native Martian facility, eliminated all opposition, and fulfilled their mission without a single casualty. Hundreds of natives dead at no cost.

Machine gun fire echoing through the walls broke his concentration. Releasing a frustrated sigh, he placed the datapad on the desk and glanced out the windows of the lab. SS guards stood at attention, but they'd be of little use protecting him. Any minute, he expected the message to evacuate.

The flashing green light on the control panel stole his interest. Clearing his throat, he brought the microphone closer to his mouth. Tempering his excitement, he pressed down on the button beneath the flickering indicator and waited.

"New Berlin one-nine-five-six, confirm authentication."

Wagner tapped the code into the console. "Authentication confirmed, London two-zero-one-eight. Stage three successful, London. Core Cadre detected but no interference. I believe they may attempt to disrupt stage four."

A pause stretched out on the comm channel broken by crackling noise. An explosion sprinkled dust from the ceiling onto the control panel. Wagner hated those prolonged silences with his counterparts but had come to accept them.

"Minimal disruption to the timelines detected, New Berlin. No adverse conditions spawned. Proceed to stage four."

Grenade explosions echoed from the corridor directly outside his lab. He fixed his SS uniform and wiped his lips. He had a matter of seconds at best.

"Understood, London. If I may, Subject One is on the loose and beginning to impact my tertiary projects. Is this having any effect on the desired outcome? Permission to terminate, if possible."

"Negative," the voice snapped, increasing in volume. "Anna Bailey is not to be interfered with under any circumstances. Any deviation from this order will result in penalties. London, out."

The line went dead, and Wagner dropped the mic back onto the panel. Sighing, he trudged to the door. Although he couldn't connect the dots himself, it appeared his first Hollow creation Anna Bailey still had a part to play. He just hoped it didn't involve murdering him before he had the opportunity to see his grand schemes come to life.

"Herr Reichsführer," Obergruppenführer Horn said, meeting him at the entrance to the laboratory. "We must evacuate now. The guards will not be able to hold her off for—"

The lab rocked from another explosion. Wagner stumbled but gripped the doorframe for balance at the last minute. Nodding at the Obergruppenführer's words, he slipped his Luger free and allowed the two soldiers outside to flank him. They moved at speed to the door leading out into the corridor and paused as one pulled it open.

Grunts, groans, and knuckles pounding flesh rattled out, interrupted by the occasional gunshot. One of the SS men hurled a smoke grenade to his left and, with a shout, ushered them onto the right. Breaking into a jog, Wagner pushed on when he heard that voice over all others bouncing against the corridor walls.

"Reichsführer!" Anna Bailey screeched. "Death has come for you. You may run, vermin, but you will never escape me."

The hatred in her voice dripped bile from her words and sent a shiver down his spine. Increasing his pace, he paid little attention to the guards around him, uncaring if they fell behind in the hopes they could at least slow his predator. Cries of agony rang out from bare metres away, but he didn't reduce his speed until he reached the hangar bay door. He paused long enough at the entrance to glance back and spied the silhouette of Anna Bailey plod forward at a steady pace. Eyes burning into his, she dragged a pummelled and disfigured SS soldier by his shattered throat. After dumping the body, she burst into a charge. He dived into the hangar bay as the SS guards opened up on her.

Heart pumping while agonised screams bellowed from the corridor, Wagner crossed the distance to the waiting transport and threw himself in. Lights in the hangar bay flickered. One of his soldiers flew through the hangar bay entrance, body flailing until he thumped onto the ground. Wagner banged the hatch shut, but rather than take his seat, he pressed himself against the window port. Anna Bailey stepped into the room.

At seeing his craft shudder to life, she unslung the MP 40 hanging from her shoulder and unleashed a barrage of fire. Bullets pinged against the hull of the vessel. Wagner flinched. The ship rose a metre, and alarms blared to signal the roof opening. Anna tossed her weapon and clenched her fists. Rather than retreat into the safety of the corridor or search for an EVA suit, she broke into a sprint and vaulted at the rising ship. With a reverberating thud, she latched onto the side and hauled herself over to the sealed hatch.

Shocked at her actions as the vessel continued to rise, Wagner pulled away but found himself mesmerised at the hate-filled eyes gazing through the reinforced glass. She appeared as angelic as the day he first clasped eyes on her, but all hints of a friendly, disarming smile had long since faded. Holding onto the hatch with her right hand, she balled her left fist and smashed it against the window with enough force to crack it.

Wagner trembled when she struck it again and fumbled for his pistol. He raised it, but her hand crashed through the glass and grabbed him by the collar. Luger tumbling free, he screamed when she slammed him into the hatch. Fingers reached around his neck and tightened.

Atmosphere seeped from the vessel as they rose beyond the confines of the hangar bay. Holding her breath, body shuddering, Anna refused to let go, her vice-like digits cutting off his air supply. Panicking, Wagner attempted to batt her relentless grasp away. Anna remained unfazed, even as the cold and lack of oxygen impacted her body.

The ship veered, spinning about in a circle. It tilted to the right, and the entire craft rocked. Anna's grip loosened and then slipped free. She dangled from the side of the ship before losing her hold and tumbling below. Gasping, Wagner reached for one of the emergency facemasks under the seats and pulled it across his face. He sucked in air as the transport levelled off and resumed its ascension. Atmosphere still escaping the craft, he stumbled to the hatch and glanced back at the base. Studying the surface, he couldn't see any sign of Anna Bailey.

Experience told him she'd live to fight another day.

**LEVEL 1, OUTSIDE FORWARD BASE ZULU
07:02 MST**

69

BLOOD RED STEEL

DAY 1

McCabe hit the copper sand with a thud, rolled, and swung his Lee-Enfield up. Continuous streams of lead poured from the gun emplacements above, pounding the terrain ahead and to his flanks. Under the sheer volume of bullets spewing from the base, the enemy was unable to fire back from whatever hidden positions they occupied. He took a second to glance back up at the battle-scarred base and saw the company stream down the ropes, dropping one at a time into all-round cover.

When First Platoon gathered around him, he signalled to advance, and they crawled forward. From the intelligence Mad Jack provided, they had a rough idea of the Nazis' potential locations. It still meant sweeping the area thoroughly until they located them. Their only advantage in engaging them outside was their ability to bring the Weapons Platoon to bear if needed. Mortars could be deployed and fired with a moment's notice.

Volleys of shots forced McCabe's EVA helmet into the dirt. Bullets whizzed overhead, and return fire cracked back from the Bren light machine guns. The gun emplacements on the base altered their aim and pounded an area roughly one hundred metres ahead. His platoon spread out and sought cover behind rocks or dips in the landscape.

"What have we got?" McCabe said, dragging himself behind a set of jutting stones.

"Three positions that I can make out," Colour Sergeant Brown said. "But I don't have eyes on them. Bug holes, if I you want me to make an educated guess."

McCabe cursed under his breath. One of their nastier actions while out in the field had been hunting werewolf and Wehrmacht units through the man-made tunnels they used to conceal themselves, house their bases, and store their equipment. The sheer extent of some of the so-called bug holes amazed him and led many in the old MEF to believe the Nazis were supported by the Martians.

The Wehrmacht possessed a finite number of soldiers spread across the territory of the five colonies. Building hundreds, if not thousands, of kilometres of passageways to hide in and launch attacks from was beyond their capabilities. Infiltrating those tunnels and engaging in close quarters combat had led to most of the high casualty rates within the battalion.

"All right, you know the drill, Jim," McCabe said. "Give me three mortars on each position, a Bren mag after, and then we'll go in to mop up. First Platoon on me to the right, you take centre with Second and have Sergeant Fleming clear the left with Fourth. Third and Fifth in reserve and Weapons Platoon on standby."

"On it, Bill."

Keeping his head down, McCabe waited for Brown to relay his orders. The base gun emplacements continued chattering fire on the enemy and then died a split second before the soil shook. Three mortar bombs each struck around the bug holes, blasting chunks of stone and sand high into the air and ripping apart anyone unlucky enough to be out in the open.

When the haze of dust cleared, the Brens opened up, pouring lead out into the area while the platoons fast-crawled closer. As the Bren fire died off, McCabe pulled a grenade from his belt, yanked the pin out, and tossed it. The grenade exploded somewhere within the crater, and with a nod to his platoon, he surged forward and hurled himself in, Lee-Enfield raised.

The mortar rounds had smashed the bug hole wide open, leaving tatters of what once had been an enemy machine gun and its crew, revealing the passageway beyond. He threw another grenade down in case any defenders rushed to confront them. After it exploded, he slid his way down and dropped into a tunnel about high enough for him to stand upright in and wide enough for two people to walk side by side.

Flicking on the torch on his EVA suit, he peered left and right, scanning for any enemy soldiers. Second and Fourth platoons slipped into the corridor from their respective positions and readied themselves. Without a spoken order, they fixed their bayonets. All knew what would happen next should they run into any Nazi or Martian personnel.

BLOOD RED STEEL

Taking point, McCabe led the way down the passageway to the left. He kept his rifle raised and continued checking the corridor for booby traps or evidence of mines. Every fifty metres or so, they came across a lamp drilled into the rocky wall with directions in German spray-painted below it. From the scrawlings and his experience with hunting the Nazis, he anticipated coming up to a junction or nexus point soon. Relaying orders to his platoon with hand signals, McCabe pushed on, switching off his torch when he spied light at the end of the tunnel. Remaining quiet, the platoon crept closer and came to a halt on McCabe's order.

Inching onwards, McCabe studied the junction point. He noted five other tunnels branching off in multiple directions, two of them towards the base. Crates and boxes lined the perimeter in between. Staying tight against the wall, he tried to scope any enemy when bullets lashed out and smashed the rock beside him.

Dropping to a knee, he fired blindly into the cavern until his sights landed on the Germans storming out of a passageway to his left. Slipping a fresh clip into his rifle, he called for the Bren and readied himself. Waiting for the shots to die off, he stormed out of the tunnel. Dashing to the nearest set of crates for cover, his men pushed up behind and fired back.

Cries thundered as enemy lead hit some of the platoon. McCabe ripped a grenade free, tugged the pin, and threw it. He waited for it to detonate, then charged headfirst. Panicked shots rang out but flew wide. Bursting through the smoke, he lunged at the first Nazi coming into view. Sharpened steel of his rifle's bayonet punched through the chest of the German's EVA. Twisting, he yanked the blade free. He slashed down against another Nazi fumbling on his knees. The bayonet cut through the helmet's oxygen tubes and buried down into the base of his skull. Bullets zipped past and hammered their disorientated rivals.

The MOF soldiers pressed their advantage and closed the distance. Slashing and swiping, they clashed with the Nazis. McCabe avoided the butt of a rifle, ducked, and drove his bayonet forward. The German soldier pulled back but lost his footing and tumbled into one of his colleagues struggling with Private Patel. All three hit the sand together, but McCabe fired, shooting them both in the bellies. Patel drew his knife and sliced through the oxygen tubes on their suits and booted one visor with enough force to crack it. Leaving the two to suffocate to death, McCabe kicked their weapons away and glanced about for a new target.

The MOF had cleared the junction. Flustered shouts echoed from at least two tunnels. Over their private comm channel, he split his men into two groups and ordered them to seek out any prowling Nazis or militia. Taking the tunnel on his left, McCabe took point again and waved his men on.

In the flickering lights, they crept onwards to locate and destroy their enemy.

LEVEL 2, FORWARD BASE ZULU
09:11 MST
DAY 1

Running his blood-slicked fingers across the Bren magazine, Jenkins unclipped it and tossed it away. Moving as quick as his hands allowed, he slapped a fresh one in and aimed at the hole in the corridor floor. Between him and the opening, he estimated at least twenty bodies rested, all slumped across each other, a few laying within hand's reach.

The pain from the bullet fragments in his leg kept him conscious, even if he had run out of bandages. Small as the various nicks were, he struggled to stop the bleeding, although he blamed it mostly on the relentless wave of attacks the enemy launched. At any moment, he expected them to detonate an explosive on the exterior wall rather than storm up through the breach. So far, he had yet to see a shadow cross the outer window to finish him off. He didn't understand why they persisted in such futile assaults. Any half-competent officer could see he had a clear field of vision. The Nazis and Martians showed either surprising gall or immense stupidity.

His hands ached, his ears rang, and his leg throbbed, but still Jenkins kept his finger on the trigger and his eye on the sight. From time to time, cracks of gunfire resonated through the walls, floor, and ceiling. On occasion, garbled comms came over his radio. Aside from that, he was alone, with only the dead for company. Another choir of ghostly faces to haunt him on the rare occasions he dreamed anymore. His thoughts drifted to Mary Bradley, the woman he had courted before enlisting, when a banging noise snapped his attention to the airlock at his rear.

He grabbed a grenade and looped his finger under the pin, vowing to pull it should the Nazis try and attack from behind. The familiar sight of a bulking EVA suit froze any action. Heaving himself up and keeping the Bren pointed down the corridor, he stumbled backwards against the door. Wounded leg and numb feet fighting for balance, he thudded on the metal and grimaced. After darting a quick look at the breach, he glanced through the airlock window.

Through the EVA visor beyond the reinforced airlock window, Jenkins made out the features of Sergeant Fox from D-Company. He pointed at the breach in the wall. Pushing up against the glass, Jenkins noted a thick patch of what looked like plastic secured around the gaping crater. Fox undid his helmet, showing they had somehow restored atmosphere, and flashed a thumbs up.

Still holding his Bren, Jenkins tugged at the bolt. He stumbled back against the doorframe. Fox and six more soldiers shoved past and took positions aiming at the hole in the floor. Firm-handed, Fox eased the light machine gun from his grip and settled him back against the massive, armoured door to the right of the airlock.

"Jesus, Jenkins, you look like shit," Fox said, smiling as he applied a new bandage over his leg. "Is that what passes for presentable in your company?"

"Apologies, Sarge. If I'd have known you'd be here so soon, I would've had a shower and a shave."

Laughing, Fox handed him his canteen of water and glanced back down the battle-damaged corridor. His smile faded at spying the dead surrounding Jenkins's former position. Taking a knee, he returned his attention to him.

"How bad is it out there, Sarge?" Jenkins asked.

"The bastards have us completely overrun and pinned down," Fox said, pausing to spit. "They've seized Level 1 and most of this floor except for the areas around the medical bay. If you can believe it, they entrenched themselves in every level between here and C&C, albeit with varying degrees of success. Looks like those shit-hawks tunnelled right in underneath us. Constant jamming means we can't find out what's going on elsewhere too. It could just be us or the other colonies. No way to communicate with the fleet and find out."

"You here to launch an attack and clear this level?" Jenkins asked, eyeing the six other soldiers in firing positions.

"Nah," Fox said, accepting his canteen back. "Got word you were out here on your Tod. Figured be worth seeing if you're still alive, considering you're only half worthless. Or so the Colour says."

"Cheers, Sarge."

"There's something else, too," Fox said, jabbing a finger at the door. "Been looking at where all the enemy's moving to. Most of 'em seem to head straight for the centre of the base soon as they get in. Every floor from here to Level 9. My theory is they're trying to find a way to launch an attack directly on Level 10. Take out C&C. Lop off the head of the snake if you will."

"Doesn't make sense, Sarge," Jenkins said, grabbing his Bren and forcing himself back up. "That's storage, innit? There's gotta be an easier way. Hell, they've already got a foothold on Level 9. How hard can it be?"

"That's the thing. I don't think it's a storage area. Looking at the base's internal layout, I reckon—"

Words died in Fox's mouth when the reinforced door creaked, shuddered, and started to slide open. Resting his Bren on his hip, Jenkins aimed at the opening crack in the doors, envisioning a company of Nazis all frothing at the lips, ready to surge out like a pack of rabid dogs. Fox's soldiers turned their rifles on the door, except for one keeping aim on the hole.

Jenkins backstepped and waited. When the door

slid open, no enemy hordes poised to strike. Instead, he spotted rows of metal crates all stacked neatly on top of one another, forming wide-opened corridors between them. A huge, black, cylindrical object dominated the centre of the room, stretching from behind the containers all the way up to the ceiling, which extended at least into Level 4 by the height of it.

Baffled, Jenkins glanced at Fox when he heard noise, something echoing from somewhere in the massive storage area. A lone voice. Singing. The voice sounded faint from where he stood. It croaked at full blast, bouncing off the walls and crates.

"*In the year of Our Lord, Two Thousand Eighteen, we compressioned our way to New Berlin. Hollowed alive, in seventy-five, in a war that was birthed in sin...*"

"What the hell?" Jenkins mouthed, taking a step closer to the opened door.

Using hand signals, Fox ordered two of his soldiers to remain guarding the breach. Sending two with Jenkins to cover the left flank, he took the right. Nodding, Jenkins led on and swept along the first corridor surrounded by crates. He gazed up and down, left, and right, seeking any hidden enemies.

"*The Reichers struck us in our beds, put their guns against our heads.*
Battered, butchered, and filled us with lead..."

Reaching the end of the avenue, Jenkins stopped and focused straight ahead. The voice became clearer, indicating the singer lingered closer to the room's perimeter than its centre. Gesturing at the two privates to remain close, he pushed on, the eeriness of the song and the lack of any other noise putting him on edge.

"*How the Second Battalion cried, when we saw how our mates died.*
Left the Rec bloody, savage, and gory.
We took it out on the Volk. Slit their fecking throats, tied the noose and pushed 'em from three stories..."

As he rounded the next corner, the voice became sharper. Homing in on the sound, Jenkins nodded to a position directly ahead. He recognised the Irish accent of the singer. More than that, the actual voice. He'd heard it somewhere before but couldn't place it.

"Hashbrown McGee came from Derry City.

The Reichers cut him from stem to sternum.

So we gathered Volker families.

Forced them onto their knees and made the Reichers watch while we burned 'em."

Jenkins paused when Fox and his team came into sight on the far side of one of the rows of crates. He pointed in the direction and indicated their closeness. Fox gave a nod. In perfect time, they converged on the source, still wary of any traps.

"Bulldog Donaldson came from somewhere outside Hull.

They shot him while he took a shower.

We hunted Reichers through their caves.

Smashed up Volker graves and burned down their church with a flamethrower."

Resting in a clearing devoid of crates, Jenkins spotted the singer perched up against a wooden box and lowered his Bren. Two soldiers, one wearing British battledress, the other in an Irish uniform, sat side by side, surrounded by a sea of Nazi and Martian bodies. The singer's face lacked colour, a rifle in his hand while his head wobbled. The much stockier British soldier slumped unconscious beside him, but Jenkins noted the rise and fall of his chest showing he lived, at least for the moment.

"Nordie Pritchett was pretty much a dick.

He was...was...he was my friend, you damn assholes!"

A round burst from the rifle, causing Jenkins to lean back, but the bullet struck an unmoving corpse. The singing died, and in the drowning quietness of the storage room, he made out muffled sobs.

"He was my friend, you goddamned Nazi pricks."

"Friendlies," Jenkins called out. "Friendlies over here. Stand down."

The soldier snapped his rifle up for a few seconds but lowered it, allowing it to rest across his legs. Wary of the soldier's mental state, Jenkins took a few cautious paces, keeping his Bren low. He took careful steps across the mat of corpses. Pools of blood tarnished empty shell casings. The assortment of Nazi and Martian dead all bore a variety of horrific injuries ranging from bullet holes to stab wounds.

Waving on Fox and the rest of the privates, Jenkins stopped a metre from the battered soldier. Vacant eyes met his gaze, and he flashed his teeth, showing red splashed across his gums. Jenkins wasn't sure if it came from a wound in his mouth or because he'd taken a bite out of the enemy. Either way, he kept a slight distance between them and dropped to a knee.

"Jenkins," the Irishman said, smiling. "You took your sweet time. What do you think of my song? I reckon I'm a much better singer than you."

Something about his words and the voice froze Jenkins. He knew he had heard it before. Memories raced across the forefront of his mind, various battles all ripping apart until a single image lingered. A Black Visor staring down while another injected his EVA suit with an unknown chemical that knocked him unconscious.

"We're the good guys, asshole," the Irishman said, and Jenkins leapt up.

Stories McCabe shared of the Black Visors' antics zoomed to the forefront of his thoughts. His finger twitched against the trigger of the Bren. The stocky soldier lifted his head and his rifle at the same time, pointing the barrel right at him. Although he was heavy-eyed and trembling from an unseen wound, Jenkins didn't risk it and slipped his digit away.

"Easy," the British soldier said. "He may be a borderline drunk and a sociopath, but he's all right. In small doses."

"Dub," the Irishman said, patting his chest before nodding to his colleague. "This mammy's boy is Big Mo. We've met before, Jenkins, back when you were a private."

"I remember," Jenkins said through gritted teeth.

Although he had limited interactions with the Black Visors after the attack on the RLA base prior to the Battle of New Berlin, their infamy spread. On the rare occasions McCabe mentioned them, Jenkins absorbed every syllable, trying to learn more about the mysterious operatives who claimed to work for their common paymasters, MAJESTIC-12, known currently as MARSCORP. On every conceivable level, he didn't trust them, but they were technically on the same side. With a wave, he urged on one of the privates with a med kit, who quickly knelt beside Big Mo and began checking him.

"What happened here?" Jenkins asked, looking back at the sea of bodies.

"Bastards came up through the floor," Dub said. "You'll find other holes throughout the room. I'd recommend sealing them all now before they make another attempt. Or at least dump a couple grenades through 'em."

At his words, Fox ordered the three other privates to fan out and locate the breaches while he drew closer. Big Mo winced when Private Dobyns probed the gash at his side, and Dub flinched at his friend's discomfort. For a moment, Jenkins thought he planned to lunge at Dobyns, but he eased himself back against the wall. After applying a bandage, he moved to check Dub. Again, the Irishman tensed as if to attack but stopped himself and lifted his shirt, revealing a variety of purple bruises and a bloodstained dressing plastered to his side. Dobyns completed the same task and turned to Jenkins when finished.

"They have stab wounds. No internal bleeding, though. Recommend getting 'em back to the medical bay, Corporal."

"We don't have time," Dub said with a grimace as he dragged himself up and nodded at the large, black cylindrical object in the centre of the room. "We need to secure that. Or else we're dead. All of us."

"What is it?" Fox asked, stepping closer.

"It's a giant pile of mind-your-own-damned-business," Dub said, flashing his reddish teeth again. "Same deal as last time, boys. You do what we say, and you all get out of this alive. Well, some of you."

Jenkins closed the distance, preparing to ram the barrel of his Bren into Dub's gut. Fox's firm grip on his forearm stopped him. Regaining his composure, he shook Fox's hand free to glare at Dub. The infuriating Irishman stared back, unflinching.

"We can't go into details," Big Mo said, face scrunching as he, too, stood at full height, towering over all of them. "We can say that's what this attack is really about. That thing and the others like it in some of the other Forward Bases. Six in total, to be exact, although MARSCORP only has three of 'em. The outcomes for the other ones have been predicted, but not here. Not in Forward Base Zulu. It's imperative we hold this installation at all costs, specifically this room here and the floors above and below it. We'll need your help to do it."

Exchanging glances, Jenkins gave Fox the slightest of nods, and both men stepped away from the circle of death, out of earshot.

"What do you think?" Fox said in a hushed tone.

"I think they've lost their marbles. Lieutenant McCabe didn't exactly trust them, but he made out they were on our side. At least to a certain degree. One thing he couldn't deny was they were passionate about killing Nazis, which ranks them slightly in my books. Your shout, though, Sarge. You're senior NCO."

"Okay," Fox said. "I'll call it in to Mad Jack. In the meantime, secure this room and keep an eye on those two."

Giving a final glance at the Black Visors, Fox stalked off, fidgeting with his comm. Eyeing the two men staring at him, Jenkins gestured at Dobyns and ordered him to assist the other privates with searching for holes and sweeping for any remaining enemies. The Black Visors lowered their eyes and stared down at Jenkins's boots. Dub checked his watch and, nudging Big Mo, they met his gaze again.

"You might want to take a step or two to your right there, Jenkins," Dub said, patting his pockets until he pulled out a grenade.

He considered standing his ground out of defiance. Remembering the various cryptic things McCabe mentioned about the Black Visors, he reluctantly obeyed. After taking a few paces away, he came to a stop. Dub yanked the pin out and, holding the clip down, readied his hand to throw. Big Mo lifted his gun in anticipation.

Baffled, Jenkins was about to query their actions

when a boom thundered, rumbling the floor and shooting a cloud of dust into the air. He blinked and spotted the rough circular gap in the concrete where he'd stood seconds ago. Dub tossed the grenade down. An explosion bellowed, followed by the shrieks of wounded men. Big Mo bounded over and fired five rounds into the hole before stepping back.

"Clean up in aisle seven," he said with a grin.

Rubbing a hand over his eyes, Dub shook his head. "Christ, Mo, it wasn't funny the first ten times."

"Ah, it is a little bit, mate. Gotta break the tension somehow."

"Do I look like I'm tense?"

"Nah, bruv. You look like you're in the middle of a nervous breakdown, though."

"Prick."

"Alco."

"Kermit the Frog–lookin' wannabe."

"Ten-pin bowling ball–headed twat."

Shaking his head at the Black Visors' bizarre behaviour, Jenkins hunkered down against the nearest crate and stared at the breach. He had no idea how they'd known the enemy was about to drill up through the floor at that exact moment, but he recalled how they managed to save Mad Jack and McCabe outside New Berlin.

Stomach tightening, he listened to every word they said and waited for Fox to return.

MEDICAL BAY, LEVEL 2, FORWARD BASE ZULU
11:09 MST
DAY 1

The soldiers holding the medical bay doors crumpled and fell when bolts of green energy ripped through their chests. Watford heaved the wounded man in her arms onto the waiting stretcher, nodded at the orderlies to proceed, and focused on the door. The entire medical bay overflowed with the injured, and with the Nazis and Martians advancing, they still had a hundred more patients to evacuate. Additional soldiers rushed to the door and began firing, but more green flashes flew back in answer.

"Come on," she roared into the throng. "If you can walk, make for the emergency exit. If you can carry someone, do so. We need to get everyone out now."

Fighting Bill shoved past her, pistol in hand. He half-jogged, half-ploughed his way through the limping crowd, slowing down when he reached the main entrance. Another soldier tumbled as Fighting Bill raised his gun and fired. The growing stack of allied dead surrounding the door showed they didn't have much time.

Watford turned to assist with another stretcher when a blast from the door sent her crashing into a line of evaluating personnel. She hit the ground but immediately fought to regain her balance, turning in time to see a cloud of smoke blanket the area where Fighting Bill and the soldiers had stood. Groans rang out, and the fleeing wounded intensified their efforts to reach the emergency exit.

On wobbling legs, she pushed herself forward and stumbled to the entrance. Fumes clearing, she spotted dozens of heavily injured men laid out on the cots, abandoned to their fate. She turned to scream for assistance when she spotted the bodies stretched out near the smouldering door. Fighting Bill rested amongst them, his uniform and face scorched and blackened.

Jutting pieces of metal embedded deep into his flesh. She dropped to a knee and checked for a pulse, finding only the lightest of ones. Blinking open his eyes, Fighting Bill stared at the ceiling before his gaze rested on her. He reached out a burnt hand, gripped her collar, and tugged it.

"Protect the wounded," he said and closed his eyes.

His hand slipped free, and his pulse faded into nothing. Glancing around, Watford pleaded for help. Aside from her fellow combat medics struggling to heave the gravely injured, they were on their own. At least sixty men rested on the cots while Doctor Fawcett performed emergency surgery on one. Many would die waiting for assistance that wasn't coming, but death would come sooner if the Nazis seized the place.

Green bolts struck the doorframe beside her, and she tumbled back. Fear tore through her veins as she fought to focus her thoughts and remain in control. Her hands scrambled for something, anything, to hold off the enemy, and they rested on the barrel of a Lee-Enfield. She cocked the weapon and raised it when a hard-faced Nazi stormed towards the door, his gaze moving left and right while he searched for a target.

At the last possible moment, his gaze crossed onto Watford sprawled on the floor. A smile cut across his face, and he adjusted his Schmeisser MP 40 barrel. Firing first, she wiped the grin right off his face when her bullet caught him square in the chest and sent him floundering backwards. He stumbled into a Martian who raised his ray gun. Exhaling, she shot twice more.

The Martian crashed down motionless and added to the growing stack of enemy dead outside. Adrenaline coursing through her veins, Watford altered her aim. More silhouettes raced towards her, flashes of green bursting out in her direction. She fired until she emptied her clip and then grasped at the murdered British soldiers around her, desperate to find more ammunition. Unable to retrieve spare ammo, she hauled herself up and shouted for her colleagues to take cover.

She swung the butt of her rifle like a club, pounding it against the first German through the door, knocking him down. A second Nazi leapt over him and caught the body of the Lee-Field as she batted it again. Powerless to raise his gun in time while jostling for the weapon, he slammed into her, ploughing her back onto an empty cot.

Stained hands wrapped around her throat and eyes brimming with hatred stared into hers. She choked and gasped for air. Bucking wildly, she managed to slam her knee into his groin, causing the Nazi to howl and loosen his grip. Watford shoved him back, grabbed an overturned tray, and pounded him across the face with it until he tumbled down.

After snatching up a scalpel from the cot, she threw herself forward, landed on him and jabbed the blade into his throat. The German shuddered and grasped at her, so she pulled the scalpel free and jammed it in again. Blood spurted across her face when she tore, cutting his neck open from right to left.

Stumbling off him, she snatched at his MP 40 while panting for breath. She squeezed the trigger in short bursts, hammering the enemies who raced through the entrance, killing them all. When the weapon fell silent from an empty magazine, she tossed it away. Spotting another shadow race towards the door, she pounced over the dead and threw herself shoulder first into him.

Landing on top of a startled Martian soldier, she batted his ray gun away, balled her fist, and smashed him full force on the nose. The cartilage shattered under her knuckles, blasting crimson across his coarse skin. She struck again and jammed her left hand down on his neck while she grabbed his weapon.

Whipping her hand back, she shoved the barrel into his face and pressed the stud she guessed as a trigger. Energy flashed out and vaporised his skull, leaving a small, scorched crater on the flooring. She tried to shoot again when another Nazi raced up the corridor. Nothing happened. Panicking, she drew back and hurled the ray gun before the German could fire. It struck him on the knee, causing him to lose his balance and stumble.

Desperate for a working weapon, Watford ducked low before he reached her. She patted the mutilated corpses spread out until bullets sliced over her head. Forcing herself lower, she turned and rolled back into the doorway. Members of the Freikorps raced past and plunged into the oncoming enemy. As she looked on in amazement, two women no older than her lunged at the downed German. One stabbed him with her rifle's bayonet while the other smashed an axe into his face. Head lolling, the Nazi slumped. Screeching incoherently, the duo took off without a sideways glance, disappearing into the corridor.

Chest heaving, she grabbed the closest Lee-Enfield, cocked it, and dragged herself up against the wall nearest the door. She glanced back down the hallway and then across the medical bay. None of her colleagues had taken shelter and continued clearing the injured men still stranded.

"Mavens, Cooper, on me," she said. "Fighting Bill said to protect the wounded, and that's what we'll bloody well do. Everyone else, get these boys to safety."

Brief cheers reverberated, even from the injured men confined to their cots. Privates Mavens and Cooper joined her, combing the dead for suitable weapons. They passed out ammo clips, grenades, and water to one another. After shifting the corpses, they took up firing positions aiming out the door in the direction of the enemy. Shots echoed, but from the lack of advancing adversaries, she credited them to the Freikorps soldiers. Another small group sprinted past to join the fray.

"I am a soldier," Watford said under her breath and readied herself for the next attack.

NEW BERLIN COLONY
12:41 MST
DAY 1

Shells started exploding the minute the atmospheric troop transport reached the surface. Lockhart didn't waste time dawdling. He had the engines powered up the moment they commenced their ascent from the underground hangar bay and took off as soon as they approached the topside. The craft bolted straight up before he executed a swerving evasive manoeuvre. Tugging on the dual-grip joysticks with a wild glee, he spun his vessel about at tight angles. Anti-aircraft flak exploded, but Lockhart didn't experience the slightest tingle of fear. In the cockpit, locked behind a reinforced armoured hull, he felt untouchable, even if he had crashed during the Battle of New Berlin.

"Where are they, Cheech?" he said, levelling transport off the and dodging another round.

His co-pilot, Lieutenant Pedro "Cheech" Gonzales, hummed to himself and tapped at the consoles in front of his station. "Somewhere to the east. Must be camouflaged 'cause I can't see a thing."

"I'll find the bastards," Lockhart said, veering the craft off.

Incessant jamming over the last few hours wreaked havoc on the MOF's operations, from communicating with the various colonies and installations to interfering with navigation. Coupled with the near-constant bomb attacks within New Berlin, everyone was on a knife edge. To find out if the Cutline defences had been overrun, Lockhart had orders to fly to the orbiting fleet in the hopes they knew more. But he saw no reason to leave an enemy anti-aircraft battery intact if he could help it.

"There," Cheech said, jabbing a finger at the cockpit window. "About a klick to the south. By those hills."

"I see it," Lockhart said and tweaked his course.

Faint whisps of smoke leaked from somewhere beyond the target area. Gritting his teeth, Lockhart hammered the throttle forward and spun his craft through the thin Martian atmosphere, rocking and dodging from the intensified anti-aircraft fire. Sensing the vibrations in the hull from his every action, he could almost feel the ferocious power of the shells he avoided. He kept his gaze focused on the target area and swooped the atmospheric troop transport into a nosedive half a klick away.

"What in the hell are you doing?" Cheech said, knuckles turning white from gripping his controls.

"It's okay" Lockhart said, their craft bombing towards the rapidly approaching Martian surface. "I read about it in a book."

"A book?! What book?"

Lockhart yanked on the joystick, pulling it back tight at the last moment. The vessel straightened off, hovering metres from the coppery sand and throttling full speed at the hills. Grinning at the abrupt blast of adrenaline pumping through his body, he released a triumphant howl.

"Maybe it wasn't in a book," he said, throwing a glance at the flak exploding far above them. "It could have been a dream."

"A dream? Damn it, Lockhart, are you drunk again?"

"I'm not sober, if that's what you mean."

Before Cheech could respond, Lockhart increased their altitude at the sight of the target area looming ever nearer.

Anti-aircraft fire dropped to intercept them, but Lockhart continued bucking and rolling his ship, his thumb closing on the button to launch his missiles. He waited until the last possible moment, lined up the perfect shot, fired, and yanked the joystick back to surge up into the sky.

Colossal booms thudded against the hull of their vessel, rattling the frame. He glanced out of his window port and spotted flames and clouds of smoke tearing across the hillside. Secondary explosions trailed nearby from ordnance detonating. Whooping in delight, he sank back into his seat and guided his beloved ship higher through the atmosphere.

Cheech made small talk while he checked the various consoles and displays on his control panel. For the most part, Lockhart gave the minimum in terms of replies. He relished the serenity of such a large flying machine breaking free of the planet's gravity and the sheer joy of seeing millions of twinkling lights blinking back.

Falling into the orbit of Mars, they ran their system checks, located the fleet, and attempted a link up with the nearest orbiting satellites. Even at the high altitude, the satellite connection appeared patchy, struggling to replay any data from the planet-wide jamming field.

Contacting the fleet came easy enough. Within seconds, comms requesting updates, demanding reports, making personal enquiries, and seeking the location of various units bombarded them. It took Lockhart and Cheech ten minutes to sift through everything that came at them at once. Sending an acknowledgement to the flagship, they followed instructions to set course for an immediate briefing.

After setting the autopilot to the task, Lockhart sank back into his seat and studied the updates still pouring into his tablet. In silence, they scanned the various pages, switching to their main displays from time to time when the satellite uplink refreshed, providing the closest thing to a real-time insight into what was happening back on the surface. If the reports were to be believed, it was a grim assessment.

The eastern sector of the Cutline had been

overwhelmed. Undermanned outposts awaiting the bulk of their soldiers had fallen relatively quickly. American and European forces outside their respective colonies were in complete disarray and scrambling to establish some sort of defence against the rapidly encroaching Wehrmacht. The Soviets in the southern sector appeared to be in a steadier position.

Although forced to fall back from the Cutline, the Russians were regrouping for a counterattack against enemy units in their area of operations. Comparatively little fighting ravaged the other sectors. Whether that was a case of time or a deliberate action to lure away reinforcements, Lockhart couldn't tell. He reached under his seat, pulled out a beer bottle, cracked the cap off, and took a mouthful.

"Really?" Cheech said. "We'll be docking in two minutes. You want to smell like booze in front of the top brass?"

Wearing a lopsided grin, Lockhart moved a hand under again and produced another beer. He tossed it to Cheech and laughed when his co-pilot's shoulders slumped, and he, too, took a swig. They gazed out the cockpit window in silence for a few minutes.

"It's bad down there, isn't it?" Cheech said.

"Yeah, it is."

"I've...I've never seen any action, you know? I mean, not like this. Not like what you've been through."

Distorted faces rippled through Lockhart's mind. Hideous laughter tore through his skull, and pain reverberated up his body as he relived the beatings. The torture at the hands of sadistic Nazis. His stomach tightened and rolled at the eyes of dead men buried deep in his thoughts. In a flash, their bodies slumped against a blood-splattered wall, gruesome swastikas carved into their flesh. Masked soldiers stood over the corpses and then lifted him to safety, each one a blur.

He turned to glare at Cheech for reminding him of things better left forgotten, but his colleague met his gaze with wide-opened eyes and pursed lips. Despite their similar rank and Cheech being six or seven years older than him, he'd forgotten that the horrors of Mars were new to his co-pilot, and he sighed away his frustrations.

"You'll be fine," Lockhart said, returning his attention to his main screen. "You want to know my rules for staying alive on that damned hellhole?"

"Yeah, sure."

"Rule one: Be crazier than the other person. More than half the time, it works every time."

"That doesn't make any sense, Lockhart."

"Rule two: If you're gonna die a horrible, painful death, it's better to do it with a bellyful of beer. I mean, it's not exactly gonna help much with the pain, but...you know."

"Right," Cheech said, fingers working across his console. "We're approaching the North Carolina, so let's stick a pin in this for a little while. Maybe permanently."

"Your loss," Lockhart said, deactivating the autopilot and regaining manual control. "I got, like, a bunch of other rules. I call 'em 'Lockhart's laws on living...and shit.'"

"Wait, are they rules or laws?"

"Who cares," Lockhart said, easing back on the throttle. "They're whatever I say they are. That's like a metaphor for life or something."

Sighing, Cheech shook his head and focused his attention on his displays when the North Carolina came into view. It always took Lockhart's breath away when he had the opportunity to survey her. Out of all the ships in the original invasion fleet, she was the last one standing. Although crippled and bearing the wounds of the SS attack two years earlier, to many, she was the epitome of resistance. Still in one piece and operational after taking multiple mortal injuries.

Many of the crew weren't so lucky. He remembered finding his father's body while the ship shuddered under constant bombardment. Hardly any of the original crewmembers worked there anymore, but outside of Kaiser Wilhelm's beerhall in New Berlin, it was the closest thing he had to home.

Flashes of light on the port side of the craft caught his attention. He blinked and watched, almost in slow motion, when the hull ruptured and burst all along three interconnected sections. Shards of metal, flailing bodies, and supplies seeped out into the darkness of space. Alarms wailed in the cockpit, forcing Lockhart to pull away from their approach vector while the common comm channel lit up with chatter. He brought his atmospheric troop transport to a safe distance and waited.

"What in the hell was that?" Cheech said, skimming through the fresh batch of comms. "Are we under attack?"

"No," Lockhart said, his heart growing heavier as he studied the sensor read-outs. "Looks like an internal explosion to me. Remember rule one? The enemy got there first. I'll bet you a steak dinner they planted a bomb. Mark my words."

Silence reigned. The two pilots sat side by side and finished their beers.

OUTSIDE FORWARD BASE ZULU
15:49 MST
DAY 1

"To the left! To the left," McCabe shouted, directing the platoon darting amongst the pockmarked surface.

Columns of rock and sand launched high from the Nazi artillery shells. Screams cut in across the common comm channel, but McCabe ignored them. After hours of stalking the tunnels and engaging in brief bouts of close quarters fighting, he believed he had located a command post buried in the bottom of the hills to Forward Base Zulu's east. They had tried to storm it via the underground passageways, only to be pushed back twice. The strength of the enemy's defence made him review his plans, so he opted for a two-pronged approach.

He planned to use mortars to hammer the command post before launching a simultaneous attack above and below ground. It didn't guarantee a swift victory. If he could give the Nazis a bloody nose, it might buy the soldiers within the base more time to concentrate their efforts on retaking the massive installation.

"Everyone down!" he said and threw himself into the nearest crater.

Explosions rippled along the top of the closest hill. In succession, the blasts wandered right across it, stopping on the coppery soil in front of the target. He shoved his head up and squinted against the cloud of hazy sand mixing with the smoke and draping them in a fog. An unnatural silence descended across the strip of land, guns on both sides falling silent.

When the haze faded enough, he looked across the battered hill. Small tendrils of fumes seeped from the rockface across several different points. Recognising the sign of an atmosphere breach, he waved his soldiers on. Fire Support Groups belted short bursts of 7.62mm rounds at the area where they suspected the door resided. Sections of men leapt from their cover and dashed ahead. After a brief delay, concealed Nazi guns fired back.

Gritting his teeth, McCabe pushed himself up and, staying low, he sprinted on. Bullets zipped past him in a brutal hailstorm. Wounded men clawed their way to safety. Field medics dashed about, snatching who they could. Another volley of mortars pulverised the top of the hill, killing some of the enemy fire, so he dived behind a set of rocks for cover and spurred his soldiers on. Keeping his head down, he scanned the hillside and focused on the concealed entrance.

Pulling his revolver out, he glanced back at the men storming closer to the bottom of the hill. Lead blasted back and forth. Despite casualties, most of them remained intact. Strings of explosions threw him back onto the ground and rocked the soil beneath him. Wondering if the Nazis had struck with artillery, he forced himself back up. A voice cut over the common comm channel.

"Panzers! Panzers at three o'clock!"

Icy fingers clawed their way around McCabe's gut. He pushed his head up enough to spot eight enemy tanks gunning towards them, barrels shuddering as they launched shells. Explosions ripped across the landscape, carving bodies apart and flinging limbs through the air. Guttural howls of the wounded tore over the comm. Their advance stalled. Soldiers scrambled for any cover they could find.

"Weapons," he said, changing the channel. "Weapons Platoon, I need panzerfausts up here now."

"We don't have any, sir," Company Sergeant O'Driscoll said, "and we're nearly out of ammo. Only a handful of mortar rounds left."

Cursing to himself when another volley struck, McCabe switched frequency again. "Jim, do we have any anti-armour attachments for the Lee-Enfield's?"

"Negative, sir," Colour Sergeant Brown said. "Shit all left in the stores. Unless we've taken any of the stores on the other levels, it could be a while."

"Damn it," McCabe said and thumped his fist off the soil. "We need to pull back."

Issuing orders to the platoon leaders and sergeants, he joined in the action to pump the maximum amount of lead at the Nazi guns as possible. Without anti-armour rounds to stop the panzers, it was a futile effort, but it kept the weapons on the hills at bay. Swirls of gas spurted free from smoke grenades detonating up and down the lines. McCabe reloaded his revolver and sprinted into the fog engulfing the company. Panzer rounds struck the surface around him, the constant explosions and obscured vision reminding him of the suicidal charge on New Berlin colony.

Somehow, the surviving members of the company made it back to Forward Base Zulu. The heavier guns perching out of the walls rattled to life, blasting at the panzers halted on a ridge. Shells lashed out at the base. At this distance, they did little real damage. The company kept low with their rifles raised in case any of the enemy infantry tried to advance on their position. In teams of three, they ascended the ropes dangling from the breaches to get their wounded tended to, take on food, and reequip.

"This is turning into a shitshow," Brown said, strolling up to him.

"We've been caught with our pants down, all right," McCabe said, studying the hilltops. "Unless we re-establish air superiority, it's a matter of time. We don't have the manpower to scour each of those tunnels. Until we cut them off, they can keep pumping fresh soldiers and ammo into the base."

"If it weren't so tragic, I'd be laughing," Brown said. "We had Fritz on the run for two years with a fraction of the men. Twenty times that number in reinforcements, and they're whipping us like dogs. If it's bad here, it must be chaos back in the colonies."

McCabe pulled out a packet of cigarettes, paused, and slipped them back into the compartment. After all that time, he still couldn't program himself to stop reaching for a cigarette when outside a stable atmosphere. His chest tightened at the thought of a sweet nicotine hit to steady his nerves.

"Come on, Jim," he said as the last of the company clambered upwards. "Hopefully Mad Jack has stabilised the situation over the last few hours. Who knows? Maybe there's a fleet of transports on the way with reinforcements and ammo."

"I'll believe it when pigs fly, sir."

Laughing, even though no joy dwelt within him, McCabe grabbed the rope and started climbing up.

LEVEL 0 (BASEMENT AREA), FORWARD BASE ZULU
18:01 MST
DAY 1

Gripping the rim of the breach tight, Generalfeldmarschall Brandt hauled himself up. A dozen of his Wehrmacht soldiers stood waiting, but he waved off their attempts to help him up. He rose, straightened his spine, pulled back his shoulders, and tilted his chin up. They each snapped their heels together and saluted. General Fischer dragged himself through the hole straight after and took his place at his side. Waving his hand, Brandt dismissed the salute and glared around at faces.

"Where is General Schwarz?"

The crowd split apart until he had Schwarz in his line of sight. Oberst Walu stood at his side, and both men marched towards him. With every step, Brandt eyed Schwarz, his subordinate's smug grin angering him. Clenching his fists at his side, he waited for the general to come to a stop.

"Give us the room."

Every soldier in earshot turned and dashed away at his command. In the wide-open basement area they finally controlled, it wasn't practical for everyone to withdraw, but they gave him enough space to do what needed to be done. Allowing the seconds to slip by, he glared at Schwarz to increase his discomfort.

"General, I want a full report on why this base hasn't been taken."

"Herr Feldmarschall, if I may—"

Raising his hand, Brandt cut him off. "I have no desire for excuses. You have had fifteen hours to take Forward Base Zulu in the name of the Reich. Aside from early moderate successes, no progress has been made. I would know why, General."

"The Allies," Schwarz said, averting his gaze. "Their levels of resistance have been unusually high. I've thrown endless waves of my men at them, and they continue to fight for every inch of ground. They are remarkably disciplined, Herr Feldmarschall."

"You've *thrown* men at them," Brandt said, lips pulling back in a snarl. "Are you a Red Army commissar to simply *throw* men at machine gun nests? Have you learned nothing from the lessons I've taught you over these years, General?"

"I must protest!" Schwarz said, locking his gaze on him, face burning puce. "My men are doing everything in their power to dislodge the Allied forces here. We have pushed them back to the eastern side, for the most part. It is only a matter of time before we crush them."

"Time," Brandt said, glancing at Fischer. "How much more time do you need, General? A day? A week? A month perhaps? While you contemplate the next words that leave your mouth, think of this: the entire southern pincer commanded to envelop New Berlin has stalled because of you. Taking this installation would cut our supply lines in half. The other objectives have been accomplished, and yet, here we are. Bogged down while the drive to New Berlin slows. If this goes on much longer, the entire crusade to liberate New Berlin may falter entirely."

"Herr Feldmarschall, I give you my word—"

"Seize this base now," Brandt said, closing the distance and jabbing a finger into his chest. "Crush the British, French, Jewish scum, and traitor filth. Do it today, Herr General. Do it now."

Snapping his hand to his head, Schwarz took a step back. "It will be done, Herr Feldmarschall. I will not fail you."

"You'd better not," Brandt growled as Schwarz scurried away.

Shaking his head, Brandt turned to Fischer when a black-uniformed SS soldier dragged himself up through the breach. He stood and made to break into a jog when his gaze fell upon the two officers.

"Herr Feldmarschall," he said after saluting. "Some unexpected guests request an immediate audience."

Peering past the SS soldier, his gaze rested on the hole and the person wriggling up through it. He noted the rank and medals pinned on the SS uniform. Curious at the surprise appearance, he scratched his chin. The new arrival didn't even look up, but instead turned and offered a hand to a larger man struggling to climb his way through. He wore a finely stitched hand-made suit with a single swastika pinned to the lapel. Both men upright, they turned to face him.

"Herr Reichsführer," he said, gobsmacked, before turning his attention to the other man. "Herr Bormann. I thought you two were dead."

"Rumours of our demise have been quite exaggerated," Bormann said, offering his hand.

Brandt extended his own and shook. He studied the wide face beaming back, utterly bewildered in his presence. Everyone believed Bormann to have died back in Germany, trying to escape the Asiatic hordes sweeping through the capital. In all the time he had spent in New Berlin, he had never heard or seen Bormann at the Führer's side. Reichsführer Wagner, he could almost expect; the former SS leader had a reputation for being slippery. But Bormann after all that time?

Taking his hand back, Brandt eyed the two men. They

represented a serious threat to his authority. He was Generalfeldmarschall by force of will alone, unconfirmed by the Führer. The reorganised Wehrmacht answered to him due to his ruthless crushing of opposition and the liquidation of any higher-ranking officers threatening to usurp his power. Bormann as a party hack, and Wagner, once the Führer's anointed right-hand man, complicated the issue.

"I have many questions," he finally said. "However, the fact you are in this place at this time speaks to the urgency of your visit. What can I do for you, gentlemen?"

"You have the Führer's attention," Bormann said. "He follows your progress and endeavours with great interest, Brandt."

"Generalfeldmarschall!" Fischer said and took a step closer. "You will address the Generalfeldmarschall by his title."

Holding up his hands, Bormann allowed a smile to cross his face. "No disrespect intended. I would be more than happy to use any honorific you desire, *Herr Feldmarschall.*"

"You imply I do not deserve my rank?" Brandt said, the anger within him welling.

Fearing it was the moment they attempted to strip him of his powers, Brandt inched his hand closer to the Luger pistol strapped to his waist. The Wehrmacht belonged to him. For two years, he had rebuilt it from the ground up. No one save the Führer had the right to take it away from him, and even then, there were always...options.

"I merely mean nothing exists without the Führer's blessing, which you have. For the moment."

"Is this why he's here?" Brandt said, nodding at Wagner. "Should I do something that displeases the Führer, you have my replacement waiting in the wings?"

"Not at all," Wagner said, shaking his gloved hands. "You misunderstand, my dear Generalfeldmarschall. I believe my good friend Herr Bormann has gotten sidetracked. We are not here to replace or undermine you in any way. We seek temporary refuge, a place to rest and collect ourselves. The Wehrmacht is yours. We will not interfere with your plans in any capacity. You have my word."

Brandt sensed Fischer eyeing him from the side. After years of collaborating, he could almost hear his subordinate's thoughts. Those men were not to be trusted in the slightest. Yet, even if they spoke reassuring words, their physical presence in the middle of a warzone baffled him. Neither one had any battlefield experience.

"Who do you seek refuge from?" Fischer asked.

Bormann opened his mouth to speak, but Wagner raised his hand and got there first. "I suppose the least we can do is be truthful about our unexpected visit. Anna Bailey. We have come here for shelter from Anna Bailey. She has been hunting us. Until I can get access to a certain technology, we require the Wehrmacht's protection and that of my former SS and the Native Martian militias under your control."

"Anna Bailey?" Fischer said. "The British spy? Does a half-Jew woman strike fear into your heart, Herr Reichsführer?"

Wagner's flesh burned red at those words, and he shifted his attention to Fischer. Before he could respond, Brandt lifted his hand to bring the focus back to him. The last thing he needed was for the situation to descend into petty name-calling.

"You have my full support, Herr Reichsführer, Herr Bormann," he said. "Whatever you need. In the meantime, I will have my men organise food and beds. I'd recommend staying here in the basement area. Most of Forward Base Zulu may be in German hands, but some areas are contested. For the moment, at least."

Waving at a pair of dawdling soldiers to approach, he grabbed Fischer and escorted him away. He gave orders for Bormann and Wagner to be seen to and continued across the floor until they were out of earshot. Closer to the stairwell leading to the upper levels, gunfire echoed through the stone.

"I don't trust them," Fischer hissed.

"Neither do I. I believe they have ulterior motives for showing up here, but we must not act until we know what they are. Keep an eye on them. Until we know what they plan, I suggest we focus on seizing this base. This must be our primary concern."

"Very good, Herr Feldmarschall. If I may show you to your temporary command post? We have multiple updates on the course of the attack across all sectors."

Nodding, Brandt allowed Fischer to lead the way. He peeked back at Wagner and Bormann, who took seats on recently assembled cots for the wounded. Whatever they were up to, he would find out. Providence sided with him. Destiny commanded he reconquer the five colonies.

Nothing and no one would stand in his way.

LEVEL 2, FORWARD BASE ZULU
19:34 MST
DAY 1

Jenkins rammed his blade into the face of the Nazi and drew back, blood splattering his already filthy uniform. Pain cut through his shoulder, and he crashed into a crate. Rolling, he spied a screaming German preparing to hammer him with the butt of his rifle. Swiping his knife, he caught the Nazi across the leg. With a heave, Jenkins dived and shoved his weapon straight through his chest, stabbing until he ceased breathing.

Ferocious fighting raged. The Black Visors' ability to predict breaches seemingly ended when the enemy blew at least a dozen holes across the storage area and stormed through. The sheer audacity of somehow massing troops all along the ceiling of Level 1 and pouring through caught them all by surprise. Every part of the storage area lay as a blood-soaked, pockmarked wasteland.

Pulling himself up, Jenkins sheathed his knife. He grabbed one of the Lee-Enfields at his feet, cocked it, and took aim. A Martian running to stab one of his comrades tumbled from Jenkins's round. He turned to select another target when a flash of green lit up his vision. Slipping on blood, he crashed to the ground. The ray gun bolt struck the container behind him and punched through the hull. Heart pounding from the closeness of the shot, he aimed his weapon and fired. Screaming, the Martian slammed backwards against a crate, crimson spraying from his chest.

Light machine gun fire thundered out, forcing his head down. Rounds pinged and ricocheted off the metal boxes. He crawled across the blood-slicked floor and dragged himself up behind the relative safety of a steel crate. Across from him, stationed closest to the black cylinder spire, Dub and Big Mo fought off a Martian attack like crazed berserkers. Even wounded, they swung their rifles back and forth, clubbing with the rifle butts and stabbing with bayonets. Jenkins aimed again, exhaled, and fired, killing one attempting to launch himself at Dub.

After checking no one had him in their sights, Jenkins ducked low and dashed across the corridor. Lead swept past, forcing him down again. Grenades from Sergeant Fox obliterated the Germans surging up through the nearest hole. Nodding his thanks, Jenkins rushed onwards. After taking aim at a Martian lunging at Big Mo, he fired.

The Martians around the Black Visor flopped dead, allowing him to turn his focus to assisting Dub wrestling with an enemy on the floor. Big Mo cracked his foot off the back of the Nazi's head and repeated the effort until the man released Dub. The two men joined forces in kicking his face into a bloodied pulp.

"Are the charges set?" Dub asked, stooping low.

Looking up, Jenkins snatched his radio and called through to Sergeant Fox, busy driving back another Nazi assault. With the attackers dead or forced to retreat, he flashed a thumbs up. Again, Jenkins looked up and studied the array of explosives placed all along the ceiling under the direction of the Black Visor operatives. His stomach churned at the prospects of what they were about to do next and the sheer madness of it all.

"Smoke," Big Mo said, and Dub fished the detonator out of his pocket.

Jenkins relayed the order, and within seconds, smoke grenades detonated. Heavy clouds sprayed out, covering the room in fog. Gunfire decreased in intensity. Studying the enveloping mist for signs of the enemy, Jenkins waved at Dub and Big Mo and darted across the corpse-laden floor to the nearest storage containers. Deadly rounds cracked out from somewhere to his left, but all flew wide.

He nearly ran headfirst into the metal wall of the container and squinted to check for the chalk markings they had scrawled across it. Big Mo patted him on the shoulder and pointed to his right, showing a vague arrow. More bullets erupted, but all sounded like panic fire. They followed the arrows until they located one pointing upwards with a rope dangling beside it.

Tugging on it to check it held secure, Dub gestured at Jenkins. Unsure if the offer was out of politeness or to see if a hidden sniper could spot them in the thinner layers of smoke above, he almost refused. Realising time was of the essence, he grabbed the rope, dug his boots into the wall and hauled himself up. Muscles straining from the effort, Jenkins fought through the pain of his leg wound and dragged himself past the top of the first container and up onto the one stacked above it.

Wary of how exposed he was as the smoke thinned out, he climbed on until he spotted a hand reaching down from the opened door of the third stacked container. Sergeant Fox drew him inside and, in turn, hauled Dub and Big Mo too. Panting, they all sat by the door with two of Fox's soldiers.

"Everybody in?" Big Mo asked.

"Everyone who's still breathing," Fox said.

Dub pulled out the detonator and held it aloft for all to see, thumb resting on the trigger. "Show time."

Strings of ear-splitting bangs boomed overhead. Violent thuds struck the top of the metal container with enough force to cause the structure to wobble. Chunks of concrete smashed downwards. The ceiling split apart and crashed. Screams faded. The ground gave way from the secondary controlled detonations. Most of the floor blasted away, save for the few strategic points they left in place across the metal beams intersecting at various sections.

They each held their breaths, refusing to move for around ten seconds. Jenkins glanced at the dented roof and then over at Dub, who forced a weak smile. Both Black

Visors reached out, shoved the door open, and peered out. Big Mo shimmied aside and waved at Jenkins to take his spot.

Jenkins crawled over and peered down, shocked at the vast swathes of the obliterated floor, uneven piles of rubble, and storage containers covering Level 1. Reinforced girders where the floor used to lay crisscrossed and intersected at several other points throughout the frame. He didn't spot any movement or hear sounds of survivors from the devastated hellscape below.

Looking up, he spotted the same metal beams stretching out along where the ceiling had been. Again, multiple key spots remained intact, allowing the surviving MOF soldiers above a clear line of sight down for two levels. Flashing a thumbs up, Jenkins nodded at Fox, who snatched his comm and started speaking. Ropes with harnesses attached dropped down from the allied positions.

Jenkins waited until one dangled at the door and tugged on it. He studied the huge black spire reaching from beyond the devastated ruins of the Level 1 storage area stretching high above.

Not for the first time, he pondered its purpose.

COMMAND & CONTROL, LEVEL 10, FORWARD BASE ZULU
21:56 MST
DAY 1

McCabe sat leaning up against the wall of the crowded C&C and sucked on his cigarette. Knees perched up, he held his right hand against his outer thigh to keep the violent shakes invisible from the dozens of NCOs and officers around. To everyone else, he wanted to appear as taking a moment to enjoy a cigarette before Mad Jack gave them an update. In reality, the unknown terror gripped him. After tapping ash, he took another long drag and prayed for the smoke to somehow steady the shudders and quell the inexplicable fear coiling around his chest.

When he smoked his cigarette down to the butt, he

quickly lit another. Willing his right hand to stop shaking, he focused on the bandage covering his aching left one. In his mind, he heard the familiar chorus of screams and explosions that plagued his dreams. Faces of allied and enemy dead merged into one contorting mass of agony, burned deep into his thoughts. More than anything, he wanted to rest his exhausted brain but knew those images would haunt him.

"Cuppa tea, sir?" Brown asked, bringing him back to the present.

"I'm okay, Jim," he said, leaving the cigarette dangling from his lips while he rose.

He shoved his right hand into his pocket and took another series of rapid inhalations. Brown looked him over and then glanced about. Confirming no one else was in earshot, he took a step closer.

"Permission to speak freely?"

"Since when have you ever needed permission, Jim?"

Flashing his pearly white teeth, Brown rummaged through his pockets. He pulled out his own packet of cigarettes, lit one, and inched nearer.

"You look like shit, Bill. Even more so than normal. Everything all right?"

"Yeah," McCabe said, flicking the last of his cigarette away. "Tired. Haven't been sleeping much since we got back. And then all this shit. When does it ever end?"

"Probably when we exterminate every last one of those Nazi assholes. Even then, they've got the natives all stirred up. Never seen anything like it in my life. We'll need a shit tonne of reinforcements if we're ever going to keep a lid on it."

Nodding, McCabe pulled his right hand out. With the tremors ceased, he ran his fingers across his stubbly cheeks and made a mental note to shave when he had the chance. He patted Brown on the shoulder and, stepping towards the gathering crowd, guided him closer to where they anticipated Mad Jack's arrival.

"We'll get through this, Bill, if that's what you're concerned about," Brown said, keeping his voice low. "We always do. From Normandy to Belgium to Germany, we've always pulled through."

"I'm not worried," McCabe said. "Just tired."

The room came to attention when Mad Jack stepped out of his office. A quick wave of his hand sent all to a position of ease. He marched up to the table they all surrounded, dominated by the 3D model of the base resting on a strewn-out map of MOF-controlled territory. He showed his notes to one of his adjutants, who began moving various coloured pieces across the map and adjusting the forces located within Forward Base Zulu.

"I'll keep this brief," Mad Jack said, making a point of looking them all in the eye. "The good news is we've established limited communications with the fleet by piggybacking on transport ships orbiting over the jamming field. I'm also pleased to announce all the five major colonies remain in MOF hands."

No one made a sound. Mad Jack fell silent. Dusting a spec of imaginary dust from his uniform, he straightened his shoulders and took in a deep breath.

"The bad news is we are unable to exercise our air superiority by using the fleet to commence orbital bombardment. Interference from the jamming signal disrupts the targeting systems of our long-range missiles and so far, the fleet has been unable to devise a workaround. Although the colonies remain intact, there have been numerous terrorist bombings against MOF personnel and installations. The Jewish civilian population have also been targeted. Except for Forward Base Zulu, the eastern portion of the Cutline defences have been bypassed. Two Wehrmacht battlegroups are in the process of launching a pincer movement against New Berlin while the Yanks attempt to hold back an assault on their own colony."

Chatter broke out at Mad Jack's revelations. Everyone, McCabe included, leaned in closer to the map, studying the enemy movements. Even if New Berlin was suffering from werewolf attacks, they still had more than enough soldiers and equipment to oppose and halt the Nazi advance on the colony. A fraction of their total strength had won the original Battle of New Berlin, yet he saw no MOF groups massing to man a defence. From his calculations, the Nazis and their Martian militia allies were mere hours away.

"Are we withdrawing, sir?" Lieutenant Barrymore said, pointing at the various enemy positions across Forward Base Zulu. "Unless we receive substantial reinforcements, I don't see how we can hold out for much longer."

"We'll hold this installation until the last man and the last bullet," Mad Jack said, placing his hands on the desk. "I have requested additional men and supplies. Major General Hamilton advised this may take some time. Until then, we are to dig in."

Another round of murmurs erupted. Various officers looked at one another and shook their heads. No one had an issue with fighting to defend their countries. To those men who made up the original MEF, none wanted to die for a shadowy organisation that reneged on their promise to send them home.

As if sensing the shifting tension, Mad Jack straightened his posture and raised his open palms. "I understand this may not be the news you want to hear, but it is the only update we received. I have full faith Major General Hamilton will provide all available resources once the colonies have been secured. Until then, we will do our duty to the letter. We will hold Forward Base Zulu. Now, there is one final matter to discuss. Colonel Henke, at your pleasure."

Groans replaced hushed whispers when Henke strode over to Mad Jack's side. Despite the fact he outranked Mad Jack on paper, no one took the West German leader of the Freikorps seriously. Although McCabe had fought alongside him, he understood why. Years of continuous bloodshed made soldiers of the former MEF wary of anyone with a German accent, allied or not.

Henke reached out and slowly pulled some boards free in the centre of the model of the base, removing five floors in the internal sections. After applying glue to the MOF markers, he fixed them to the inner walls of the compartment and then waved his finger up and down, showing the newly vacant space in the interior.

"These floors have been destroyed," he said. "They were the series of detonations we all heard a few hours ago. We believe one of the primary objectives of the Wehrmacht was to seize control of these central areas. That would account for the path their various infiltration units have taken and the positions we currently hold."

"Why, sir?" McCabe said, scratching his chin. "I mean, why attack Forward Base Zulu to just blow up the centre of it? Surely, if they wanted to kill us all, they'd refocus their efforts on breaching the outer walls and venting the atmosphere out."

"They weren't responsible for the destruction of the central floors," Henke said. "The Black Visors were."

"Do we know why they blew it up?" he asked, trying not to grind his teeth.

"No," Henke said, firing a glance at Mad Jack before returning his attention, "but we have received certain... coded transmissions indicating there is a piece of technology housed within the interior of this installation which is of interest to MARSCORP."

"And MARSCORP never thought to tell us before we relocated here?" McCabe asked, leaning across the table.

"You forget yourself, Lieutenant McCabe," Mad Jack said, forcing him to stand upright again. "It is not our place to dictate what MARSCORP does or doesn't tell us. Like it or not, while on this planet, we work for them."

In that moment, McCabe wanted to lash out, smash the base model to pieces, upend the table, and swing a punch at Mad Jack. Clenching his jaws tight, he took controlled breaths to fight the volcanic anger building within his chest. Focusing on his breathing, the rage began to subside, and he kept his mouth shut. No matter what he said, there was little he could do to change their predicament. Waiting a few seconds, he gave the slightest of nods.

"Yes, sir. Understood."

After clearing his throat, Henke again pointed to the interior of the base. "It appears the Black Visors have collapsed the floors of these levels in an attempt to halt the enemy's advance and prevent them from seizing this asset. However, several Wehrmacht teams have breached the inner walls and are trying to use the metal beams previously supporting the floors as walkways. We are under orders to reinforce this central area at all costs, and only then may we proceed to clear the rest of the base."

"This is madness," Barrymore said, shaking his head. "We have isolated units spread across the base, and we're to leave them unsupported? They'll be completely destroyed if they're not already. And all to protect an asset we know nothing about alongside these...Black Visor maniacs?"

"This may be madness," Mad Jack said, "but these are our orders. Lieutenant McCabe, since you've experience with the Black Visors, I'm putting you under Colonel Henke's command. A-Company and the Freikorps will immediately secure the interior, assess the situation, and report back. I'll take the remainder of the Second Battalion, and along with the base security personnel, we'll reinforce our defensive lines. Any questions?"

"No, sir," the small crowd groaned in response.

"Very good. Dismissed."

As everyone trudged away, Henke fell in beside McCabe. They strode on together for a moment before the West German officer placed his hand on his forearm. Out of earshot of Mad Jack or the other officers, they paused.

"I know you have strong feelings about these Black Visors, Lieutenant. Do you anticipate their presence producing any problems?"

"The fact they're here suggests a major problem, sir," McCabe said. "I've never trusted their agenda, but the things Dub spoke about have stayed with me. The strange thing is, a part of me believes him, and if he is telling the truth, then there's something going on far beyond our level of understanding."

"Agreed," Henke said. "I suggest we focus on our mission but keep our eyes and ears open. If the Black Visors have returned, then the asset must be protected from the enemy at all costs."

Giving a slight nod, Henke started walking again and made for the exit. McCabe followed a step behind, not looking forward to delivering the news to his sergeants that they were on the move again after the battle earlier in the day. For one moment, the tiredness and pain faded when the image of Noid flittered through his thoughts.

In the hell he found himself in, the idea of seeing her again made it all worthwhile.

154KM EAST OF NEW BERLIN COLONY
23:22 MST
DAY 1

"It shouldn't take this long to move from beyond the Cutline to reach New Berlin," General Schulz said, lowering his modified binoculars from his EVA suits visor. "That idiot Brandt must've run into an obstacle."

"That he has," Myers said, peering across the darkness blanketing the planet. "He's gotten bogged down in Forward Base Zulu. And MOF units out on manoeuvre have been launching sporadic attacks on the main thrust. Not enough to stop the left pincer, certainly enough to slow them down. We've also received some limited air support from suicidal pilots flying by the seat of their pants. Altogether, it's added about a full day onto Brandt's schedule when they should have been here hours ago."

In the dim light, Schulz could barely see Myers standing mere centimetres away. Only the dampened glow from the transport carefully concealed behind a boulder allowed him to make out a brief outline. He raised the binoculars and marvelled at the night vision filter turning the darkened nightscape into an eerie green hue. Once again, he glared east, willing Brandt's Wehrmacht to hurry up so Myers would relent and allow them to return to the colony.

"I still don't see why you insisted we come out here," Schulz said, shifting his gaze across the terrain. "The two of us and your pilot won't be able to stop them. Why haven't you mobilised the forces at your disposal?"

Myers waved his hand dismissively and lowered his binoculars again. Sighing, he turned and faced Schulz, forcing him to do the same. Even in the dark, he somehow sensed that malicious smile and those cruel eyes beaming.

"All in good time, Herr General. All in good time."

Shaking his head, Schulz opened his mouth to

107

protest when the faintest flicker of illumination caught his attention. Turning east again, he pressed the binoculars against his visor and increased the focus. It took a few attempts, but he zoomed in on the glow in the distance and made out the shape of a panzer with its high beams aimed low. Another three followed in a line.

"Reconnaissance," he said. "This must be the advanced tip of the pincer. It seems they're making their way to the valley beneath us, and from there, it's a straight run to New Berlin. You were correct in your assessment, Mr. Myers. I suggest you relay this information to the colony immediately."

"You need to relax, Herr General," Myers said, giving him a forceful pat on the shoulder. "I know what I'm doing. Come, step closer to the edge."

With great reluctance, Schulz complied. Using the night vision on his binoculars, he studied the rocky sand and traced Myers's steps. They inched nearer to the precipice and came to a halt beside a set of rocks. Myers took a spot and gestured at Schulz to join him. Wishing the deranged American would hurry up with his theatrical performance, Schulz took his seat and kept his gaze centred on the approaching vehicles.

"A little bit closer," Myers said, the pitch in his voice increasing. "Pay close attention, Herr General. You're about to witness history."

As the panzers pushed deeper into the valley, Schulz wondered what he was meant to be on the lookout for. Some new weapon, perhaps? A new landmine or long-range missile? Whatever it was, he had no clue why Myers wanted him to bear testimony. Surely someone higher up the MOF food chain would have been more appropriate than a former Wehrmacht commanding officer. Growing bored at simply tracking the four panzers, he shifted in his seat, but Myers raised a hand and pointed down into the valley. Schulz reeled his gaze to the spot but spied nothing more than rocks and sand.

Green flashes lit up the night, and he flinched. In another eyeblink, the lead panzer exploded. He dropped his binoculars in time to see another flare strike the rear vehicle. Popping from ammunition cooking off within the damaged tank grew. Swinging the binoculars back, he noted the two remaining panzers halting, barrels rotating to locate a target.

This time, he concentrated on the second panzer, determined to see what type of weapon was being unleashed. To Schulz's shock, green lightning struck the turret, punched a hole through the front and emerged out the rear. Panicked soldiers scrambled to climb out of the smouldering vehicle. Another shot smacked one soldier and blasted a lump out of his chest, sending him spiralling onto the sand. The third tank exploded when a beam tore through its engines, engulfing the metal beast in searing flames.

Three surviving soldiers fired their K98ks into the darkness. Through the night vision filter, he made out their faces contorting as they screamed at one another and ducked behind the nearest cover. They shot another volley and huddled together, heads peeking at the rocks and hills.

"Keep watching," Myers said.

Acidic sickness warped Schulz's stomach. Those men may have cast their lot with the traitorous Brandt and his renegade Wehrmacht, but at one time, they had been his responsibility. He held no desire to stand by and watch German soldiers slaughtered like lambs. Before he could protest, Myers shushed him and nodded down at the valley.

A figure emerged from the shadows and came to a stop five metres from the cowering Germans. They each lifted their rifles and unleashed a barrage. The new arrival stood motionless. Surprised at the stranger's indifference, he focused on the EVA suit they wore but couldn't identify it. It didn't look like the bulky one most of the MOF used, often white and smeared with red and brown khaki. Likewise, it wasn't the streamlined one he or Myers donned. Although it retained a beefy quality, it appeared more solid and angular.

"It's armour," he said.

Gobsmacked, he witnessed the Wehrmacht soldiers

empty their clips at the figure. Every bullet that struck the armoured suit ricocheted into the night. Surprised as the Germans appeared, to their credit, they rose to their feet and pulled their knives free. Glancing at one another, they readied themselves and, blades held high, they raced at the newcomer.

An energy bolt leapt from the stranger's unusual rifle and crashed through the lead soldier, decapitating him, and bringing his two colleagues to a frightened halt. When the body collapsed to the soil, both men lost their nerve and tumbled to their knees. The metal-encased figure lowered his weapon, slung it across a burly shoulder and strode towards them.

Closing the distance, he reached down, and wrapped a metallic hand around one of the soldiers. After lifting the German up, he shook him slightly and tightened his grip. The soldier's body fell still, head slumped at an awkward angle. He tossed the body away, drew his foot back and kicked the last survivor to the sandy ground. Begging for mercy, the man threw up his hands, pitiful cries echoing through the valley. The metal beast lifted its boot and stomped down on his skull, splitting it apart like a watermelon.

Horrified, Schulz dropped the binoculars and fought the urge to spew in his suit. Lips clamped tight and eyes watering, he turned his attention to Myers. Even with blurry vision, he sensed the pure, unadulterated delight from the MAJESTIC-12 operative.

"What a show! Am I right?" Myers cackled.

Stomach churning, Schulz turned away from the valley and concentrated on the dim lights of their transport. "What have I witnessed Mr. Myers? What is that thing?"

"That, my dear General, is the future of modern warfare."

Desperate to put distance between himself and the murder scene, Schulz stumbled back to their ship. His foot caught on stones, and the uneven landscape nearly caused him to trip, but he kept the vessel's lights as his guide and ambled on. Myers fell into step beside him and threw an arm over his shoulder. Waves of revulsion added to the growing turmoil in his stomach.

"The armoured EVA suit you saw is a prototype," Myers said. "It's what we call an Exo-suit, kind of a like a reinforced tank, but on your body. The weapon we've named an HK-11. It can fire three particle beam shots a minute, but also uses standard 7.62mm ammunition for intervals in between. I know three energy bolts in sixty seconds isn't great but look what two of my soldiers did in that time. Can you imagine an entire army equipped with such gear? I certainly can."

They reached the transport, and Schulz hauled himself in first. He waited until Myers sealed the door, then whipped off his helmet. Somehow, having it off caused the bile in his belly to recede. Taking a deep breath, Schulz steadied and forced himself to meet Myers's gaze.

"You didn't have to murder those men to make a point, Mr. Myers," he said. "A simple demonstration on a firing range would have sufficed."

"Oh, please, Herr General. You're thinking in old-world terms. They weren't your people. Your people are the Mars Occupation Force. Our enemies are your enemies. Our friends, your friends."

"Butchery is still butchery."

"Really," Myers said, rapping his hand on the cockpit door to take off. "I can't believe I'm getting lectured on morality by a card-carrying National Socialist. Don't you and yours have an entire philosophy on killing people in the name of the state? Oh, right. I forgot. It's only butchery if it's a certain type of subhuman. Can't waste good ol' premium Aryan breeding stock when the gene pools have been so diminished after two years of war."

Anger tore through Schulz with volcanic explosiveness. As the transport rose, he unstrapped himself and tossed his helmet to the deck. While Myers sniggered, Schulz ripped the EVA suit off and kicked it away. He grabbed the Luger strapped to his waist, pulled it out, cocked it, and aimed right at Myers's head. Infuriatingly, that caused Myers to laugh more. He raised his hand not to ward off a bullet but as if to get him to stop telling a hilarious joke.

"Was it something I said?" he said in between fits of

giggles.

"Do you really think I won't kill you here and now, Mr. Myers? You won't be the first man I've ever shot, but I have no objection to you being the last. I'd welcome a firing squad at this stage."

"No," Myers said, wiping tears of laughter from his cheeks. "I don't *think* you'll kill me, Herr General. I *know* you won't."

The last tether to reality snapped within Schulz. Driven by anger, he tightened his fingertip on the trigger. He didn't care if they lined him up against the nearest bulkhead and shot him. Myers needed to die. No doubt in his mind existed. He'd be doing the entire planet a service by removing such a parasitic, manipulative sociopath.

The bullet never fired. He commanded his finger to pull the trigger, but it refused. Myers's glee grew the more Schulz struggled. His index finger declined to obey. He tried to switch digits, but his hand rejected all attempts to comply. Baffled at what was happening, he saw Myers contain his laughter, although the hellish smile lingered.

Hand shaking from the effort, Schulz watched in horror as the barrel of the pistol turned inwards. Against his efforts, his own hand placed the gun against his forehead. He tried to scream and call out, but the words wedged in his throat. Legs refusing to move and rooted to the spot, he stared at the Luger jammed against his skull.

"I am more than you will ever know," Myers said, smile fading. "I am more than you will ever be. Now, like a good little lapdog, you will sit and be silent."

Without hesitation or effort, Schulz uncocked his gun, slipped it back into its holster, and took his seat. Through no conscious command of his own, his hands strapped the belt back on and then rested on his legs. Sitting bolt upright, unable to move anything other than his eyes, he stared at Myers.

"Careful of those thoughts too. I can hear them as clear as day."

Fighting the growing terror bubbling within, Schulz closed his eyes and thought of home.

THE APPLICATION OF TERROR

LEVEL 2, FORWARD BASE ZULU
06:13 MST
DAY 2

Resting against the cold, copper-coloured wall, Jenkins peered down into the darkness beneath him. In the hours since the Black Visors had overseen the obliteration of the floors, MOF soldiers had used the doors of the storage containers and any other scrap metal they could pilfer. In teams, they created crude walkways along the beams left intact. Twice, the Nazis attempted to scale the walls to reach the girders along what was once the floor of Level 2. Both times the MOF soldiers shot them down like sitting ducks. Since then, the enemy had changed strategy. Instead, they focused on blowing holes in the walls to attack the various walkways head-on. So far, the MOF held.

Red flares lit up from the opposite side of the room and sailed downwards, casting flashing lights along the walls until they struck the rubble-filled bottom. Jenkins spotted several bodies stretched across the shattered piles of stone and scorched storage containers, mostly Germans and Martians. At least three of their own lay amongst them, likely more. Lieutenant McCabe's arrival helped bolster their defence of the base's interior, but he had yet to land eyes on his commanding officer. Priority came down to detecting where the enemy planned to breach next and holding the holes they had already blown.

"See anything?" Dub asked from beside him, his own gun pointing down.

"I thought you could tell the future," Jenkins said, scanning the devastation. "Shouldn't you know where Fritz will attack next?"

"It doesn't work like that," Dub said. "What I know is based on probabilities and looking for patterns. I can make educated guesses on certain things. Nothing more."

"How in blimey did you know they were gonna blow a hole exactly where I was standing earlier then?"

Dub shrugged. "I was showboating a little. I had a rough idea based on what I'd seen down there."

"I'm starting to understand why Lieutenant McCabe doesn't like you, Dub. Can't you for once say what you mean?"

The Black Visor operative shifted in his seat, and Jenkins thought he planned to storm off, which wouldn't have bothered him in the slightest. Instead, he pulled out his canteen and splashed water on the metallic walkway forming a small puddle. Curious at his actions, Jenkins adjusted his weight and moved away from the edge of the path hoisted along the metal beams.

"You see this?" Dub said, circling his finger over the water. "This is time."

He placed his fingertip in the centre and swirled it. "This is you, Jenkins. Right here. Let's say, one day, you wake and decide to join the British Army, right?"

Dragging along a line, Dub created a small stream to the right, beyond the puddle. He paused and dipped his finger back into the middle. With a pull of his digit, he formed another one at a forty-five-degree angle.

"This new deviation is you waking up on the same day and deciding against joining the army. Every decision you make creates a new line, a new variation. If you make toast for your breakfast instead of cereal, you end up late for the bus and get fired. If you go left instead of right in a firefight, you get a bullet to the head or step on a mine. Are you with me so far?"

After checking the flickering flare didn't reveal any skulking enemies, Jenkins gave a single nod. He hadn't quite understood what Dub was getting at. Intent on providing McCabe with some intelligence, he focused, hoping to provide insight into his thinking. Dub placed his hand in the water and dragged it along the walkway until it left nothing but an unrecognisable damp smear across the metal.

"Linear time is a man-made construct, Jenkins. A way for us to try and perceive the passage of years or record our civilisation's progress. In reality, every action has an equal and opposite reaction. You join the army and end up on Mars. Never enlist, and you wind up working as a cobbler married to Mary Bradley. Or Mary Jenkins, I should say."

The very mention of his lost love's name caused Jenkins to flinch. His mouth gaped open, wary he'd never told anyone about her in all his time on Mars. He eyed the Irishman with wide-eyed shock. Dub pointed again at the drops of water.

"Time is a stream, and the Annunaki have the ability to study every droplet of water. They know how to manipulate it to bring about their desired outcome. Essentially, it's like building a dam and rerouting water to the ideal location. Everything we're doing, Jenkins, every single action and move we make, is to keep the stream flowing the way we want it to. Events must happen in a certain order, or we've lost the war before it's even started."

Rubbing his forehead, Jenkins processed Dub's words. After an exhausting day of near-constant fighting, hardly any food, and no sleep, he struggled to comprehend the information laid out. On one level, he understood the essence of what Dub was telling him, but his exhausted, logical mind refused to keep up.

"Forget it," Dub said, standing up. "You'll understand when it counts, Jenkins. I don't know what's worse for you boys. Suffering horribly for years in the wars to come or enduring all that pain only to find out most of you were destined to die in this God-awful place. Pawns, like me. Locked in a game of interstellar chess between the

Annunaki and the Core Cadre."

"You're saying we all going to die?" Jenkins said, sitting bolt upright.

Dub turned to walk away but paused. Shoulders slumping, he returned his attention. For the first time, Jenkins noted the drooping, exhausted eyelids on his blood-spattered yet pale face.

"We all die, Jenkins. Every one of us. The ones whose names are on my list will have died for a reason. That's the sad, cruel part of it all."

"What list?"

Grimacing, Dub shook his head and turned again. "Another time. I have to do something I haven't been looking forward to...talk with that asshole McCabe. Your relief is coming, so try to get some shuteye."

As Dub walked away across the pathway, a million questions flooded through Jenkins's mind. He stopped himself from calling out for fear of giving away his position and cursed his brain for only springing to life after the fact. What list? What was going to happen next? Were all his friends and comrades about to be killed?

Halfway across the path, Jenkins spied Dub slow as someone passed. In the darkness, he couldn't make out who it was. He did note they stopped and leaned in close, exchanging a whispered conversation. The new arrival nodded and proceeded on to where Jenkins sat. Only when she stepped closer did he recognise the former Army of David leader, Zofia Nowak.

"Captain," he said, curious at why an officer would stray so far from the command post.

"Corporal," she said, taking the spot beside him and drawing her gun. "You will sleep now."

"Excuse me, sir...ma'am, I—"

"Captain is fine."

"Yes, Captain. I mean...well—"

"Spit it out, Corporal."

"Yes, sir...Captain, I...Why are you here, ma'am? Sir... Goddammit. I—"

"We suffered many injuries today, and Lieutenant McCabe is currently redeploying who he can to defend the breaches. Apparently, a handful of the Mars Occupation Force regulars have concerns about taking orders from a woman, so here I am. Reassuring fragile male egos by being less useful. Sleep, Corporal Jenkins. I trust you have no strong feelings about sleeping beside a woman?"

Even in the dark, Jenkins sensed his entire face turning red. He hoped she hadn't noticed, but at that moment, he could've sworn his flesh lit up brighter than a flare. Steely eyes burned into his, and rather than risk any more embarrassment, he mumbled his thanks.

Nestling his gun, he rolled over to grab even a few minutes sleep.

LEVEL 3, FORWARD BASE ZULU
08:34 MST
DAY 2

Leaning against a wall, McCabe was studying a hand-drawn map of Forward Base Zulu when a series of explosions lashed out. He dropped to the walkway and gripped it for dear life, experiencing a rush of fear as the metal plates rumbled. Chatters of machine gun fire gushed out. Seeing he wasn't going to tumble to his death, he peeked his head up enough to notice four breaches in the walls perfectly aligned with the Level 3 walkways. Clouds of smoke poured out. Gasmask-wearing Martians rushed through, particle weapons blasting.

Aiming at the closest enemy, he shot twice, catching the Martian in the chest, and sending him plummeting off the metal sheeting. He fired again and turned when plodding boots boomed out behind him. Some resting MEF privates had sprung to their feet and charged at the smouldering breach, bayonets levelled. They smashed into the line of intruders forcing their way through, swiping the sharpened steel attachments at the end of their rifles.

Hauling himself up, McCabe emptied the rest of his clip at the remaining invaders and rushed to join the fray. Rounds ricocheted off the plates beneath him and struck the walls. Foggy swirls leaked from the rupture ahead, obscuring his vision except for the flashes of Nazi weapons carving through his men. He grabbed a grenade, yanked the pin, and threw it full force through the hole, out into the corridor beyond. Shouts of warning rang out just before it detonated, smashing scuffling soldiers to the floor.

A punch to the gut dropped McCabe. He rolled in time to avoid a bayonet aimed for his chest and kicked out, knocking the German back a few paces. Cutting his hand again from shoving the blade away, he launched his fist and struck his opponent in the groin. Somehow, he pushed himself up, caught the groaning soldier by his webbing, and shoved him off the walkway.

Fiery green energy chewed to his left. He sprinted and dived right at the Martian, who fumbled for the knife strapped to his waist. They hit the ground, and McCabe headbutted the flailing soldier. He snatched his own knife, pulled it loose, and rammed it into the enemy soldier's chest, twisting until the light in his eyes faded. Yanking the blade free, he wiped the seeping blood from his reopened wound across his shirt. He rushed the breach and slammed his shoulder into another advancing Nazi.

He took the blow and struck McCabe with the butt of his weapon, stumbling him backwards, nearly falling off the ledge. An allied bullet punched through the German's face, and he fell into the smoky corridor. Having forced the assault back, McCabe waved the surviving soldiers to the hole and glanced about.

The MEF and Freikorps units held the breach in front and to his right. On the left, the enemy limped through and began firing on positions across from them. Without his needing to give the order, the men around him pumped back murderous lead, taking out three of them in an eyeblink. The rest huddled behind the corpses of the fallen and shot back, killing a young corporal to McCabe's right. Ducking low, he reloaded his Webley and fired non-stop until he emptied his weapon.

"Sir," Private Matthews said and pointed at the towering spire in the centre of the room. "Look up there."

McCabe followed Matthews' gaze and spotted two Nazis scaling the column en route to Level 4. Noting ropes dangling down from the intersection walkways above, he cursed. By some means, the invaders had broken through and were threatening to cut the MEF positions in half.

"Matthews, you're a good shot, aren't you, lad?"

"Yes, sir," Matthews said but slapped his hand across the back of the soldier standing next to him, "but Lakes here is better."

"All right, Lakes. Shoot those Jerrys."

"On it, sir," Lakes said and dropped to a knee.

Taking careful aim, Lakes exhaled and squeezed the trigger. The first bullet struck the Nazi on the left in the back and sent his body reeling below. He fired another round and caught the second one in the back of the head. Shots rang out from above, pelting the walkway with lethal lead. Waving them to the hole, McCabe stepped through into the scarred corridor beyond.

Slaughtered bodies and tattered limbs carpeted the floor. Heavy black smoke choked his lungs and stung the back of his throat. Everyone dropped low. Soldiers closest to the door fired back at the intruders. McCabe glanced left and right to get his bearings, but also to give him time to form some sort of a plan. The stretch of hallway was too long to hold if the enemy massed against them. They had virtually no cover from above if the Nazis and Martians dug in.

Flashes of yellow and orange pulled McCabe's attention to the end of the corridor on the left. Guns rose, and fingers eased against triggers. Blood-curdling screams cut deep into the flayed remains of McCabe's soul, and he readied his Webley. The blaze lit up again, illuminating the entire smoke-filled section of hallway. Swirling masses of burning figures rolled, clawed, and crawled along the floor. Horrid, ear-splitting screeches bounced off the walls. No one fired. Years of war had given everyone an ear for a German screaming for life.

Searing flames lashed out again, bathing the last writhing Nazis and stilling their burning bodies. The MEF soldiers maintained their readiness. No one acted to offer a mercy kill to the hated enemy. Too many of their own had fallen for them to care.

"McCabe!"

The voice ripped through the smoky air above the last dying whimpers of the enemy. He recognised it even with bullets whizzing in the storage area beyond. The Irishman's voice, the cocky, smarmy one that rattled through his brain, stoking his temper. Dub.

"McCabe!" Dub said again. "Tempted as you are, don't shoot. I'm coming out. The corridor behind me is clear."

"Keep a watch, but don't fire," McCabe said to his soldiers. "He's one of us. Allegedly."

Through the tendrils of smoke, Dub emerged, wearing a stained and tattered Irish Army uniform, a flamethrower resting in his hands. Same smug grin across his face, cold blue eyes locking onto McCabe. Behind him, a bruised-looking Big Mo limped, eyes like slits as if fighting to stay conscious.

"So, you got the promotion after all," Dub said, pointing at McCabe's collars. "I told you, didn't I?"

His words took McCabe back to those last moments in the lab with the Compression Matrix when Dub handed him the futuristic weapon he called an HK-17. Doing his duty, he passed it over to his superiors but never heard anything about it since. Seeing the damage the Martians' particle weapons wrought, he wished the MOF had something close to that firepower. Knowing the bureaucracy, though, it most likely lingered on a shelf somewhere.

"Why are you here, Dub? Why now? Why this place and time?"

"That's Core Cadre business, not yours," Dub said, face curling into a sneer. "Right now, I'm giving you the advantage. We can clear Level 4, drive those Nazi twats back, and push down into Level 2. If you're game, that is."

"Where's the rest of your team?" McCabe said.

"Busy," Dub said, pursing his lips while he shifted his weight.

A thought struck McCabe. He didn't pretend to know Dub well. Those days during the Battle of New Berlin gave him at least a partial insight into his behaviours. Without his balaclava, he noted the lines furrowing across his brow, the momentary break in eye contact, and how his signature cocky grin slipped.

"How's Noid keeping?" he asked.

Eyes widening, Dub planted his feet solidly and glared. Sensing a shift in Dub's mood, McCabe decided to go on the offensive and allowed the slightest of smiles to cross his own lips. Big Mo stepped forward and patted Dub on the shoulder, pulling his attention back.

"Come on," Big Mo said. "We need to go. Lieutenant McCabe, are you with us?"

"Yeah," McCabe said, signalling his men to move. "I'm with you. Lead on, boys."

Fixing the straps of the flamethrower tank on his back, Dub fired one last scowl and turned to take point. Of all the things he expected to face, McCabe never thought he'd have the pleasure of getting under Dub Loughlin's skin. Using his overt protectiveness of his teammates against him could prove valuable, if not entertaining.

Despite everything going on, he made a mental note and waved his soldiers on.

LEVEL 0, FORWARD BASE ZULU
10:41 MST
DAY 2

Brandt extended his fingers, clenched them into a fist, and slammed it hard onto the map-laden table. Officers around him flinched. None spoke a word in challenge. Gathering himself, he stood upright, anger rushing through every atom in his body. No one dared meet his eye.

"Oberst Walu," he said, frowning at the liaison officer. "Repeat what you said."

To his credit, Walu, of all the men around him, didn't appear fazed in any way. While everyone else gave away tell-tale signs of their discomfort, Walu's face remained as unreadable as copper-coloured granite. Tilting his chin up, he cleared his throat and spoke.

"Yes, Herr Feldmarschall. The pincer attack on New Berlin has stalled. Preliminary reports indicate both battlegroups have suffered massive casualties and are retreating."

Hearing those words a second time did little to soothe Brandt's nerves or allow the information to process in his brain. He stared down at the map where the counters should have stood, but instead, lay strewn across the table. For some strange reason, the urge to laugh nearly took him. It was as if fate itself had chosen him to be its jester. Cursed to fail no matter how righteous his crusade.

"Who gave the order to retreat?" General Fischer said, his voice far more restrained.

"I'm uncertain, Herr General," Walu said and slipped his updates onto the table. "The reports were chaotic. More communications from individual units than any cohesive command update. The one theme they had in common was that a concealed enemy force ambushed both battlegroups simultaneously and inflicted devastating losses within the opening seconds."

"An airstrike?" Fischer said. "Surely the Allies haven't found a way to cut through the jamming signal so soon?"

"There were no reports of aircraft spotted, Herr General. Indeed, this was my first question. Reports suggest the attack was ground-based. Even more interestingly, the enemy possessed particle weapons."

"We've been betrayed!" Brandt said and shoved his finger at Walu. "Your accursed people have sided with the MOF. Is that it, Oberst? You supply them with weaponry despite our protection and assistance?"

"I must protest, Herr Feldmarschall," Walu said, staring him head-on. "Under no circumstances have my people thrown our lot in with the invader. Of course, there are those who dissent. Even they would not risk their people's wrath by openly giving the MOF access to our technology."

"This was something else," Wagner said, approaching the table.

Brandt turned about, ready and willing to focus his anger on someone more deserving. As his plan for the reconquest of the colonies unravelled, he knew he had little time to act. His rivals would be sharpening their knives, prepared to strike him down and assume the mantel of

Generalfeldmarschall. He had risked everything on one massive offensive, which was crumbling before his very eyes.

"The SS," he said, lowering his hand to his Luger. "Your people have betrayed the Reich yet again, Herr Reichsführer."

"No," Wagner said. "This was something much worse. The future has arrived, Herr Feldmarschall. The future I envisioned so clearly h—"

An explosion burst through the room, knocking the surrounding officers into the table. Brandt struck the corner, the pointed end jabbing him in the stomach, and he crumpled over. Machine guns bellowed to life. He spun about, searching for the source of the detonation with his watering eyes. Had the MOF launched an undetected counterattack from outside?

Men raced about, disappearing through cloudy pillars of smoke. Muzzle flashes lit up and died. Wagner grabbed Brandt and hauled him up while the rest of his general staff roared into their radios, demanding an explanation. Another detonation rocked the basement, throwing soldiers off balance. Through the haze, Brandt thought he spotted a flicker of movement and drew his pistol.

"I demand to know what's going on now!" he shouted at his befuddled staff.

"Reichsführer!"

That single utterance blanketed the noise of the gunfire and sent a shiver down Brandt's spine. The sheer hatred dripping from that animalistic voice made him take aim through the clearing fog as he sought the owner. Unable to locate anyone, he turned to ask Wagner when he noticed the Reichsführer's pale face, widened eyes, and gaping mouth.

"Who is it?" Brandt asked.

Sounds of flapping clothes in the wind preceded a violent thump. Brandt flinched when the body of a German soldier plummeted to the concrete floor a metre away. Levelling his gun, he shifted about, edging closer to the downed man. Below his solar plexus his innards oozed from a fist-sized gap. It didn't remind him of any bullet wound, bayonet strike, or shrapnel damage he recognised. If anything, it almost looked like someone had ripped a clump of flesh out with their bare hand.

"Reichsführer!" the voice said again, closer.

Hearing it clearer that time, he noted the distinct English accent with the slightest of American twangs. A woman? How could an Englishwoman have made it so far into the underground basement undetected, and why would she be searching for Wagner? Tentacles of smoke cleared enough for Brandt to spot her. Statuesque, she stood alone in a single dark jumpsuit with pockets across her legs and chest. Closely cropped hair and eyes as dark as hell itself fixed on Wagner. Mauled corpses rested at her feet. From what weapon, he couldn't tell.

"Anna Bailey," Wagner mouthed, rooted to the spot.

When Brandt's gaze rested on her dripping red hands, it struck him. He couldn't spot a pistol strapped to her waist or shoulders. The remaining soldiers in the vicinity raised their weapons. None made any attempt to gun her down or apprehend her. Transfixed by the spectacle, Brandt lowered his Luger, unsure how one woman could be responsible for such devastation.

"Your time has come, Reichsführer," Anna said, teeth bared like a lion. "You cannot evade your past. You will never escape me. Fall to your knees here and now, and I'll grant you a quick death. Resist, and I will kill every last man in this room and bleed you slow."

Despite speaking low and clear, Anna's voice boomed off the walls, drowning out the gunfire leaking from the upper levels. Whether it was her poise or the unmistakable confidence in her voice, Brandt found himself mesmerised by the sight. He shook his gaze free and stared at Wagner, who backstepped, nearly crashing into the overturned table. Rifles cocking snapped the tension in the room. Anna took off like a lightning bolt.

In swirls of motion too quick for Brandt to comprehend, Anna closed the distance to the nearest offending soldier. She dipped below his aim, dropped, swung her leg about, and lifted him from his feet. Anna steadied herself straight away, and while the soldier flopped towards the floor, she pounded his chest with the force of a jackhammer, ploughing him hard onto the concrete. His ribcage shattering from the blow triggered a release of angered shouts from the surrounding soldiers, who opened fire.

Brandt flinched when Anna executed a diving run, jumped up, and speared the nearest soldier. She snapped his rifle off him, rammed the butt into his face, raised it, and bashed it again into an SS officer who tried to grab her. Spinning about, she clutched his shoulders and used him to take the force of a cascade of shots. His chest exploded in red, but again, Anna was off. He tracked her every movement with terrifying awe, shocked at her reflexes. It was as if she moved faster than the bullets themselves and sensed the trajectory of every shot.

She launched herself at another rifleman, swatted the barrel of his K98k away, and rammed a fist at his throat. He collapsed like a sack of potatoes, body writhing on the cold concrete floor. Anna didn't stop for a breath. Firing, two soldiers rushed to close the distance, their bullets ricocheting as she dodged and rolled.

Throwing her arms out at the last minute, she ploughed through the men with her extended limbs, knocking them off their feet. Swinging onto her back, she hammered her right elbow at the jaw of one of the soldiers. The second one grasped at her, but instead of fighting him off, she clutched his shoulders. She hauled herself closer and smashed her forehead against his face. He screamed and tried to fend her off. Anna rose and stomped her boot down on his throat, silencing him. The remaining soldier pulled his knife. When he lashed out, she snatched his wrist, yanked the blade off him, and stabbed it into his eye. She held him for a few seconds before shoving his lifeless body away.

Horrified at the blood-soaked scene, Brandt emptied his gun. Anna swerved around every bullet he and the dwindling number of soldiers unleashed. He reloaded, but rather than fire, he grabbed Wagner and pushed him towards the door. Snapping out of his shocked daze, Wagner complied and fled to the nearest stairwell.

"Reinforcements," Brandt said. "We need more men

now!"

Backing away to the stairs, he fired another fast-paced barrage. Anna may as well have been a ghost or a vengeful poltergeist. Her body twisted and contorted in ways he couldn't ever have imagined, sailing through the crossfire with ease, bullets no more a concern to her than a drop of rain on a cloudy day. SS soldiers stormed down the stairs, shoved Wagner in, and took to a knee. MP 40s raised, they poured fire at the elusive enemy agent, even as she ran down the remaining Wehrmacht men still standing.

Reaching the entrance to the stairwell, Brandt glanced back. Anna disappeared behind a stack of crates, but the SS pumped bullets in her direction, intent on keeping her head down while they stormed forward and attempted to flank her. Unwilling to take any chances, Brandt slammed the airlock door shut, trapping them all in the basement, and locked it. Pressing himself up against the reinforced window, he peered through, spotting the SS soldiers. Guns raised, they approached the boxes at his periphery.

"What is she?"

Fixing his dishevelled uniform, Wagner nearly collapsed onto the bottom step. "She's a prototype. The mother of a new generation of warriors. She is beyond magnificent."

"Magnificent?" Brandt said, tearing his gaze away to stare at him. "Did you not see how many of my men she killed, Herr Reichsführer?"

"Marvellous in every way," Wagner said, dabbing a handkerchief across his sweaty forehead. "I admit, she's not behaving how I envisioned due to unfortunate interference by the Core Cadre, but her children are beyond perfection. You'll meet them very soon, Herr Feldmarschall."

"Marvellous," Brandt said and slapped another clip into his Luger. "That thing's presence has put our seizure of this base in jeopardy, Herr Reichsführer. If she retains control of the basement area, then we are cut off from our reinforcements and supplies. Sandwiched between the MOF and a sociopathic killing machine who desires for nothing more than to murder you, my men, and me along with it."

Thoughts of his offensive grinding to a halt flashed before Brandt's eyes. He had dreamed of the successful outcome ever since being carried from New Berlin, wounded in the last fight to retain control of the colony. Everything he envisioned melted away, replaced with disgrace, failure, and shame. Wagner couldn't have cared less. He placed his handkerchief back in his pocket and dragged himself up, gripping the railing for support.

Shocked at what he witnessed, Brandt decided to rid himself of at least one more complication. The Luger in his hand started to rise when a dreadful thump boomed from behind. He spun about and nearly dropped the weapon when he saw Anna's eyes burning through the airlock window. Fresh blood dripped from her face, making her appear like a predator smeared with the lifeblood of its latest devoured kill. She raised a saturated hand and slammed the head of a decapitated soldier against the reinforced glass. Emotionless, she waved it side to side and tossed it away.

"Reichsführer!" she shouted and pounded against the metal.

Brandt turned to snatch the SS officer in the chance that killing him would appease her murderous rage. When he faced the stairs, Wagner was gone. He glanced up and spotted him, racing up the stairwell two steps at a time in a bid to flee.

Without dithering, Brandt took off after him. As he ascended, he looked back at the airlock, but Anna had disappeared. Considering it only a matter of time until she breached the basement area to pursue her prey, Brandt increased his speed.

He didn't stop until he reached the Level 1 checkpoint.

LEVEL 4, FORWARD BASE ZULU
12:55 MST
DAY 2

Swinging his flamethrower about, Dub bathed the hallway in fire and shifted back behind wall cover. Terrible screams screeched out. Enemy soldiers rolled and bucked

127

on the floor. McCabe flashed a thumbs up at his team, and they fired a round each, silencing the burning and scorched men. Under normal circumstances, he would have been content to let them suffer, but the constant screams bouncing off the walls distracted him too much, chipping at his resolve. Of all times, he couldn't afford the overwhelming loss of control to seize him.

"Softie," Dub said, shouldering past him to take point once again.

Flamethrower levelled, Dub walked carefully forward, weaving between the flaming corpses. One well-aimed shot could engulf him in flames too. Despite the risks, he showed no hesitation in being the first one to push onwards, trailed by Big Mo. Egged on by the selfless behaviour, the MOF soldiers clung closer than they should have, regardless of the danger. McCabe kept his gun at the ready as they sifted their way down another liberated corridor on their trek to the central storage area. Big Mo scurried past Dub when they reached the intersection. After glancing both ways, he pulled back against the wall.

"Clear," he said.

"Good," McCabe said. "It should be a straight run to the breach from here. With the stairs held from Level 2 up to Level 9, it gives us one hell of an opportunity to advance against the lower levels once we clear these bastards out."

They pushed on and followed the corridor, slowing to check for any boobytraps in the rubble littering the floors. The closer they got to the breach leading into the interior, the louder the sound of battle grew. Dub signalled to stop. Staying low, he half-crawled, half-dragged himself over the piles of wreckage across their path, Big Mo ever at his heels.

Unwilling to let him out of sight, McCabe traced his route and waved at his men to follow. Blasts of flame swept out, trailed by the screams of burning men. McCabe shoved through the last mound of debris and spotted four men doused in fire screeching and rolling on the floor. While Big Mo shot them point blank, Dub charged the gaping hole leading to the metal pathways.

Particle blasts lashed out, striking one of his men.

Ducking low, McCabe pressed onwards, following the two Black Visors into the fray. He paused at the wall and peeked in. Dub hunkered down behind a makeshift barricade of sandbags and sprayed another fiery burst at two fleeing Martian militia fighters. Both tumbled, arms thrashing when they struck the floor and clawed at their burning skin.

Confirming the MOF still held the walkways above and below, McCabe waved his men on to seize the far breach. Already, soldiers from Level 5 climbed their way down ropes. Suppressive fire battered the lower levels. After securing the last entrance into the interior area, he assigned guards and a patrol to locate any other enemy positions in the base's exterior corridors.

Sweat drenching his face, he sauntered back across the walkway, the odd bullet pinging the metal panels beneath him. He returned to where Dub and Big Mo rested behind the sandbags. Undoing his helmet, he took a seat opposite, steel crates shielding him from any stray rounds.

"How about we skip the games this time," he said, fumbling for his cigarettes. "Why don't you tell me why you're here."

"That's irrelevant," Dub said, loosening the flamethrower straps from his shoulders. "You're not on the list anymore, so it doesn't really matter."

Slipping a cigarette into his mouth, McCabe allowed his first encounter with Dub and his Black Visor cohort to flitter through his mind. He remembered staring into the blackened helmet visor glaring back and hearing words similar to what he just spoke. Something about a list which didn't include his name. He struck a match, took a long drag, and leaned against the wall.

"In '54, you said I was on the list. Something about me being the reason you got locked up instead of executed. I don't suppose you intend on telling me what this is all about?"

"The flow of the Stream has changed, and it can't be helped. You'll still be why we get banged up, not shot, but in an indirect way. You'll find out soon enough, McCabe. Sooner than most of us would like."

Exhaling a mouthful of smoke, McCabe considered pressing Dub on the matter but decided against it. He did contemplate beating the information out of him. Although they weren't exactly world-class fighters, all four Black Visors had taken a thrashing from the renegade fugitive Anna Bailey and lived to tell the tale. Tempting as it was to see how badly he could batter the Irishman, he refrained and took another drag.

"So, what now?" McCabe said. "What's next on your top-secret plan that somehow involves me and my men getting shot at and potentially killed?"

"Easy," Dub said, grimacing as he forced himself up. "First off, we need to break the enemy. With our help, you've regained momentum. For events to follow the pattern we need, it's essential we smash their resolve immediately. Utterly crush their morale. After that, I need you to escort me and Big Mo to the medical bay on Level 2."

Placing his left hand on his side, Dub groaned. He reached out his right and helped Big Mo to his feet. Lips tightening, they squeezed their eyes shut as if such simple movements caused inscrutable pain.

McCabe noted the cuts and bruises across their faces and their haggard postures. Slivers of sympathy cut into him, and he gave the slightest nod of understanding rather than offering a challenge.

"How are we to break them?" he asked. "We're outnumbered and outgunned. I saw those tunnels they dug outside the base. They can pump as many reinforcements and supplies as they need. Unless we regain air superiority or a steady influx of our own replacement personnel, we won't be able to hold out for much longer."

"Follow me," Dub said and limped to the nearest smouldering body.

Exchanging nods, the Black Visors kicked at the burning corpse until it rolled off the walkway and plummeted below. They repeated the exercise with the other smoking carcass and hobbled back to the breach. Dub lingered at the hole and pointed out into the corridor, a grim nod coming from Big Mo.

"Lieutenant McCabe," Big Mo said. "Order your men

to bring some of those dead Nazis inside. Any Martian cadavers you can find too. We'll also need chains. Long ones. You'll be able to find them in a storage room on Level 6. I can give you directions."

"What?" McCabe said, meeting Big Mo's gaze. "Bodies? Chains? What in the hell do you plan on doing?"

Big Mo opened his mouth to speak, but Dub reached out, grabbed his upper arm, and gently squeezed, silencing him. As he limped closer to McCabe, his dark blue eyes burned deep into his, smouldering with a darkness that chilled him to the core.

"Terror," Dub said. "We're going to apply terror tactics and break the militia. Order your men to do what we asked and I'll explain."

Mulling over Dub's words, McCabe gave a reluctant nod and signalled his soldiers. In pairs, they heaved the enemy dead back onto the walkways and dumped them at Dub's feet. Curious eyes gazed at the Black Visors and then at the corpses. They backstepped to their previous positions, keeping a lookout in the corridors or at the enemy-held bottom level. Big Mo stepped back. Dub hobbled over to one of the bodies, drew his blade, and dropped to a knee.

"An obvious fact for you, McCabe," he said, leaning in closer to the lifeless face of the dead German soldier. "The Martians only really know about you...us, the MOF, MEF, Allies, etcetera, from what the Nazis told them. I'm sure you, of all people, are aware of the National Socialist propaganda machine. All sorts of stories. We're *Übermenschen*. Filthy, degenerate monsters. Sometimes though, if you want to defeat a monster, you become one yourself."

"I don't necessarily agree with tha—" McCabe said and trailed off when Dub sank his blade to the cadaver's face.

Steady-handed, he carved lines into the forehead. McCabe recalled similar etchings when they'd rescued the pilot, Lockhart. Once he finished cutting the Star of David into the skin, he eased his knife around the corner of the corpse's eye and popped it out of his skull, ripping it free and tossing it below. Retching resonated from the corridor. One of the onlookers vomited.

"We did stuff like this during the Reicher Rebellion," Dub said, using his blade to cut open the shirt before working new lines across the exposed chest. "After those neo-Nazi scumbags shot our friends in their beds, we hunted them all down. Made sure they understood the concept of terror before we liquidated them."

"We didn't stop there," Big Mo said, refusing to make eye contact as he, too, knelt beside another cadaver and drew his knife. "We marked the sympathisers too. Wanted to make sure every time they looked in the mirror, they realised the price of defying Terran rule."

Shaking his head in disgust, McCabe turned away and waved back anyone still gawking at the gruesome spectacle. Revulsion tore at his stomach at the barbarous acts committed in his presence. He recognised the need to hunt down and exterminate the enemy, but even in his most blinding rage, never once had he considered punishing civilians, regardless of their background. The courts could deal with non-combatants. A fine line existed between justice and revenge. He had no plans on crossing it, even if the future iteration of the MOF seemed open to it.

"Tell me how butchering dead men will break the enemy," he said, pulling another cigarette loose.

"Like I mentioned," Dub said, glancing over the words '2ND BATT' carved into the skin, "the militias only know of war from Nazi propaganda. They haven't fought amongst each other in a millennium. Certain rules against the desecration of mortal remains are one of the cornerstones of their beliefs, and they've no concept of barbarity. We're about to obliterate them psychologically."

Disgusted at such grotesque acts, McCabe turned away and walked back to the breach. Although he found the mutilations abhorrent, he also wasn't beyond using anything that could turn the tide of the battle in the MOF's favour.

Deferring once again to the Black Visors' superior knowledge, he glanced down and listened to the random shots ringing out.

MEDICAL BAY, LEVEL 2, FORWARD BASE ZULU
15:51 MST
DAY 2

Exhausted, eyes stinging, and hands shaking, Watford forced her eyelids to remain open and rested her finger on the trigger. The tide of enemy attacks had slowed over the past few hours, but every time she was certain the worst had passed, another assault began. Although they had succeeded in evacuating most of the seriously wounded back into areas resolutely under MOF control, the medical bay became the focal point for units cut off from the main body of soldiers. Stragglers limped and crawled their way there, many on the brink of death.

Hours ago, Mad Jack himself had ordered them to withdraw. Doctor Fawcett, too focused on tending to the injured, refused to speak with him. Likewise, Corporal Owens had led a small band of the wounded to a field hospital set up on Level 4, so it forced Watford to make the call. She believed in the chain of command, but everything in her gut told her Mad Jack's decision was the wrong one. In a fit of temporary madness, she took the comm and disguised her voice. Gunfire howling in the background, she did her best imitation of now deceased Fighting Bill.

It worked. She didn't know why or how. For some reason, Mad Jack bought it and ordered them to hold the medical bay and protect the wounded until he could send reinforcements. The rest of her fellow combat medics congratulated her, even if the end game was most likely a court martial should the truth ever came out. Still, in her heart, she knew it was the right thing to do. At the very least, it bought time for the injured.

"Tag," Smack said, causing her to flinch. "You're out, Watford. Grab some sleep. I'll take it from here."

The thoughts of laying down and snatching a quick rest filled her mind, but she shook her head. No matter how fatigued she was, it struck her as wrong to abandon her post. If the Nazis attacked and something happened to Smack or someone else while she slept, she could never forgive herself.

"I'm okay," she said, maintaining her gaze on the shadowy corridor outside. "Relieve someone else."

"I have," Smack said, hunching down beside her and aiming her rifle into the hallway. "You're the only one too stubborn to grab a cuppa tea or snatch a few minutes sleep. You're no good to anyone burnt out, Watford. Step away. I got this."

The urge to protest grew within Watford, but she sensed Smack staring. She turned and noted one arched eyebrow and eyes focused right on her. It reminded her of a similar look her own mother used to flash when she made a decision and Watford had no say in the outcome. Sighing, she gave a nod and heaved herself up. Her joints cracked, and she shook the stiffness out of her limbs. After patting Smack on the shoulder, she strolled across the maze of cots.

She spotted Private May, also known as Mayday, struggling with a trolley and went to assist her. The smaller woman halted, placed her hands on her hips and nodded at the nearest vacant cot. Relenting, Watford threw up her hands, tossed her bag to the floor, and fell onto the mattress. She shifted herself into a comfortable position and, snuggling her rifle, closed her heavy eyelids. In seconds, sleep took her.

Somewhere between dreams and consciousness, Watford's mind took her to strange, fantastical places. Even as her last thoughts faded and she dived deeper into a slumber, images of MOF soldiers in armour lingered. Like locusts, they converged on Mars, turning the red planet into one swirling mass of grey. Pained sobs and agonised wails cleaved through the gunfire engulfing the world.

Her viewpoint shifted until she floated in space, amongst the stars. Earth, or what the MOF designated Terra, on her left and Mars on her right. Small black dots appeared on the sun, slowly growing. She watched them expand until the sun's light dimmed, casting a shadow across both worlds.

Narrowing her gaze, she stared at the darkness until it struck her that whatever it was, it wasn't consuming the sun. Moving ever nearer to the planets, its sheer size blotted out the sunshine. Fear took her. She tried to flee, but in the vacuum of space, she couldn't move. Helpless, she floated there. The colossal storm cloud swept closer and closer...

"Watford? Watford? You all right?"

Snapping her eyes open, Watford glared at the medical bay lights blazing down on her. Panting and slick with sweat, she pulled her Lee-Enfield tight against her. She glanced about, spotting Mayday hovering over her, forehead crinkled while she shook her.

"I'm fine," Watford said, looking around and remembering her location.

"You sure?" Mayday took her hand back. "Looked like you were having one hell of a nightmare there. Kept talking in your sleep. What's an Annunaki?"

"A what?" Watford said, sitting up.

"Annunaki. You kept saying the Annunaki were coming. Is that a breed of dog? Like a Pomeranian or something?"

"I don't know," she said, rubbing her sweat-slicked face. "Was I out for long?"

Mayday glanced at her watch and then back at her. "About five minutes."

Groaning, Watford sat up just as a violent blast raged and tossed her from the bed, face-first. She struck the cold concrete, a copper-taste filling her mouth. Ears ringing, she snatched her rifle and pushed herself up. Clouds of dust and smoke hung over the entire medical bay. She spotted flutters of movement as her fellow combat medics rushed to grab their patients and ease them back onto their cots. Blinking, she wondered what had caused the explosion. Stumbling around the overturned beds, she searched for anyone amidst the mess. She came to an abrupt halt at the gaping hole in the floor.

Two hands reached through the breach and gripped the edges. A grey-faced Nazi hauled himself up and altered his grip to drag himself through when he paused at seeing Watford standing over him. Time froze when they locked eyes. Watford forced herself to react first. She lowered the barrel of her Lee-Enfield, took aim, and fired. His skull exploded and sprayed across the concrete before his limp body disappeared back through the breach.

"They're coming through the floor!" she screamed and inched nearer.

Muffled shouts followed another head extending up, gripping a grenade. Watford aimed her rifle and emptied the clip, causing the body and bomb to disappear. Seconds later, it exploded, triggering a chorus of howls. Edging closer, she peered down, spotting torn and distorted bodies on the level below, but no other attempts to climb in. She grabbed the nearest overturned cot and dragged it over the opening. It wouldn't stop a concerted effort to break through, but it might buy them time.

Shrieks burst out from across the medical bay. Watford turned in time to see a Nazi ram his bayonet through Mayday's chest and kick her to the floor. Slapping in a fresh clip, she knelt, aimed, and fired three times. The German soldier dived behind wreckage for cover, but she surged forward, keeping her head low, and took shelter behind an upended bed. A grenade came sailing through the air and landed where she had been seconds ago. It detonated as she flattened herself. More cries moaned out from patients still on the ground, tangled in blankets and toppled cots.

Watford pushed herself up and aimed. The Nazi dashed between the beds. Three shots went wide, but one struck him in the waist, slamming him into the wall. Surprisingly calm, given the shock of the blast, she darted again, dropping to a knee when she spotted her target slump awkwardly. He stopped trying to reach for his MP 40. Blood leaking from his mouth, he held up his hands in surrender. Without conscious thought, Watford slapped in another clip, cocked the Lee-Enfield, and fired. The bullet exploded through his heart, and he tumbled over. Staying low, she turned to seek out Mayday and find the other breaches.

Anguish seized her when she came upon Mayday's body. Blurry-eyed, she fell to her fallen colleague's side, Lee-Enfield slipping from her hands and thudding down.

Out of instinct, she rolled to her back in time to see a blurred figure drop onto her, using his weight to pin her legs. Blinking her eyes clear, she swung her fist at the German, but he blocked. Wrapping his hand around her throat, he slammed her head against the concrete and choked her. She tried to break his grip, but the smiling Nazi tightened it.

"English bitch," he growled, leaning his weight down.

Desperation coursing through her, Watford intensified her efforts, trying to scratch and tear at his face. The German pulled back out of her reach, shaking her throat, and squeezing the life out of her. Heart pounding and dizzy from the lack of oxygen, she nearly missed Noid rushing up behind her attacker. He spotted it at the last minute and half-turned. She rammed her knife into his back, instantly breaking his grip as he clasped at the wound.

Gasping for air, Watford rubbed her aching throat. Noid grabbed the Nazi by his hair, yanked his head back, and ran the blade across his neck. Waterfalls of blood spilt across his uniform. She tossed him aside and, grinning, dropped to a knee to help Watford up.

"You all right?" she asked, her voice less harsh than normal.

"I'm fine." Watford snatched up her Lee-Enfield. "Are they the only ones who got through?"

"I think so," Noid said, peeking her head over the sea of overturned cots. "I dropped grenades on the hole near Mayday and took out a few of the bastards trying to climb up. We should check around and make sure there aren't any other breaches."

"Agreed," Watford said, massaging her aching neck. "Once we have that done, we need to get the wounded out of here. Whatever it takes. I'll remain in case any of our boys show up, but Doctor Fawcett and the rest need to be evacuated."

"You're one tough chick, Watford. Okay, let's do it. So we're clear, me and Smack will stay behind with you. This is where we need to be."

Something about Noid's words struck her as final. She couldn't decode the strange look she gave her. When their gazes met, she nodded in reply. Taking a deep breath, she forced herself to her knees.

Shadowing Noid, they crossed the devastated ruins of the medical bay.

LEVEL 1, FORWARD BASE ZULU
18:29 MST
DAY 2

Reichsführer Wagner stood by the gaping hole in the wall leading into the rubble-strewn Level 1 storage area. Across the wreckage of concrete and containers, he noted the bodies of the Wehrmacht killed in the earlier attacks. He could differentiate with ease. Most were intact, wearing whole, if not stained, uniforms. The new additions were something else entirely.

Shattered and burst carcasses dotted the macabre landscape, mostly broken apart from the fall. Each one bore the same handiwork, similar to their counterparts dangling from the chains above. Looking up, Wagner scanned the dozen or so corpses with chains around their lopsided necks, swaying where the ceiling used to stand. Every one of them oozed blood from the variety of wounds inflicted. He recognised the Star of David carved into the foreheads of every victim. After that, the injuries varied. For the most part, eyes, ears, noses, and digits had been hacked off, often tossed down afterwards like a hellish rainstorm.

The messages sliced into their flesh intrigued him more than anything. Words like "2ND BATT WAS HERE," "HOLLOW JUSTICE," and "MOF RUNS MARS." Of them all, one seemed directed at him. Simply "WAGNER" carved into the chest of an unfortunate with a knife buried into the centre of his name. In all his time, Wagner had witnessed plenty of what could be termed brutality, but he had never seen it inflicted on his own people. The change in tactics fascinated him, not so much for its originality than its effectiveness. The Native Martian militia refused to fight.

He turned away from the scene and peered down the corridor where the wounded stretched out. For the third time in the past five minutes, Oberst Walu shouted and cajoled the latest batch of Red Blade militia fighters into advancing. Although he couldn't speak the Native Martian dialect, he grasped a sense of the conversation from their tones and body language. Walu commanded them to continue the fight on Level 2, but these reinforcements were terrified. They took one look at the hanging bodies and flinched when another, a native, plummeted down, splattering across the ravaged concrete and contorted steel.

The new group pulled away, backstepping towards the corridor they'd come from while Walu waved, urging them on. He looked each one in the eye, spittle forming on his lips, and gestured again and again in the direction of the enemy. Upstairs, rapidly deteriorating Wehrmacht forces fought to hold back the MOF push, their only hope to stem the tide refusing to fight.

"Who is the ringleader?" Wagner said, approaching the band.

All backs straightened at his words, and Walu came to attention. "They are my soldiers, Herr Reichsführer. I accept full responsibility for their conduct."

"At ease," Wagner said and looked over the mob. "I'm not looking for someone to blame, Oberst. I want to know who the ringleader is so I can understand their concerns."

Wide-eyed, Walu glanced over the reinforcements, lips trembling. The militia spoke fluent German, so there was no need to translate. They understood Wagner's words clear enough. After a few seconds, one of them stepped forward. Even for a native, he loomed over his comrades, his head scratching the corridor ceiling. Struggling to make eye contact, he cleared his throat and fidgeted with his copper-red uniform.

"Forgiveness, Herr Reichsführer. We cannot continue this fight. They are not people up there, but beasts. These Terrans share no concept of the honourable combat that you and your brother National Socialists have taught us about. Look what they do to those they capture. Have they no respect for the dead?"

Wagner allowed a small smile to break free, which

amplified the soldier's squirming. He ceased all attempts at holding his gaze and, even towering over him, somehow appeared to make himself smaller. As he grabbed at the edges of his shirt, his lips quivered.

"I mean no disrespect, Herr Reichsführer. We wish to stand side by side and fight with our Aryan brethren to liberate Big Red from the Terran mass murderers and their Jewish-Bolshevik hordes. We know they have your beloved Führer in captivity. But this...this is madness. To commit such actions..."

"I understand," Wagner said, reaching out and patting him on the forearm.

With his free hand, he snatched his Luger, flicked off the safety, pointed it at the native's head, and fired. Brain matter sprayed across the wall and ceiling. The native collapsed back into his horrified colleagues. Wagner levelled his gun at the closest one, capturing the attention of all in attendance.

"You will advance now, or I will execute every last one of you for treason."

To back him up, the wounded Wehrmacht men in the hallways lifted their guns and took aim. If the militia raised the particle weapons in their hands, Wagner expected to die in the first volley. The moment he glanced over their faces, he knew they wouldn't. Broadened eyes, shaking lips, and thumbs away from the firing studs spoke louder than words. Walu let out a series of harsh commands. Heads dipping low in compliance, the mob marched forward into the darkening tunnel.

"My apologies, Herr Reichsführer," Walu said, eyeing the body at his feet. "You have my assurances. I will take far more effective measures should this situation arise again."

"No apologies necessary," Wagner said, holstering his pistol and turning away from the corpse, "but I do need a way out of Forward Base Zulu. With the basement area inaccessible, it is imperative I make it to the observation post in the hills. Can I enter the tunnels any other way?"

Rubbing his chin in imitation of the gestures his colleagues made, Walu nodded. "I believe so, Herr

Reichsführer. There's a secondary access hatch roughly one hundred metres from the south side entrance. We had one installed prior to the attack in case any of our soldiers needed to storm the outer walls. It will lead you back to the OP, but with Anna Bailey inside the perimeter, I cannot guarantee your safety."

"Indeed," Wagner said, his own thoughts derailed by her name.

Somewhere below, or possibly even on their level, Anna was on the loose. They hadn't received any updates on her location since her attack. With their forces still cut off from their supply lines, it added to the tension. Wagner could almost sense her gloved fingers tightening around his neck while she choked the life out of him.

"Very well," he said. "Make the arrangements to..."

He trailed off at the shouts rumbling up the corridor. For one terrible moment, he thought Anna had located him, but in seconds, he recognised Generalfeldmarschall Brandt's voice. At first, he expected him to come storming through the littered hallway in emulation of his predecessor, blustering and shouting like an enraged buffoon. Instead, the tone of the shouts sounded more pained than angered. He gave Walu a nod to carry out his orders and turned to face the approaching Wehrmacht commanding officer.

"I've been betrayed," Brandt said, face glowing red and his eyes dazed and unable to focus. "Was it the SS, Herr Reichsführer? Was it one of my own men? My rivals, perhaps? The natives even? We were so close. Victory was within my grasp!"

Pulling his hands in tight, he thumped his chest. Confused, Wagner observed the spectacle and glanced at the rows of soot-faced wounded sprawling across the hallway, soaking up the sight. Heads bobbed low at the words of their commander. Those capable of walking dragged themselves up and hobbled away, back towards the basement.

"Come with me," Wagner said and, taking his arm, guided him closer to the breach.

Brandt rubbed his eyes at the scene of the dangling bodies on display, but rather than trigger, it sobered him.

Redness seeped from his flesh. Those familiar cold eyes hardened. Another screaming soldier came flailing from above and smashed onto the wreckage. Taking a deep breath, Brandt pulled his shoulders back and snatched something from his pocket. Breathing out, he handed Wagner a set of folded papers and waited until he unfurled them before speaking.

"It's official. Our entire thrust against New Berlin has been eliminated. Tens of thousands of men gone. Vanished into thin air. Annihilated. The attack on Eisenhower Colony has faltered. The MOF are moving reinforcements against us in all sectors. Within hours we will be pushed back. Again."

"Such is the will of Providence," Wagner said, his iron-hard heart unmoved by Brandt's failures. "If this truly is the end, I have no doubt you will do your duty up to the final moment."

In a slow motion, Brandt pulled out his Luger, resting the barrel in his palms. For a moment, Wagner thought he planned to emulate his mentor and threaten him with death or blow his brains out right there. Instead, he holstered the weapon and looked him right in the eye.

"I'll ask you this once, Herr Reichsführer. Has your SS betrayed me? Is this all part of your plan? Do you know if the MOF has some kind of super-weapon, one capable of destroying my battlegroups at a finger snap?"

Wagner took a step closer, ensuring to maintain unbreakable eye contact. "The SS continue to serve at the Führer's discretion. The minority under your command have not betrayed you, Herr Feldmarschall. I cannot speak for the ones imprisoned in New Berlin, but I do not see how they could have impacted the outcome of this battle in any tangible way."

Keeping his gaze focused on Brandt, Wagner studied him for any signs of disbelief. The words he spoke were most likely true. He was still the Reichsführer and commanding officer of the SS, in name at least. Considering his absence for the last two years, it wasn't beyond the realm of reason that the Führer's methods had changed, even if the end goal had not. Their beloved leader had sanctioned the

SS turning on the Wehrmacht back in New Berlin. It was entirely possible he, at the very least, didn't object to MAJESTIC-12 planning to destroy the Wehrmacht forces beyond their control and remove a thorn in their side.

"Very well," Brandt said, eyeing him back. "We'll embrace our destiny together then, shall we?"

Extending a hand, Brandt pointed down the corridor to the nearest rallying point. Wagner followed his gaze, then glanced back up the hallway in the direction of the Level 1 stairwell. He took a pace back and shook his head.

"I'm afraid, Herr Feldmarschall, that I have other business to attend to. It is of the utmost importance I—"

"I insist."

Hand still outstretched, he held his ground. Wagner contemplated outright refusal but decided against it. With Anna Bailey roaming free and hunting him, he needed the protection of the Wehrmacht. At least until Walu could facilitate his escape.

Giving the slightest of nods, Wagner turned and started walking, all the while sensing gloved hands tightening around his neck.

APPROACHING FORWARD BASE ZULU
20:03 MST
DAY 2

Anti-aircraft fire spewed out from six positions, tracer bullets sparkling in the receding light. Lockhart let out a roar of laughter and pushed his atmospheric troop transport into a dive, avoiding the criss-cross of rounds eager to slice his ship to pieces. Behind him, in the personnel compartment, nervous gasps broke out at the sudden manoeuvre. Pulling on the joystick, he levelled the craft off, maintaining it bare centimetres over the sandy surface and making it far harder for the enemy guns to target him.

"Careful," Cheech said. "I can't see shit out there, and the jamming is wreaking havoc on the imaging sensors."

"I see all," Lockhart said with a grin and jolted the craft up two metres to avoid a sand dune.

Shaking his head, Cheech worked his fingers across the control panel and again tried to contact Forward Base Zulu. They'd received patchy comms from the base over the last few hours. On their approach vector, the jamming became more prevalent. The last thing any of them needed was a perimeter gunner to open up when they attempted to land. Especially with the additional cargo they held onboard.

Flak from the anti-aircraft fire exploded above, rocking the vessel. Unfazed, Lockhart pushed the throttle forward. The surge of speed exhilarated him, even as he scanned the darkness for the base. Without their navigational controls due to the interference, he was mostly flying by the seat of his pants. He had a rough approximation of where the base resided, and the enemy fire told him he neared it, but he needed to find it soon to execute the last part of his manoeuvre.

"There," Cheech said. "Northeast of our present course."

"I see it," Lockhart said, tugging on the joystick.

In truth, he didn't, but he had learned at a young age it was all about confidence. People always respected confidence, and sooner or later, he'd locate the base. Or not.

"Pull her a bit more to port," Cheech said.

"I know what I'm doing."

Lockhart reached for his beer. After taking a swig, he altered his course accordingly. Squinting, he could nearly make out the base rising over a line of hills. Cheech sent another transmission and gave a thumbs up when it connected, then advised of their imminent arrival and warned the base defenders to prepare for an emergency landing.

Yanking on the joystick to ascend, Lockhart released a triumphant whoop as, on cue, Forward Base Zulu lit up. External guns poured fire out onto the enemy units and gun positions laying siege. He doubted it would do much good in destroying the besiegers, but it captured their attention. At the very least, it forced their heads down.

"You're too high," Cheech said. "Christ kid, we need

to be level if we're to reach the emergency pad on the top. Level off!"

"Oh, ye of little faith," Lockhart said and jammed on the joystick, slamming the craft down at a forty-five-degree angle.

Surprised gasps and chatter broke out again from the men in the rear compartment when the ship lurched. A single red light flashed from the emergency landing pad on the top of Forward Base Zulu, guiding them in. Gripping the throttle, Lockhart eased off slightly but kept his ship's speed up. Last-minute anti-aircraft rounds spewed out again. Every shot flew wide.

"What are you doing?" Cheech said, voice raspy. "Slow down. You'll kill us both."

"Correction, kill us all," Lockhart said and flicked the cap off a button on the side of the throttle handle. "On my mark, fire landing thrusters at full power for a three-second burst and then reduce to one-quarter."

"Have you lost it?"

"Possibly. You ready?"

"Yeah."

"Ready. Ready. Mark."

In a moment of synchronised perfection, everything came together. Lockhart cut the throttle and simultaneously triggered the emergency thrusters at the front of the transport, designed to lessen the impact of a collision. The vessel jolted from the sudden blast of inertia smashing into their momentum. Like he had envisioned, the landing thrusters steadied the craft. He glanced out the side of his cockpit window port and smiled as he aligned perfectly with the pad. The enemy fire lessened when his ship descended for a soft touchdown.

"You utter maniac," Cheech said when the transport thumped onto the pad. "If you ever, *ever* try anything that stupid again...make sure I'm your co-pilot."

"Deal," Lockhart said and undid the straps of his harness. "Hold tight and keep the engines warm. I'll get everyone out and oversee the wounded being hauled in."

Shoving on his helmet and connecting it to his bio-suit, he made for the cabin door. He banged on the release and flashed a thumbs up at the pale-faced Soviet officer sitting by the airlock door. Rapid bouts of Russian caused the surrounding men to drag on their own helmets. Lockhart approached the airlock and peeked out. Spotting a green light flashing by the main airlock into the base, he gripped the door release. Confirming everyone had their helmets on, he gave it a pull and hopped out onto the landing pad.

The Russians followed as he jogged across the pad. The airlock door swung open. In single file, men carried stretchers towards the waiting transport. Looking them over behind their helmet visors, he recognised a few of the leadership. Colonel Penford's unconscious form was the first in line, with the corpses of Captain Chastain and Sergeant Major Howells right behind.

Lockhart paused at the door and approached the officer urging on his soldiers. "Keep 'em moving, sir. The sooner we get 'em loaded, the faster we can be back for more."

"I'm not a sir. I'm a sergeant. I work for a living," the soldier said before his gaze dropped to the rank markings on Lockhart's bio-suit. "Apologies, Lieutenant. I didn't mean anything by it."

"Of course, you did, but I don't take anything personally. Hell, I'm drunk off my ass half the time. Tell you what, buy me a beer next time, and we'll call it quits. Carry on, Sergeant."

"Yes, sir."

"Oh, and Sergeant?"

"Sir?"

"It's Captain. Captain Lockhart."

As the Russians filed into the airlock, Lockhart squeezed through the mass of traffic to rally on the rear echelons of the evacuees. Glancing at the pained faces and the blood bags attached to protrusions in their EVA suits, he had a horrific glimpse into the fighting raging within the base. The Soviets came to a halt at the inner airlock door and turned. Backs against the wall, they stood easy. Their officer and NCOs prowled up and down the line. Lockhart waved on the last batch of wounded when someone roared out.

"Boris? Boris, is that you?"

A soldier with British markings on his EVA approached the Russians, on course for a stocky new arrival. The Soviet NCOs converged and held up their gloved hands, but the soldier shouldered through them and came to a stop in front of his colleague. Three other British soldiers on security duty fell in beside him.

"Jesus, Sergeant Alexeev. It's good to see you. Are you reassigned back to the Second?"

The Russian officer stormed over and threw himself between Alexeev and the British soldier. Helmet to helmet, they glared at each other, and Lockhart sensed the mood in the room shift. Signalling for the last wounded men to hurry, he kept his gaze focused on the scene, wondering what was going on.

"Stand down," the officer growled. "This man is a prisoner of the USSR and has been assigned to a penal battalion. You are not permitted to speak with him."

"Peter Jenkins," Alexeev said. "You must stop this."

"Like hell, Boris," Jenkins said. "A penal battalion? They're going to throw you at a machine gun nest unarmed like the last war. How is that going to help?"

"It is Soviet business and, by definition, not your business," the officer said. "In fact—"

The officers' words died when the butt of a Lee-Enfield smashed into his helmet with enough force to crack the visor. He crashed to the floor. His NCOs surged closer, but they all stopped dead in their tracks at the sight of four rifle barrels pointed at them. Jenkins pulled his foot back and booted the fallen Russian officer in the stomach, causing him to yelp. He placed his boot right on the damaged visor and pressed down, more cracks forming from the pressure. With no atmosphere in the airlock, the Russian wouldn't last long if it shattered.

"Damn it, Boris," Jenkins said. "If you really want to die, just say so, and I'll put a bullet in you right here. No one deserves to suffer that much before dying, especially someone who hasn't done anything wrong. Have you a death wish, Boris?"

"*Nyet.*"

"Good. Come with me. The rest too," he said and turned his attention to the officer under his boot. "Thanks for the reinforcements, dickhead. If I were you, I'd scarper back to that transport. I hope you don't mind us taking your guns too. Every bullet counts."

With a nod, the three other British soldiers stripped the Soviets of their weapons and ammo. Jenkins gave the helmet one last crunch and then lifted his foot away. With rifles still aimed at them, the Russians picked up their officer, backstepped to the airlock, and broke into a sprint. Aware the wounded had been evacuated, Lockhart stood there, unsure if the British were going to rob him of his pistol or even shoot him as a potential witness to mutiny. Instead, Jenkins lowered his rifle and tipped his hand off his helmet in salute.

"Captain."

"Corporal."

"You're doing good work, sir. I'll buy you a beer if I make it through this. If you're old enough, that is."

"I reckon I should get you a drink on account of... well..."

"I won't say no, Cap. Mine's a whiskey. Until that day, sir."

Baffled at what he had witnessed, Lockhart saluted back. Jenkins dropped his hand and ordered the outer door sealed after his departure. Lockhart dashed outside and raced back to his ship.

Pushing the scene from his mind, he turned his thoughts to their return flight and climbed into his transport.

LEVEL 3, FORWARD BASE ZULU
10:39 MST
DAY 3

Gunfire raged all around, but Jenkins kept his gaze centred on the narrowing surroundings of the vent. Every movement echoed louder than the bullets slicing back and forth between the MOF and the defending Nazis desperately trying to hold their positions in Level 2. Controlling his breathing, he crawled on, eyes searching for the aperture that vertically dropped. In theory, it would lead them to the rear of the enemy toehold on the east of the base. Forcing the thoughts of being buried alive far from his mind, he reached out a hand. Instead of solid metal, he touched nothing.

Tensing his body, he came to a complete halt, as did the small group of Freikorps volunteers behind him. He pulled the rope free from his shoulders and looked up, gaze narrowing as he searched for the grate from the blueprints they had studied. Locating it, he fidgeted until he rolled onto his side and tightened the knot. After tugging on it to confirm it held steady, he glanced back at the shadowy features of the men and women waiting.

He reached over the space between the drop and the other side of the perpendicular vent and grasped the edge. Aiming to not tumble headfirst down the shaft, he manoeuvred his legs first and, mumbling a prayer, began climbing down. At any point, he expected the rope to give way, hurling his screaming body all the way down to the basement. By a miracle, it held. In the darkness, he prodded along the walls, seeking the access vent for Level 2.

Seconds dragged on like hours, but he finally located it. After climbing to safety, he tugged on the rope three times and waited. It seemed like a lifetime until everyone reached Level 2. Once assembled and stretched out end to end, they only had a short portion to trek. Jenkins repressed the urge to whoop with delight when he saw the light cut through the vent access.

Peering through the narrow slits, he confirmed the immediate area clear. Silently, he pushed the mesh free. Without any delay, he shimmied his way through, dropped to a knee, and scanned the corridor, Lee-Enfield at the ready. Although the chatter of machine guns exploded from nearby, no one occupied that section of the hallway. The rest of the Freikorps emerged and moved into all-round cover. Jenkins took point and, with his rifle raised, he darted to the end of the corridor.

He paused at an intersection and recognised the

identical layout to the MOF-held area above, then peered to the right. Dead and wounded Germans and a handful of Martian militia fighters lay stretched out across the floor. Protected by rows of battered sandbags, a section of the enemy poured machine gun fire up through the stairwell, grinding any attempt at breaking through to a standstill. Relaying the information to his team, Jenkins pulled a grenade free from his belt. He tugged the pin, tossed it at the enemy section and ducked back behind the wall for cover.

The blast silenced the guns. Pained screams took its place. Bolting around the corner, Jenkins charged straight at the smoking emplacements. The wailing wounded made no attempts to stop him, raising their hands if they could. With the Freikorps right behind, he closed the distance, lunging with his bayonet, when a battered Nazi emerged from the ruined sandbags.

Two more pushed bags from their bodies and scrambled for their weapons. Former members of the Army of David lowered their guns, snatched the axes and knives from their belts, and fell upon the bloodied enemy. Agonised wails reverberated through the corridor. Sharpened steel cleaved through flesh and bone, blood splattering the walls.

Sifting through the wrecked emplacement, Jenkins ordered the wounded occupying the floor stripped of weapons and herded together. After confirming no other survivors eluded them, he posted the Freikorps to guard both directions and made his way to the stairwell.

"Clear!" he shouted. "Repeat, the area is clear."

Victorious roars boomed back in response. The MOF soldiers above proceeded with caution, guns raised as they worked their way down the winding staircase. At the lead, the brawny figure of Alexeev waved when his gaze met Jenkins's. Everyone increased their speed, flowing past him to take their places for the push against the enemy occupying the level. Alexeev still wore the faded prison fatigues he arrived in. Even though the Russian rarely showed his emotions, Jenkins reckoned there was a gleam in his eye at the AK-47 in his meaty hands again.

"You ready, Sergeant?" Jenkins asked.

"Yes."

"Good," Jenkins said, pulling the crudely drawn map from his pocket and flipping it open. "You take the left flank—clear any pockets of resistance and make straight for the southern stairwell. Hold it and lead a recce on the eastern one if you can. I'll go right. Lieutenant McCabe thinks there's a command post between here and our lines guarding the medical bay. If I can break through, we can launch a pincer on the eastern side, and we'll drive the bastards back down another level. Watch out for breaches in the walls, though. We've sealed most but not all, and if they get desperate, they could blow some new ones."

"I understand, Peter Jenkins."

Half-expecting him to dive straight into his mission, Jenkins began turning when a hand thumped down. He met Alexeev's gaze and did a double take at the Russian squeezing his shoulder. The slightest of nods followed before Alexeev broke away and bellowed in Russian and English for his team to move. Surprised at the closest thing to a thank you he'd ever received from his colleague, he ordered soldiers to guard the stairs. Standing with the bulk of the Freikorps unit, he waved them on down the corridor.

They moved quickly but slowed when they approached airlocks or discarded equipment, watching out for tripwires. Once, a Freikorps volunteer forgot to check her surroundings and lost her legs when she stepped on a mine, dying a minute or two later. From time to time, they came across bodies strewn across the floor, most of them MOF, likely left where they had been killed in the initial attacks. The stench intensified the further they worked their way through the corridors closest to the exterior walls. Rotten meat, sweat, and sulphur clouded the recycled air.

One of the scouts peered through an airlock window and beckoned. They all ducked low. Jenkins crept up to it and peeked through, counting two heavily bandaged Martian militia, surrounded by a variety of unconscious comrades with blood-slicked, tattered clothing. Both men lounged against the wall as if unable to stand under their own power, oblivious to the presence of Jenkins and the Freikorps. Signalling at his band to ready themselves, he eased a hand onto the handle. Gently pushing it down, he expected resistance at any point. To his surprise, he tugged the airlock door open.

"Keep one alive," he said when the Freikorps rushed through, bayonets and blades keen for more blood.

Three of them impaled the soldier on the right, gouging his body across the chest and stomach until he collapsed, whimpering at their feet. A hatchet to the skull silenced him. They battered the other Martian to the ground, clubbing him until he curled into the foetal position.

"Get him up," Jenkins said, and the two nearest Freikorps soldiers complied while the rest spread out to guard the intersection beyond.

"Translate this into German for me," he said and cleared his throat. "Where is the command post?"

Bloodied gashes weaved their way across the Martian's tanned, almost reddish skin. Wide-eyed, he glanced at each of their faces, offering no opposition to his arms being pinned against the wall. He looked Jenkins in the eye and replied in German.

"He says he doesn't know," Private Levi said. "Says he and his platoon have been left here for hours. They were supposed to be relieved, but the Germans never came. After his platoon died from their wounds, he and his friend were planning on escaping. He's asking to surrender, Corporal."

"Tell him we'll talk about surrender after he tells us where the command post is."

Levi broke into another bout of German, and again the Martian answered. "He's saying he doesn't know, Corporal. He arrived in the second wave of reinforcements and was posted straight here. Hasn't done any fighting, according to him."

"Like hell," Jenkins said. "How did he get all those wounds on his body, then? Cut himself shaving? What about his dead mates?"

Returning his attention to their prisoner, Levi opened his mouth to speak, when Jenkins lunged out his hand.

He jabbed his fingers onto one of the bandages covering a wound on his chest. The Martian howled and writhed from the pressure but couldn't break his grip free.

"The command post?" Jenkins said, prodding his fingertips deeper into flesh. "Where is the command post?"

Through clenched teeth and scrunched eyes, the captive responded in bursts of broken German.

"Corridor on the left," Levi said. "Sounds like somewhere around section 2-C. There or thereabouts, from what he's describing."

"Good," Jenkins said and took his hand away.

The Martian slumped, his legs buckling, and heaved for breath. Jenkins grabbed him by the back of his neck, slipped his knife free, and rammed the blade through his heart. Blood spilt onto the floor, and he stepped aside as the Freikorps allowed the dying man to collapse.

"Kill them all," Jenkins said, sheathing his knife and nodding for the Freikorps to prepare to move.

Spacing out, they cleared the rooms they passed one by one. For the most part, they found minor storage rooms stacked with various sets of cleaning or engineering equipment. The billets they investigated were all empty, except for the odd body, murdered by the militia's ray guns or the Wehrmacht's bullets.

Enemy fire spewed when they crossed into the corridor approaching the command post. From behind a rugged line of broken furniture and sandbags, green blasts zipped out and ploughed into the Freikorps soldiers to either side of Jenkins. Lead pounded out, wounding the Freikorps too slow to dive for shelter. Dropping to the floor alongside the bodies, he aimed his Lee-Enfield. Rolling in behind a stack of discarded metal ammo crates, he shot back.

He emptied his clip and slapped in a new one. Another Freikorps soldier fell, clasping at his stomach as he crashed. Strange battle cries erupted from somewhere behind Jenkins, and a thunderstorm of bullets ripped out. He turned in time to see Captain Nowak lead a new charge, the captured machine gun balancing on her hip while she ran.

Shocked at the brashness of running headfirst into

enemy fire, Jenkins pulled the last of his grenades free and hurled them at the barricade. A wounded Nazi managed to toss one grenade back, but the second exploded in his hand, tearing him apart and showering the defenders with shrapnel. Even the grenade that landed closer didn't deter Nowak. Squeezing the trigger in three-second bursts, she zipped past Jenkins, screaming, and leapt straight into the cloud of smoke covering the enemy position.

As members of the Freikorps sprinted by, he joined in the fray, remembering the Army of David's suicidal charges on the Wehrmacht lines during the Battle of New Berlin. Outgunned and with little heavy weaponry, they stormed the Nazi defences repeatedly. Despite taking substantial losses, they swarmed the enemy and shoved them back inch by bloody inch.

Hopping over the devastated barrier, Jenkins saw silhouettes rush and slam into each other. Smoke stung his eyes, but he avoided a knife slash from a shadowy figure lunging at him. He thumped the butt of his Lee-Enfield to counter. Cursing in German, his opponent swatted it away again and jabbed, but the blade missed his stomach by centimetres. Throwing all his weight behind it, Jenkins slashed his bayonet, catching the Wehrmacht soldier across the side of the head, steel biting deep into his jaw.

Screaming, the Nazi tumbled. Jenkins anticipated and thrust the bayonet down, impaling him through the belly. He twisted, drew it back out, and slammed it at his heart. Pulling the trigger, he blasted a small cavity into his chest. Sharp, agonising pain cut across his back. Almost blinded by the shock, he tumbled to his knees.

Out of sheer instinct, he caught himself and rolled, the agony intensifying with his weight on the wound. He wondered if he'd been shot until he noted the metal bar in the Martian's hand. She raised the weapon again, but a Freikorps soldier swept out of nowhere, swinging a hatchet and carving through her waist. She tumbled backwards as the Freikorps soldier pressed on, pushing the enemy back.

Groaning and wincing, Jenkins dragged himself up in time to see a Nazi attempt to stab at the same Freikorps soldier who saved him. He took aim and fired once, the bullet catching its target somewhere through the chest. Shrieks echoed off the walls, bombarding his ears. Smoke and sickening scents tore at his throat and nostrils. To focus himself, he concentrated on the hallway ahead, knowing they had to press their advantage to link up with the medical bay.

He shoved through the bodies locked in mortal combat, jabbing with his bayonet, and taking pot-shots when he could. He hammered the butt of his rifle into the back of the legs of a Martian choking one of the Freikorps and walloped him across the side of the head when he fell to his knees. Sidestepping from a blur of motion, he turned in time to see Nowak race past him, swinging a machete. She buried it through the face of a Nazi stabbing one of her men, pulled the blade free, and ran it through his torso, knocking him to the floor.

Shots rang out, and the Freikorps ducked. Jenkins noted two Wehrmacht soldiers kneeling outside the door of the command post. They took hasty shots and missed their targets. One of the Freikorps snatched up a ray gun and fired a blast back, causing the two men to dive out of the energy beam's searing path.

"Forward!" Nowak screamed and dashed on alone to meet the enemy.

Jenkins took off after her, managing to fire the last bullet in his clip, hitting the soldier on the right through the head. The remaining one, hands trembling, struggled to load in a new magazine. Nowak closed the distance in time. She swung the machete, ploughing it straight into his skull, shattering his jaws. Blood bubbled from his mouth. She yanked the blade free and kicked his body away. Not wasting any time, Jenkins pressed up close to the doorframe and risked a quick glance into the room beyond. Shots blasted back in answer.

"I see at least seven," he said, loading a fresh clip. "Four on the left, three on the right. Could be more, and I'm out of grenades."

Without uttering an order, Nowak turned and extended her hand. A grizzled West German NCO limped closer to her, pulled two German-style grenades from a belt looped across his chest, and fell in beside her. She handed them to Jenkins, who tore the cords and tossed them into the room, turning his back from the opened door. The room boomed from the explosion. He threw himself in headfirst, firing as he ran and catching at least one Nazi emerging from behind a desk.

The rest of the Freikorps unit followed close on his heels, two of them falling from a sudden barrage. Swinging his attention to the corner of the room, Jenkins fired at an SS officer huddling. The bullets went wide, so he rushed around the overturned, smouldering desks and closed the distance. The SS officer raised his pistol to fire, but with blood seeping from a large gash on his arm, he couldn't lift the weapon again. He mumbled something in German, and the gun tumbled from his grip while he slouched back against the wall. Jenkins rammed his bloodied bayonet into his chest, twisted, and struck again, repeating the action until the SS officer fell on his side, lifeless.

When he spun about, the Freikorps had spread out across the devastated command post. Shattered radios hissed and spat sparks. Small flames licked papers and the edges of broken tables. Some hacked at Nazis lying at their feet, but none of the enemy remained alive.

"My compliments," Nowak said, sheathing her machete. "It seems you British still have some fight left in you."

"Thanks, Captain," Jenkins said, unsure from her flat tone if she meant it as an insult or a joke. "Lieutenant McCabe ordered us to press on to the medical bay. Shall we proceed?"

"Indeed," Nowak said, picking up a discarded MP 40. "I haven't had my fill of Nazi blood today. Tell my Freikorps to take on water, and then we move out, Corporal."

"Yes, Captain," he said, but she had already stepped away from him.

Watching her tend to one of her wounded men, he passed along the order.

MEDICAL BAY, LEVEL 2, FORWARD BASE ZULU
12:04 MST

DAY 3

"I'm out of bullets," Watford screamed and emptied the last of her clip at the growling German stumbling through the door.

She stood to stab him with her bayonet, but he tumbled onto the pile of broken and oozing corpses half blocking the door. Hand shaking, she eased herself down, catching sight of the layers of blood and grime staining her bare arms. Adrenaline kept her going. So did the collection of pains throughout her body. Readying herself for the next attack, she glanced at the various barricades they had erected across the medical bay, mainly to block the door and the multiple holes blown into the floor.

"Here," Smack said, handing her an enemy ray gun she called a 'particle weapon.' "Better than nothing."

Watford pulled the bayonet blade free from her empty Lee-Enfield. Holding it in her left hand, she took aim with the ray gun, thumb resting on the firing stud. Leaning against the metal frame of an overturned cot, she focused on what was once the door but had become nothing more than a gaping hole in the wall. A Martian she thought dead twitched on top of the pile of bodies, and she fired out of surprise. A bolt leapt from her gun without recoil and smashed him in the back, eviscerating his flesh and slicing him in half.

"Six-second recharge time on these things," Smack said, "so pick and choose your targets. Got it?"

"I understand," Watford said, yawning. "Any idea when your friends are getting here? Between you and me, I don't think we can hold out much longer."

"Soon," Smack said, clasping her shoulder. "A little while more. We're nearly there."

"I hope so," she said, looking back across the ravaged wasteland of the medical bay over to Doctor Fawcett.

To his credit, the man worked non-stop on the injured under his care. They had managed to evacuate the walking wounded and those who could be treated in the field hospital, but Fawcett refused to surrender anyone he didn't think he could save or who needed immediate surgery. While bullets and bombs destroyed his once pristine medical bay, he continued doing all he could as the combat medics fought to hold back the tide of advancing enemy.

The room rocked. For a horrific moment, Watford thought the ceiling was about to collapse in on them. The far wall opposite her cracked and tumbled inwards. Grenades followed and skittered along the floor before exploding, sending chunks of cots and burning bedding into the air. She swung her aim from the door to the breach. Blasting on their MP 40s, a mix of SS and Wehrmacht soldiers stormed through. Watford fired, the swirling green energy bolt smashing the lead SS officer and tearing a chunk out of his chest.

Spreading out, the Germans darted across the room, firing with every step. Aware the ray gun bolts could eat through metal and stone, Watford tracked one Wehrmacht soldier trying to flank her. She fired again, the bolt vaporising his head as he attempted to shoot. Smack pressed the stud on her particle weapon, narrowly missing when her target threw himself flat. Another barrage of grenades soared through the air. Smack grabbed her by the shoulder and hauled her away when one landed nearby. The blast sent the two of them crashing face-first into another overturned cot.

From the moment she struck the ground, Watford knew something was wrong. Searing, fiery pains ate across the flesh of her back. She clamped her jaws to stop from screaming, strength fading from her body. In desperation, she turned to Smack, only to see her colleague lying on her back, eyes closed and a gash on her head. Whimpering from the agony of movement, Watford pressed her fingers against Smack's neck and detected a pulse. She snatched up her ray gun, looped her arm under Smack's shoulder, and attempted to drag her away.

Bullets pounded the wreckage to her left. She raised her weapon and fired at the screaming Nazi rushing towards her. The blast flew wide. He leapt over the rubble and adjusted his aim. As his finger curled on the trigger, a blur of motion sliced through the air and struck him in the waist, causing him to lose his balance. Noid jumped over a pile of debris and landed on the fallen soldier. She pulled her knife from his side and slammed it hard into his throat.

Another torrent of lead sprayed out, so she ducked down and crawled over. She frantically scrambled closer, eyes widening at the sight of the unconscious Smack as she, too, checked for a pulse. Too weakened to even speak and advise, Smack was knocked out but not dying. Watford lifted her weapon. She fired at three more of the charging enemy, the bolt slashing the arm off one and hurling him backwards.

The world slowed. Six seconds until she had another shot, but in that time, the enemy would have a clear line of sight. Dazed, in pain, and exhausted, Watford sat there, eyes on her next target, willing the weapon to charge faster.

"I am a soldier," she said, ready to meet her maker.

She pressed the firing stud, but nothing came out. Five more seconds. She tapped again anyway as those barrels levelled on her. For no reason at all, she couldn't help but smile, even as two angered faces contorted into snarls bore down on her. She pushed the button again. Nothing.

Fresh cracks of weapons fire exploded out. Unblinking, Watford waited for the rounds to punch through her body, ending her life. They never came. Instead, they slashed through the two approaching soldiers and knocked them backwards, spurts of blood spraying through the air. The remaining Nazis ducked low or pulled back, shifting their fire in the direction of the emergency exit, the last doorway the MOF controlled.

Cringing from the pain still eating into her flesh, Watford shifted her weight and glanced back at the door. Rows of MOF and MEF personnel in their nations' distinctive battledress poured through, throwing walls of lead at the diminishing enemy force. Within seconds they cleared the room, killing the last of the Nazis before securing the various breaches.

She flinched at the sudden movement from the body-stacked door closest to her but lowered her charged weapon at seeing a woman in a Freikorps uniform stepping through, brandishing a machete for some reason. More Freikorps followed, with one British soldier directing them across the room. Cheers rose from throughout the medical bay. For the first time in what seemed like an eternity, Watford realised she would live to see another day.

Freikorps soldiers set a battered cot upright and eased Smack onto it before helping her and Noid up. Noid went to a knee beside her friend and took her hand, gently checking her for other wounds. Still in shock from her near-death experience, Watford mumbled her thanks. Holding her ray gun tight, she glanced about and caught Noid staring, an eyebrow arched.

"Christ, you ok?" Noid said.

"I could use a bath and a bed. Oh, and wine."

"No, I mean your back. You're covered in shrapnel."

At her words, the pain in her skin strengthened. Every breath heightened the sense of the tiny jutting pieces of metal cutting into her. Despite the agony and the light-headedness, she nodded. Staring down the barrel of a gun and surviving somehow filled her with a sudden gratitude for breathing.

"I guess it takes nearly dying to appreciate being alive," she said and turned when an officer came into view and marched towards her.

Her joyous mood soured when she recognised Lieutenant Barrymore, the one who had humiliated her on her first day of arrival. Holding her ray gun, she did her best to salute and somehow not tumble over. Forehead crinkling, he stared at the particle gun in her hand and then at the Freikorps soldiers picking through the debris around her.

"Who gave this woman a weapon?" he snapped.

"The last owner didn't need it as much as I did, sir," Watford said, dropping her hand when he didn't reciprocate her salute. "He's over in that pile behind me if you'd like to see if he has any objections."

Barrymore looked past her at the stack of enemy dead slumped inside the door and out in the corridor. Eyes turning to slits, he looked her up and down and took a step closer. Jabbing his finger, he snarled.

"I remember you, missy. You're one of those uppity nurses, aren't you? Hand over that weapon and go clean a bedpan."

The urge to raise her ray gun and fire a bolt into his groin threatened to overwhelm her, but Watford stayed her hand. After everything she had done and suffered through, the least she expected was a measure of respect. Even after the endless courage she and her fellow combat medics had shown in protecting the wounded, they were still considered nothing more than glorified orderlies.

"What's all this about?" another voice said.

A taller officer strolled up and took Barrymore's side, glancing from her to him. Resting his gaze on Barrymore, he pulled out a cigarette and lit one, making no attempt to saunter on. Covered with dirt across his face, it took Watford a moment to recognise him as an officer with A-Company named McCabe.

"This *nurse* has a weapon!" Barrymore said, spittle forming on his lips.

"Yeah, I can see that, Dave," McCabe said, pointing back at the corpses of the enemy dead. "I'd say she's pretty damn good with it too."

"Don't start, Bill. You know the regs."

"Try explaining the regs to Captain Nowak over there," he said. "Half the bloody Freikorps are women. And if you ask me, I'd gladly take a dozen of these combat medics into battle than those green-as-shit new MOF recruits. Tell the stick up your arse to take the stick out of its arse and take a walk, Dave."

Barrymore glared at McCabe but, shaking his head and mumbling to himself, stalked off. With a small smile on his face, McCabe turned his focus to Watford and gave her the slightest of nods.

"Name?"

"Private Watford, Shirley, sir. Combat Medic."

"One of Fighting Bill's lot," he said, exhaling smoke. "Where is the old bugger anyway?"

"Dead, sir. Died in one of the first attacks."

McCabe's gaze tightened. "That's interesting, Private

Watford. Could've sworn we were getting reports off him up to a few hours ago. Care to shed any light?"

Watford's stomach swirled at his words. Already, she envisioned the court martial sitting at their desks in judgement, ready to throw the book at her for refusing to evacuate and impersonating an officer. Everything she had worked for up in flames. Yet regret didn't sting at her. Deep down, she knew she had done the right thing. Men were alive because of her deception. For that, she wouldn't apologise.

"It was me, sir," she said, lowering her gaze and accepting her fate. "We had too many wounded here, and if we abandoned them, the Nazis would have murdered them where they lay. I couldn't leave them, so I lied and said we had the situation under control and held the enemy back as best we could. The deception was mine and mine alone, sir. I accept full responsibility. Please don't punish anyone else in the platoon."

McCabe dropped his cigarette and stubbed it out with his boot. "Relax, Watford. Far as I'm concerned, you did the right thing. The fact you ladies, excuse me, *soldiers*, held out for so long on your own is nothing short of a miracle. I commend you on your bravery, Private. Corporal Jenkins?"

The thin British NCO with the Freikorps soldiers jogged over to McCabe's side. "Sir?"

"Corporal, mind if I borrow your rank markings?"

"Not at all, sir," Jenkins said, tearing off the markings and handing them over.

McCabe accepted them, stepped closer to Watford and extended a hand. Fatigued from her efforts over the last few days, it took her bewildered brain several seconds to register the act. Confused, she accepted the markings and ran a grimy thumb over the two arrows representing the rank.

"Consider it a battlefield promotion, Corporal Watford," McCabe said, nodding to take them. "We have this room secured. When the last of the wounded have been moved, I want you to take your people and get 'em fed and rested. We'll have more casualties before this battle is through, and it'd be a weight off my mind knowing I have you and yours in the fray. And get your back seen to. You've half a grenade sticking out of you."

Stunned, Watford grasped the markings, straightened up, and saluted. McCabe returned the gesture and then waved her off, giving another small grin as he turned to walk away.

"Hey, old guy," Noid said, standing up from the wreckage where she minded Smack.

Surprised at Noid's outburst, Watford hobbled a few steps, expecting McCabe to explode at the insult. Instead, he froze mid-step, turned back, and jaw gaping open, he stared. Unsure of what was going on, Watford decided to err on the side of caution.

Rallying the rest of the combat medics, she ordered them to the field hospital for a good meal and, crumpling to the floor, passed out.

MEDICAL BAY, LEVEL 2, FORWARD BASE ZULU
13:01 MST
DAY 3

Against his will, McCabe found himself unable to keep from staring at Noid. In all the bloodshed and madness he experienced, thinking of her gave him the slightest of reprieves. In her presence, all the ugliness, anger, and pain faded. Until Dub and Big Mo arrived, he had never thought he'd see her again. It was almost too good to be true.

"Noid," he said, his brain unable to process anything else to say.

"Miss me?" she asked, wandering around the mass of wreckage.

Dub hobbled to his injured friend's side. "Smack!"

Stepping closer, McCabe noticed the blonde-haired Black Visor unconscious on a damaged cot, a bandage fixed to her head. Eyes widened and lips scrunched tight, Dub checked her for wounds and grabbed her hand, resting it against his forehead. Big Mo limped behind him and started shouting for a medic.

163

"I didn't think I'd see you again," he said, stopping a pace from Noid.

She ran a hand behind her right ear, pushing an invisible curl that didn't exist due to the shaved sides of her head. Colour flowed to her normally pale cheeks, and when she smiled, his heart skipped a beat. Pulses of warm, flowing energy cascaded through every atom in his body, and he wanted nothing more than to lean in and kiss her. The presence of so many soldiers, the stacks of the dead, and the fact the enemy still lurked nearby held him off.

"We were always destined to see each other again," she said, her smile fading, "but I'm afraid this is the last time. We've nearly completed our mission here, and when we're done, we're going back home. We won't be coming back after that. There's another war we have to fight."

"I understand," McCabe said, commanding the muscles in his face not to reveal the utter disappointment crushing him at her words. "Well, feel free to look me up when you get back to 2018. I'll be an old man by then, but technically your mind is seventy years old, thanks to all the...Hollow...compression stuff. Won't be that much of an age gap."

He hoped for a laugh, but the smile disappeared from her face. She dipped her gaze and eased her hands onto the front of his battledress, pulling him closer. When she looked up, tears stained her eyes, a renegade one slipping down her cheek.

"That's the thing..." she said, trailing off to wipe the tear away. "Your name isn't on the list anymore, Bill. I checked and rechecked and triple-checked. It's not there. Gone. Erased."

Dropping her head, her body twitched, and she pressed herself into his chest, emitting a muffled whimper. McCabe wrapped his hands around her, and uncaring of who gaped, he pulled her tight. She slipped her arms around his back and hugged him. The scent of her hair zapped him back to the moment when they'd first kissed, and the entire world and war melted away. Unsure of the meaning of her words, he held her until she loosened her grip, wiped her tears, and stared up at him.

"I'm sorry," she said. "I'm not really the feelings type. Never have been in all my years. Until I met you. It's stupid."

Moved by her honesty and overpowered at touching her skin, he tightened his hold on her hands, pulled her in close, and eased his lips onto hers. Indifferent to who stared on, he lost himself in her, lips moving in time, tongues gently probing. He slipped his hands across her waist and drew her closer, her own hands wandering past the side of his head and interlinking around his neck. The energy between them increased, grips tightening, body contact building until everything outside receded into nothingness.

Breaking away, Noid gazed up at him, skin lightly red and clammy. She slipped a finger across his jaw and bit her lower lip, leaning in long enough to plant one more hard kiss on him before she nipped his lower lip in her signature move. Dizzy and intoxicated from her presence, McCabe ran a fingertip to his lip and smirked, the moment ruined when Dub cleared his throat.

"Tell him," Dub said, easing a conscious Smack to her feet. "Better to rip the plaster off quick and be done with it. He deserves to know."

Noid turned at his words, her gaze narrowed and lips pulled back. "Shut the hell up, you demented, egg-headed asshole."

In response, Dub raised his middle finger and guided Smack closer, working their way around the twisted metal and broken shards of wood. Familiar with Noid and Dub's antagonistic relationship, McCabe said nothing. They glared at each other before she returned her attention to him.

"Tell me what?" he asked, stomach tightening at the answer.

"No," she said, squeezing her eyes closed.

"I'll tell him," Dub said, his own lips curling into a wolfish snarl. "I may not like this plastic paddy, but he deserves to know what's coming next."

"Shut your face," Noid growled, opening her eyes and meeting McCabe's gaze. "I'll do it."

Shifting her weight, she ran her hands against his side. Lip quivering, she opened and closed her mouth, attempting to force the words out. She coughed, shook her head, and looked him dead-on.

"The cylinder spire thing we've been protecting in the interior is called a conductor. One of the reasons we had to come back is some of our people have been trapped here due to an incident back in 2018. The only way we can get them and ourselves back home is to temporarily activate the spire. If your name's not on the list..."

"Okay," McCabe said, "I'll help you. Whatever you need."

"I know you will," she said. "That's the thing, though. This is as far as a lot of you will ever go, Bill. In all the variations, all the various possibilities and potential futures, a lot of you never make it past this point. Even in the scenarios where you refuse to help, few as they are, your people end up dying somewhere else. The Core Cadre lied to us. Lied about you."

News of the possible deaths of him and his men sobered him, but the effects wore off quick enough. Although he trusted Noid's words and had no wish to die so far away from home, he was still a soldier, and it came with the job. If their assessment was correct and he had no way of escaping it, he didn't see the point in getting bogged down in overthinking. He'd always believed in fate since a young age, and if it was his time, so be it. He planned to fight up until the last breath of air escaped his lips.

"It is what it is, then," he said, shrugging. "It'll be a cold day in hell before I curl up in a ball and let the fear of dying slow me down. Come on. We have work to do."

Interlinking his fingers with Noid's, he flashed her a smile. She reciprocated and nodded. Relishing her touch, the smile on his face grew, the fear of death far from his thoughts.

Together, they made for the entrance leading to the field hospital, the rest of the Black Visors in tow.

PART 4

RECONSTRUCTING FALLING STARS

APPROACHING FORWARD BASE ZULU
16:49 MST
DAY 3

Tugging his MOF-style field coat tighter, General Schulz peered out the transport window port and studied the base looming in the distance. With every passing second of their approach, it came more and more into view. Its size impressed him, though not so much as the amount of damage it had received during the siege.

Vast chunks of the exterior walls lay exposed to the elements. Craters from artillery shells pockmarked the landscape around it, and mangled carcasses of panzers dotted the perimeter. Yet, for all the destruction, according to the reports, most of the fighting had taken place within the walls of Forward Base Zulu and in the tunnels underneath.

Turning his gaze away, he looked across the rows of smiling men lounging in their seats. Each one wore the red and black khaki of the Mars Occupation Force. Two years earlier, they had served the Führer in the Wehrmacht and the Volkssturm. All of them had fought in the Battle of New Berlin, most of the older men in the last war back home. They quietly rejoiced at their newfound freedom after years of imprisonment and what the victorious Allies

167

called de-Nazification. Challenges lay ahead, though. Schulz doubted it would take long for their true identities to become known by the serving members of the MOF or even, God forbid, the Freikorps.

Bloodshed would inevitably follow. Of course, he had explained that to the malevolent Mr. Myers, but the American brushed his worries aside and told him not to be concerned. The inability to worry came easily to a deranged individual like Myers. To Schulz, commanding officer of the once-proud Wehrmacht, it was all he could do.

They were his men, his responsibility. He had no issues sending them to fight and die in the name of the Reich. Having them gunned down by the MOF as soon as they arrived made no sense. He wanted nothing more than to kill Myers, but his dark powers or whatever he used to control him stayed his hand.

"Nearly there," Myers said, unstrapping his harness.

The transport lurched, but Myers stood all the same. Grabbing the ceiling handles for balance, he worked his way over to Schulz. Without any concern for decorum or personal space, he leaned across him and gazed out the window. Uncomfortable with his proximity, Schulz shifted in his seat, leaning as far away from him as he could.

"You're in for one hell of a show," Myers said, pulling himself back upright. "The moment is so close I can taste it. And you get to witness it all, Herr General. The new Mars Occupation Force, forged from the greatest warriors Terra has ever produced. All of one singular vision and mindset, carrying our banner side by side into the future."

In no mood for another one of Myers's head-scratching preambles or self-indulgent tirades, Schulz nodded. The transport slowed and came to a full stop in the air, the engines underneath the craft firing as it descended to within jumping distance of the emergency launch pad. Green lights flashed over the airlock, and Myers gave him a thumbs up.

"Captain Koch," Schulz said. "Move your platoon out."

"Yes, Herr General," Koch said and began rallying his soldiers.

Schulz waited until they exited the vessel before

trailing after them with Myers right behind. He landed with ease on the pad and, glancing at the barren copper desert surrounding the base, followed his men into the waiting open airlock. After Myers banged the door shut, the transport took off again in anticipation of the next one hovering overhead, ready to land another platoon. A lieutenant with a British flag on his EVA suit opened the inner hatch and, with three of his soldiers behind him, entered. He undid his helmet, prompting Schulz to do the same. Eyebrows furrowed, he glanced over the new arrivals until his gaze landed on Schulz's rank markings.

"Sir," he said, saluting. "Apologies, we weren't aware a general was arriving. I'll contact Lieutenant Colonel Wellesley immediately and have him report to you."

"That won't be necessary," Myers said, pulling his own helmet loose. "Lieutenant?"

"Lieutenant Barrymore, sir. Sorry, sir. Just got the word from the colonel to get up here and sort it out."

"No apologies needed, Lieutenant," Myers said, wearing his most disarming smile and stepping closer to pat him on the shoulder. "Now, we best vacate the airlock so the rest of our men can enter. We've close to two battalions ready to join the fight."

"Yes, sir," Barrymore said and gestured his men back into the corridor. "If you'll follow Corporal Bradley, he'll lead your men to the staging area on Level 2. I'll contact Colonel Wellesley and make him aware—"

"I'll speak with him directly, if you would be so kind," Myers said. "General Schulz will remain here until the rest of our men have landed."

"Of course, sir," Barrymore said and turned to face him. "Schulz, eh? Didn't think any more West Germans arrived with the fleet. Haven't seen many of you around town, aside from the Freikorps."

His gaze rested on the West German flag on Schulz's arm, then moved to study the line of soldiers filing out. Even so, his brows dipped into a frown, and his eyes turned to slits as he scrutinised faces and uniforms. Most of the former Wehrmacht men did their best impressions of a friendly smile, but Barrymore's face turned a shade

169

paler in the final few seconds.

"Schulz," he said, once again focused on him. "General Schulz."

The penny dropped, and Barrymore reached for his pistol, but Myers raised his hand, freezing him to the spot with his demonic abilities. Barrymore's eyes widened. No other part of him moved until Myers snapped his fingers. Leaving his gun holstered, Barrymore shook his muscles free and glanced at the two men, lips moving to speak, but no words coming out.

"You'll remain here with General Schulz," Myers said, leaning in close to his ear. "No harm will come to him, and you will order your men to lead every single one of his soldiers to the staging area without incident. If I find even one of them has been interfered with, I'll pop every blood vessel in that cranium of yours with the snap of my fingers. Nod if you understand."

Barrymore bobbed his head, and with a wave, Myers gave him back control of his faculties. Gasping for air, he backstepped away from the MAJESTIC-12 operative. Knowing how intrusive Myers's powers could be, Schulz gave the British officer space while he gathered himself. Outside, transport engines hummed closer to the emergency pad, signalling Schulz to place his helmet back on.

"Well, General Schulz," Myers said, stepping through the airlock door. "I leave everything else in your capable hands. Report to me at once if anyone hinders my plans. Understood?"

"Yes," Schulz said, motioning at the distressed Barrymore to replace his own helmet.

"Very good, Herr General. Carry on."

The inner hatch sealing reverberated through the room. Keeping Barrymore in his line of sight, Schulz crossed the room and waited by the wall. The light over the outer door flashed green as it registered the oncoming Wehrmacht platoon.

"What is he?" Barrymore said, the horror of standing in the presence of a Nazi replaced with something much worse.

Schulz had asked himself that same question many times since finding himself trapped in Myers's orbit. He had heard rumours during the war of the SS leadership's obsessions with the occult. Never anything credible and nothing coming close to explaining Myers's fearsome abilities. Meeting Barrymore's gaze, he noted the sickly paleness of his face behind the visor and spoke the only explanation springing to mind.

"He's the devil, Lieutenant Barrymore. That man is the devil incarnate."

LEVEL 2, FORWARD BASE ZULU
19:01 MST
DAY 3

Following a sandwich on stale bread, a ten-minute snooze, a cup of lukewarm tea, and two cigarettes in rapid succession, McCabe felt even worse than he had an hour earlier. Eyes stinging from fatigue, he rubbed a hand over his stubbly face. After applying a new bandage to his still-aching left hand, he glanced at the Second Battalion units massing for the push to drive the last infiltrators out of Forward Base Zulu. Of the thousand Second Battalion soldiers who arrived at the base, including the MOF replacements to bolster the former MEF veterans, less than half were capable of fighting.

Since the siege broke out, a quarter of their number had been killed outright, with another quarter wounded and ineffective. Needing to maintain soldiers to guard the various breaches, stairwells, C&C, and the spire in the interior, that left over two companies comprised of three hundred men in total.

Out on the barren plains of Mars, he could have crushed an enemy many times that number with ease. Indeed, hunting the werewolves and the reorganised Wehrmacht, they had on multiple occasions. But here, within a confined space, constrained with movements and unable to use the mortars that had proved devastating in every engagement with the enemy in the past, their advantages lessened.

171

"Come on, lads," he said, walking between the various platoons. "Get it together and hurry it up. One last push and the first round of pints is on me!"

That got a semi-enthusiastic cheer, mostly from the inexperienced MOF replacements who didn't realise there was no pub in Forward Base Zulu. The veterans, still in the uniforms of their home countries like him, heeded his words all the same, though, dragging on their EVA suits and filling their pockets with as much ammunition as they could carry. Near the breaches lining the exterior wall, sealed over with a single layer of transparent plastic of some form, the engineers finished bolting the rope harnesses into the ceiling.

"I always knew I was gonna cop it climbing two stories up on a faraway planet," Colour Sergeant Brown said, sauntering up beside him. "What about you, Bill?"

"Definitely doing something stupid, but I figured I'd be drunk," McCabe said, eyeing the desert beyond the covered holes. "Any sign of Lieutenant Barrymore? Sergeant McGee has his company ready, but it's not like Dave to be late."

"No idea," Brown said. "Tried calling him after Mad Jack sent him to the roof, but he's not answering. Want me to send a runner?"

"Yeah, double time."

Brown stalked off to grab the nearest soldier and task him with the unenviable ordeal of jogging eight levels up to deliver a message and eight floors back down in record time. As he did, Jenkins came into view, helping one of his lads secure the equipment on his backpack.

Of all the people he thought could survive the barren wastes and brutal close quarters combat on Mars, McCabe had placed Peter Jenkins at the bottom of the list. Somehow, though, the lad survived situations men twice his age and experience couldn't overcome. The way the Second Battalion got thrown into the forefront of every action, Jenkins would most likely outlive them all.

"Corporal Jenkins," he said, and without missing a beat, Jenkins darted over to him, wincing slightly from his leg wound.

"Sir?"

McCabe stared at his young NCO and allowed a few seconds to pass before speaking. "What's this I hear about you assaulting a Soviet officer?"

"Which one?"

"What?"

"Which one, sir? I pulled a knife on one back in New Berlin and smashed the other one's visor in upstairs. Which one are you talking about, sir?"

"Christ, Jenkins," McCabe said, rubbing his temple. "Are you looking to get put up against a wall and shot, lad?"

"No, sir. In all fairness, the last one resulted in me getting Alexeev, thirty extra heads, three rifles, and a revolver, so I reckon it's a trade-off."

As much as he didn't want to, McCabe allowed the smallest of smiles to cut across his face. He had found out about Jenkins's actions minutes after they happened. Rather than burden Mad Jack, he offered to ensure Jenkins received his just deserts. He reached into his pocket and slipped a wrapped piece of cloth free.

"You're a good soldier and a solid leader, Jenkins, but you need to leave the officer bashing to me. If it happens again, either do it so it never gets back to me or accept the consequences. Now, there's one last thing to cover."

He extended his hand and gestured at Jenkins to do the same. Nodding to proceed, he watched as he unwrapped the cloth and held up the sergeant's stripes in his fingers. Jaw aghast, he ran his thumb across the fabric and met McCabe's gaze.

"Since I gave your corporal's markings to Watford, I figured you could use a new set," he said. "All joking aside, lad, I recommended you for platoon sergeant weeks ago as Sergeant Blake's replacement. It's all official now. You'll be a fine sergeant, of that I have no doubt. Well done, Peter. I'm proud of you."

For once in his life, Jenkins was speechless. He lowered his hand and, gripping the markings for dear life, he bobbed his head. Wanting to give him a moment to collect himself, McCabe patted him on the shoulder and ordered him to carry on attending to the platoon when ready.

As he stepped away, a stream of MOF soldiers in red and black flowed down the corridor, marching in step into the staging area. McCabe glanced over the pristine, immaculate uniforms, studying the faces of the NCOs plodding along at the side, unable to recognise any of them. Considering he hadn't met even a fraction of the reinforcements in the months the Second Battalion had been out in the field, he didn't find it unusual. What stuck out was that each of them bore the West German flag. Highly unorthodox since MARSCORP refused to allow them to serve in the MOF and confined them to the paramilitary Freikorps.

Curious at the spectacle, he sought out Colonel Henke, standing amongst his Freikorps officers. He pushed through the crowds of men readying themselves for battle and, catching Henke's attention, pointed out the new men.

"Excuse me, sir," he said. "As one of the West German liaison officers, were you aware of any reinforcements being sent by your government?"

"Reinforcements?" Henke asked, scrutinising the rows of men lining up in parade formation. "I'm afraid you're mistaken, Lieutenant McCabe. A small delegation of translators, lawyers, and academics arrived with the fleet. No members of the military. MAJESTIC-12 were quite adamant about that. 'Too many Krauts as it is,' I think was their exact phrase."

"That is the West German flag on their arms, is it not, sir? Are they Freikorps?"

"They most certainly are not," Henke said, stepping away from his officers and approaching the replacements.

He caught the attention of a freshly shaved sergeant in his forties who, in perfect precision, executed an about-turn and saluted in the MOF style. McCabe sauntered closer to eavesdrop on the conversation. Except for Henke and some of his men, a handful knew he understood German, which he used to his advantage.

"Name and unit," Henke said in German, accepting salute and lowering his hand.

Rather than answer, the sergeant boldly reached into

his pocket, produced an envelope, and handed it over. Forehead creasing, Henke accepted it and, glaring at the still-silent sergeant, he opened it. He lowered his gaze to the contents of the letter, eyes flicking while they scanned the text. After a few seconds, his head jerked up. Eyes gaping and jaw dropping, he looked over the massing soldiers and stared at the sergeant.

"Is this true?" he asked.

"Yes, Oberst."

Rubbing his mouth with the back of his hands, Henke backstepped away. The sergeant saluted again and returned his attention to the men still marching into the staging area. Closing the distance, McCabe noticed his eyes were as wide as saucer plates while he gaped at the growing formation. He handed Henke a cigarette, slipped one in his own mouth, and lit them.

"What was that about, sir?" he asked, eyeing the sergeant who had his back turned.

"We may have a problem, Lieutenant," Henke said, voice barely over a whisper. "I will tell you, but I need your word as an officer you will restrain yourself and your men until we can formulate a plan. Do you agree?"

Alarmed at Henke's expression and tone, McCabe nodded. "You have my word, sir."

Maintaining his gaze on the new soldiers, Henke handed him the letter. McCabe spoke and understood German a lot better than he could read or write it, but he picked up enough key words to churn his stomach. He recognised the two signatures at the bottom of the document too. Mr. Myers, the MAJESTIC-12 leader, head of MARSCORP, and the one-time commanding officer of the Wehrmacht who surrendered New Berlin, General Schulz.

"Those men are former Wehrmacht and Volkssturm," Henke said, his tone still low. "The same ones we fought against in the Battle of New Berlin. According to this letter, they've each been thoroughly vetted and de-Nazified and are to be considered full members of the Mars Occupation Force by official order."

Those words struck McCabe harder than any bullet or shrapnel splinter ever could. Flashes of his men cut down by machine gun fire and shredded apart by artillery shells flooded his mind. Bodies stacked high across a desolate wasteland of brick and steel. Horrors that haunted his every waking moment and pursued him into his dreams.

He knew Henke and the original West German contingent had served in the Wehrmacht in the last war. Something he struggled with, even if he held a grudging admiration for Henke's abilities as an officer, but the news was too much. If his men, the former members of the MEF, realised the soldiers who killed their friends and comrades in the Battle of New Berlin were present, it would lead to bloodshed and anarchy. Not to mention the security risk of such men betraying them and aligning with their old allies on Level 1. Stunned by the level of unparallel stupidity, he grabbed his comm and brought it straight to his mouth.

"Top Hat, this is Knight Four," he said into the receiver. "Message Priority One, over."

"Knight Four, this is Top Hat," Mad Jack said without missing a beat. "Aware of situation. The order stands. Over."

"With all due respect, if the Freikorps—"

"You are not to divulge this information to the Freikorps under any circumstances, Knight Four. This comes directly from MARSCORP's personal representative, Mr. Myers, and you will respect the chain of command. Do I make myself clear?"

Something dawned on McCabe at that moment. The slightest inflections of Mad Jack's voice and the excessive language he abhorred when not breaking into one of his colourful yet anti-climatic speeches. The chain of command. He glanced at the two signatures on the document, and it occurred to him.

Although the Mars Occupation Force took its orders from their MARSCORP paymasters, for all intents and purposes, MARSCORP was still a civilian body. For any type of military action, they needed Major General Hamilton to sign off and issue the relevant instructions is subordinates and so forth. Mad Jack had given him pening.

"I understand perfectly, sir," he said.

176

"Good. You don't have much time, Knight Four. Top Hat out."

Henke tapped his thumb against the missing signature and nodded his understanding. Whatever Mr. Myers was up to, they had to act fast before his Wehrmacht goons could entrench themselves in Forward Base Zulu. They had the advantage in numbers, but they still needed to drive the enemy out of the base. What better way than to wear down the new recruits and let them battle it out with their former allies before turning on them?

"I believe I have new orders to issue," Henke said. "Can you get a runner to deliver a discreet message for me?"

"Yes, sir," McCabe said.

Looking over the two platoons massing nearby, he stalked off to grab the fastest runner he could find. Once again, he found himself a pawn in a game of chess between players whose motives he couldn't pretend to comprehend. Unlike the last time, he intended to do more than follow orders. If the powers that be wished him and his men to fight beside the same beasts who murdered their colleagues, they were in for a rude awakening.

They could imprison him on Mars for the rest of his life, but they could never take away his principles.

LEVEL 2, FORWARD BASE ZULU
22:10 MST
DAY 3

Digging his feet in, Jenkins tugged on the rope, allowing his body to stand almost horizontal on the exterior wall of the base. Not for the first time, he cursed his decision to enlist in the army. He cocked his left leg over the rope and turned, his entire body facing the rugged Martian landscape two stories beneath. The rope between his legs slacked ever so slightly, the grips on his EVA boots the only thing stopping him from tumbling. More rope eased through, his footing loosening.

"I really don't think this is going to work," he said into the battalion comm channel. "Seriously, there's still gravity, and I've a full backpack on. I'm slipping."

"You'll be all right," Colour Sergeant Brown said. "Give it a bash, lad. It's worth a shot."

"Gravity doesn't work this way, Colour."

Head leaning more towards the surface, Jenkins scratched his boots against the wall, edging closer to the Level 1 breach. According to Brown, he should be able to peek through without exposing his body to the bullets of any prowling enemy soldiers closest to the hole. When Jenkins pointed out they could still shoot him in the face, Brown slapped him on the shoulders and told him he had to earn his new rank. Even as he suggested they tie him from his boots and lower him down that way, Brown shrugged it off, chuckling behind his visor as if it was all for his entertainment. Jenkins wasn't amused.

"Like, you could have at least tied it from my back," Jenkins said, inching closer to his target. "Makes more sense than having to perform acrobatics while dangling off a building, Colour."

"Good point," Brown said. "I'll remember that for next time."

Cursing to himself, Jenkins dug his boots into the wall and leaned down a few centimetres. The floor of the corridor within came into view, but he didn't detect anyone standing nearby. The rope eased between his gloved hands, tilting him further and bringing more of the hallway into picture. He shifted his helmet to gain a better vantage when the world spun. The rope slipped from his hands and bounced off his groin before his body flipped, swinging right side up and dangling outside the breach. Two Nazis lounging against the wall froze when he groaned. Jenkins reacted first, grabbing his Lee-Enfield from his shoulder, cocking it, and taking aim.

He fired the first round, catching the German soldier in the chest and sending him crumpling, air and blood seeping from his damaged EVA suit. The second enemy reached for his own weapon leaning against the wall, but Jenkins had him dead in his sights. The Lee-Enfield ed again, the bullet smashing through the visor and ing through his face.

ill dangling, Jenkins swept his gaze, seeking out

anyone else lounging nearby. At seeing no one, he slung his weapon. He used his momentum to swing over to the breach and caught hold of the edge, allowing him to land his foot. After climbing through, he scanned the corridor again and held the rope tight for the rest of his platoon to climb down.

Outside, clouds of smoke and dust covered the hills to the east. The atmospheric troop transports pounded the landscape with relentless fury, aiming to screen the MOFs excursion on the exterior walls. With luck, it would tie down the reserves they believed holed up in the networks of underground bunkers there. Within ten minutes, two full platoons stretched out across the exposed hallway, men securing both airlocks in preparation for the advance.

Issuing orders to the various section leaders, Jenkins pushed on to the airlock leading towards the southern passage. He peered through the reinforced glass, studying the ravaged corridor beyond. Although the walls were intact, discarded ammo canisters, damaged equipment, and even the occasional body lined the floor. Signalling at Private Hughes to take point, he backstepped. Along with the rest of the platoon, he raised his weapon.

Hughes placed his hand on the handle and eased it down. Flashing a thumbs up to show it unlocked, he gently pushed it open. At the last possible moment, Jenkins spotted the fishing line tightening when the airlock door shifted. He opened his mouth to roar a warning and turned to shove as many away as he could when the booby trap detonated. The shock of the blast sent him tumbling back several metres until he crashed down with a thump.

Moans echoed out, and when he lifted his dusty helmet, he made out chunks of Hughes's scorched body around the airlock. Most of the platoon dragged themselves back up, showing surprisingly few injuries. Ears aching from the popping sound, Jenkins stumbled forward, Lee-Enfield raised and leaned up against the opened door.

Whoever had set the trap fixed the bomb on the inner section of the airlock door, confining most of the blast within the sealed corridor. Alarms wailed from the base's automated system, registering the sudden drop in atmosphere from the breaches, so Jenkins ushered on his platoon. If the Germans and Martians didn't know they were coming before, they certainly did now.

Four simultaneous blasts reverberated from around the base, heralding the attack from Level 2. Using improvised explosives to destabilise the enemy defence emplacements around the strategic stairwells, the new West German units no one recognised would be surging down. Their overall aim was to keep the focus on their own attacks while Jenkins and the rest of the Second Battalion and Freikorps infiltrated from the exterior.

"Come on, lads," Jenkins said over the comm. "Get your arses in gear. Let's move it!"

Breaking into teams, First Platoon pushed on. They tread a careful path around the wreckage at their feet, wary of concealed mines but moving quickly. Jenkins changed channels, listening to the various updates coming through from the different platoon leaders reporting back, surprised at hearing German cutting through from time to time.

The Freikorps and former West German MEF soldiers always used English to communicate. Either they were picking up interference from the defending Wehrmacht units, or the new West German contingent hadn't been updated on the unofficial expectation.

Hazy smoke burst from an intersection ahead. Flashes of movement caught Jenkins's attention. Fumes spewed out, filling the area with a dense fog. He fired and dived onto the floor.

"Get down!" he said, enemy machine gun rattling to life.

From the mist, bullets chewed out, cleaving through the MOF soldiers still standing. Bullet-riddled bodies tumbled, dead before they hit the ground. Screeches mixed with the wailing alarms and the *rat-a-tat* of lethal fire spewing. In such a tight corridor, being pinned down meant certain death. The only advantage lay in the smoke grenades blinding the gunners as much as them.

"Corporal Burgan," he said. "Where's my bloody Brens? Rothchild, get that grenade attachment on. Light the bastard up."

Huddling behind wreckage and fallen bodies, the MOF soldiers shot back. The Brens rumbled to life seconds later, spitting death into the swirling white cloud. He glanced back and spotted Rothchild, jostling to fix the grenade attachment onto his Lee-Enfield. Timing it for when the Brens chattered, he raised his gun and fired. The grenade swept into the fog and exploded with a deafening boom, silencing the enemy weapon. Jenkins leapt up and charged straight ahead, Lee-Enfield seeking out any movement.

Trembling hands reached out from beside the charred remains of a machine gun. Sidestepping, Jenkins slashed with his bayonet, the steel biting into flesh. He then thrust, burying it hard into the dying German's chest, twisted, and drew it out while the man collapsed, dead. Stalking the area around the intersection, he stabbed the other two charred corpses and called up the remainder of his men.

To their left sat a hallway heading to an external access hatch used by the maintenance teams. He dispatched Burgan and his section's Alpha Team to clear it. On their right lay the corridor leading to their objective. Like the rest, discarded instruments of war and the bodies of the fallen littered it. At the end, it would lead them right up to the southern stairwell. From there, it was a stone's throw to the interior section housing the bottom of the spire that Forward Base Zulu was seemingly built around. With distance between them and the exterior breaches, he ordered his men to remove their EVAs.

Taking the lead again, Jenkins urged on his soldiers, Sergeant Alexeev a step behind. They weaved around piles of rubble, twice barely missing concealed booby traps. The closer they approached the hallway leading to the stairwell, the more the noise of furious fighting grew. Every three or four seconds, grenades detonated, pierced by the constant screams of the dying. One last explosion threw them all off balance. It knocked out the flickering lights, throwing the entire area in darkness broken by the muzzle flashes of weapons blasting close by.

The sudden bleakness brought on memories of hunting werewolves through tunnels. Jenkins pushed such claustrophobic thoughts away. Torches and flares lit up ahead, casting orbs of blinking light, showing friend and foe clashing at point blank range. Unable to gain a clear shot, he ordered his platoon to advance and, unleashing howls, they charged.

Bayonets smashed through grey, stained Wehrmacht uniforms. Bullets banged and popped. Bodies tumbled, grasped, jabbed, snatched. The blackened area near the stairwell became a free-for-all. Shimmering lights shifted and wheezed, casting ghoulish glares off confused, petrified, and angered faces.

Jenkins thudded his bayonet into the chest of a sneering Nazi. A fist flashed from his right, connecting with his cheek, and sent him stumbling backwards. Rather than fall, he slammed into a mass of grappling men and swung his rifle, slicing through the face of his attacker. Private Dobyns tumbled, another German ramming his blade into his guts.

Shots ringing out buried Dobyns's screams. In the frenzied light, Jenkins could see his jaws twitching wide. He rammed the butt of his gun and caught the attacking Nazi, but he disappeared beneath a sea of boots. A gunshot close to his right ear deafened him to the maddening wails and groans of the injured.

Spinning about, he avoided the swipe of an axe. The strength of the strike tore the Lee-Enfield from his hands. As men banged into him from either side, he lunged at the German and swung his head at his nose. Cartlidge exploded under the force of the blow, and the axe plunged away. A rifle butt crashed towards his head from the left. He ducked, drew his knife, and stabbed, running the blade up to the hilt in flesh.

Ears still ringing, he turned. Two muzzle flashes lit up. At least three soldiers fell beside him, one of them Private Heaney. Deeper into the swirling darkness he ran, closing the distance on the shooters. When he leapt and jabbed, the attackers lay on the blood-soaked floor, their heads already caved in. He rolled and dodged a bayonet thrust, swiping with his knife in turn. The serrated metal edge ate through calf muscle, splashing blood as the enemy soldier collapsed. Nearly slipping, he ran his blade through the soldier's chest and shoved him back. Another volley of shots cut down silhouettes struggling bare metres away.

Ripping his knife free, Jenkins glanced about. He saw Alexeev pinned against the opposite wall, dragged himself up, and sprinted at the Wehrmacht soldier. He pounded the blade into his side, but the German cocked his head back, catching him in the face and blurring his already unsteady vision.

A blow to the head knocked him backwards. Again, he stumbled into a brawling pair and held his balance, then blocked another punch and jabbed. The Nazi grabbed his wrist and shoved the blade away. Desperate to gain an advantage on his stronger enemy, Jenkins forced himself in close and ploughed his knee into his groin. Wrist freed, he buried his knife through the fleshy part beneath the Nazi's jawbone, forcing his head back at an awkward angle.

Seeking out Alexeev, he stumbled across the slippery floor and swiped when a Martian lunged. His blade carved across the Martian's chest, who lashed out his hand, catching him across the side of the head. Roaring, Jenkins dived, smashing him back into the wall, giving him a chance to pound his knife below the man's ribcage. As the Martian slumped, Jenkins struck him one last time and released his grip.

Breathing heavily, Jenkins turned in time to spot a figure on the opposite side of the hallway taking aim at him with a pistol. Through the flickering lights, he saw no battling men or enemy soldiers he could throw in the path of the bullet.

Priming himself to launch a desperate charge, Alexeev heaved himself up off the ground between them. His body slumped, and a hand grasped at his side. He half-ran, half-fell into the German. A shot rang out, and they thumped to the floor.

"Boris!"

The Nazi squirmed under Alexeev's unmoving body pinning him down. Jenkins stomped on his wrist, dipped down, grabbed the Luger, and shoved it against his head. He pulled the trigger once, shattering his skull.

Scanning for anyone poised to attack him, he placed a hand on Alexeev's shoulder. After shaking him and getting no response, he pushed his colleague onto his back and screamed at Alexeev's lifeless eyes staring up, a bullet wound in his chest and a collection of bloody stab wounds across his stomach and arms.

Without warning, the lights burst on to full power, illuminating the battle scene. For a split second, everyone stopped what they were doing, stunned by the savage brightness. Seeping corpses littered vast swathes of the floor. Four defending Germans stood flanked by at least thirty MOF.

One of them threw up his hands in surrender, but it prompted the killing frenzy. The MOF mob descended on their enemy like brutal predators, using bare hands, knives, and rifle butts to beat them to death there and then. Chests heaving and blood dripping from their faces and uniforms, they stepped back only when they had annihilated the last defenders. Trying to steady his breathing, Jenkins crossed the carpet of brutalised men, grabbed his Lee-Enfield, and glanced up at the stairwell.

The whole way down lay covered with the motionless cadavers of MOF soldiers, broken by the odd grey uniform of the Wehrmacht. Scorch marks on the walls and floor showed where they had stormed down at point blank range in an almost suicidal attack to take out the heavy guns pinning them down.

Glancing back at Alexeev's lifeless body, regret tore at him. Strangled by sorrow as the scene took hold, he wished he could've reacted faster and taken the bullet himself. Half-dazed, he slipped the Luger into his belt and tried to think of something to say. His mind stayed blank. Sadness building within him turned to anger as the death of his friend seized him. Gritting his teeth, he wanted to scream like a madman and beat the remains of the dead German to a bloody pulp.

He turned his gaze back to the corridor, looking over the allied and enemy killed, lying motionless. Widened eyes gaped from those who still had faces and mouths contorted into hellish snarls. Retching sounds broke the groans of the injured. Three of his men emptied their stomachs at the spectacle. He raised his rifle overhead, drawing all eyes to him.

"We press on. We don't stop until every last one of these Nazi bastards lies dead at our feet. Kill them all!"

"Kill them all!" the MOF hollered back, except for the new West German contingent.

Guessing they were unfamiliar with the Second Battalion's words, he lowered his weapon and sought out an officer or NCO. A short stubby man with a scar covering the left side of his face stepped away from the West Germans. Recognising his sergeant's markings, Jenkins nodded and offered him water from his canteen. When he declined, he glanced over them. They bandaged their wounded and grabbed what ammo they could from the dead.

"Your lads did well out there, Sergeant," Jenkins said. "You attached to Colonel Henke's Freikorps boys?"

"Most of us have served in one capacity or another," the sergeant said, his face solid as granite. "We are all MOF now, yes?"

"Yeah," Jenkins said and extended a hand. "I suppose. Jenkins. Sergeant Peter Jenkins."

"Richter," he said, shaking back. "Sergeant Otto Richter. On your order, let us commence the final offensive, Sergeant Jenkins."

"All right then," he said and turned to stare down the end of the corridor. "C'mon, lads, let's give Jerry a swift kicking. New Berlin is ours!"

"New Berlin is ours!" they cried back, the West Germans louder than anyone else.

LEVEL 1, FORWARD BASE ZULU
03:29 MST
DAY 4

The relentless barrage of bullets pounded the sandbag walls, forcing Wagner even closer to the floor. While Wehrmacht units crawled onwards, intent on holding their positions against the advancing enemy, he dragged himself away. As a Reichsführer, it was his role to lead, not get involved in combat. The Führer himself decreed it, and who was he to question his will?

Creeping low, Wagner backtracked to the intersection and threw himself behind the safety of a wall. Rounds still cracked out as the two sides battled for supremacy. He glanced in both directions, searching for Walu and his ticket out of Forward Base Zulu. The sheer ferocity of the MOF's attacks astounded them all. Like men reborn, they assaulted along every point, often engaging in hand-to-hand combat to seize a position from the die-hard defenders.

Luger in hand, he walked down the corridor to his left. Red Blade militia units bowed their heads as they raced past, gun-toting officers trailing, lest they attempt to avoid the fight. He eyed them all and spurred them on with every claptrap propaganda phrase that sprang to mind. Deep down, his thoughts focused on escape and survival. His work was far from complete. An empire beyond imagination stood at the cusp of its inception. He, the supreme architect, needed to watch it bloom and grow. Only in the future could he be free of his deranged creation, Anna Bailey.

An explosion straight ahead threw him down. The wall burst open, showering chunks of copper concrete across the floor. Shocked by the sudden devastation, he scrambled over to a stack of empty ammo crates and dragged himself behind it for any meagre cover it offered. Through the smoke and dust, MOF soldiers emerged, their rifles and machine guns seeking out any target. Terrified at the thoughts of capture, he took a deep breath and rolled onto his front, pressing himself tight against the wall and closing his eyes.

Boots thudded past, English-accented men shouting orders back to one another. One set plodded their way right up to his head. A sharp prod of a barrel dug into his back, but Wagner remained frozen. He waited for the bang of the gun and the searing pain of a bullet. It never came. The soldier jogged away, back in the direction he had come to trap the beleaguered Wehrmacht and sandwich them between two lines of fire.

Wagner exhaled when his lungs threatened to burst. He stayed still, awaiting the bullet from a lingering soldier. Gunfire rising in intensity, he risked lifting his head and peeked out. This section of the corridor remained devoid of any soldiers, so he dragged himself up. Gun in hand, he took off.

The entire base rocked from another succession of explosions. Grabbing the wall, Wagner steadied himself, fearing the flooring was about to give way. He stumbled onwards, back in the direction of the exterior walls, hoping Walu had retreated there instead. If the native officer failed to wait for him, Wagner would need to make his own escape, somehow procuring an EVA suit and finding an appropriate place to scale down the outside of the structure. With luck, he could either find the tunnel access or even make the crossing to the OP by himself. Considering the ferocity of the fighting, he hoped the MOF didn't have as many lookouts scrutinising the flat land surrounding the base.

Focusing on his imminent freedom, Wagner turned a corner and froze. A lone soldier stood in the centre of the corridor, staring right at him. Wagner raised his pistol and, forcing his hand to remain steady, took aim. Not recognising the unusual uniform, his gaze flitted to the flag on the soldier's arm. Irish?

The click of a gun cocking at the back of his head stayed his trigger finger. A pistol barrel pressed into the base of his skull. Two women stepped from his left and right, aiming pistols at his head. In a flash, he recognised all their faces, the ones the Core Cadre had sent to interfere with his plans back in New Berlin. The Black Visors.

"You were right, you Nazi tosspot," the Irishman said, a small smile creeping across his face. "We did meet again."

Offering no resistance, Wagner allowed one of the women to take the gun from his hands. Despite the hopelessness of the moment, he tilted his chin up, determined not to let them see his fear. He had a destiny. Regardless of whether they killed him or not, the wheels of time were in motion. They could stop him, but never the future he had so painfully crafted.

"I must admit, I didn't expect to see you so soon," Wagner said, switching to English. "Since our last engagement, I've taken the time to read up on you all. You must be the one they call Dub, which would make this *fräulein* to my left Smack, Noid to my right, and I assume Big Mo with the pistol to my head. Am I correct?"

"Correct," Big Mo said, jamming the gun harder.

"Very well," Wagner said. "Now the introductions are over, do you intend to murder me?"

"Tempting," Dub said, stepping closer. "Very tempting, but we've kinda made a deal with a friend of yours. She helps us with a little something, and in return, we give her you. Sounds fair, doesn't it?"

Grimacing, Wagner glanced at both women, wondering if somehow he could disarm one before Big Mo splattered his brains across the ceiling. In the end, he decided against it. The fact Anna Bailey hadn't presented herself showed she wasn't nearby. That alone could buy him time to escape if they weren't going to kill him there.

"You know my death won't achieve anything," he said. "What's done is done. The Stream has been opened. The Annunaki will rise, and only what I have set in motion will prevent our race's destruction. You know this. I can see it in your eyes."

"Maybe you dying won't help the war effort," Dub said. "It sure as hell won't hurt it, you sadistic SOB."

Dub gestured, and Wagner turned to face the corridor he had come from. The raging gunfire faded. Flanked by the Black Visors and prodded by Big Mo, he walked at a slow pace, hoping that somehow a stray band of Wehrmacht soldiers would come to his rescue. If no one showed up to aid him, he had one chance to survive any encounter with Anna Bailey, and it hinged on Mr. Myers.

"Have you met your forebearers yet?" he asked, trying to scan for a reaction out of his peripheral vision.

Smack did turn to glance back at Dub and Mo, but Noid kept her gaze focused on him, gun at the ready. A hand grabbed him by the arm, stopping him in his tracks, and shoved him up against the wall. He raised his palms and studied their faces. Dub stood in the centre and closed the distance, fingers easing on his knife's grip while the other three kept their guns trained on him.

"What do you mean forebearers?" Dub said, eyes turning to slits.

For emphasis, he slipped the blade free and pressed the point into Wagner's stomach. Wagner had known many killers in his time as commanding officer of the SS, and he recognised the look in Dub's eyes. Although he may have promised Wagner's life to Anna, he wouldn't hesitate to inflict damage beforehand.

"Your Hollow brothers and sisters," Wagner said, eyeing the blade. "I assumed that's why the Core Cadre sent you back to this time. To interfere with the first batch of your brethren."

"Wait a minute," Big Mo said, head tilting to the side. "We're the first batch. The ones activated in '75. What the hell are you talking about?"

Realising he had them baited, Wagner allowed a smile to cross his lips and gestured at the knife pressing into him. Dub removed the pressure slightly but kept the weapon poised to strike. Each of the Black Visors pressed closer, Noid acting as lookout.

"I'm afraid that's incorrect," Wagner said. "We activated the first batch of Hollows months ago in the American Zone. They are quite proficient, I might add. A true testament to the spirit of what I'm building for our species."

"It can't be," Smack said, glancing at her colleagues.

"Shit," Dub said. "That must be what our Anna warned us about before we left. Oh, Christ. I think I know what he means."

"Care to fill us in?" Noid said, checking the corridor.

Dub pulled his knife back and sheathed it. He turned away and met Smack's gaze before staring back at Wagner.

"It's the Young Guns," he said.

"No way," Big Mo said. "Those utter psychopaths? No chance, mate. It couldn't be. We were the first ones."

"Remember what Holly told us back in the MARSCORP building?" Dub asked. "She said we'd met before right after she broke my nose. The Young Guns went rogue right after we got banged up in prison in '76. It's not outside the realm of possibility they were active far longer than we thought."

"It does explain why they were adamant about getting Anna out of New Berlin in '54," Smack said. "Shit, if this is true, then we need to get out of here quick. If we can avoid a run-in with those maniacs, we should."

"It's been written," Wagner said.

Dub grabbed him by the back of the neck and threw him forward. Delighted at seeing his captors emotionally off balance, Wagner offered no resistance and started walking. The Black Visors fell in around him. From casual glances, he noted their furrowed brows and increased attention to the hallways in front and behind them.

If said Young Guns were members of the first incarnation of the Hollow Programme, Wagner looked forward to seeing them in action again.

LEVEL 1, FORWARD BASE ZULU
09:44 MST
DAY 4

A bullet sliced through Private Matthews, forcing Watford to raise her ray gun and fire off a blast. The Germans ceased shooting and ducked for cover, buying her time to run for the wounded lad. She stopped herself when he flopped back lifelessly, his entire body ripped apart. Rounds smashed into the sandbags she huddled behind, but the remnants of the platoon she fought with responded in kind. She waited for her weapon to charge, fired another blast at the enemy barricade, and dipped back down.

Bolstered by much-needed reinforcements, the MOF was slowly pushing the invaders back inch by inch. Already, they had secured most of the external corridors and shoved them back into their holdout in the Level 1 storage area. They still controlled access to the underground basement, but as soon as they cut that, it would only be a matter of time before the MOF crushed them.

Two grenades flew and landed behind the Nazi gun

emplacements. A Wehrmacht soldier grabbed them and tried to fling them back, but an MOF bullet punched through his chest and sent him flopping backwards. The explosion shredded the sandbags, and metal debris and limbs hurtled against the walls. Releasing a battle cry, the nine remaining soldiers of the Second Battalion C-Company, Second Platoon charged, firing a volley into the smoke, and swiping with their bayonets. Ray gun levelled, Watford followed.

"Clear," Corporal Owens said and waved everyone down. "Take on water, reload, and let's move."

Watford grabbed her canteen and, after offering it to her colleagues, took a mouthful. The coolness of the water dulled the tiredness in her brain momentarily. As she slipped the cap back on, the urge to fall asleep threatened. She had dozed for a half hour after regaining consciousness in the field hospital, her back bandaged. With so many MOF and Freikorps wounded, she couldn't in good conscience leave injured men unattended. When word came of the big push against the last Nazi holdouts, she volunteered, despite the bites of pain eating into her back.

Having taken on water and reloaded, Second Platoon recommenced their trek. In a staggered formation, they kept close to the walls, checking the littered floor ahead for tripwires. The base periodically shook from explosions vibrating through the stone. Sulphur and cooked meat wafted heavily in the recycled air. Bullet casings and smears of blood stained the ground, broken by discarded ammo clips, wrecked equipment, and the occasional body part.

Owens guided them down the end of the corridor, but they slowed when the gunfire grew in tempo. They hunkered down behind any cover they could find, and with hand gestures, he sent Private Collins on to investigate. Watford readied her weapon and tracked Collins as he disappeared into the darkness. Savage, pained screams bounced off the walls, sending a shiver down her spine. When Collins returned, she eased her thumb off the firing stud but maintained her focus on the hallways ahead.

"It's the Freikorps boys," Collins said. "They've pushed the last of the Wehrmacht back. It's a straight run from here to the storage area. One last push, and we'll root the bastards out."

"All right," Owens said, standing up. "Let's go have a look-see."

LEVEL 1, FORWARD BASE ZULU
14:15 MST
DAY 4

The pressure building in Brandt's skull prodded the festering anger within his chest, causing him to pace non-stop in a small circle. He ran his hands across his lips and face, sometimes digging his nails into his skin wishing the momentary pain would ease his growing frustrations. Like a wild, cornered animal, he wanted nothing more than to lash out. As his supply of manpower depleted by the second, the end stared him in the face.

The few Wehrmacht and militia survivors were boxed into the Level 1 storage area, hemmed in on all sides, every breakout attempt smashed to pieces by the MEF's growing flood of reinforcements. His failure at the Battle of New Berlin haunted his thoughts. Once again, he had been unable to score a final victory against the Allied menace. The army he had spent so much time rebuilding and reorganising was a mere shadow of itself.

"Herr Feldmarschall," General Fischer said, saluting.

Waving him off, Brandt glanced over the survivors scattered about the storage area. A mishmash of different units made up an under-strength battalion, a few hundred at best. All huddled under hastily assembled covers of brick and metal to shield them from the Allied bullets intermittently raining down from the third and fourth floors. The stench of the bodies dangling above them hung like a storm cloud over their heads.

Most survivors were wounded. Those who could, helped forge barricades around the four doors as well as fallback locations when the enemy breached. He didn't even count the native militia who remained. For all their talk and the

Wehrmacht training they received, they proved themselves poor warriors. Unfit to stand shoulder to shoulder with the soldiers of the Reich.

"Herr Feldmarschall," Fischer said again, stepping closer, eyeing the metal sheet over their heads. "I regret to inform you that we have been unable to communicate with the OP or any of our units outside the base. The MOF has commenced large-scale bombardment of the surrounding area, I believe in an attempt to collapse the tunnels. Reinforcements are unlikely anytime soon with the MOF's re-established aerial superiority."

"Of course," Brandt said and, turning, he leaned his hands on the map-burdened table. "Like everything else the Natives Martians promised, their jamming technology failed to produce long-term results. Without the ability to counteract the MOF's ships, we were doomed to failure. We have been betrayed by our so-called allies, Herr General."

"There is one option," Fischer said, lowering his voice. "I have located explosives amongst our stores. We can blow a hole in the floor, escape into the basement below, and attempt to locate an undamaged tunnel. With luck, we might be able to evacuate a portion of the men to safety."

"And then what?" Brandt said, studying the layout of Forward Base Zulu. "Flee like rats? Spend our days waging a guerrilla war until the MOF hunt us down? Hide in caves until we grow old and bitter? No, Herr General. I will not run again. I intend to make my final stand here. The Führer's name will be on my lips when I fire my last bullet and charge the enemy like a Viking of old. Valhalla awaits, my old friend."

Straightening at his words, Fischer raised his arm and open palm high. He opened his mouth to speak when a deafening bang engorged the room, shaking the very foundations of the building. The sheer force caused Brandt to slam onto the table, its legs collapsing under his weight. Face-first, he fell, ears ringing from the blast. For a split second, he thought an artillery shell had smashed them. Raising his stinging eyes, he spotted the clouds of grey smoke seeping through all four doors. Muzzle flashes ripped through the outer tendrils. The final attack had begun.

Every gun around him exploded to life. Contorted German faces snarled. They pumped round after round through the smoking open entrances. Grenades hurtled back, gliding through the fog, and erupting in crescendos about the storage room.

Men ripped apart, engulfed in flashes, limbs thrown about. Soldiers in red and black uniforms flooded through the mangled doors, bullets carving though their chests, cutting them down and smashing their bodies in small piles across the floor. Still, they came. Rifles and machine guns pounded back at the defenders, forcing heads down and buying more centimetres of ground to seek shelter.

In slow motion, Brandt absorbed it all. He rose to his feet. Lead carved past his head, less than a hair's breadth from his skull. He didn't flinch. On four sides, the enemy pressed ever inwards, a metre or two at most from the cover of their smoke grenades. Gaining toeholds nonetheless with unusual fanaticism he hadn't expected from the MOF.

An RPG ploughed into a barricade near the eastern entrance, enveloping a line of machine guns and tossing their torn operators away. A hand gripped his arm, and in sluggish movements, Brandt spotted Fischer beside him, dragging at him, mouth wide open, screaming words he couldn't decipher over the noise.

Something changed in his friend's demeanour, the face of a general of the Wehrmacht morphing into one of a mere mortal. Large, teary eyes pleaded, the grip on his limb digging hard into his skin. Over the hellish screams of the dying and constant din of battle, he focused on Fischer's moving lips until the words he spoke cut clear in his mind.

"It was me, Herr Feldmarschall. The Führer willed it. I betrayed you and allowed our men to be destroyed piecemeal."

Written on Fischer's face, he could see the entire story. The organised and systematic destruction of the Wehrmacht forces unwilling to accept the surrender and determined to carry on the fight. In his darkest moments, Brandt told himself he was fulfilling his master's will, but he finally saw it. Knew the Führer had lost all faith in him and thrown his lot in with the occupiers. The reorganised Wehrmacht would always be a thorn in the side of the MOF. After his failed offensive, they would be little more than a splinter.

"I will explain all," Fischer said. "I stand ready for any punishment you deem fit, but I cannot allow you to die here, regardless of what the Führer demands. You deserve better than that, Wilhelm. Come with me, and I'll get you out."

Brandt wrenched his arm free and stared at his colleague until he clamped his jaws shut. He grabbed his rank markings, tore them off, and slapped them into Fischer's hand. The urge to kill him rose then waned. Despite his betrayal and the deaths of so many good men, he understood Fischer had no choice but to follow the Führer's commands. No matter the bloody cost.

After clapping him once on the shoulder, he pulled his Luger from its holster, tapped off the safety, and cocked it. The promise he made himself when dragged from New Berlin echoed in his mind. Never again would he fail and live with such guilt.

Tracking an advancing MOF soldier, he aimed his pistol and fired. The bullet caught the man in the stomach and sent him floundering. Grateful to find a way of purging the violent anger from within, Brandt strolled closer, his gaze fixed on the eastern entrance. Oblivious to the rounds pinging down from above, he shot again into the spewing cloud of smoke. Another body flopped.

Three grenades bounced along and skittered towards the last sandbagged defence. One German soldier had his head blown off when he tried to snatch and throw them away. The sandbags bore the brunt of the explosion. Defenders rattled their machine guns to life and, once again, poured static fire out into the hallway. Devoid of hesitation, Brandt broke into a sprint and bounded to the defensive position.

Stray bullets cleaved left and right, but adrenaline coursed through his veins. Senses heighted, he scanned the smoking cloud billowing from the door and took aim from behind the sandbags. Men beside him cheered and redoubled their efforts to maintain their fire. The ground rocked. A hole exploded through the wall three metres from the entrance. More smoke grenades spewed cover, masking another round of explosives flung into the room from the metal walkways above. Brandt emptied his clip at the new breach, satisfied when he spotted floundering forms tumble through the clouds and crash to the floor.

When reloading, he ducked for shelter and glanced about. Dented storage containers piled amongst the bricks of the former ceiling blocked his view of the western entrance. He spied his men still putting up a fight north and south. Even as a dense cloud formed in the room, they fought like beasts in the fog, charging the enemy head-on in most cases, keen to bring glory to the Reich.

Another explosion detonated from within the room, and he noted Fischer standing near a hole in the floor, throwing a rope down into the basement area below. He would've preferred his former friend to fight and die with the little honour he had left, but he didn't begrudge him an escape attempt. They had lost the day, but someone needed to lead the remnants of the Wehrmacht, and it couldn't be him. Brandt had fled once; he would stand his ground this time.

Gun loaded, he levelled it at the eastern entrance again. Already, a handful of MOF soldiers had infiltrated and spread out, throwing themselves behind any cover they could find. Enraged, he tracked one diving for a stacked set of metal crates and fired three rounds. Two struck the soldier on the leg, causing him to trip and crash headfirst onto the crates, where he flopped over unmoving. He swung his gun to seek another target when a flitter of movement from his periphery stole his attention. Time slowed. A MOF soldier threw a grenade and ducked back down. Registering the explosive curving towards him, Brandt screamed at his men and leapt away from the guns, landing as the gun emplacements erupted.

Shrapnel lashed out but didn't strike him. Still gripping his Luger, he rolled about and tried to take aim again, but a figure stood over him, bayonet and rifle aiming down at his chest. In shock, he glanced at the face and recognised it. Blinking again, his surprise grew at the sight of Captain Koch, one of his former panzer commanders captured during the Battle of New Berlin.

He nearly whooped for joy at seeing his man infiltrating the MOF ranks when a foot kicked his pistol out of his hand, and the bayonet ate into his chest, shooting barbs of pain through his torso. Screaming as Koch twisted and yanked the blade free, he watched the lifeblood seeping from the open wound.

"Why?" he said, the taste of copper filling his mouth.

"The Führer wills it," Koch said. "You should have obeyed his command and surrendered. Soon, the MOF will be our new Wehrmacht."

Koch thrust the bayonet into his stomach, tearing through his organs, and Brandt shrieked in agony. Limbs turning to lead and eyes burning from the pain, he threw his weakened hands over the gaping wounds and rolled onto his side.

"See you in hell, Herr Feldmarschall," Koch said and took off, leaving him to die a slow death.

Gunfire, wailing, and explosions dimmed in Brandt's ears. The sheer agony of his injuries tore at his mind. Shifting his gaze beyond the storm of boots pouring into the storage area, he spotted the hole Fischer had blown into the floor. He reached out his hand to claw himself closer but pulled his bloodied fingers back to his damaged flesh. Brain growing cloudy, he rolled onto his back and stared upwards at the metal walkways crisscrossing across where the ceiling used to be.

A shadow passed across him, but halted, turned, and looked down. Bullets still raged, but the figure over him didn't flinch. Darkened eyes turned across his body, studying the wounds before meeting his gaze. Shuddering and struggling to breathe, Brandt spit up the blood welling in the back of his throat.

"Would you like to know something?" the stranger said in perfect German. "Would you like to understand what you've achieved here today?"

Brandt turned his head, spat, and nodded.

"Absolutely nothing. In a decade, you and your men won't be remembered. You'll be lucky to be a footnote in the history of the Terran Empire. If only you could see what I see. Entire worlds trembling in fear of our flag. Millions of Hollow soldiers enforcing order throughout the galaxy. True power. An everlasting Reich. Here, I'll grant you one small mercy and show you what you could have been a part of."

Delirious from blood loss, strange images occupied Brandt's final thoughts. Skies of green and red and blue and grey. Worlds with several stars beaming golden light down. Moons bigger than Earth hanging on the horizon of planets, gargantuan in their own right. Soldiers, too many to count, clad in iron and steel, laid waste to them all. Tinted visors looked across seas of bones, crushing skulls under metal boots. One flag draped itself across every star in the galaxy with Earth, *Terra*, glowing in its centre.

"Are you the devil?" Brandt asked as the images faded, the meaning living on.

"No. I'm a man on a mission. Goodbye, Wilhelm Brandt."

The figure pulled a pistol from his belt, cocked it, and aimed. Brandt wanted to scream the Führer's name in his last moments. His lips remained clamped.

A desolate bang rang out, and the pain ended.

LEVEL 1, FORWARD BASE ZULU
15:37 MST
DAY 4

Only after the "West German" contingent stormed into the storage area did McCabe and the real MOF soldiers follow. He slowed as he looked over the stream of corpses lining the eastern entrance, each one dotted with various bullet wounds. With an almost suicidal fervour, they had thrown themselves headfirst into carefully prepared machine gun emplacements and reaped the cost in lives.

Fighting persisted in the centre of the area. McCabe commanded his men to fan out, keen to keep them behind the lines of the former Wehrmacht soldiers conscripted into the MOF. Better to let them die and thin out the herd for when Mad Jack ordered the true MOF under his command to act.

He paused when he spied Mr. Myers, gun in hand, standing over the body of a dead German officer. For some reason, the MARSCORP operative gave him the creeps in every sense of the word, sending shivers down his spine at the very sight of him. Choosing to maintain his distance, he branched off. Sweeping closer to the interior of the storage area, he stayed near the crates and piles of rubble dotted about for cover.

Unrepentant fire blazed back and forth from the ring of defences around the base of the spire. Rings of metal, wood, and sandbags covered the last remaining Wehrmacht unit's intent on fighting to the final man. Sheltering beside a storage container, McCabe took aim but lowered his gun when he couldn't land a shot. The new MOF arrivals poured non-stop fire at the holdouts and crawled low across the debris-laden floor, closing the distance to fling grenades. Dozens of them lay dead already, heads blown off as the defenders fought ferociously.

"Perimeter's secure, sir," Brown said, pulling up behind him with a platoon in tow. "We did find a hole with a rope fixed leading down into the basement. Mad Jack's ordered Barrymore's lads down to check it out and secure the main tunnel in. Orders, sir?"

"Christ," McCabe said, slipping a cigarette between his lips and holding the packet out. "This is butchery for butchery's sake. What the hell are they trying to prove?"

Brown took a cigarette and lit a match. "Damned if I know, Bill. It's like they want to die."

"Could be they know something we don't."

Against all common sense, the former Wehrmacht soldiers in MOF uniforms threw themselves right into the line of sight of blazing machine guns. Small piles of corpses already formed at intervals around the enemy ring. Even more men surged onwards, using the bodies of the dead for cover while they lobbed grenades.

McCabe had seen individual acts of bravery during his career and even courageous actions from entire platoons and companies. Never anything so devoid of logic as such a monumental slaughter. He cared little for those men, knowing they had helped murder his MEF colleagues who had fallen in New Berlin, but the sheer lack of fear of death sickened him. With foresight and planning, they could've achieved their objectives with a bare fraction of the casualties. Either those soldiers had a poor commanding officer or an unyielding death wish.

Another wave of MOF uniforms gushed from the alleys between the storage containers. Guns blaring, they screamed and charged. Twenty fell within the first few steps, blood spraying a red mist through the air behind them. Most collapsed, wounded, and crying, but they clawed and fired until well-placed rounds finished them off. McCabe sucked on his cigarette and shook his head.

"At least they're making it easier for us," Brown said, leaning nearer and keeping his voice low. "At this rate, they'll barely have a company left, let alone a battalion. Their second one hasn't landed yet, which gives us the advantage."

"Why doesn't it feel like an advantage then?" McCabe said, exhaling. "They fought hard in New Berlin, but nothing even close to this level of madness. Not even the SS. I've got a horrible feeling something much worse is coming, Jim. Make sure the lads are ready."

"Yes, sir," Brown said and, turning away, ordered the platoon up closer.

Over a field of bodies, one of the MOF soldiers reached the ring of defences. Oozing blood from multiple wounds, he tossed his gun down, detached a grenade, and hurled his flailing body over the barrier. The explosion demolished a machine gun and sent men hurtling away. Piercing whistle blasts sounded, and more reinforcements charged ahead, taking full advantage of the lull in fighting.

In gruesome fascination, McCabe watched as former comrades turned on one another with merciless barbarity. Those in MOF uniforms refused surrenders and pleas of mercy, jabbing with bayonets and hacking with knives. They choked, bludgeoned, and stomped on each other as the fighting worked its way around the ring. The action moved beyond the spire in McCabe's line of sight. Flicking away his cigarette, he waited for the shots and the screeching to die off. When the last pained scream died from a lone gunshot, whistles rang out. For a second, the storage area fell strangely quiet.

"Come on, lads," McCabe said. "We'll secure the spire. Colour Sergeant Brown, report back to Mad Jack. Ask if he has any orders."

"Will do, sir," Brown said, giving him the slightest of nods.

Stepping from his position, McCabe gave a slow glance around the storage area. He noted his Second Battalion men at all the entrances and hanging back behind the still-standing line of "West Germans." Individual sections worked their way through the alleys, combing them for any stragglers and positioning themselves closer to their enemies in MOF uniforms. If the former Wehrmacht officers suspected they were being herded, they didn't exhibit it. Instead, they ordered their men to sling their weapons and begin moving the dead from the spire.

"Quite a show, wasn't it?" Myers said, strolling over.

Suppressing the urge to shudder, McCabe tried to force a smile. "It was something, sir."

"No offence intended, Lieutenant McCabe, but please don't call me sir."

"Fair enough. Anything I can help you with?"

"Yes, actually," Myers said, holstering his pistol. "What is your assessment of our latest additions to the MOF?"

McCabe looked about at the rows of soldiers dragging the dead away, both theirs and their former comrades. The words "war criminals" floated to mind, but he kept his lips shut lest he give away his hand. Bodies of Jewish civilians swinging from lampposts as the Wehrmacht retreated through New Berlin flittered at the forefront of his thoughts. Each and every one of the new arrivals soiling the red and black MOF uniform deserved to be put down. Or at least locked up for the remainder of their lives. Too many of his own men had died savagely at their hands, and the dead demanded justice.

Smiling, Myers reached out and patted him once on

201

the shoulder. The momentary touch of his gloved fingers sent an instinctive reaction to lash out, but he restrained himself. Everything about Myers fired alarm bells through his skull. He couldn't quite put his finger on why.

"No need to answer just yet," Myers said, glancing away. "I'll read all about it in your after-action report, I'm sure. Plus, the main event hasn't started. Best to keep your opinions to yourself to the very end, wouldn't you agree?"

Without waiting for a reply, Myers stalked off, hands behind his back as if enjoying a mid-day stroll through a park on a sunny day. Tracking his movements, McCabe watched him saunter closer to the spire. He climbed over one of the scorched barriers and tilted his head up, tracing the length of the spire until it worked its way into Level 2 above. Reaching out a hand, he pressed his palm against the smooth dark metal and ran his fingers across it.

Shuddering without any explanation, McCabe turned away. Brown approached. With a nod, he directed him closer to one of the battered storage containers. They lit up cigarettes. After confirming no one within earshot, Brown covered his mouth with his cigarette hand and whispered.

"We're good to for Case Orange when Mad Jack sends the word. All the platoon leaders and sergeants are on standby. Everyone knows what they need to do and how to do it."

Exhaling smoke, McCabe gave a slight nod. "Good. The second we get the word, we do it."

"You one hundred percent sure about this, Bill?" Brown said, looking around. "I mean, I'm all for it, but... well...this could be considered mutiny."

"The order to accept Nazis into the Mars Occupation Force came from Myers, not Major General Hamilton. If the general says it, that's one thing, and he can have my resignation while he's at it. It's our duty to round up these Wehrmacht assholes and keep them under guard until then. There's no way I'm letting them have free rein over Forward Base Zulu. No, I'm certain this is the right thing, Jim. We didn't fight and watch our boys die just to see their killers out and about wearing Red'n'Blacks."

"Understood," Brown said. "I'm with you. So is the rest of the battalion and the Freikorps. Let's get it done. Soon as the call comes through."

APPROACHING FORWARD BASE ZULU
17:05 MST
DAY 4

Fury unlike anything Lockhart had ever known pumped through his veins. His knuckles turned white from gripping the joystick and throttle hard to stop his hands from trembling. Teeth clenched, his gaze narrowed, and he focused on the base on the horizon.

"You're sure about this, Cap'n?" Cheech said after securing the cockpit door and retaking his co-pilot's chair.

"Damn straight, I am," Lockhart said, tweaking the volume on his headset.

"I mean...with all due respect, Cap. We could be wrong. That's a firing squad, straight up."

"We're not wrong," Lockhart said and reached out a hand to his panel.

With the flick of a switch, he activated the comm linking to the personnel chamber making up the body of the atmospheric troop transport. Voices laughing, chattering, and babbling came through their headsets. All speaking German.

"I'm buddies with some of the Freikorps back in New Berlin," Lockhart said. "They confirmed it. Aside from civies and translators, no West German military personnel arrived with the reinforcements. Think about it...it's been eight months. Someone would've seen them. And they're sure as shit not Army of David."

"I don't know," Cheech said, switching the chatter off. "We could be missing something. You really gonna bet your life on a bunch of limeys who've been under siege for a few days? Brains could be scrambled."

"Not those limeys," Lockhart said.

As Forward Base Zulu grew larger through the cockpit window, Lockhart thought once again of the horrible day in New Berlin when his transport had been shot down.

German soldiers found him, stripped, beat, and tortured him for their own amusement. His recollections were blurry at best, but he remembered McCabe risked his own life to rescue him alongside the Black Visors.

The British and French soldiers of the original MEF kept their heads screwed on, even under relentless fire and brutal combat. He trusted them more than the MOF if they were allowing Wehrmacht men to swell their ranks. In his mind's eye, he saw his father's decapitated body aboard the USAF North Carolina while the SS engaged in kamikaze attacks on the fleet, obliterating it. The Nazis killed his father, his best friend, and that he could never forgive.

With a tap on his control panel, Lockhart activated the video feed into the personnel compartment. Thirty men sat in their seats, hands flailing. They laughed, joked, and patted one another on the backs. Although all wore EVA suits, not one of them was strapped in or had their helmets on. Reducing the speed of the transport, he scanned over the surrounding area seeking out any lingering targets. No anti-aircraft weapons blared out. For all intents and purposes, the battle was over.

"Okay," Cheech finally said. "I'm with you, Cap. Who wants to live forever anyway, huh?"

"Right on, daddy-o," Lockhart said, changing the comms channel again.

He searched the channels he knew the Second Battalion used, aiming to cut through the erratic jamming signals. It took a moment, but he located a series of bleeps and worked on his controls to boost the signal. Static interference screeched. As they drew nearer to the base, the signal strength intensified.

"All units, Case Orange," a voice said over the channel. "I repeat, all units Case Orange. Case Orange."

Taking a deep breath, Lockhart keyed the comm twice to show receipt of the message and eased his hand from the throttle to the control panel. Exhaling, he moved his gaze to the video feed and the joyous Nazis he transported. He pressed down on the emergency airlock override. Those smiles turned to frantic shouts when the airlock door burst open, and the atmosphere seeped out.

Six men tumbled out the door at first, with the remainder grasping at the walls and seats, gasping for what little oxygen remained. Yanking on the joystick, he barrelled his craft to the left, tossing the remainder of the platoon out the door to their deaths. When he confirmed the compartment as clear, he closed the airlock door and repressurised the rest of the vessel. He threw a quick glance out his side cockpit window at the unmoving bodies littering the copper-red sands below.

"That was cold, kid," Cheech said, reaching a hand for the cubicle between them. "Ice-cold. You need a beer?"

"I'm good," Lockhart said, switching his gaze to the emergency landing pad on top of Forward Base Zulu. "You ain't seen nothing yet."

Jamming on the throttle, he powered his ship faster towards the pad. The transport ahead, piloted by his colleague Lieutenant Haldeman, tilted to the left midway through executing a landing manoeuvre. Its complement of Wehrmacht tumbled onto the cold concrete before the ship ascended. Those men who survived the fall scrambled up, flailing desperately to gain access to the airlock. Flicking his thumb, he opened the firing cap on top of his joystick and aligned his vessel for an attack run. The panicking Wehrmacht men didn't notice as he bore down on them.

As he pressed down on the trigger, tracer rounds burst from his transport's forward guns and carved through the mass of men. Bodies split apart from the high-calibre rounds, a few tumbling off the edges of the base and crashing to the surface below. Three soldiers managed to return fire, but their shots pinged off the outer hull. Lockhart corrected his aim and shot them down with ease. He performed two more passes over the landing pad, shooting at the fallen men until sure they were dead.

Satisfied with his work, Lockhart swung his ship about and made to follow his previous course. Haldeman had already ascended high above, keen to escape back to New Berlin and keep his record clear with deniability on what transpired. The rest of the pilots, mostly newbies, needed to be dealt with. He had checked the flight rosters and knew all their names. Aside from Haldeman, he couldn't trust any of them.

While he closed on the closest craft in the convoy, he opened ship-to-ship comms and broadcast a pre-recorded message outlining the true identities of their cargo of men and what actions needed to be taken to not be considered hostile. With luck, they'd follow his instructions and dump the Wehrmacht men to their deaths as he had and respond on the same channel. If they didn't, he was prepared to cripple their ships. He owed the Second Battalion that much.

Seconds dragged on for an eternity. Cheech pressed his headset close to his ears and pushed a button on his console. The sensor board in front of Lockhart changed, showing eight vessels in total, all on a course for Forward Base Zulu. The last two switched to green and broke formation, setting a return course for New Berlin. The remainder flickered to red and maintained their flight path.

"Six transports are refusing, Cap," Cheech said. "Pretty much saying the same thing. They're proceeding with their orders, and if we attempt to interfere, we'll be considered hostile."

"I'm already hostile," Lockhart said and loaded his compliment of ship-to-ship missiles. "Send a final general warning. Any ships approaching Forward Base Zulu, regardless of intent, will be shot down."

"Are you serious?" Cheech said, swivelling in his seat. "If we transmit it on general, the entire fleet will pick it up. They could gun us down from orbit."

"The relays may allow us to piggyback comms," Lockhart said, "but it won't work for long-range missiles, especially with the low-level jamming still in place. If we remain low, they won't get a clear shot."

"Yeah, but that means the approaching transports can stay high, and we can't get to 'em."

"I know what I'm doing, Cheech. You in or you out? I can drop you off on the surface, and you can say I pulled a gun on you if you want. No hard feelings."

"Nah," Cheech said, swinging about to face his control

panels. "I'm with you, Cap. Always figured I'd get court-martialled one day. Guess I just always thought it'd be for drunk and disorderly or punching a general or something."

Nodding his thanks, Lockhart kept his ship low while he glanced at the sensor screen intermittently cutting out from the interference. If his colleagues were smart, they would have broken formation to try and evade him. Evidently, they didn't take his warnings seriously. They remained on the same flight path, working their way ever closer to Forward Base Zulu. He narrowed his gaze when he spotted the lead craft in the distance.

"Arm missiles."

"Done," Cheech said, pressing the commands into his panel. "We don't have targeting sensors with the jamming. You'll need to do this manually."

"Easy," Lockhart said and pulled on the joystick, sending this vessel on a course with the first transport.

He locked the ship's engines in his sights and hovered his thumb over the firing button. At the last possible moment, the ship barrelled to the right, but he levelled off, anticipating such a move, and fired. The missile burst from the forward launcher and swept through the thin Martian atmosphere. Shuddering, the transport attempted to break into evasive action, but the pilot left it too late. An explosion tore through the engines and ate into the personnel compartment, sending the craft spiralling towards the surface. Lockhart waited long enough to confirm the pilots ejected before setting course for the second ship in the line.

At seeing his colleague downed, the next one wasted no time in offering resistance. High-calibre rounds burst out at a distance, zipping past the reinforced hull of his transport. Lockhart decreased altitude, aiming to come up on the other vessel's underbelly. The pilot matched him, keeping his forward guns on them. Smiling at the challenge, Lockhart hauled back on the joystick and spun his ship around, the top of his craft pointing down at the ground. He fired another missile, again targeting the engine, and veered past it as the rear of the transport detonated.

The four remaining vessels took the hint and broke

formation. He righted his ship and set a course for the nearest one on the right. Panicked calls squeaked over the common comm channel, but he increased his velocity to close the distance. His thumb was lingering over the firing button when Cheech raised his hand.

"They're breaking off," Cheech said. "They're requesting a ceasefire and pulling back to New Berlin."

"Okay," Lockhart said and decreased speed. "Tell them they can go, but we'll hang about for a bit longer. Once we're sure we're in the clear, we'll pick up those downed pilots and head back."

"You got it, Cap," Cheech said, breathing a sigh of relief.

Lockhart swung his transport about and set a course to patrol the local area while confirming the other transports were indeed returning to New Berlin. If luck still walked with him and the men of the Second Battalion, he had bought them time to subdue the Wehrmacht and make contact with Major General Hamilton to inform him of Myers's deceit.

Hoping he wouldn't have to down any more of his colleagues, he kept his thumb close to the trigger button and glanced at the sensor screen.

LEVEL 1, FORWARD BASE ZULU
19:11 MST
DAY 4

Unsure of the order, Watford waited until Corporal Owens and the other men of the unit removed their MOF uniform shirts and stood there in their dark red T-shirts. Sighing, she complied and tied her shirt around her waist. Leering eyes gazed at her figure. Too tired to ignore it, she stared back until they looked away and rested her hand on the ray gun fixed to her belt.

She pulled her backpack on and winced when it rubbed against the bandaged wounds on her back. Freeing her weapon, she glanced over the remaining men, almost daring them to ogle her again so she could pistol whip some manners into them. Averting their gazes, they fell in behind Owens and, with her bringing up the rear, marched on down the corridor to the interior storage area.

Four soldiers, also stripped to their T-shirts, challenged Owens but waved him on when they recognised him. The section plodded onwards and entered the storage area where Watford was hit with a massive barrage of shouting and roaring. She blinked and tried to make sense of the chaos. Former MEF men, distinguishable from their countries' battledress, and MOF soldiers, all in distinctive red T-shirts, rounded up other MOF soldiers, penning them in the corners of the room. A few Freikorps stalked amongst them, jabbing bayonets at the detainees while engaging in fierce exchanges in German.

Owens led them towards the massive spire jutting upwards and ordered them to halt while he sought out orders. They took a free space close to a set of storage containers. Looking across the carpet of dead bodies around the spire, Watford caught a glimpse of the fierce battle that must've raged here. She recognised Lieutenant McCabe also near the spire, flanked by NCOs and officers. All had their guns drawn and pointed at a solitary man dressed in black. Standing transfixed and unmoving, he stared at the spire, oblivious to the madness breaking out.

"What the hell is going on?" she whispered to Private Mulcahy beside her.

"The latest batch of replacements are all ex-Wehrmacht. The same ones the MEF fought in New Berlin and the other colonies. Somehow and for an unknown reason, MARSCORP sent 'em here, and the old MEF boys aren't taking it too lightly. See the fella in black over there? Name's Myers. Some sort of MARSCORP bigwig."

"Oh."

Eyeing McCabe and his small group approaching Myers, she slipped her thumb closer to the firing stud. She had every intention of following any lawful orders given, and if that meant helping to disarm the same breed of men she'd spent days fighting, fine by her. Something about Myers's demeanour frightened her on a subconscious level. He had six guns trained on him, and the Nazis he brought there were stripped of their weaponry. Yet he hardly noticed, which in turn, made McCabe and his band even more wary, ratcheting up the tension in the room.

Looking over his subordinates, McCabe furrowed his eyebrows. Taking careful steps forward, he closed the distance to Myers. Placing his pistol at the side of Myers's neck, he nudged him once, which snapped him out of his trance. His head turned slightly, seeing McCabe for the first time out of the corner of his eye. Raising his gloved hands, he turned, a smile plastered to his face from ear to ear, cold eyes staring. The sheer ferocity of his gaze brought Watford to her feet, a strange chill cutting deep into her bones.

Keeping his finger firm on the trigger, McCabe snatched the pistol from Myers's belt and stashed it into his own. He gestured at the ground. Myers stood unmoving, malevolent smile beaming out, almost magnetic in its aura. Prodding with his gun, McCabe again waved at the floor with his free hand.

"I said, on your knees!"

"I don't think so," Myers said, his voice above a whisper but somehow booming against the walls.

Something gripped Watford. Tiredness swept over her like those moments before sleep took hold. She sensed her mind slipping away into unconsciousness. In a dreamlike state, she marched towards McCabe and Myers, aware her body was moving, but uncaring she wasn't in command of her faculties. Giddiness rushed through her when she raised her ray gun. Thumb resting on the firing stud, she pointed it at McCabe. Around her, her entire section, even the MEF soldiers, all lifted their weapons and took aim at him and his cohort of NCOs and officers.

Exhaustion seeped from Watford's body, replaced by a revitalised alertness. She didn't know why she pointed her weapon at McCabe, an officer who granted her a field promotion and treated her with the slightest bit of respect, but she didn't exactly care either. Her arm held steady. Somewhere in the recesses of her mind, a lullaby her mother used to sing to her as a child reverberated and soothed her.

"What the hell?" McCabe said, eyes bulging as he

glanced around. "Stand down. That's an order!"

"They can hear you," Myers said, easing his hand over to the barrel of McCabe's shaking gun, "but I assure you, they are under my power."

The five officers and NCOs flanking McCabe raised their pistols and pressed them against the side of their own skulls, pulling the cocking hammers back. McCabe looked back, jaw open at their actions. He offered no resistance. Myers guided the barrel of his gun down to the floor. From her peripheral vision, Watford noted every soldier in the vicinity, MEF, MOF, Wehrmacht, and Freikorps, standing motionless, weapons levelled and at the ready. Her curiosity piqued at what could make enemies band together like this. The lullaby in her skull increased in volume, drowning out any concerns.

"How are you doing this?" McCabe said, backstepping. "Release my men now."

"It would take too long to explain," Myers said, smile faltering and beads of sweat collecting on his forehead. "Suffice to say, they are under my control, and they will fire if I command them to. You will not interfere with my mission, Lieutenant McCabe. Under no circumstances—"

The eastern entrance somewhere to Watford's right and out of her line of slight opened. Myers and McCabe turned and stared at the same time. Sounds of boots clicking echoed. Drops of sweat dribbled down Myers's reddening skin, the smile finally fading as he clenched his jaw. Whoever the newcomers were, they surprised the two men in equal measure.

A man pushed through the crowd, shoving past Watford. He had a shaven head and wore an Irish Army inform. Smack and Noid trailed behind him, and for a moment, Watford experienced a sense of relief. The lullaby in her skull grew louder and louder, overriding her thoughts. She blinked for the first time in what seemed like minutes and noted her hand shaking from the strain of holding her weapon outstretched for so long.

"You," Myers said through clenched teeth, sweat pouring down his face. "I've seen you. I know you. You're—"

The Irishman swung a fist, connecting with Myers and

knocking him to the ground. The lullaby receded within Watford, lingering as a bare whisper, but the cloud draped over her brain evaporated. She still couldn't move, but the strains in her muscles made themselves known again, and with the noise gone, she wondered what she was doing. Panic set in at being unable to command her limbs. She fought to lower her weapon. An unseen glue kept her arm in place.

"It's not possible," Myers said, crumpled on the floor.

The Irishman pulled back his boot and kicked him in the stomach. "Oh, but it is *Dennis*. Your Jedi tricks don't work on us anymore, mind-walker."

The sensation of a strike to her own belly snapped Watford and the men around her free. She lowered her ray gun, rubbed her stinging eyes, and shook her aching leg muscles loose. The soldiers nearest the Wehrmacht got the drop on them again, swinging their guns about before they attempted to escape. They offered no resistance and, exchanging puzzled glances, tossed their weapons down.

"Dub," McCabe said, staring at the Irishman. "What in the blazes is—"

Grabbing Myers by the neck, Dub wrenched him up and forced him onto his knees. Still confused at what had happened, Watford held her ground, moving her gaze from the groaning Myers to her friends, Noid, and Smack. She took a step closer, but the women strode away without looking at her and made for the spire. Noid drew her knife and ran the edge of the blade along her palm. Lines of blood seeping free, she pressed her hand against the spire's metal frame and pulled it away. Watford gasped. A glowing blue square of light appeared where Noid had touched, revealing components and buttons of some kind. Smack eased her fingers into the blue square and tapped at a control panel that emerged out of nowhere.

"Clear the area," McCabe said. "Secure the prisoners, guard the entrances, and tend to the wounded. Everyone else, give us space."

"Not her," Dub said, and when Watford looked at him, his gaze locked on hers. "Or Owens. They can stay. Both of 'em have a part to play. Bring Big Mo in with the prisoner, too."

At a loss on why Dub asked them to remain, Watford stepped closer to Owens, whose eyebrow arched. He gave her the slightest of nods when she fell in at his side. Shuffling her weight from side to side, she looked back at the eastern entrance. A stocky soldier in British battledress plodded through, prodding a bound SS officer on with the muzzle of his gun. As soon as he reached the spire, he shoved the SS officer down beside Myers.

"You," Myers said again, staring at Dub. "I didn't know it was you. I've seen your face many times. Our paths are linked. Do they know yet?"

"Know what, mind-walker?" Dub said, slapping him across the back of the head.

"That you'll lead them all to their deaths? Fire and blood lie in your future, Darren Loughlin. New Berlin will be wiped off the face of the planet. Your friends' lifeless eyes stare back at me. I see it all. The strands connect and interweave. You foolish, foolish child, you've already done it, haven't you? You've opened the Stream on your side. That's why you're here, isn't it? That's why you came back."

"You're the abomination," Dub said, stepping closer, lips peeling into a sneer. "You tell me, you little prick-bollocks."

Closing his eyes, Myers bowed his head. The colour returned to his clammy skin, but his forehead crinkled, and he scrunched his eyes tighter. Shuffling for grip, the SS officer glanced about but said nothing. Watford eased herself closer, questions about what was going on burning within her. McCabe caught her attention and shook his head. Remaining still, she took in the spectacle and Noid and Smack at work on the console.

"You've doomed us all," Myers said, opening his eyes wide. "You have opened the Stream in your time. Are you even aware of the consequences? Terra and Mars are not ready to face the Annunaki. You've sent us on a collision course for war...decades, centuries before we can face their might and prevail."

The mention of the word "Annunaki" triggered Watford's

memory of the bizarre dream in the medical bay. Intrigued by what it meant, she focused her attention on Myers, hoping to glean any information from his interaction with the Irishman. Dub sauntered around from behind Myers and came to a stop facing him. He took to a knee and reached out a hand, cupping his chin and digging his fingers into his skin with enough force to cause him to flinch. Myers didn't retaliate in any way, though. For some unknowable reason, he grew powerless in the presence of the Irishman and his colleagues. The malevolent energy radiating off him was replaced with something else. Fear.

"We're not playing by your rules anymore, Dennis. I've found the artefacts and broken the cycle. My Hollow brethren will no longer be your cannon fodder. We fight for ourselves now. The people of Terra and Big Red will stand with us as equals. Not as masters with their slaves. Remember that when we meet again. If you kill us when we rebel in '76, you doom yourself to destruction. The Stream is open here and now. That's all it'll take for the Annunaki to cast their gaze back on what was once the jewel in the imperial crown. *Alea iacta est* and all that malarky, bitch."

He released the trembling Myers and stood, turning his focus to the SS officer who kept his head bowed. His boots clicked off the floor as he crossed in front of him and came to a halt. Big Mo grabbed a handful of the SS officer's hair and yanked his head back until he looked up at Dub.

"It's almost time, Wagner," he said. "I must admit, I was looking forward to gutting you like a fish. Considering the fate you're about to meet, I suppose it'll be worth it."

"So cocky and arrogant," Wagner said. "Do you really think anything you've done here will result in permanent changes? Time has a way of course correcting, as you well know. You may complicate things, but the damage is not irreversible. When you look upon my handiwork and realise the truth, think of me, my Hollow child."

Dub balled his hand into a fist and raised it to strike, but Smack calling his name redirected his attention. He jogged over to the spire and joined the huddle around the glowing control panel. Watford met Owen's gaze and shrugged.

"Any idea what's going on?" she asked.

"No clue. Best to keep our heads down, eyes open, and lips shut until someone says otherwise."

"There's wounded I could be tending to," Watford said. "Not to mention checking in on the rest of my girls."

"Manchester, isn't it?" a voice said, and when she looked up, she noted Big Mo smiling. "Your accent, I mean."

"Yeah."

"It's strange seeing you again after all this time, Watford. Surreal, even."

"Have we met?"

"In a manner of speaking. That's why you two need to be here. None of this will make sense for a very long time, but when it does is when we'll need you the most. You'll know what to do when the moment comes. Like Owens said, keep your eyes open."

Curious at his meaning and where they could've met, she opened her mouth to speak when multiple radios blared to life at the same time. She turned towards McCabe. He spoke into the radio mic and pressed the handset tight against his ears. The creases on his forehead intensified, and he nodded before passing the comm to his radioman and stepping forward.

"Listen up," he shouted, voice booming around the room. "All NCOs and officers on me."

"That means us," Owens said, taking her by the elbow and guiding her to where McCabe relocated, out of earshot of the two prisoners.

"We have a problem," he said when everyone gathered. "We have two unidentified craft on inbound. Make and model unknown and transponders switched off. Lockhart tried to intercept them, but they're far quicker and more manoeuvrable than anything he's seen, and they're making a beeline for the base. There are rumours they may be some sort of advanced unit who answers directly to MARSCORP outside our chain of command. Possibly even the same people who took out the Wehrmacht thrust on New Berlin. No matter what happens, we need to hold this position, but I won't make this an order. Volunteers only. If you stay, you're here till the end, one way or another. Make your peace now."

Murmurs chimed out. Fatigued men exchanged glances and hobbled away. Fifteen injured MOF soldiers broke ranks and limped to the eastern door. Every single man and woman of the MEF and Freikorps held their position, hurt or not. Taking his time to look the remainder over, McCabe nodded to himself. Watford remained unwavering, honoured to be amongst such heroes.

"I wish I was a man of words to describe how proud of you I am, but I'm not an orator. Maybe in another life. In the meantime, I'll dispatch orders to your individual units and contemplate buying you all pints after but keep what we need to do in mind. We hold this place until the job is done. Understood?"

"Understood, sir," the room boomed back.

For reassurance, Watford thumbed the frame of her ray gun. She looked across the faces of her comrades who had endured so much and refused to back down. It didn't matter who the inbound soldiers were.

The remaining men, no, the men and women, of the Mars Occupation Force and their allies would hold their ground.

THE DIE IS CAST

LEVEL 1, FORWARD BASE ZULU
02:09 MST
DAY 5

As MOF soldiers moved about, rounding up prisoners and manning defences along the entrances, Reichsführer Wagner kept his head bowed and his gaze low. It was a race against time to see if his Hollow soldiers could reach him before Anna Bailey did. If his forces arrived and they still managed to activate the spire, they could just as easily whisk him away to their time. In that time period, should a future version of Anna exist, she could finish the job there and then. Like everything, his fate rested in the hands of Providence.

To his right, Mr. Myers rocked his head up and down, lips moving without uttering a word and eyes widening and narrowing at irregular intervals. Wagner had little experience with what the Führer dubbed *Psykes,* having instead focused on the Hollow Programme. He had seen such side effects once before. When those walking psychic weapons strained themselves from overusing their abilities, it caused something akin to temporary insanity.

With his own eyes, Wagner had witnessed Myers drag an entire room under his power, hundreds of men. Most likely, he had never attempted a feat on that scale before, and in his cockiness, he'd nearly shattered his mental faculties. Assuming such weapons could be cultivated in the long-term, they were of obvious use in a warzone. Wagner still threw his lot in with the Hollows.

Harvesting the multitudes of experience harnessed from lifetimes on the battlefield would be the ultimate weapon. Throw in the ability to regenerate or replace the body of a soldier killed, and an unstoppable army awaited. Like anything, it depended on timing. Should he escape his predicament, Wagner would oversee it all. Become the person to perfect the Annunaki's ancient technology and flick the switch to bring millions of Hollow soldiers to life. Warriors all, who answered to him.

"We have a problem," Smack said from behind him.

"What is it?" Dub said.

"I can't re-establish the Stream. It should be working, but it's not. I followed all the instructions. It's powering up, but I can't lock in a signal for 2018. Something's blocking us."

"Christ, it can't be the London Installation, can it?" Dub said. "They can communicate with this time period, but all they've access to is Compression, not the Stream."

At the mention of his allies, Wagner made sure to keep his body language subdued. He hung on their every word. It was true, the operators he'd communicated with on multiple occasions hadn't cracked the mysteries the Black Visors had solved. If someone was blocking their ability to chart a way back to their own time, then it was worth finding out who. Even the Annunaki wouldn't be able to act so quickly had they somehow fully awoken in their time period.

"No, it's not London," Noid said. "It's a signal coming from Terra all right, but not in this timeline. It's...it's bizarre. Look."

Wagner tilted his head and glanced at Myers. If the American could regain his senses, he might be able to keep the Hollows distracted long enough for them to escape. The thin line of drool dribbling from his mouth proved otherwise. Shaking his head, Wagner pulled at his bindings to no avail. He risked a glance back at the Black

Visors. All four had their backs to him, leaning in close to the spire's control panel. Lieutenant McCabe stood nearby, facing him, but rattled off an endless cascade of orders and requests for updates, paying him little attention.

"That is weird," Big Mo said. "Core Cadre, maybe? Although, why would they be blocking us returning home? We've done everything we needed to."

"I don't think I can handle another mission," Dub said with a groan. "The fifties suck. Like, proper suck. Gaff reeks of smoke and B.O. There's feckin' Nazis everywhere. All the Brits keep calling me 'paddy.' I never thought I'd say it, but I want to get the hell out of here and get back home to our New Berlin."

"Fecking?" Big Mo said. "What is it with you and that word nowadays?"

"Smack bet me I couldn't last a week without dropping an f-bomb. Few more days, and I can curse like a sailor over a newly won bottle of Jameson."

"Can we stay on track?" Noid said.

"It's not the Core Cadre," Smack said, voice flattening. "Look at the timestamp. Can't be for real, right?"

A long-drawn-out silence followed, broken by a string of muffled curses Wagner couldn't decipher, even with his extensive knowledge of English. He threw his gaze back, aiming to spy any type of clue. Their heads blocked the control panel. McCabe flashed a glance at him and patted the revolver handle on his waist, so he turned back around.

"No way," Big Mo said, his voice strained. "I mean, I'm pretty sure human civilisation doesn't go back that long. Eight or nine thousand years, yeah, sure, but this? I don't think anything even remotely human by our standards existed back then."

"What about the Native Martians then?" Dub said. "We know they had a technologically advanced civilisation millennia before anything like that ever reared its head on Terra. What if human civilisation is far older than we thought? It'd explain the discrepancies in those texts we found."

"Shit, there's more," Noid said. "Look, it's a set of coordinates, like Compression travel. And some sort of corrupted message from a dude called...John Titor? That name ring any bells?"

"Nah," the other three said.

Puzzled at what that revelation meant, Wagner almost missed shouts from outside the eastern entrance door. Raised voices filtered in, trailed by thumps against the closed metallic doors. Guards nearby formed a picket line. Other soldiers rushed to man defences made of whatever debris they could pull together. Considering such ad-hoc barricades had done little to help the Wehrmacht, Wagner didn't put much faith in their efforts. If it was his Hollow rescue party, they wouldn't stand a chance.

A British soldier stumbled through the breach to the left of the entrance, clasping his nose, blood pumping down his face. Guns adjusted their aim at the hole, and voices called for the soldier to get out of the line of fire. He dashed away as a figure stepped into view, coming to a halt at the threshold, cold eyes gazing around the interior of the storage room. Wagner's blood turned to ice when those eyes met his. Anna Bailey had found him.

"Stand easy!" McCabe said, and gun barrels lowered. "Everyone, stand down."

Anna held her position, gaze darting about as if listing off every soldier and ranking them in order of threat. She took a single step forward when no other guns aimed at her, and again scanned the room, almost daring someone to defy her. Even as he anticipated her bloody vengeance, Wagner's heart stirred at the sheer majesty of her presence. After years of experimentation, she was his true success. The first Hollow soldier rebirthed into a body of his design. The perfect killing machine.

"Anna," Dub said, pulling up alongside Wagner. "We fulfilled our part of the bargain. The Reichsführer is yours, but there's been a complication."

Slow and methodical, Anna strode across the room. She wore a single black bodysuit with a knife hanging from her belt and no other weapons. Like the blessed old days, Wagner drank in her every movement, consumed by her living embodiment of faultlessness. She paused a few steps away but switched her gaze to Dub, causing the

Irishman to raise his open palms. Big Mo and Noid broke away from the spire and fell in behind their colleague. None of them made any attempt to close the gap between themselves and Anna Bailey.

"Complications are your problem," she said, eyeing them over one at a time. "I've come for what's mine and nothing more."

"This affects you," Dub said. "Well, the future you...I think. I can't go into detail, but there are other Hollows active in this timeline. If they are who we believe they are, then they're your people. In the future, I mean."

"Other Hollows?" Anna said, shifting her gaze back to Wagner. "My, my, Herr Reichsführer. You have been a busy little bee, haven't you? Where are they and how many?"

Wagner said nothing and stared at his creation. He flinched when her left hand snapped out, grabbed his throat, and without so much as breaking a sweat, lifted him from his knees until his legs dangled. Choking for air, he struggled against her grip, but she tightened her hold. At the moment he thought his lungs ready to explode, she lowered him to his feet. Gasping for breath, he glared, any anger within him fading at the darkness lingering in her eyes.

"Where are they and how many?" she said.

"Fewer than a hundred," he said. "Located in the American Zone near where you ambushed me. Your progeny here are referring to the unit that has been dispatched to retrieve me. Probably a handful at most. Even that is overkill. They are much more...refined than you are, Miss Bailey."

"The Stream's powering up," Smack said, pulling their attention back to the spire. "It'll take a couple of minutes, but it looks like we'll have to take a detour before we can go home. Intense Dan is on standby. We're nearly there, people."

Turning away from his captors, Wagner glanced at the spire and noted the sparks of blue electricity working their way up the smooth metal exterior. He wanted to laugh in delight at what he was witnessing. The fool Myers could think it all a mistake, but Wagner understood the truth. No different than the day he had first successfully transferred human conscience via the Compression Matrix, it was just as important. Although he hadn't unearthed all the secrets himself, it was proof the holy grail existed. In time, humanity would be able to master the most monumental power of all. The ability to transfer matter across time and space as the ancients had done.

"I've thought about how I was going to kill you for a long time, Herr Reichsführer," Anna said, stealing his attention back. "I could never decide slow or quick. Now, I find I've lost all interest in such a debate."

"So you'll let me go?" Wagner said, the glee from the activating spire bursting across his face.

"No," Anna said. "I'm just going to get it over with."

A jackhammer of a punch ploughed into his chest, shattering his ribcage, and crushing his lungs. Wheezing, Wagner tried to suck air in but tasted blood on the back of his throat. Pain engulfed his entire torso. Bone shards cut through his internal organs. He crashed down, light-headed and dizzy, wanting to scream but hacking up globs of thick, dark blood instead.

As he crumpled onto his back, his vision blurred, the carving sensation within his chest intensifying. Anna's cool, unblinking eyes gazed down, no hint of emotion betraying her chiselled features. Fighting for breath, he turned and spat up more blood, but no air entered his mouth. Heart failing, he rolled onto his side, away from the glares of the Black Visors. The room around him swirled. He stayed focused on the spire.

Life escaped him with every splatter of blood spraying across the ground. Wagner held no regrets, even as the absolute terror gnawed at his failing mind. He had seen the future, and that they could never take from him. His individual life may not mean anything to them, but his legacy would last aeons. An empire incomprehensible to such small-minded mortals. Thinking on the future Terran Empire yet to rise, Wagner focused his failing eyes on the blue shards of energy dancing around the spire. He forced a final smile.

A piercing white light washed over his thoughts, and he closed his eyelids.

LEVEL 1, FORWARD BASE ZULU
14:17 MST
DAY 5

The handle of the Bren rattled in Jenkins's hands. In his two years of non-stop combat, he had known much fear, even stared into the face of death countless times. It had never manifested itself physically. Despite all his efforts, his hands shook, no matter how hard he squeezed the wooden butt and metal trigger guard. Reports from the scattered Second Battalion on the levels above shook him to the core.

Screams of agony had been the first indicator the intruders weren't standard soldiers. Desperate radio operators called out vague descriptions of their attackers and begged for reinforcements right up to the moment the life drained from them. No matter who they threw at the invaders, those sections or platoons were annihilated, the few survivors racing back to the lines, screeching, and shrieking like madmen. Those who talked sense described metal-encased giants with ray guns pouring out lead like a light machine gun. Faceless monstrosities tearing soldiers apart with their metallic hands.

To make matters worse, Jenkins heard the actual screams of soldiers from the level above, resonating through the copper stone. It started with a barrage of bullets and ended with savage wails as the armoured beasts worked their way down to Level 1. Standard rounds so far didn't have any impact, didn't even slow them down.

Charting their progress from the cries of the dying, Jenkins anticipated them coming out at the eastern stairwell and, from there, making a beeline to the storage area. He posted guards around the other entrances in case they tried to flank them, but that was where he planned to put their mettle, so to speak, to the test.

From wall to wall, they'd laid out every sandbag they could drag into position. Brens and .5 cal Brownings covered the hallway, leading out from the stairwell exit onto the only access to the storage area on their side of the base. Soldiers with anti-tank attachments on their Lee-Enfield's readied their weapons. Mines lay concealed in the rubble all along the stretch of corridor the enemy would need to cross to approach. Grenades sat ready to be flung. For good measure, they even had a flamethrower on standby if it came to it. Whoever these armoured invaders were, they were about to walk headfirst into a fully armed and prepared defensive position manned by the toughest and most experienced soldiers on the planet. Still, Jenkins's hand trembled.

"Spotted 'em at the Level 2 eastern stairwell," Private Fitzpatrick said from his concealed spot on the floor above. "Two of 'em. Can't get a good look 'cause of all the smoke, but they're big, Sarge. On their way down now."

"Acknowledged," Jenkins said and cast an eye over the MOF and Freikorps soldiers on his flanks.

Each of them knew their duty. He didn't have to remind any to ready themselves or what needed to be done. On Mars, or Big Red as some of the MEF veterans called it, you adapted and survived or you died. Eyes lowered to the sights on their weapons, and men pulled cases of ammunition close. Easing his finger onto the trigger, Jenkins readied himself and focused on his breathing. He thought of Alexeev's dead body lying stretched out in a corridor and used the anger as fuel.

Someone thumped down beside him and cocked their weapon. He turned and spied Captain Nowak take aim down her Lee-Enfield's sight. Confused at her presence, he opened his mouth to speak, but she got the first.

"You fight well, Sergeant Jenkins. Although I fight better. I thought you could use another gun on this line."

"Em...thanks, Captain. Are you sure you should be here, though? You know, in case they br—"

"You are skinny," she said, gaze locked on her sights.

"Excuse me, Captain?"

"You should eat more."

Turning to face him, she rested her rifle and patted at a compartment on her belt. She pulled out something covered in paper, unwrapped it, and thrust her hand out. Jenkins looked down at the sandwich and then back at her unblinking gaze.

"Eat," she said, waving the sandwich. "I can make it an order."

Wanting to be polite, he tried to think of a way to respectfully decline, but his stomach chose that moment to growl. Conceding, he accepted the sandwich and took a bite. His mouth salivated at the taste of fresh chicken and lettuce, and without any decorum, he devoured it within seconds, nodding his appreciation. The smallest of smiles crept up the side of Nowak's face, and she returned her attention to the corridor ahead.

"If we live through this, I will cook for you," she said.

"Thanks, Captain. But you really don't—"

"Take a hint, Peter Jenkins. And you may call me Zofia."

Unsure of what was happening, Jenkins tried to think of a response when clunking sounds boomed down the stairwell. Heavy boot thumps moved in time, snapping his attention back and getting louder with every step. The wails from above had long since stopped, and every man and woman to his left and right fell quiet. For one long moment, no one drew breath. All listened to the banging of armoured boots on the metal frame of the staircase. The sound dulled as the first foot struck the concrete floor. Heavy footsteps rang out, working their way to the open doorway leading into the corridor ahead. Mumbling a silent prayer, Jenkins readied his trigger finger.

Two figures emerged into the hallway at the same time, causing Jenkins to flinch. At first, he thought they wore modified EVA suits. As his eyes adjusted, he made out the polished metal armour. The bolts locking individual pieces into place, the tinted visor allowing an excellent field of vison to either side, and those strange, black semi-automatic weapons in their hands. Both armoured beasts turned to face them head-on but made no effort to raise their guns.

"Fire!" Jenkins shouted, and the gates of hell exploded open.

A thunderstorm of 7.72mm and .5 Cal rounds raged out at the duo. Mines and grenade explosions ravaged the area around the stairs, chunks of splinters smashing into the walls. Anti-tank bombs hit the enemy soldiers, engulfing them in fire. In three-second bursts, Jenkins emptied his magazine, rammed in another, and blasted away at the cloud of smoke. Additional grenades lashed out, throwing more dust, fumes, and shrapnel. Another anti-tank round struck its target, lashing out flames. Jenkins drained his second magazine, loaded a third, and called for a ceasefire.

The guns on the line fell silent. Every soldier who needed to reloaded fresh clips or readied more grenades to throw. From the smoky haze, he prayed to see the outline of the two monstrosities draped out on the floor, preferably in pieces. The fog cleared, and his heart sank at the sight of them still standing in their original positions. Neither one with so much as a scratch on their armoured torsos or limbs.

"Our turn," a child-like voice boomed from helmet speakers.

"Fire!" Jenkins said, and again the MOF's guns raged to life.

Unbothered by the storm of lead pinging off them, the enemy soldiers raised their weapons. They pulled back on the top housing of their guns, reminiscent of pumping a shotgun, and took aim. Two fiery stars of green energy leapt out and smashed the barricade, obliterating five men and two Brens outright. They then squeezed their triggers and sprayed back their own hell storm of lead with deadly accuracy, blasting skulls apart with ease.

Jenkins pounded on the trigger as the armoured soldiers trudged forward, every one of his bullets bouncing off the metal frames and ricocheting. When one of those enemy guns turned on him, and he spotted the cocking motion, he snatched up his Lee-Enfield, grabbed Nowak, and dragged her away. Deadly green energy sliced through his position and Bren, leaving a scorch mark where the sandbags used to lie. Grenades exploded at the feet of the two armoured hulks. Neither flinched, and in response, they sent another wave of blasts into the deteriorating barricade.

"Retreat," Jenkins said and, dropping to a knee, fired off a shot. "Everyone pull back!"

Half the soldiers manning the defence lay dead, vast chunks of their bodies missing and seared. Others had holes punched through heads from deadly accurate bullet fire. Those who could rose and shot back at the advancing enemy, unleashing everything they had in a vain attempt to slow them. Men collapsed, screeching when lead chopped them down, but even wounded on the floor, they kept firing, refusing to relent.

Nowak at his side, Jenkins grabbed at anyone he could and hauled them back. He emptied his clip and, backstepping, loaded another. The two enemy soldiers crossed the smouldering wreckage of the barricade and slowed at the spectacle of the wounded at their feet who were still firing at point blank range, even though their bullets did nothing to halt them. Private Shearson, his guts spilling over his lap, pulled a grenade free, tore the pin and rammed it against the knee of the soldier on the right. The detonation ripped his head and arm off, spraying blood across the walls but not leaving a dent on the knee joint.

"Leg it, lads!" Jenkins bellowed. "Double time! Everyone retreat!"

The armoured soldier on the left lowered its weapon and reached out a hand towards one of the fallen. It lifted a badly disfigured Freikorps soldier by the throat and, with the slightest of flicks, cracked his neck. After tossing the body against the wall, it raised its foot and stomped down on the head of Corporal King, splattering his brains and skull under its metal boot.

Horror coiling around his stomach, Jenkins threw down his empty Lee-Enfield and snatched the captured Luger from his belt. Half-running, half-stumbling backwards, he fired non-stop until the gun clicked. Unsure of what else to do against such unstoppable juggernauts, he turned, pushed Nowak ahead, and fled at full speed back to the last layer of lines outside the eastern entrance. He rejoined his soldiers at the barricade, which housed far fewer heavy weapons than they had stood with.

Sounds of thudding boots echoed ever closer.

LEVEL 1, FORWARD BASE ZULU
14:59 MST
DAY 5

With most of the Wehrmacht prisoners evacuated, the few remaining uninjured MOF and Freikorps soldiers within the storage area took position near the entrances and breaches. Everyone else manned the barricades set up around the four corridors surrounding the area. From the reports Watford overheard, the outcome seemed grim. Whoever those new attackers were, they were reportedly like walking tanks with modified particle weapons that spewed bullets too. In a slow, methodical fashion, they had shattered the hastily assembled outer defences and plodded ever onwards to their target.

"My men are getting cut to pieces!" McCabe said, turning the force of his anger on Dub. "You need to do something now."

"Where are we with the Stream, Smack?" Dub said, ignoring him.

"Five, ten minutes, maybe. I'm not sure, but I'm working as fast as I can."

"Damn it, you need to listen to me," McCabe said, grabbing Dub's arm. "I'll order my men to stand down if I have to. They're throwing everything they have at those... things, and it's not putting a dent in their armour."

Dub yanked his forearm free and stared McCabe down. "They're called Exo-suits, and it's not like we were expecting any Hollows to show up in this time period, McCabe. Yeah, they're pretty much impervious to anything short of a missile strike or..."

Trailing off, he shifted his gaze to Watford. She tilted her chin up at his attention, ready to play her part if needed. His gaze moved to the weapon in her hands, and she, in turn, lifted it higher, grasping his meaning. The particle weapons favoured by the Martian militias had already proven themselves capable of slicing through flesh, steel, and stone. It stood to reason it'd work on the bullet-resistant armour these Exo-suited soldiers wore.

"Sergeant Watford," he said. "I—"

"It's Corporal, actually," she said, cutting across him.

"Apologies. Corporal Watford, join the eastern entrance and hold 'em back."

"That'll work for one entrance," McCabe said. "We have three others."

"I know," Dub said. "I have an idea. Time to get stupid."

"I'll come with you, dickhead," Noid said, snatching up her Lee-Enfield.

"Cheers, wench," Dub said and turned back to the spire. "Mo, cover Smack. Anna, this won't mean anything to you, but those soldiers are the Young Guns out there. Stop them, but—"

"Try not to kill them," Anna said, inspecting her bloodied hands. "I'll do what I can, but I make no promises. The Stream will be here waiting for you when you get back, Mr. Loughlin."

"Where are you going?" McCabe said as Dub and Noid rushed past him.

"To pick a fight with a bunch of sociopathic killers," he yelled and raced out the western door.

Watford took off across the room and headed for the breach by the eastern entrance. Bullets sliced back and forth with unstoppable fury. From the left, green energy blasts zipped back, pounding the barricade beyond the door. She slowed, wary of the sheer volume of rounds pouring out from the defences. Keeping her aching back against the wall, she eased herself into view of the bullet-riddled corridor the enemy came from.

She froze at the sight of the two Exo-suited soldiers twenty metres away, plodding on in a slow and steady course. Lead pinged off their unblemished armour. They moved their guns with ease, switching between standard ammunition and the particle blasts that chewed through everything in their paths.

In the last few seconds, the MOF gunfire had died off from the relentless enemy barrage. Taking a deep breath to steady herself, Watford took aim at the soldier on the right. She exhaled and pressed down on the firing stud. A swirling bolt leapt from her weapon and ripped a chunk out of the wall bare centimetres from the soldier's helmet.

Cursing her lack of accuracy, Watford dropped her hand and counted as the ray gun recharged. For a moment, the enemy soldiers halted their advance and stopped firing. When the recharge light on her weapon pinged green, she made to aim again, but two fiery bolts smashed the wall ahead. The wall absorbed the brunt of the energy discharge, but she was in direct sight of the two armoured soldiers. Dipping to a knee as bullets pounded, she raised her hand and fired again.

The blast ploughed into the soldier's upper chest near their shoulder, causing them to fall on their knees, weapon slipping from their hand. Scorch marks lined the armour around a section of burnt visible flesh. The second soldier shot back, but the MOF defenders let out a roar at finally seeing one of the enemy wounded and hammered on their triggers. Rounds pounded the downed soldier. One bullet found its mark, smashing through seared skin and sending the injured soldier crashing backwards.

An angered howl erupted from the remaining one, who attempted to increase their pace. Hampered by the Exo-suit, they moved no faster than a brisk walk. Watford ducked when another blast lashed out, disintegrating chunks of the wall behind her. As her enemy closed the distance, she raised her weapon to fire again when a searing, agonising pain cut through her shoulder, and she tumbled, slamming her head in the process. Dizzy and with bullets whizzing past, bare centimetres from her skin, she spotted the blood leaking from the hole on her shoulder.

Gritting her teeth, she raised her weapon and pressed down on the stud. The bolt shot out and caught the Exo-suit above the left knee, tearing through the reinforced armour. The enemy soldier crumbled, sweeping their weapon about, and taking out at least three more defenders. Distorted cries rang out from within the suit. The soldier grasped at the burning wound, gun hitting the ground in the process. Watford levelled her weapon again, fighting through the pain eating into her and held it aimed at the enemy's head as it recharged.

When the light turned green, the tinted visor rose, and the contorted face of a screaming girl appeared, a child of fourteen or fifteen. Thin faced, she appeared minuscule in such bulky armour. Watford's first instinct was to crawl her way over to the screeching teenager. Seeing what she had done to her fellow soldiers, she hardened her heart to mercy and pushed the firing stud. The energy blast smashed the girl in the face, obliterating her skull and slumping her body.

Growing more light-headed by the second, she held up her ray gun for someone to take. When Private Patel slipped it from her grip, and other hands pressed down on her wound, she closed her eyes.

"I am a soldier," she said, her comrades lifting her.

LEVEL 1, FORWARD BASE ZULU
15:11 MST
DAY 5

The doors to the northern and western entrances exploded at the same time, throwing soldiers about. Clouds of grey smoke blasted out. Pulling out his Webley revolver, McCabe dashed towards the western door and took position behind one of the barricades. Green energy bolts sliced through the fog and slammed into a machine gun emplacement, vaporising two Freikorps soldiers and their weapon. Smoke grenades detonated beside the door. Through the haze, two mechanical figures stepped through, covered head to toe in armour. Bullets pinged harmlessly away. They strode on, sweeping their guns around and shooting in controlled bursts.

McCabe fired, every one of his rounds striking the armoured attackers but doing no damage. While reloading, he watched as they trudged forward, switching between firing their particle blasts and standard ammunition, cutting down his soldiers with ease. An energy bolt flashed out from behind him but flew wide, drawing one of the Exo-suited soldiers' attention. Private Patel, armed with a

Martian weapon, leapt behind a container. Green energy zipped back in response and ate through the metal walls. Unsure of what else he could do, McCabe raised his gun to fire again just as Anna Bailey sprinted onto the scene.

While dashing straight for the enemy soldier on the right, her body weaved and ducked like she could see the bullets faster than a standard human eye. After closing the distance, she jumped and executed a perfect spinning roundhouse kick, booted foot smashing off the side of the helmet. The blow did no damage to the tinted visor but sent the Exo-suited soldier tumbling down. Dropping to a knee, she grabbed at the soldier's weapon. Metal hands held tight. She rolled away as the other soldier aimed and fired a particle blast, narrowly missing her.

Volleys of shots rang out from the north side of the room, both blasts forcing Anna's head down. All four Exo-suited soldiers converged on her, ignoring the harmless lead that smashed them from all angles. Desperate to aid her, McCabe holstered his pistol and looked at the nearest one with its back turned. Uncertain of any meaningful action, he leapt and slammed into the back of one of the soldiers, throwing his arms around the visor, aiming to blind them. The soldier attempted to shake him off and took their hand off one of their weapon's handles to strike him. McCabe pulled his head back but clung on while tugging at the helmet in a bid to somehow wrench it free.

Anna used the distraction and bolted at the nearest Exo-suited soldier. She ducked below the stream of bullets unleashed at her, rolled, and drove her foot into the knee joint. The soldier raised their weapon to strike her with the butt. She threw herself behind and, again, thrust her boot against the back of the knee with enough force to cause them to stumble.

An armoured fist caught McCabe on the side of the head and knocked him off. The soldier turned and started to level his gun, but a green energy blast struck the left arm, and it staggered backwards. Head aching, McCabe dragged himself up and hurled himself at the soldier, his momentum knocking them off balance. They fell, struggling for the particle weapon.

The MOF bullets spewing out ceased as McCabe and Anna fought amongst the enemy. Volunteers braved the return fire and hurled themselves onto the grounded Exo-suited soldier in a bid to weigh it down. A body crashed into McCabe's shoulder as he struggled for the weapon, spraying warm blood across his face, and knocked him down again. MOF and Freikorps soldiers piled on and tried to wrench the gun free. Their opponent refused to break its grip.

Face bruising from the punch, McCabe forced himself up again and grabbed at the arm. The downed soldier swatted him and the mass of squirming soldiers away. It fired its particle weapon at point blank range, splitting lumps out of the soldiers clambering to keep its legs pinned down. Smoking bodies struck the floor. While Anna continued to run rings around the three others, two more Exo-suited soldiers strode through from the southern entrance and raised their guns. His men scattered at the sight of the deadly particle weapons and rushed back to their makeshift defences along the storage containers.

Sergeant Fox grabbed his hand to haul him away but stumbled back, a smouldering hole where his chest used to be. McCabe turned in time to kick the enemy gun away, spraying bullets out into the centre of the room, past the spire. A metallic hand lashed out and thumped him in the stomach, winding him and ploughing him backwards. Light-headed, he gasped for breath and tried to roll. An armoured fist cracked him in the face and bounced his head off the concrete.

Groaning, McCabe pushed his hands up to deflect the oncoming blow, but the fist slammed through the attempt and crunched his nose. The copper tang of blood filled his mouth while shards of pain cut deep into his skin. Eyes watering, he attempted to roll over and crawl away, but a hand grabbed him by the leg, flipped him over, and clobbered his face again. The strength oozed from his flesh. Woozy and unable to raise his arms in defence, he took the next strike, sure his skull split in half.

Noise of the fighting faded. Screams, bangs, and explosions seeped away with his already blurring vision.

Even the pain became less intense with every punch as his brain started switching itself off. In between metal hands obliterating him, a strange sense of acceptance crept inwards, the exhaustion of his years of fighting catching up. All that existed for one moment was the Exo-suited soldier beating the life out of him. So much so that he barely noticed the second one creep up behind. The new one reached out. For a second, McCabe envisioned it as the death blow, the last thing he'd see before his soul slipped from that world into the next.

Through stinging, blurry eyes, he saw the new soldier grab his attacker by the wrist, holding it centimetres from McCabe's swollen and bloodied flesh. With a swing of a hand, the new arrival threw the Exo-suited soldier onto his back, snatched the gun up, and pointed it right at the helmet visor. A green flash obliterated the front of the visor, devastating energy vaporising the skull within.

Cocking the weapon, the soldier spun about, grabbed McCabe by the shirt, and dragged him to his wobbling feet, armoured body covering him from any stray rounds. Bewildered, McCabe clung to his saviour for support while his legs threatened to give out. The soldier turned, the visor rising for a second, long enough to spot Dub's bloodstained, grinning face before disappearing again.

"You look like dogshit, McCabe," he said, then took aim and fired at one of the Exo-suits trying to pin down Anna.

The particle blast struck one on the back, eating through the rear plates and sending the operator flailing. As the three remaining ones spun about, Anna took advantage and dashed at the legs of another. Letting out a roar, the unmistakable voice of Noid rang out as she, too, wearing an Exo-suit, fired a particle blast and dived right at one. They crashed down, rolling about, grasping at each other's helmets.

"Check on Smack," Dub said. "I'll cover you. There's more than eight in the building. A second group is working its way towards us now, and they're ready for us. We don't have much time."

While Noid continued to battle one of the soldiers,

the two others ignored Anna's attempts to interfere and turned their guns on Dub. He shepherded McCabe on, his body between him and the particle weapons, and fired a shot at the soldier on the right, narrowly missing. Guns taking aim, he shoved McCabe over to the spire and threw himself down. Flashes of green zipped over his helmet. McCabe tumbled against the spire, blood dripping from his face across the scorched floor. Strength failing, he stumbled along the perimeter until he reached Smack. Big Mo raised his gun in challenge but lowered it when he recognised him.

"You look like you've been hit by a bus, mate," Big Mo said and snatched at his pockets for a bandage.

McCabe waved him off and turned his attention to Smack, whose fingers danced across the control panel. "No time. Dub said they've got reinforcements coming. You lot need to get out of here while you can."

"Hang on," Smack said, unblinking. "Nearly have it... and...there!"

Ripples of blue energy twirled along the exterior of the spire. Low-pitched humming noises emanated from within, and the scent of ammonia electrified the air around the glowing structure. To the left of the control panel, sparks coalesced, taking on an almost liquid form, and slowly expanded outwards, creating a crude circle almost up to McCabe's head height. He backstepped from the swirling mass and glanced back at the two Black Visors as smiles crossed their bloodied and battered faces.

"We did it," Smack said. "We can get out of here. Get the others and let's go."

Big Mo raised his gun and stepped out from beyond the spire but ducked as a stray particle blast lashed out. Crouching, McCabe worked his way along the side of the spire until he absorbed the scene. One of the enemies lay on the ground, a stump where the arm should have been, while Anna knelt over, hands working to tear away the helmet. Dub and Noid still fought their respective enemies, guns on the floor as they resorted to hand-to-hand combat, sluggish from the restraints of the Exo-suits. The surrounding MOF and Freikorps soldiers had since ceased their firing, most likely deeming it useless and either retook positions along the entrances or stared on at the spectacle.

Spotting his chance, McCabe half-ran, half-limped towards the nearest discarded particle weapon. Legs straining from the effort, he tumbled to the floor while Big Mo called out from behind. He grabbed the gun and cocked it like he had seen the others do. He raised the barrel in the direction of the four remaining combatants, aware he had no way of differentiating between them.

"Dub! Noid!" he shouted, searching for a sign or reaction.

"Here," Dub said, his visor raising as he punched his adversary in the chest, creating space between them.

Releasing an exhale, McCabe aimed and fired. The energy burst leapt from his weapon without recoil and smashed his target on the side, knocking them off their feet. He cocked again, but Noid and her foe still battled it out. Too focused on the fight, she didn't reveal herself. Dub trudged closer to give aid as a crescendo of particle blasts erupted from the southern entrance. McCabe clawed across the floor, gun aiming in the direction of Noid and her opponent, and he halted when he gained a better view beyond a storage container.

Three more Exo-suited invaders burst in, guns raised while they waited for the recharge. McCabe swung his weapon about, took aim and fired, catching one in the stomach, and sending it crumpling back into the corridor. He dragged himself up and bolted away. Two shots launched back in answer. Dub and Anna joined the fray and, together with Noid, forced the soldier down.

A series of metal-fisted strikes smashed the visor open, revealing the face of a young woman, barely more than a child. She screamed and struggled against the Black Visors pinning her down, but Dub reached inside the suit and flicked something. The plates around the chest, arms and legs slid apart, allowing him to grab her by the neck and haul her free. Anna delivered a single, full-force blow with enough strength to knock her unconscious.

"Children?" McCabe said.

"Not unlike the Nazis to experiment on children, is it?" Dub said and shoved McCabe to his side, protected by his own Exo-suit's armour.

After Noid snatched up her fallen weapon, they all took aim and headed for the swirling lights on the spire. The two other Exo-suited invaders spread out, beyond their line of sight to flank them. McCabe spotted one at the last minute when it emerged from behind a pockmarked pile of rubble and fired. He opened his mouth in warning, but the particle blast struck Noid on the side before the words left his lips. She hit the ground, muffled screams leaking out from the helmet. Dub returned fire, but the attacker disappeared, and the shot flew wide.

"Noid," McCabe said and dashed over to her.

Heaving, he pushed her onto her back and pounded on the visor. An entire section of side armour melted through, revealing scorched red skin. The visor opened, showing Noid's contorted face, forehead lines crinkling, and teeth bared in agony. She fidgeted within the Exo-suit, and the armour split apart. Bullets lashed out. The enemy soldiers switched to standard ammo, no doubt in a bid to target him or Anna. Dub took a knee, the rounds pinging off his chest, while Anna dropped and laid flat behind Noid's damaged suit.

Using Dub for cover, McCabe reached in and scooped Noid out, her side raw and speckled with blood. She winced at the movement and clamped her teeth. He wanted to tell her something, anything to ease her suffering, but as the lead rained out, he kept his mouth shut. As Dub rose, he dragged Noid to her feet, and together, they pushed on to the spire.

McCabe followed, his weapon tracking the Exo-suited soldier to the right, when a blistering pain ploughed through his stomach. Shocked, he glanced down at the oozing red hole. The agony intensified at the sight, and his legs gave out from under him. He fell, the gun slipping from his grip. He slapped his hand over the wound, warm, sticky blood leaking through his fingers. Seconds later, his brain caught up and registered he'd been shot.

The world slowed. Anna leapt from her position

and sprinted at the soldier on the right. Even in slow motion, her precise movements, the way she anticipated all the lines of fire and avoided them with breathtaking accuracy astounded him. He rolled his head over and spotted Noid screaming his name, full-on fighting against Dub's extended arm, barring her from running to his aid. Nodding, he wanted to transmit he'd be fine. The wetness inching along his back from the larger exit wound told him another story. With his free hand, Dub gestured at Smack and Big Mo to enter the Stream, but all their eyes were on McCabe.

Shouting inaudibly, Dub grabbed Smack first and shoved her through the portal, which enveloped her entire body. He threw his arm around Big Mo's neck and pushed him through. Only Noid remained, fighting like a wild animal, and even ducking under his arm until he yanked her from the back of her uniform collar while bullets lashed out.

McCabe wanted to tell her it'd be fine. He enjoyed the small amount of time they'd spent together. It meant more to him than she could ever know. Minutes of pure bliss in her presence had gotten him through uncountable life and death situations. By being herself, she had brought rays of hope and joy to his life. He desired those words to leave his lips, but a tiredness seeped over him. Not just from this wound but the many other unseen ones he had suffered through in his long and exhausting life. Sleep beckoned. As his eyes grew heavy, he saw something which surprised him.

Noid held Dub's particle weapon in her hands and fired at the enemy while he trudged back towards him. In slower motion than could've been real, Dub crossed the distance, scooped up McCabe and spun about. Half-dazed, he gazed up at the tinted visor, trying to comprehend the risk when the Black Visors were on the brink of escape.

"She likes you a hell of a lot more than she does me," Dub said as if reading his thoughts.

Steps from the barricade around the spire, and the world spun again. McCabe tumbled from Dub's arms and slammed onto the concrete, spikes of pain across his face and chest, shaking the cobwebs from his brain. Noid screamed and fired, prompting him to glance back. A smouldering hole lingered on the back of Dub's armour. He rolled to his side, but a second particle blast struck, and he unleashed a high-pitched screech of utter agony. McCabe crawled closer to the Exo-suit as Dub opened it and climbed out, his back and sides scorched red, his face pale and clammy.

"Go," Dub said, his eyes squeezed shut, fingers touching a grenade on his belt. "Get Noid out of here, McCabe. They can carry on the mission without me."

"No chance in hell," McCabe growled and snatched Dub's uniform by the shoulders. "No way I'm letting you have one up on me by dying first."

With the last of his failing strength, McCabe heaved, dragging Dub's limp body along the stained floor. Taking another breath, he pulled again, hauling him closer to the barricade. Noid unleashed another shot and, after cocking the weapon, grabbed Dub and dragged him over the wall.

Reaching up a hand to pull himself over, for a second, McCabe touched Noid's skin. She spun about and caught him, heaving him halfway over the wall, when another burst of pain ripped through his back, catching his breath in his throat, and causing a dark mist to cloud the periphery of his vision.

Noid's lips moved. He couldn't hear her words. Even as bullets ricocheted around her, he took one last look at her eyes and smiled. He gave one final thrust, the last of his strength. His hand connected with her uniform and knocked her off balance. Holding a wilting Dub, she stumbled backwards, eyes widened in those last seconds when she realised his actions.

She plunged into the mysterious depths of the Stream and disappeared, never seeing the final round that struck Lieutenant William McCabe in the back of the head.

LEVEL 1, FORWARD BASE ZULU
15:41 MST
DAY 5

"Sir!" Jenkins shouted, leaping from behind the Bren emplacement and dashing straight for the spire.

One gun rang out as Anna Bailey silenced the other, but it still pumped bullets and particle beams at anything moving. Undeterred, Jenkins raced across and half-jumped, half-fell over the barricade as the strange blue energy dancing around the spire died. He stumbled over the wreckage of the surrounding ground until he dropped beside McCabe's fallen body. His heart shattered at the sight of the gaping hole in the back of McCabe's head. Even before his fingers pressed against his neck for a pulse, he knew his mentor and colleague was gone.

Sinking against the barricade, he rubbed his stained hand over his mouth, looking from the gap through McCabe's forehead to the blood and brain matter spilling onto the floor. As Anna silenced the last enemy soldier, the sudden quietness registered. Gazing at the battered remnants of the man who had kept him alive more times than he could count, a heart-breaking sadness rose from within. Tears clawed at his eyes, but with his men dotted around the storage area, he refused to let any slip free, lest they see. Lumps of ice forming in his stomach, Jenkins peeled his gaze from McCabe's unmoving corpse. Someone else climbed over the barricade and thumped down beside him.

"He was a good man," Nowak said.

Fighting to maintain his composure, Jenkins couldn't think of anything to say and nodded in response. Warmth embraced his skin, and he glanced down to see Nowak's hand on his, squeezing it tight. He looked at her and reciprocated, the pain within subsiding when she met his gaze and tugged him to his feet. Turning away from the remains of his friend and mentor, he squeezed Nowak's hand once more. He slipped his grip free and surveyed the scene.

Anna Bailey stood over the last fallen Exo-suited soldier slumped at her feet. Slowly, the remaining MOF and Freikorps soldiers emerged from their cover, heads low and weapons raised as if anticipating another assault. Jenkins rose and, climbing back over the barricade, he pulled his comm from his pocket and reported back to Mad Jack in the C&C. He tried to keep his voice level when he stated McCabe's death using his Knight Four call sign. The ripple of emotion refused to stay buried.

"Secure the area," Mad Jack said after a moment's hesitation. "We don't know if there's any more of those metal buggers about."

"Understood, Top Hat," he said and pocketed the comm.

Maintaining an emotionless mask as best he could, Jenkins ordered the remaining privates and corporals back to the entrances. Every one of them gave him a grim-faced nod, knowing that should any more of the armoured enemy show up, they stood little chance of holding them back until Anna collected and passed out the scattered particle weapons. The MOF soldiers took them in awe. Cocking each one, they jogged to their respective positions, more of a spring in their tired shuffles. On his orders, Privates Duplantier and Patel, former MEF men, wrapped McCabe's body in a blanket and carried him away to receive the proper burial he deserved. Colour Sergeant Brown fell to his knees, head bowed low, his men coming to his aid.

"Are they dead?" Jenkins asked, nodding at the unmoving Exo-suited soldiers when Anna strolled up.

"Two of them live."

"Okay," he said and pulled his revolver free, but Anna's iron grip slammed on his wrist.

"They are not yours to deal with," she said, her cool gaze staying his hand and her hand forcing the weapon back into his belt. "They are my concern. Delegate some of your men to bring them to the tunnels in the basement, along with bio-suits and what rations you can spare. I'll take them with me when they regain consciousness. They won't be a threat to you under my protection."

A variety of different replies came to Jenkins's mind. He rejected each one. Although he didn't believe Anna had the authority to give him orders, he had seen first-hand what she could do, and she was rumoured to be formerly MI6 before her captivity. Slipping his hand free from the pistol handle, he gave her a nod in answer.

"The more important question should be what you intend to do with him, Sergeant," she said, glancing over her shoulder.

Following her gaze, Jenkins realised he was looking at Mr. Myers uncurling from a foetal position amongst the wreckage. Whipping his Luger out, he leapt past Anna and closed the distance. Whatever unnatural abilities he held, Jenkins sensed from the bottom of his gut it was better to put him down amidst the chaos of the battle scene and claim it as enemy fire. As he approached, gun pointed at the man's head, Myers raised his palms. Drops of blood dripped from his nostrils, and his pale skin lay slick with beads of sweat.

"I assure you, killing me will not be in your best interests, Sergeant Jenkins."

"Really? Seems like it is to me."

"I'm drained," Myers said. "Pushed myself too hard, too quick. But I have enough left to keep you and your men alive if you give me your word that you'll escort me to Colonel Wellesley after. And tell the truth, Peter Jenkins. I'll know if you're lying."

Particle blasts boomed from the southern entrance again, trailed by the familiar screams of wounded men. Keeping his gun aimed at Myers, Jenkins slid along the nearest storage container and risked a glimpse. Three more Exo-suited soldiers stormed through, weapons blazing, ripping through the already battered defences.

"There's more coming," Myers said. "You can save the lives of every still-living person in this room, and all it will take is your word."

"Fine," Jenkins said. "I give you my word."

Myers stretched out his hand in the direction of the entrance. Fingers trembling, he exposed his palm, the drips of blood from his nose turning into a full-on stream. He closed his eyes and clenched his teeth.

"Sleep."

The three advancing enemies tumbled face-first onto the floor, no particle blast scorch marks lining their armour. The firing ceased, and for the first time in days, an eerie silence reigned in Forward Base Zulu. Myers slumped against the storage container wall and ran a shaking hand under his nose, holding it there to stem the flow of blood.

"There's four more about a hundred metres away in the northern corridor. They'll be asleep for the next few hours, but I strongly suggest you chain them up. If they awaken before we find a solution to our mutual predicament, they'll slaughter every one of your men with their bare hands. I won't be able to protect any of you then."

"We held our own," Jenkins said.

"Only because their prototype armour is slow and clunky, limiting their movements and counteracting their hand-to-hand combat skills. A defect I believe will be rectified in the next iteration of the Exo-suit design. Make no mistake, Sergeant Jenkins, those Hollow soldiers take after their mother. Unencumbered with armour, you'll be dead before you even know what's hit you."

Jenkins glanced at Anna but heeded Myers's words. He ordered his men to strip the Hollow soldiers of their suits and bring them up to Level 10, where plenty of vacant rooms resided to lock them in.

"Your part of the deal now, Sergeant," Myers said. "Take me to Lieutenant Colonel Wellesley."

Tempted to shoot Myers anyway, Jenkins dismissed the thought and extended a hand. Myers took it and, body trembling, stood on uneasy feet. Despite his sweaty, shaking, and bloodied appearance, he removed his hand from under his nose and flashed a grin.

"I'm glad to see you're a man of your word."

Grabbing him by the arm, Jenkins dragged Myers towards the eastern entrance. He would be Mad Jack's problem. Although he held out hope Mad Jack would give the order to shoot him.

If that happened, it didn't count as him breaking his word.

4KM WEST OF FORWARD BASE ZULU
17:35 MST
DAY 5

"Whadda we got?" Lockhart asked, swerving the

243

transport about.

"Ten bogies on inbound," Cheech said, fingers dancing across his controls. "Flying low, all coming from New Berlin, I reckon. Not attack formation, though. Registering as standard atmospheric troop transports, unlike those other ships."

With a tap on his control panel, Jenkins brought up the information Cheech transmitted to his console. According to the computer, each one registered as a transport with the New Berlin ID code. It could mean they were ferrying soldiers to quell the Second Battalion's refusal to obey orders or...well, mutiny, but it made no sense. To keep all those ships in a linear formation reduced their ability to effectively use their weapons and made it all the easier for him to target with a handful of well-aimed missiles if need be.

"How long till intercept?"

"Two mins, Cap."

Lockhart lowered his ship's altitude in a bid to come up under their bellies and hide his approach vector. Even with his use of his vessel's proximity to the surface to confuse their sensors, any able pilot should have spotted some glitches on the scanners. Anyone with even the remotest common sense would have ordered the convoy to break into either an attack or defensive formation. Or at least send one ship ahead to investigate. If the approaching craft spied him, they weren't acting like they perceived him as a threat. Their mistake.

"What do you reckon, Cheech?"

"Not sure, Cap. Either they wanna draw us in close and attempt to swarm us last minute, or they know something we don't."

"Recheck sensors," Lockhart said, "and confirm they're receiving the ship-to-ship message we've been broadcasting."

The sound of Cheech working furiously on his panel echoed over the dull hum of the engines. Lockhart flicked the safety off his joystick and readied his thumb over the missile launch button. In less than a minute, they'd be within firing range, but everything about the scene struck him as wrong.

"Sensors are good, Cap, and yeah, they're receiving the message we got on repeat. Oh wait...what's this?"

Lockhart glanced at his co-pilot, but Cheech continued without prompting.

"Got something coming in on one of the lower bands... hang on....Message reads: Do not fire. Allies approaching. MEF stands with Second Batt. New Berlin in chaos. Requesting orders from Mad Jack. Repeat, do not fire."

"What?" Lockhart said. "That's gotta be a trick. Open comms."

Cheech flicked a switch on his panel and flashed a thumbs up. After clearing his throat, Lockhart activated his comms mic, thumb still hovering over the missile launch button. In seconds, he'd have a clear line of sight on the oncoming vessels.

"This is Lockhart to lead atmospheric troop transport. You will reverse course immediately, or we will open fire."

Static rang back until a click chimed through, and the familiar dull echo of a transport engine purred in the background noise.

"Lockhart! It's good to hear your voice. It's Evans here. You're not gonna believe the day I've had, buddy."

Without a moment's doubt, Lockhart recognised the voice. Lieutenant Evans was one of the rare decent pilots who survived the attack on the North Carolina during the invasion. Although they had flown together on multiple missions, they weren't exactly close, but Lockhart still rated him as a straight shooter with a good head and a knack for flying. He wasn't someone stupid enough to fly in convoy formation with a hostile opponent in wait.

"Evans, stand down and reverse course. I will open fire on you."

"Hold your fire, Lockhart," Evans said. "Hear me out. Word got back they're conscripting the Wehrmacht into the MOF. The MEF veterans and some of the newbies lost their shit. Entire units are refusing to obey orders. We're friendlies here. I got MEF boys looking to link up with the Second Batt. Solidarity and all that."

"Bullshit," Lockhart said. "You expect me to believe

you got three hundred bodies packed into those transports all set to fly over for a beer and a hotdog?"

"Bit north of a three hundred. Got 'em crammed in here like sardines. Some of 'em were eager to get outta New Berlin if you catch my drift. And no offence, kid, but if I was aiming to pull the wool over your eyes, you reckon I'd be stupid enough to fly in a line with my belly showing and guns cold while lit up like a Christmas tree? Give me a bit of credit."

As the incoming craft approached on his sensor screen, Lockhart weighed up the options. If it was some type of an elaborate ruse, it was a risky one. At any point, they could have broken formation to attack. Ten to one odds were very much in their favour. Something about Evans's voice, the sincerity, and the common sense of not giving him such easy targets played on his mind.

"Okay, Evans," Lockhart said, easing off on the throttle. "I'll hold off on opening fire on the condition you and the rest of the convoy set down first and switch off your engines. I got a flat piece of land on sensors about a klick east. Play nice, and I'll send word. Let Mad Jack make the call. Fair?"

"Okay," Evans said. "We're coming down now."

Pulling on the throttle, Lockhart brought his craft to a stop and hovered a metre off the surface, titling up, weapons ready if Evans tried to speed by him and make a break for Forward Base Zulu. Cheech tracked the convoy's progress as it flew past, and Lockhart fired the engines again. Hanging back, he made sure he had a clear line of sight with the rear transport's engines. True to his word, Evans led the convoy down onto the proposed landing site. Once grounded, all the ships deactivated their engines.

"Well, I'll be..." Cheech said. "You reckon they're serious? MEF boys all flocking to Zulu? Shit must really be hitting the fan in New Berlin."

"Not sure," Lockhart said. "Call it in. See what Mad Jack wants to do."

"On it, Cap."

Chewing the inside of his lip, Lockhart's thumb reached for the missile launcher cap to reapply the safety when multiple lights pinged on the periphery of the screen. As the readings cleared, he counted at least six more vessels coming from the direction of the American Zone. Instincts flaring to life, he considered blowing all the downed craft to pieces and launching after the intruders when Evans cut over the comm.

"I know you can see them, Lockhart," Evans said. "Trace their trajectory. They're flying here, not heading for Forward Base Zulu. You can intercept and scan if you want, but they're all weapons cold. I told you, the MEF boys are losing their minds. You'd think it was being told they weren't going back home with the fleet that'd tip them over the edge but seeing Nazis in MOF colours was the final straw."

Lockhart stayed his thumb when Cheech, eyes widened, nodded, and switched off his comm.

"Mad Jack says bring 'em all in, but land on the external launch pad. Whatever's going on in C&C, it sounds like it's kicking off. Reckon Evans may be telling the truth after all."

"We'll see," Lockhart said, flicking the firing cap back on. "All right. Let's wait for the rest to join, and then we'll all head back to the barn."

LEVEL 10, FORWARD BASE ZULU
00:28 MST
DAY 6

Grimacing from the struggle of movement, Watford limped into the packed C&C area, observing the assortment of gathered NCOs and the officers who lived. She noticed far more national uniforms than the red and black MOF colours, something which caught her off guard. Either the MEF veterans had switched back to their original battledress en masse, or they'd gotten a noticeable injection of reinforcements in the few hours she'd been recuperating in the field hospital.

In truth, she wanted nothing more than to return to that lumpy bed and sleep for at least another day. Every part of her body ached, not just her throbbing shoulder and stinging back. The painkillers Doctor Fawcett prescribed did little to quell the dull ache in her bones and skull. Still, with the base finally secured and patrols outside confirming no other sight of the enemy, Mad Jack ordered his senior leadership team to assemble to deliberate something of importance. Considering Fighting Bill was dead and Corporal Owens was seconded to an infantry platoon, that left her as the closest thing to a representative of the combat medics.

Trying to mask the pain from her every movement, Watford worked her way through the growing crowd towards the back end of C&C with all the monitors, consoles, and maps. Thankfully, a battered-looking French sergeant offered her his seat. Although in most circumstances, she would have declined, the building pain within her demanded she get off her feet, and she accepted his offer. She sank back in her chair. Mad Jack finished conferring with Colonel Henke and stepped behind his desk. Sergeant Jenkins stood to the left, a comm in hand, with Captain Nowak at his side. They eyed Mr. Myers, who slumped in a chair, his chin and nose caked in dried blood.

"I'm guilty of many things," Mad Jack said in a low voice that somehow rumbled across the entire room. "When, after two years' service, Major General Hamilton told me and the other battalion commanders we would not be returning home with the fleet still in orbit, I accepted it. I, like many of you, wished to return home, but I accepted the order in the belief they would send us when the next batch of reinforcements arrived. When there would be more than enough to secure this planet. I was wrong."

Murmurs broke out through C&C. Soldiers turned and whispered to one another. Many nodded at his words and folded their arms. With a flash of his palm, Mad Jack silenced them all.

"I have fought for and served my country since the day I joined the British Army," he said. "In that time, I've done everything asked of me. I have led men to their deaths and ordered men to die far from home on battlefields that will be forgotten in a generation. But to stand side by side with the same butchers who killed my boys, the same murderers who terrorised the Jewish population of the colonies, this is too much. I will not wear the colours of an organisation that wishes us to serve alongside Nazi war criminals. Who wish to wage war against a misguided people who want only to defend their homes, as you or I would, and kill for the fulfilment of an entrenched elite that saddles up to the old man in the tower, Adolf Hitler himself."

To rising chatter, Mad Jack removed his red and black khaki shirt and tossed it onto the floor. All the officers and NCOs flanking him wearing the same colours repeated his movements, throwing their shirts away in disdain. Watford glanced around, and of the few still in MOF uniforms, herself included, they had all stripped down to their red t-shirts.

"As many of you no doubt know," Mad Jack said, shifting his gaze across the room, "our actions in disarming the Wehrmacht have had a ripple effect. Word of our activities has spread across the colonies and incited widespread disobedience from the MEF veterans, and indeed, some of our MOF replacements, at what is viewed as a series of illegal acts against the Martian populace. Quite simply, we came here to eradicate the Nazi threat. Not fight side by side with them against a people who look and bleed just like us. Crushing National Socialism is one thing. Acting like them and starting a war against the indigenous population for reasons known only by an elite is something else."

Cheers rang out from throughout C&C. Enlisted and officers alike clapped at his words and slapped each other's backs in agreement. Having spent days fighting the militias, Watford doubted if many had any deep sympathy for the Martians, but all agreed with the sentiment. Moved by his speech, she joined in the applause. Although she was one of the MOF replacements he spoke about, a new arrival like many of her ilk, she held the MEF in high regard. They had endured far more pain and bloodshed than any of them, cut off and isolated, wondering if every day may be their last.

"At this moment," Mad Jack said, adjusting a radio microphone on his desk, "I am about to commence speaking with Major General Hamilton, where I will insist MAJESTIC-12 and MARSCORP honour their agreement with the MEF and send us home with immediate effect. Empty ships float in orbit, ready to take those of us who have survived back as promised but never delivered. I have asked each of you to be here as representatives of your various countries, units, battalions, and regiments to bear witness."

Bursts of static echoed when Mad Jack flicked on the radio loudspeaker. He took the mic in hand and brought it to his lips. After clearing his throat, he tilted his chin up and pressed the button.

"This is Lieutenant Colonel Wellesley," he said. "Acting commanding officer of Forward Base Zulu and commanding officer of the Second Battalion, Third Brigade. Message for Major General Hamilton."

Static whined out over the speakers. No one dared make a sound. Watford leaned forward in her seat, keen not to miss a single syllable. The interference droned on for four or five seconds until the line cleared.

"Damn it, Jack," Hamilton croaked over the comm channel. "What in the hell are you doing over there? This is madness. Are you that eager to be lined up against a wall and shot, man?"

"Sir," Mad Jack said. "It is my duty to inform you all my senior officers and NCOs are present, as well as representatives of other battalions. They are all listening to our conversation. I am speaking with you now to insist you repatriate the soldiers of the Mars Expeditionary Force back to their homes on Earth in accordance with what was promised us."

"Insist?" Hamilton said. "Insist? Who are you to insist? By God, this is treason. Outright mutiny! Jack, I am ordering you to hop on the next transport back to New Berlin for immediate arrest and court martial. If you report back to me in the next few hours, I may see fit not to shoot every single one of your co-conspirators."

"I'm afraid I can't do that, sir," Mad Jack said without delay. "We were sent here to fight Nazis, and now we're being asked to serve alongside them. Whatever MARSCORP's agenda, it is not in keeping with the oath I swore. Major General, again, I ask you to fulfil the promise made and send us home. It's been over two years, sir. We've done our duty."

More static interference churned out. Everyone's gaze remained fixed on Mad Jack, whose face lay emotionless as he stared at the microphone in his hand. Someone struck a match to light a cigarette, causing heads to turn and glare at the offender. The radio crackled again, and the line steadied.

"Now, hear me as clear as day," Hamilton said, voice rising. "Every one of you will stand down immediately. You will arrest Lieutenant Colonel Wellesley and present yourselves at New Berlin for disciplinary actions. Refuse to comply and consider this: I have three ships of the fleet in orbit over your position. With the flick of a hand, I can and will order them to open fire and wipe Forward Base Zulu off the face of Mars. If you doubt my resolve, carry on with this fool's errand, and I will show you the true depths of my retribution."

"No, you won't, sir," Mad Jack said without missing a beat. "We have the device known as the spire under our control, along with Mr. Myers. I have it on good authority you won't destroy this spire object. Please also note that Mr. Myers is too...depleted to utilise his abilities for now. We have measures in place. Should he return to his full potential, he will be neutralised with the Hollow soldiers who murdered my men."

The static rang out for far longer than previously. Soldiers shifted their weight from side to side, glancing at one another. Fingers stroked chins and cheeks. Hands massaged necks. The smell of cigarette smoke grew stronger, but no one spoke. Finally, the line cleared.

"Damn it, Jack," Hamilton said. "Don't make me use the MOF against you. The last thing I want is to order soldiers to shoot their fellow countrymen. I can't send you home, and for that, you have my deepest apologies. The MEF has seen far more than it should have, and we can't take the risk. The MOF, on the other hand, signed twenty-year contracts for this mission. By the time they go back, we'll have safeguards in place to ensure their compliance. I'm sorry to be the one to tell you and your men this news. Maybe in a couple of years when things settle down on the political front. Then we can find a way. But not now and not anytime soon. I don't want to sacrifice the lives of any more young people to remove you and your men, but I will if I must."

For the first time since the transmission began, noise broke out amongst the ranks. Jaws dropped, and eyes widened. Gasps rang out, hands clasped over mouths, and tears welled up in eyes. Confused, Watford glanced about at the sea of faces and only then understood the true extent of their shock. She, Shirley Watford, had willingly signed on for a twenty-year contract. The men of the former Mars Expeditionary Force had not.

"A compromise," Myers said, shocking everyone at his sudden outburst.

Hands shaking, he grabbed the desk and hauled himself out of his seat. Sergeant Jenkins raised the comm to his lips while Nowak reached for her pistol. Mad Jack held up a hand, halting them. Barely able to stand upright under his own power, Myers leaned on the desktop. He shuffled closer to Mad Jack and extended a hand. Eyeing him, Mad Jack handed over the mic and nodded.

"A compromise," Myers said again into the receiver. "MARSCORP is satisfied we've achieved all our objectives, minus a few unexpected blips. Mistakes have been made. Ones we should have anticipated, but I see no reason to cause a further rift in the Mars Occupation Force. We certainly don't have time for a civil war or another insurrection. Let's look at the facts, shall we?"

"Proceed, Mr. Myers," Hamilton said, his tone far more subdued.

"We can't send the MEF back due to security considerations," he said, meeting Mad Jack's gaze head-on. "It's a non-starter. A complete and utter deal-breaker. It will not happen, not yet. In a few years? Yes, I see no problem with that once relevant safeguards are in place. Maybe even a year or two. Until then, I propose we release the MEF from their contracts and demobilise them. Set each of them up with an allowance and a roof over their heads in whatever colony they choose. Spend their days relaxing in the artificial sun, soaking up a few beers, and catching up on some well-deserved rest and relaxation until the day comes when we can send them back. How does that sound?"

"No," Mad Jack growled. "The moment we hand over our weapons, you'll throw us in prison. Hell, you'll almost certainly use the Wehrmacht to do it. No, Mr. Myers. I reject your plan."

"Okay, okay," Myers said, waving his hand and forcing a smile. "Autonomy then. You and your men stay here. Make Forward Base Zulu your temporary accommodation. Over two thousand of you were tasked with defending this base, and as you can see, there's room and facilities to house at least five times that number. Keep your weapons if it makes you feel better. And as you mentioned, you'll still have the spire under your control, so we won't be able to obliterate you from space."

"What of the Cutline?" Hamilton said.

"The Cutline was a failed experiment," Myers snapped. "Nothing more than a badly drawn line on a map. What do you say, Lieutenant Colonel?"

Mad Jack's gaze tightened, and the lines on his forehead creased. He took a step closer to Myers and glanced back at his retinue. Most of them shrugged, seemingly as baffled as Watford was at the offer. If the spire was of such importance to MARSCORP, why surrender it to men who could use it as a bargaining chip? It made no sense to her.

"You'd give us this base?" Mad Jack said, voice level. "Now there's a poisoned chalice if ever I've seen one. Half the installation is in ruins, our stores obliterated, and we're sitting on enemy lines. Do you intend to starve us to death or wait until we're all weak from the hunger to finish us off?"

"Nothing of the kind," Myers said, his grin growing. "If you agree, I'll arrange for teams of engineers to restore this base to her former glory. I'll have shipments of food, equipment, and even weapons to cover the needs of your future community. Those same engineers will also show you how to set up aeroponics bays, similar to the ones New Berlin uses to feed her entire population. You'll be self-sufficient for all intents and purposes."

"And the Martians?"

"The Native Martians won't bother you. Not for a long time, if ever. What they've experienced at your hands is something that will torment them for a generation. Even if they do attempt an attack, you defended this base with a fraction of the support you'll have."

"What's the catch?" Mad Jack said.

Shrugging, Myers turned his gaze on the assembled officers and enlisted men. Angered stares greeted him, but no one shouted him down. At the very least, they listened to his proposal, if some of them didn't fully support it from the shaking of their heads.

"It's not so much a catch, per se, but it is something to take into consideration on your part. If you agree, we'll also be relocating the Freikorps and certain former members of the Army of David, along with their families and other undesirables."

"You mean the Jewish population?"

"Not all of them," Myers said. "Just the troublemakers."

Scuffles broke out when some of the Jewish members of the MEF and Freikorps stormed out of the ranks and made a beeline for the desk. Their colleagues held them back from charging at Myers, but they shouted and cursed him all the same. From Watford's perspective, it sounded like Myers was proposing to remove anyone who stood any chance of resisting his agenda and dumping them there, far from where they could stir up a resistance.

"A poor choice of words," Myers said, holding up his hand as if that would restore calm. "I merely mean, we will be reorganising the colonies and the MOF over the next few weeks and months and wish to offer any dissenting voices an alternative place to live. The decision belongs to you and your men, Lieutenant Colonel. It is the best one on the table, unless you desire to witness more death and destruction."

Mad Jack snatched the microphone off Myers, and with a nod, Sergeant Jenkins grabbed him and hauled him back to his seat. Looking over the room, he sighed and leaned a hand onto the desk. The lines on his forehead tightened, and Watford couldn't imagine the burden. With a word, he could decline and incite a civil war across the colonies.

Countryman against countryman, friend against friend, brother against brother. In the end, the former MEF men would most likely lose. They stood at a fraction of the number that had crash-landed on Mars and waged war against the Nazis. Far too many had died, and they lacked the ability to restock their dwindling ammunition and food stores.

On the other hand, to acquiesce meant surrendering hope of returning home on the whims of people who had lied and betrayed them. Even if Myers stayed true to his word and repaired Forward Base Zulu and gave them all the stores and supplies they needed, what type of life would that be? Exile would be a poor life for demobilised soldiers with too much time on their hands.

"I won't make this decision for you," Mad Jack finally said, switching off the comm and setting down the mike. "I leave it to your own consciences on what to decide. We'll meet back here in an hour, and I'll hear what each of you has to say before we come to our verdict. Make no mistake, though, we have three options. Rejoin the Mars Occupation Force and accept the consequences of our actions today. Take up arms against our fellow countrymen and go to the gallows as traitors. Or agree to exile, trying to build a life here in the hopes that, one day, they will send us home."

Colonel Henke dismissed everyone in attendance, and, shoulders sagging, Mad Jack fell onto his chair and moved his interlinked fingers to shield his face. Watford stood, not envying anyone their choice, but her decision rested clearly in her thoughts. As much as she lacked trust in Mr. Myers and MARSCORP, she had signed on to the Mars Occupation Force for the next two decades. Like it or not, she was a woman of her word, and she planned to play her part, maybe even influence events behind the scenes, if she could, in time. She had her orders after all, and she intended to obey. Running a hand over her new rank markings, she smiled to herself.

She was a soldier.

EMERGENCY LANDING PAD, LEVEL 10, FORWARD BASE ZULU
10:49 MST
DAY 6

Lowering his hands as bayonets prodded air around him, General Schulz clambered aboard the last transport waiting to leave Forward Base Zulu. One other occupant sat in the entire compartment. For a second, he considered turning about and requesting another ship, but angered faces of MOF soldiers glared from behind their EVA visors. Sighing, he pulled the airlock shut, ignoring the middle-fingered salutes and the variety of colourful profanities shouted about his parentage and his mother's occupation.

He considered taking the seat nearest the door. Myers's unblinking gaze and unwavering smile heralded his desire for company, so Schulz sank into the seat opposite him. When the light over the airlock door turned green, and the engines of the atmospheric troop transport fired up, they removed their EVA helmets.

"Well," Schulz said. "That was an exercise in futility. I'm told three-quarters of the two battalions fielded for this operation are dead."

"Not quite as futile as you think," Myers said, reaching under his EVA suit to jostle for his pockets. "Their sacrifices will assure the integration of the rest of the Wehrmacht into the MOF. Who cares if they died believing the spire would resurrect them? The most important thing is I've confirmed something that will be of great importance to my colleagues in MARSCORP."

He produced a small, square, silver device and, with the flick of his hand, revealed a tiny series of colourful lights. With the tap of a button, a sequence of squiggly lines appeared on the miniature screen. Its meaning meant nothing to Schulz. For all he knew, it was a child's toy.

"We knew the Stream could be used to transport matter from one point in space to another," Myers said.

256

"Hell, you Nazis proved it when you got lucky and escaped from Germany all those years ago. We also theorised it could be utilised to allow matter to traverse time as well, and now we have our proof. In the future, we won't be reliant on the Compression Matrix anymore. We can send actual people from point A to point B, anywhere, anytime we want. The only thing we need to work out is the how. So far, all our experiments have failed. Yet these…Core Cadre or Black Visors or whatever you want to call them, achieved what we could not."

Growing bored with Myers's musings, Schulz fidgeted in his seat and wished he'd selected somewhere close to a window port. He would have appreciated seeing the devastating scene first-hand where so many Germans had given their lives for such a pointless mission. Whether it was at Brandt's orders or his own, the least he could've done for them was take in the sight where they'd fought so valiantly.

Bare minutes after taking off, their transport descended back to the surface. At Myers's prompting, Schulz reattached his helmet and watched as he made his way to the airlock door. When their craft landed, he leaned against the window port and waved. He unlocked the door and stood aside. A bulky figure in an EVA suit stepped through, glanced at Schulz, and made his way to the far corner of the compartment. After Myers sealed the airlock, the transport rose again. Eyeing the new arrival, Schulz removed his helmet along with Myers when the lights flashed green. Their new guest did not.

"Herr Bormann," Myers said, "meet General Schulz. General Schulz, Herr Bormann."

Forehead creasing at the introduction, Schulz stared at the visored face for confirmation. Bormann had been reported dead since the last days of their evacuation from Germany over a decade ago. Never once had he heard any reports of him surviving, let alone joining them on Mars. Yet Myers's gleeful face and widened smile showed his excitement.

"I'm sure you two will have plenty to discuss when we get back to New Berlin," Myers said.

Seeing no reaction from Bormann, Schulz shook his head and looked away. In no mood for another one of Myers's tirades about his sadistic future plans, he cleared his throat and attempted to shift the conversation to more practical matters.

"Do you really think it's wise leaving so many potential enemies alive and in a fortified position?"

"In an ideal world, we'd have them all liquidated," Myers said with a light-hearted shrug, "but they could still prove useful. Some of them carry the Hollow gene, so when we perfect the body replication methods, at least we'll have additional guinea pigs to experiment on."

"You don't foresee any issues with leaving a heavily armed group of malcontents on your border?"

"Not at all. If anything, it's better to have all your enemies in one place rather than have them blend in. At least this way, we can keep an eye on them. And until we can activate all six planetary spires, there's no point wasting resources. We have three so far. Another three, and we'll be able to open the Stream Corridor, but it could take years, even decades to locate. We're patient, Herr General."

"And Anna Bailey? Do you intend on allowing her to roam free yet again after everything she's done?"

"The Mother of Hollows still has a part to play, Herr General. It's better she does that out there, rather than within our walls."

Schulz ran a hand through his sweat-slicked hair and rested his head against the bulkhead. The riddles Myers spoke in invoked a slight headache. More than anything, he wanted to get back to New Berlin and cleanse himself of the last few days in a bath or a shower.

"I'll never understand you, Mr. Myers," he said, closing his eyes and wishing he could sleep, "and I hope I never will. Dare I ask what is to become of me and my men?"

"Exactly as promised," Myers said, the sound of his harness unlocking, forcing Schulz's eyes open.

He crossed the compartment and plonked onto the vacant seat beside him. Disgusted at the proximity, Schulz leaned away. Undeterred, Myers placed one leg over the other, sank back, and rested his hands on his stomach. Bormann, sitting in the corner, remained motionless and silent.

"There'll be blowback, of course," he said. "Confusion and dissension in the ranks, but in time, we'll integrate your soldiers into the Mars Occupation Force. As soon as the recent upheaval abates, I'll be relying on your men to utilise specific skillsets that our current assets are reluctant to employ, for the most part."

"Such as?"

"Ethnic cleansing, mostly. I've identified certain Native Martian populated areas that may contain the location, or at least clues to, the other spires. Nothing your boys can't handle."

Regretting the day he had ever laid eyes on the monster, Schulz looked away, shaking his head. Myers would put SS officers to shame with his bloodlust in the name of power. In his weakened state, Schulz wondered if he could reach across and strangle him to death there and then and do the entire planet a single act of goodness. As he glanced again, that same disgusting smile shone back.

"You're welcome to try," Myers said, "but it'd be a shame to lose you, Herr General. We have much work ahead of us, and you know what? I like you."

Bowing, Schulz averted his gaze. Against a beast who could read thoughts and control people's minds, he had no chance. Not yet. But someday. One day, an opportunity would present itself, and he vowed to take it and rid the world of such a creature as Myers.

"Be careful you don't miss," Myers said, closing his eyes and easing himself against the seat for a snooze. "I never do."

HANGAR BAY, FORWARD BASE ZULU
13:34 MST
DAY 7

Leaning against the observation window, Jenkins peered down onto the hangar bay. He watched the steady stream of transports coming in or moving back out to the external launch pad. In a non-stop flow, engineers, under the watchful eyes of MEF soldiers, poured into the base, repairing damage to the exterior, rebuilding floors, ceilings, and airlocks, and refurbishing the vast assortment of equipment damaged in the fighting. Entire transports were dedicated to delivering food supplies, gardening paraphernalia, and, surprisingly, weapons.

At no point had Jenkins expected Myers to follow through on his word when the majority voted for exile. So far, he had. The many MOF personnel who arrived to assist them were downright supportive if anything. Even though they no longer wore the same uniform, they treated each other as comrades in arms with no ill will for the events of the last few days.

The Freikorps and the civilians were a different story. It became clear very quickly that many of them had no choice in their relocation, being forced in some cases at gunpoint to board the ships taking them from New Berlin. According to overheard conversations between officers, the Jewish families and ethnic Germans designated undesirables petitioned Mad Jack hourly, demanding to be brought back to their homes. He had tried to intervene, but the pilots refused, stating they had been told they'd be shot down if they returned anybody.

It only added to the sense of gloominess clinging to the air in Forward Base Zulu. They were trapped there. All of them. MEF, a handful of MOF defectors, Freikorps, Army of David, and ethnic Germans, or Volk, as some called them. Destined to rot in a prison with all the amenities and food they could ever want, in the hopes one day, someone would see their plight, liberate, and send them home.

Captain Nowak, or Zofia, as she insisted he call her when not on official duty, had certainly made her thoughts known. She rallied the Freikorps and her former Army of David fighters to protest the injustice of their forced relocation. The more radical elements within both organisations demanded armed resistance. Yet, for all her bluster, Zofia took no measures that would impact the influx of materials and much-needed stores into Forward Base Zulu. In time, it was possible hostilities could erupt, but for all her angered speeches, she gave an equal number appealing to the refugees to give their new home a chance. Bide for time and play the long game.

In a million years, Jenkins didn't think he'd ever truly understand her. He had to admit, though, he enjoyed her company. She could be curt, overly direct, and lacked any filter to her thoughts, but she was the strongest woman he'd ever encountered. Despite the perpetual scowl she wore as a mask, she was one of the most caring people he had come across in all his time, compassionate to the members of her community and the MEF veterans. He smiled when he thought of her tapping her holstered pistol earlier in the day and insisting he come to her quarters in the evening so she could cook for him.

"Sergeant Jenkins," a voice said, snapping him out of his thoughts.

He turned and stood to attention, bringing his hand to his head in salute.

"Sir," he said.

"Knock it off," Lockhart said, flapping his hand.

"Yes, sir," Jenkins said and lowered his hand.

"I mean it," Lockhart said. "Enough with the sirs and the salutes. You're like three years older than me. It's weird. Here, take this."

Grinning, Jenkins accepted the hip flask and flicked open the cap. He detected the scent of whiskey and took a small slug before handing it back. The warmth worked its way down his throat and chest and, for a moment, eased some of his worries.

"I didn't see you at the funeral," Lockhart said as they stepped away from the observation window back to the corridor. "Colour Sergeant Brown, he, uh...had a lot of nice things to say. Very moving."

"I couldn't," Jenkins said, forcing the bitter sadness back down into his gut. "Lieutenant McCabe and Sergeant Alexeev were good people. Great leaders. They didn't deserve to die here. Not like that. I'll pay my respects in my own way and in my own time."

"I understand," Lockhart said and gestured at the wall. "So, what'll you do now? Here, I mean. How are several thousand disgruntled soldiers going to pass the time?"

"There's still Wehrmacht out there," Jenkins said when they stopped at a stairwell. "The Second Battalion was sent here to root out the Nazis, and as far as I'm concerned, the job isn't done. We'll take care of the reorganised Wehrmacht and whatever's left of the werewolves before we decide what to do about the ones in the MOF. What about you?"

"I'm a pilot," he said and took another drink. "I fly. That's all I know. As I hear it, you boys have a couple of transports allocated and not enough pilots to fly 'em. I was thinking of hanging around for a bit. See what trouble I can get up to."

Another smile crossed Jenkins's face, and he patted the lad on the shoulder. He opened his mouth to speak when his radio chimed. Holding up his finger, he grabbed the handset and pulled it up to his lips.

"This is Knight Four. Go ahead."

"Knight Four," the radio operator said. "Top Hat's received reports of a convoy north of here heading out past the Cutline. Looks like werewolves fleeing the colonies. Wants you to check it out."

"Message received," Jenkins said. "Tell Top Hat I'm en route for briefing. McCabe's Marauders are on standby."

"Acknowledged, Knight Four."

"McCabe's Marauders," Lockhart said. "Catchy."

"It's the only word I could think of that started with the letter m."

"Didn't think of 'machetes,' then?"

"No," Jenkins said, repressing a smirk and throwing his hand around the young pilot's shoulders. "Come on. I could use a pilot, and I reckon there's a thing or two I can show you. Between the two of us, maybe we'll find a way off this big, red rock."

"All right, I'm game," Lockhart said. "You had me at 'Let's go shoot werewolves.'"

Laughing, Jenkins pulled his hand back and shook his head. The weight of the many, many dead comrades lifted from his shoulders, at least for a few seconds. Trapped on Mars for an unknown amount of time, it occurred to him that sharing moments like that with friends and doing his duty were all he had to look forward to, but it was better than compromising who he was. The demobilised soldiers of the MEF had their own destinies to craft, building new lives on the blood-red sand and soil.

Shoulder to shoulder, Jenkins and Lockhart marched on to continue the hunt for werewolves on Mars.

The End

About the Author

Damien Larkin is an Irish science fiction and fantasy author. His novels Big Red and Blood Red Sand were published by Dancing Lemur Press and went on to be longlisted for BSFA awards for Best Novel. He spent seven years in the Irish Reserve Defence Force and currently lives in Dublin, Ireland.

Website:
www.damienlarkinbooks.com
Facebook:
www.facebook.com/DamienLarkinAuthor
Twitter:
www.twitter.com/Damo_Dangerman
Instagram:
www.instagram.com/damo_danger_larkin

Other great science fiction titles!

CassaStar
By Alex J. Cavanaugh
To pilot the fleet's finest ship...
Print ISBN 9780981621067
eBook ISBN 9780982713938

"...calls to mind the youthful focus of Robert Heinlein's early military sf..."
- Library Journey

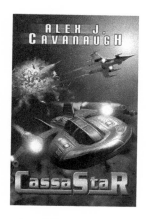

Revolution 2050
By Jay Chalk
Samuel Moore is living a dystopian lie...
Print ISBN 9781939844439
eBook ISBN 9781939844446

"...we once again need reminders that each generation must fight for its own freedoms or it will lose them." –
Gordon A. Long, author

Lost Helix
By Scott Coon
Lost Helix is the key...
Print ISBN 9781939844682
eBook ISBN 9781939844699

"...the ride is an entertaining one." –
SF Reviews - Don D'Ammassa

Printed in the USA
CPSIA information can be obtained
at www.ICGtesting.com
LVHW091106120923
757863LV00004B/26